Angelguard

Angelguard

Not all the spirits are good

Ian Acheson

LION FICTION

Published by Lion Fiction
an imprint of
Lion Hudson plc
Wilkinson House, Jordan Hill Road,
Oxford OX2 8DR, England
www.lionhudson.com/fiction

ISBN 978 1 78264 002 8
e-ISBN 978 1 78264 003 5

First edition 2013

Acknowledgments
Scripture quotations taken from the Holy Bible, New International
Version Anglicised Copyright © 1979, 1984, 2011 Biblica, formerly
International Bible Society. Used by permission of Hodder &
Stoughton Ltd, an Hachette UK company. All rights reserved "NIV" is
a registered trademark of Biblica. UK trademark number 1448790.

A catalogue record for this book is available from the British Library

Printed and bound in the UK, Feb 2013, LH26

For Fiona

Acknowledgments

Thank you, God. Through this journey Your ever-watchful and inspirational hand has been plainly evident. May this story bring You glory.

To Fiona, my wife and best friend, thank you for your graciousness in allowing me to chase my dream. I couldn't have done this without your belief in this story and in me.

Dan and Jake, our boys, thank you for loving me.

To my constant writing companion, Brandy, our much-loved pooch. It amazes me how God created an animal with such selflessness and desire to make us humans happy.

Thanks to Tony Collins, Jan Greenough and the team at Lion Hudson for making this story the best it can be. You've spoilt me and taught me so much in the process.

Thank you to Paul Bootes, founder of Koorong, for taking thirty minutes of your weekend to share your wisdom and for the introduction to Tony. One of many occurrences during this story's gestation that can only be described as a "God-thing".

Thanks to the late Clare Booth Steward, my first editor, who helped me believe this story was publishable and who taught me the basics of writing and self-editing.

And finally, to those of you who will give up a few hours to read this story, thank you. I am so grateful.

Cast of Characters

HUMANS

In the UK

Thierry Le Bon
Ruth, his wife
Mikey, their son
Charlotte, Thierry's sister
Jerome, Charlotte's son (deceased)
Danny and Joanna Connolly
Jack, their son, godson of Jack Haines
Major Bill Lancaster, SAS

In Australia

Jack Haines
Sarah Haines, Jack's wife
Grace and Catherine, Jack's infant daughters
Jane, Jack's sister
Louise Haines, Jack's mother

In the USA

Loren Summers
Ray Malone, Loren's boss
Candice Malone, his wife
Tom Mayer, Loren's ex-husband and Ray's colleague
Taylor and Luke, Loren's children
Stephen Haines, Jack's younger brother

In Europe

Leopold Grosch, Belgian industrialist
Marie Verheyen, Belgian deputy prime minister and Grosch's mistress
Zhou Chau, hitman and wireless technology expert
Vincent and Farkad, Grosch's henchmen

Pienaar, Swartbooi and du Preez, South African mercenaries
Colonel Charles Smithson ("Smitty")
Mr. Ballack, head of security for the G8 Summit

ANGELS

Tagan, leader of the European region
Athaniel

Guarding the Le Bons

Elijah
Hannen
Andola (later redeployed to guard Zhou Chau)
Jolane (also guarding Zhou Chau)

Guarding Loren Summers

Arlia
Emur
Landen
Grindor
Mylee

Guarding Jack Haines

Darius

DEMONS

The Fallen Angel
General Thrasos, Chief Warlord of the Fallen Angel
Lord Bacchazar, demon in chief for Europe, the Middle East and Africa
Volkyre, his adviser
Drakkin
Chonnggi
Tetak
Sergeant Slyzor
Zeldax
Agramon, demon in chief for the Americas and Asia
Grazag, Tom Mayer's keeper

Chapter 1

London, January, the present

"It's time!"

The voice was resonant, powerful, yet warm. Thierry, rising through the mists of unconsciousness, longed to hear it again.

Yet even as he stirred, the being was gone, the golden glow fading. He felt a pang of sadness. He wanted more time, to draw closer, to soak up the warmth and love...

"Nurse! I need a nurse in here!" A loud male voice jarred.

"Coming, doctor," a woman's voice responded. "I'm just finishing up here."

The doctor was checking Thierry's body, feeling his arms and legs and opening his shirt to examine his chest. Thierry tried to open his eyes but the light was too bright. What happened? Why was he here? His head was pounding.

He heard a curtain being drawn.

"Good. Nurse... Evans, is it? I need you to clean this head wound before I stitch it."

"That all?"

"Yes. We'll get him down for some X-rays as soon as we can. And overnight for observation, if you can find a bed on a ward."

"That won't be easy. It's a madhouse out there."

"Are they still coming in?"

"No, I think that's the last of the casualties. They're still bringing out the dead – the Whittington's acting as a temporary morgue."

"Right, I'll get on. It's going to be a long night."

Thierry heard it all, vaguely. Beyond the curtain there were hurrying feet, the clatter of trolleys, raised voices. He grimaced from the vise-like pain in his head.

"Can you help me?" he whispered through dry lips. "My head…"

"It's OK, luv, you're gonna be all right. Just have a headache for a while." She was swabbing the side of his head, her touch gentle but firm.

There was a pain in his side, every time he breathed in. Like an iron band round his ribs. Like… his mind went back… like playing football, a few years back, his team against Dartford United, the collision with their number nine, two cracked ribs…

Football! Recollection came flooding back. He'd been watching a football match! Jerome's Christmas treat – his excited face grinning up at his uncle, yelling for his team. The Blues did well in the first half… then, right on the half-time whistle, the blast knocking him forward – a noise like the end of the world, screams – then nothing. Nothing. Waking up here, in pain.

His eyes flew open and he tried to raise himself on one elbow, only to fall back with a strangled gasp of pain.

"Jerome! Where's Jerome?"

"It's OK, calm down." He squinted against the light and saw the nurse, a solidly built West Indian, bending over him.

"You've taken a bad knock on the head. I'll get you something for the pain. The doc's just coming back to stitch your head."

Thierry closed his eyes and waited, his mind probing at the muddled memories. He remembered walking to the stadium, Jerome skipping alongside him. He remembered parts of the game. Then a noise like thunder, then nothing.

"Now then, Mr. Le Bon." It was the doctor's voice. Thierry looked up.

"What happened to me?"

"Hold still." The doctor was expertly suturing the head wound, which gaped pink against Thierry's dark-brown skin. "It was a bomb – a big one. Blew the stand apart, killed nearly everyone in it, lots of others injured. You're one of the lucky ones. Someone must be looking out for you. Only a handful got out of the West Stand alive."

"Jerome – my nephew…"

"I'll ask the nurse to see if he's on our lists anywhere. If not, I'm afraid you'll have to wait for police reports. Everyone's pretty busy tonight. We'll see if we can get you a bed on the ward. You've had a nasty knock on the head." The doctor spoke rapidly, and pushed the curtain aside as he hurried away.

Thierry was drifting in and out of consciousness. He had no strength to call for help as he fell sideways and vomited over the side of the bed.

* * *

"How's our patient?" The voice was concerned. A tall blond angel gazed in through the window of the hospital room, unseen by the hurrying medical staff and the victims lying on trolleys. Over eight feet tall with snow-white hair and piercing blue eyes, he wore a silver cloak, which swung back to reveal a three-foot scabbard hanging from his belt.

"Lucky to be alive, Tagan, sir," reported a second angel, as dark as the first was fair. "His head struck a concrete ledge, and his ribs were broken when an advertising hoarding landed on him." He clenched his fists. "Hannen did a tremendous job – he moved the hoarding to cover Thierry and protect him. He took a bad knock himself, from a demon who tried to stop him. He's nursing his sword arm as we speak." Both knew their comrade would heal fast. Angels did, as a rule.

"And Thierry?"

"His body will take a little longer to mend. But his spirit…"

"I know, Athaniel. Losing his nephew will cause him more pain. How that affects him remains to be seen. It could turn him further away. And he is vital to our purpose." The angel paced up and down by the window, deep in thought. "He needs guidance as well as protection. I will order Elijah to join Hannen as his guard."

"Yes, sir." Athaniel hesitated. "Did you know Lord Bacchazar himself appeared at the scene?"

"His presence did not go unnoticed. I cannot recall when last the old warlord supervised an attack in person. Today's events must be important to him." Tagan looked heavenward.

"Gabriel and Michael have called a conference of all the leaders of the continents. I must speak to Elijah and Hannen and get their views."

"Elijah was in the stand opposite and saw it all. There were over a thousand demons to our one hundred knights, and we had no intelligence of their plan, so we could not prevent it. But we will have our revenge!"

The dark angel drew his sword and raised it menacingly. It shone with a brilliant radiance, which did not come from the leaden January sky. It was a huge weapon, fit for an angelguard of Athaniel's standing – right hand to one of the most senior in the angel kingdom.

"You will have your day, my friend." Tagan smiled briefly at his subordinate's intensity. "But for now we must be vigilant if we are to prevent another attack, and lay our plans with care. I will seek out Hannen and Elijah. Stay here till they relieve you."

Tagan turned, took two paces and sprang silently into the air, white wings opening out of his back to carry him swiftly into the sky above.

Athaniel returned to his duty at the window with renewed diligence.

* * *

It was dark when Thierry awoke, and the silence told him that he had been moved to another room. He tried to lever himself up on his elbows. *Wow! That hurt! Must be time for more painkillers.*

In the gloom he could make out three other beds, and a light coming from a half-open door. He pressed the call button. Where was Ruthie? Did she know what had happened to him? His head felt clearer suddenly. When the nurse appeared he was ready with questions.

"What's the time? Does my wife know where I am? Can you find out about my nephew? Jerome Sanders – he's six."

"Hold on a minute, one at a time," said the nurse, switching on a dim light above his bed.

"Pain relief first." She turned him expertly and administered an injection.

"It's a quarter past ten. You've been here for about four hours. I don't know about the boy, but your wife's outside. I'll fetch her."

Thierry's heart leapt. Ruthie!

A woman in a black leather coat appeared in the doorway, glanced around the room and came swiftly over to the bed. In the dim light he could see that her eyes were swollen with crying, and tear tracks marked her smooth brown skin. To Thierry she had never looked more beautiful. She bent and kissed him tenderly.

"Hi, baby," she said, touching his face gently. "How're you feeling? Sorry it took me so long to get here. I had to get a sitter for Mikey. And then it took forever to find out which hospital you were in, and the traffic's chaos. They said I had to wait till you woke up—" The words tumbled out and she stopped to draw breath. "Oh, thank God you're alive!" Tears sprang to her eyes again. She clung to his hand as if she would never let it go.

"Ruthie – where's Jerome?"

Ruth hesitated and Thierry saw the answer in her eyes.

"Oh, no… Charlotte…"

His sister. She would never forgive him. He'd promised to take care of her little boy. Thierry felt as though he was drowning in an ocean of guilt. He wanted to cry out but he didn't have the strength. The pain in his head and his side faded away as the drug-induced mists closed over him again.

"I'm sorry, babe." Ruth's quiet sobbing was the last thing he heard before he lost consciousness once more.

* * *

Hours passed. He was dimly aware of Ruth leaving. Nurses came and went. He drifted in and out of sleep.

Then suddenly he was wide awake, and struggling to breathe. It was pitch black – where had the lighted doorway gone? Where were the other beds? He seemed to be caught in a nightmare, blind, deaf, unable to escape, yet writhing under a weight, which crushed the air from his lungs. His whole body was in agony. A chill ran up his spine. *Where am I? Am I dying?*

A sulfurous smell stung his nostrils, and he felt hot breath on his face. Something was looming over him, threatening him, enveloping him in darkness.

Then right on the edge of audibility he seemed to hear faintly a distant screeching sound, a crash, and the weight lifted. He drew a shuddering breath and it was clean, cool air, free of foul odors. Something touched his brow gently, and he relaxed, sighing, as peaceful, dreamless sleep received him again.

Like a lightning bolt, three white knights had crashed into the black cloud surrounding Thierry's bed. The demons screeched and hissed, furious at being taken unawares, as the bright blades slashed at them. Athaniel and Elijah forced four of them back, while Hannen darted forward and grabbed the last by the throat as he crouched over Thierry's sleeping body. The demon twisted in the air and drew his own sword, but Hannen smashed it from his grasp, leaving him defenseless. Black wings unfolded and the demons fled, disappearing through the ceiling like smoke in the wind.

Athaniel sheathed his sword. "You two arrived at the right moment. I couldn't have taken all of them."

Elijah's sword was still glowing with the heat of battle. "Let's finish them!"

"No, Elijah," said Hannen, placing a restraining hand on his arm. "Our task is to guard Thierry. Athaniel will report to Tagan."

The dark angel nodded his understanding and left. Hannen laid a gentle hand on Thierry's brow. "Sleep peacefully, my friend. You are safe."

* * *

A week later Thierry was at home, though his head still ached intermittently, his ribs were healing and the livid bruise on his left shoulder made movement painful.

Ruth was taking a phone call in the hall, though she didn't seem to be doing much talking. When she came back into the room he could see she'd been crying again.

"How are they?" he asked.

"Your mum's really struggling, but she's holding it together for Charlotte. Troy is doing it tough too." Troy was Charlotte's ex. "They know what happened to Jerome now. They found him under a pile of rubble. Darling, he would have died instantly – a huge piece of concrete struck his head. He wouldn't have known anything about it."

Ruth put her arms round Thierry, holding him gingerly because of his bruises. To Thierry the pain in his body was trivial compared to the pain in his heart. Why couldn't he have saved him? Why did Jerome have to die while he lived? Why had he even suggested the trip in the first place – a little boy's first live football match, watching his beloved team play at home? It was all his fault.

His arms tightened around Ruth, and then he pulled away to look at her.

"It was strange, Ruthie," he said. "I remember looking up, just before half time. The sky was really black – as if all the clouds had gathered over the stadium. I could see blue sky all around it – just this one big black cloud over us. It felt menacing – as if something was going to happen."

Ruth looked at him doubtfully.

"I know, it sounds crazy. But it was real. Then the ref blew the whistle and – wham! Everything just went blank. I didn't have time to grab Jerome or anything."

Tears were streaming down his face.

Ruth kissed him. "It's good to talk about it, babe. Let it all out. It'll help." She held him for a while longer, and then left him to rest. He still slept a lot during the day, and often Ruth would sit beside him, holding his hand, ready for the moment when he would wake up shouting for Jerome, reliving the explosion and his fear. Sometimes as he slept he half-heard her murmured prayers – for him, for Charlotte and his mum, and for all the other families who mourned.

He dozed and woke to the same anguished thoughts. I survived – why not Jerome? Anger welled up inside him. God! You could have stopped this pain, this heartache! Why take such a little boy away from his mum, whose life is already so tough?

He found he was beating his fist on the arm of the sofa. *If I could get hold of the person who did this, I'd kill them with my bare hands!*

His fury exhausted him. *If only I'd never taken him there. If only…*

His clenched fist relaxed. *If only…*

Healing sleep claimed him again, and Hannen gently withdrew his hand from Thierry's arm.

The angelguard was watchful.

* * *

Not far away, in a disused warehouse, a meeting was taking place.

The building had been empty for years, and to human eyes it was dark and deserted now. But in a far corner a huddle of black creatures were arguing noisily. Suddenly the group scattered as one of their number was thrown bodily across the building and crashed against a wall. A second followed, landing on the first. Raucous laughter and hissing broke out among their fellows. Then a misshapen form hobbled out of the group, waving a crooked walking-stick.

"Spineless cowards!" he croaked. There was another burst of laughter, quickly hushed as another creature stepped out of the shadows. This one dwarfed the others, standing eight feet tall, and wielded a huge sword with a muscular arm. He let out an ear-splitting roar, which caused the two ejected beasts to cower against the wall.

"I don't want to see you two cowards again, until you each present me with the hide of a white knight!" snarled the demon lord. The scars that disfigured his face throbbed a deep crimson. "If another mission is interrupted by the haloed ones, do not think to return unless in victory. If you fail, then die fighting the enemy, not in fleeing. Do I make myself clear? Now go, before I feed you to the monsters of hell myself!"

The two struggled to their feet and shakily took flight through the warehouse roof.

Others flew up beside them, mocking and crowing.

"Be silent!" bellowed the huge demon. "Let this be a lesson to you all. Failure will not be tolerated. We must not let the white knights prevail. We tasted victory at the football stadium. Let us savor it again." He sheathed his blade.

"We have noted the presence of the angelguards around one survivor – a man named Le Bon. He or his family may be of some importance to the enemy. We do not yet know why. But we should do away with them before the white knights can awaken their spirits. I want them under attack by every means – mentally, physically, and emotionally. Do you hear me?"

There was a mumble of agreement.

"We must outwit the white knights. I have battled with them often enough to know they are not easily deterred. Away with you! Drakkin has a base in a vacant shop close to Le Bon's house. Go and keep watch."

The remaining demons took flight, passing through the physical barrier of the roof as though it were mist. Only two remained: the powerful monster and the elderly one with the walking-stick.

The huge beast spoke first. "Volkyre, wise old sorcerer. Why the white knight interest in Le Bon, do you think? What role does he play in their plans?"

"Lord Bacchazar, take my counsel. Their presence around Le Bon is only small. He may just be wavering on the brink of belief, and the white knights are encouraging that. I would not concern yourself, my lord. More significantly, I hear that the plans for Los Angeles and Sydney are now in place. Both will be marvelous victories. And it is time for us to plan for the biggest strike of all. More and more will suffer, more will come to doubt, to fear, to succumb to evil."

Volkyre's voice rose to a quavering shout, flecks of black spittle flying from his curling lips. "And, Lord, what a great day that will be. You will stand alongside the Most Evil One, as commander of this earth-shattering victory!"

Bacchazar merely smiled.

Chapter 2

Los Angeles, January, a week later

Loren Summers breezed into the cavernous arena. It was abuzz with activity in preparation for tonight's fundraiser. Dressed professionally in a black skirt-suit, she smiled; seeing it all come together gave her a strong sense of pride. She had been responsible for its creation.

Scanning the crowd of workers and not seeing a familiar face, she made her way towards the front—

THUD!

A short young man knocked her off her feet.

"Oh! Sorry, sweetheart – didn't see you there!" he said in a Texan drawl. He helped her up.

"That's all right, no harm done," Loren said, brushing her skirt down.

Loren moved on briskly towards the stage. The Texan called out to her, "Sorry again!" and mumbled something to his co-worker who stood at the opening of the front-of-house mixing pit, leering as his eyes followed her long legs.

Arlia, the white knight who accompanied Loren, paid little attention to the men. Her attention was focused on the two huge reptilian creatures that sat atop the nearby speaker boxes.

They promptly jumped off, landing directly in front of the angel, halting her progress. They stood upright, their massive torsos blocking the white knight's path.

Releasing her wings to accentuate her size, and looking intently from one demon to the other, the angelguard spoke. "I mean you no harm. Out of my way!"

"Ha, ha, ha, ha!" The two hoodlums broke up in hissing laughter, momentarily relaxing their stance.

"You mean us no harm, then?" one replied sarcastically, sticking his ugly head right in the angel's face so his crooked beak was inches from the angelguard's perfectly shaped nose. He blew a cloud of foul gas into the glistening turquoise eyes.

The white knight stood motionless, meeting her enemy's hate-filled stare.

The demon's veins were bulging in his oversized neck. "Of course you're not going to harm us. If anyone is going to be harmed, it's going to be *you*." The other snickered.

The white knight stood still, continuing to make eye contact with the aggressor.

"So what's your business, then?" the demon demanded angrily, holding up a clenched claw, talons bent forward, ready to inflict pain.

"On guard duty, that's all." She shoved the offending claw away. "You understand that, I presume?"

The demon rose to his full height, his face narrowed and his body taut, whilst his partner moved in closer.

Moments passed as the three stared intensely, all primed to strike on the slightest movement.

CHOMP! The demon feigned a bite. The angel didn't flinch.

He slowly moved aside, allowing her to pass. As she was almost beyond them, he reached for her—

SLASH! A white streak sliced the air, ending with a sword at the demon's throat, forcing him to release his grip on her arm. He gulped.

"Hold your horses!" he growled through gritted teeth. The sword lowered but the intensity on her face didn't, nor did she relax her fighting stance.

"One more thing before you go."

"Yes, and what's that?" Still she hadn't moved.

"What name do you go by, you stuck-up—?"

"Arlia is my name. Remember it… as the day will come when I will be standing over your corpse. The next time I draw my sword in your presence, your head will roll! Be warned." She re-holstered her gleaming weapon.

"Huh, I look forward to the day our swords meet," he spat back.

Arlia ignored that final comment. She took note of the other six demons in the arena as she hustled forward. They watched her approach attentively.

Arlia was expecting this, but she knew no trouble would start.

Not yet, anyway.

The demons returned to their watchtower in the mixing pit, their long tattered black overcoats swinging past the two Texan sound engineers, who were on their hands and knees bolting on an addition to the electronic mass under the panels.

"How long is this going to take?" asked Arlia's interrogator, exasperated, his eyes fixed on the two humans.

"It is nearly complete, Sergeant Slyzor. Before we were rudely interrupted, I heard Max say it should only be another few minutes," hissed the other.

"Well, about time!" Slyzor said. "I can't wait to see my blade slice that lousy angel trash in two!"

He took a deep breath, his vast shoulders rising.

"Tonight is going to be a great victory," he announced, "Our army is a thousand strong, and they," pointing first in the direction of Arlia, then at the stage, "don't stand a chance."

The two demons turned their attention to the two men below them.

"That's it, Max. Timer set. We're ready to rock'n'roll," said one.

"Good, good, Rick, my good friend. Mr. King will be pleased with us," said the second one.

A roadie from the stage came over and addressed them. "Hey, Max, have you finished rigging up all the sound cables, as we need to take them under the floor to the stage?"

Max popped his head up. "Yeah, Vince, we're almost done. Give us a couple of minutes and we'll start joining them to the stage."

"Great, Max! We're ahead of schedule. We should be able to knock off early, the way we're going." Vince was pleased. "Keep up the good work, guys."

* * *

"Roger, you have my word," Ray Malone said, gripping the handset tightly. "You will have a full report on all of these transactions by the end of next week."

He listened to the response, loosening the button to his shirt collar, sweat beads running down his neck.

"Looking forward to seeing you tonight. Till then, Roger."

He hung up and slumped in his chair.

He grabbed his cell phone from his desk drawer and dialed a number.

"Tom Mayer…" answered a male voice through the speaker.

"Tom, Ray. We got a problem. I just got off the phone from Roger McDowall. He spent twenty minutes interrogating me about a series of 'suspicious', to use his words, transactions the audit team has discovered. And guess what? They happen to amount to a cool fifty million dollars."

"Whoa, cool it, slow down a little," Tom replied.

"Don't tell me to relax, Tom. We're talking about fraud here, and that could get me jailed!"

"Yes, yes, I know. But yelling and screaming at me isn't going to help you."

Malone got to his feet and went to sit on the edge of his desk. He was short and solid, with a weathered face.

"You do have all the backing documentation safely locked away, don't you, Tom?"

"Of course I do, Ray. All safe and sound in my New York office."

"I need to pull together a report for McDowall, so I require a detailed investment strategy from you for each of the amounts transferred. You can produce that for me, can't you, Tom?"

"Yeah, no problems, Ray. Will get that to you ASAP next week. I'm working out of New York, so it will be fine. Don't you worry, you'll have everything you need to convince him of the bona fide nature of those transactions. I'd best be off. Have a great weekend. We'll talk next week."

The line disconnected.

No blasted audit partner is going to take Ray Malone down, no chance!

He was stomping around his large office getting angrier and angrier at each step he took.

I'm the best in the business and I am not finished with it yet. I've still got another good twenty years left. I'll be the next famous ad industry mogul, you watch me. No audit partner who's paranoid about being sued is going to stand in my way!

Two black shapes, invisible to the human eye, towered over him as he leant over his desk. They each had a claw on his shoulder, and one whispered in his ear, feeding Ray's anger.

Malone swung around and resumed his angry pacing. The two demons left a trail of sulfur as they followed him, inciting his rage:

"You should be angry, Malone."

"We'll get that audit partner."

"How dare he go direct to McDowall?"

"You're the best in this business."

Malone's face burned crimson with fury. He was aware of an unpleasant smell, and sniffed his own armpits suspiciously. The room was thick with a fog of sulfur and sweat.

A large shadow stepped out from behind the sofa, flanked by smaller dark figures. The leader was considerably larger, bare-chested, with thick black hair covering his torso. His only clothing was a pair of black trousers, stretched to cover his tree-trunk-sized thighs.

His grotesque face wore a look of complete disgust.

PHPHOOM! GASP!

His right arm shot out and grabbed one of Malone's shadows around the neck. The others froze where they stood. He dragged the cowering fiend by the neck and brought him to within an inch of his rock-hard face.

"GRRROWWWLLL." He sounded like a lion before it devours its prey.

"How dare you place this mission at risk!" he said. "If it falters because of your incompetence, I will personally send you to the abyss, never to return!"

His grip was tightening. The junior demon was gasping for breath, shaken like a rag doll.

He opened his mouth but no sound emerged.

"You wish to speak?" the strongman asked.

The noose-like hold on the sentinel's neck eased. He spoke haltingly. "Agramon, sir… it was not my fault. One of the others—"

"No excuses!" Agramon yelled, lifting him off the ground with one mighty paw. "I want no more mistakes. Make sure Malone isn't found out yet! It's too early. Or else, you all know what the penalty will be… " he hissed.

THUMP! The sentinel fell in a heap, his legs unable to hold him up.

Agramon turned and walked through the wall, followed by his two aides. The accused's colleague helped him to his feet.

Malone, oblivious to these exchanges, had resumed his seat behind the magnificent desk. The demons returned to their stations behind him.

He felt a sudden sharp pain in his neck as it locked up.

"Ughhh…" he cried out in pain. He couldn't move.

The demon, his face burning with anger, grabbed Malone's neck in a vise-like grip.

He squeezed a little tighter. *"Arghhh!"* Malone winced in agony. Panic hit him, as paralysis started moving down his spine.

The second demon thumped his colleague's powerful arm, forcing it to release the pressure. Malone gasped in relief.

"Wow, what was that?" he muttered to himself.

"That's not going to solve any problems, you know," said the second demon.

"I know, but it sure made me feel better!" snarled the first. "Let's get Malone back to work!"

* * *

She was in her car listening to the radio when her car-phone rang. She didn't recognize the number on her dash.

"Loren Summers," she answered, a serious expression on her face.

"Off to make ourselves beautiful for tonight, are we?" came a voice she knew instantly. Loren smiled.

"Ray, you know we women always want to look our best… one of the problems with being a woman."

"Hey, sorry I couldn't meet with you this morning. Something urgent came up."

"No problem, Ray. It gave me extra time at the arena, looking over the preparations for tonight."

"Good." Malone was sounding slightly smug. "I wanted to tell you that you've been accepted by the Board to take part in the Executive Leadership Development Program that starts next month."

A smile spread across her face.

"Are you serious?"

"As if I'd joke about it, Loren."

"Ray, I don't know what to say, other than thank you."

"Loren, you deserve it. You should have got it last year but – oh well, best not go into that."

Hmmm, what's that about?

Ray filled the silence. "It starts with a week at Insead in France. Will getting someone to mind the kids be a problem?"

"Oh, ah, it shouldn't be. Most likely I'll have Mom and Dad move in. Might even ask their father."

"Would he do that?" He paused. "He'll be too busy, surely?"

"Probably, but it's about time he starting taking some responsibility for his children. He's hardly seen them since he took that New York-based job."

"Certainly. But some guys just aren't cut out to be fathers, and I reckon Tom Mayer is just one of those men."

"Ray, he's their father, for heaven's sake. It's not about whether he's good at it or not, it's his responsibility. If he wasn't cut out for it, he should have thought more about that before he decided to have children. And anyway," Loren's voice turned bitter, "I actually think he can be a good father. He's just consumed by doing deals and bedding every pretty girl that walks by."

"OK, OK, enough. No doubt you're right. But he won't be able to help you out at the end of the month."

"Why not? How would you know?" Ray and Tom were both members of the same country club. But why would Ray know Tom's schedule?

"Oh, he mentioned something to me at the Club the other day, about having to be in New York or somewhere at the end of the month."

She had caught the slight hesitation. "Ray, it sounds like you know more than you're telling me."

"Not at all. He didn't say anything else that I can recall. Obviously, ask him."

"You bet I will!" Loren had little respect for her philandering ex.

A moment passed in silence.

"Listen, Loren, I need to keep going, more calls to do. Congratulations once again on the EDP. The Board is very proud of your achievements. And I'll see you tonight, looking gorgeous, I imagine. Bye."

Ray hung up before Loren could say goodbye.

Not like Ray to hang up like that. Hmmm.

The Saab was really purring at sixty, shooting down the Santa Monica Boulevard. Her frown soon dissolved.

Oh, wow. I got the Development Program!

"Yesss! Yesss!" She starting tapping the steering wheel, elated.

The clock on the dashboard said 3:17. Right on time for her hair appointment.

* * *

The darkness was absolute – but alive, moving, pulsating. Every few feet two red glowing eyes pierced the blackness. Hundreds of them, scanning feverishly, ever watchful.

The moving mass was scratching, hissing, shouting. Squabbles broke out, the noise intensifying, causing an eruption of barking dogs across the city that drove their owners mad, while dog-less neighbors yelled obscenities over back fences.

The noise ceased suddenly.

In an empty Hollywood studio, a herald blew a series of sharp notes on an ancient golden horn. The dark space lit up as a thousand-strong army of writhing black ghouls scrambled and shrieked into a roughshod formation.

THUMP!

The ground shook. Hushed silence. Almost in unison the demons, of all shapes and sizes, turned their attention to the far end of the studio. Those at the front took a step back, only to be pushed forward again by those whose space they had invaded.

There at the head was their leader, extending his monstrous frame. Covered in masses of hair from head to toe. Agramon. His black, beady eyes examined his silent legions.

"The time has come, my eager, murderous army," he bellowed, snorting sulfur. The crowd erupted in a chorus of snarls, growls and hisses.

He continued in his gravelly voice: "We have waited for this day for a long time and the planning is complete. All is in readiness. You all know what is expected of you—"

Agramon stopped and waited, a smirk revealing dagger-like front teeth.

The stillness was broken by a commotion from the side.

"Let me *gooo!*" screamed a deformed creature. Two bulky wolf-men were dragging it towards the leader.

"Stand to attention," demanded one of the henchmen as they stopped in front of Agramon, with a whack to the back of the demon's head as encouragement.

"No, no, no, Agra—" it whimpered. "No… it wasn't me, no, I didn't do it, please, sir—"

With a single slash Agramon decapitated the creature. Its lifeless form crumbled to the ground in a black cloud of dust.

Cheers rose from the crowd. Demons existed only for this. Kill or be killed.

"That is what will happen to any who fail," Agramon snorted gleefully, his black sword smoking as he held it triumphantly above his head. "I will personally ensure that any who fail never return. Arise now and wreak havoc on all you encounter this evening. Spare no one and be willing to die for the greater cause!"

"KILL! KILL! KILL!" chanted the crowd.

There was a flapping and clapping of wings as row upon row of demons flew off, filling the sky. An enormous black stain soon blocked out the sunset, like a large oil spill consuming the blue water of the ocean.

The streetlights cast a shadowy glow over the hills of Hollywood. A frigid night wind blew in off the Pacific. People on the streets quickened their pace, seeking refuge from the storm, and looking into the murky sky with a sense of unease.

The demonic assassins did not have far to travel to their destination, the nearby arena, for what they anticipated would be a major victory.

* * *

"Here they come, over towards the hills in the north-east corner," a tall white knight on watch duty relayed to the group of five standing in Loren Summers' office. Promptly, they moved to the windows to see for themselves the black swarm that approached.

"There must be at least a thousand of them," one said, exasperated.

"Far more than we have at our disposal. We don't stand a chance!" another said.

"Yes, Landen, you're right," Athaniel replied. "We don't stand a chance if we engage. But the plan is not to engage tonight," he said, turning back to the centre of the office.

"What? We just stand by and watch this army of murderers wreak havoc on our city?!"

Athaniel put his arms on Landen's shoulders. "Landen, I know it sounds ridiculous, almost unbelievable, but we must stick to the plan!"

Athaniel's dark features contrasted with the fairness of the others.

"Reinforcements from Denver, Colorado are on their way as we speak," the angelguard leader continued. "They will boost our numbers by three hundred."

"Oh, that's good to know. Now the odds are only three to one. That makes me feel a whole lot better! *Not!*" Landen said, stomping his foot.

"Will they engage us, Athaniel?" the watch guard asked.

"You can never tell with the enemy. They are so blood-thirsty. It doesn't take much to get them to reach for their swords.

But they are more interested in humans tonight, not our limited forces.

"The key is to keep Loren safe. Our intelligence indicates they are not yet aware of Loren's importance to our plans, so we hope they will continue to ignore her."

Loren entered her office in a stunning full-length cocktail dress, her long brunette hair now stylishly swept up. Arlia followed and, on seeing her comrades, joined them.

Loren dialed a number on her desk phone.

"Hello, Marcie speaking," said the voice through the speaker.

"Hey, Marce," Loren replied.

"Hey, babe, you all dolled up for your big night?" Marcie asked.

"Ah, yeah, I guess. You know me – always feel better in a suit rather than a cocktail dress!"

"I'm sure you'll be the belle of the ball."

"Oh, don't know about that! Hey, got some sensational news today."

"Do tell."

"Remember how I always wanted to be accepted into that Leadership Program? Well, my boss told me today that I'd got it!"

"Yay, Loz! Congratulations, babe! That's great news."

"Look, I'll tell you all about it tomorrow, as I'm kinda in a rush now. How are Taylor and Luke going?"

"All good here. Well, in fact, it's a bit of a crazy house at the moment with Bec's three, my three and your two."

"And you're loving it, I bet!"

"Naturally, nothing makes me happier than seeing all our kids having a ball."

"Marce, I better go. Give my love to Tays and Luke – oh, and Bec."

"See ya, babe. Have a fantastic night, and we'll talk in the morning about dropping the kids back to you."

"Thanks, Marce. Love you."

"Love you too. Bye."

The group of angelic beings locked arms. Their wings were held tightly within their backs.

They began quietly humming a song of praise as Loren opened her closet and took one last look in the mirror. The white radiance of the group's tunics reflected off the ceiling lights, creating a halo effect around Loren.

"Oh well, this is going to have to do," she said to herself.

It was 6:31.

* * *

Across town, Marcie, having gotten off the phone from Loren, was standing in her kitchen, deep in thought, marinating the chicken for the barbecue. Rebecca walked in, a beautiful knight glorious in all-white battle-dress following her.

"Bec, whilst the kids are out of sight, I think we should pray. I've felt uneasy all day and I sense Loren needs our prayers."

"Hmmm, let's do it, Marce," Rebecca replied. "I know to never doubt the Spirit's nudges on your heart."

A second white knight strode up, greeting the first with a warm embrace. They knew each other very well.

"How is she, Marce?"

"Sounded rushed and a bit flustered. This is a really big gig for her and she could do with the Lord's protection." Marcie grabbed her friend's hand and led her to the lounge. They knelt at the coffee table. The two white knights stood over the two women, shielding them with outstretched wings.

Chapter 3

The limousines arrived one by one at five-minute intervals, allowing the guests to disembark at a leisurely pace. The small but lively crowd – stargazers and the just plain curious – were barricaded either side of the red carpet. The first guests to make their way down the long red corridor to the front foyer of the Amphitheater were mostly unknown to the public. They were executives of large Fortune 500 companies who had paid $5,000 a seat to attend tonight's extravaganza.

The night air was thick with the demonic horde. The constant flapping of their wings generated a chilling breeze. It cut through clothes and forced the guests to hasten their progress into the theatre, many of the women protecting elaborate hair designs.

"When will this be over?" asked a frustrated bat-like creature, lining the inside of the barricade along with 100 fellow demons. They were the advance party, responsible for monitoring all activity within the venue. They shouted abuse at the humans, adding unheard tension to the chill in the air.

No response was forthcoming, so the bat screamed, "Let's get the mayhem started!" directly into the face of a camera-wielding teenage girl. He pointed his taloned claw inches from her nose. She immediately felt claustrophobic, hemmed in by the masses, nausea rising to the back of her throat.

A hush came over the crowd as one of the first real celebrities arrived. A famous Oscar-winning actress hopped out of the silver stretch, accompanied by her current actor boyfriend and her mother, who was resplendent in a simple black dress. The mother brought the crowd alive by grabbing her daughter's hand and leaving the beau behind in a confused muddle. He promptly wandered over to the fans, signing autographs and making shallow conversation, much to the crowd's pleasure.

Limousine after limousine arrived and moved on, dropping the glamorous and feted. Fifty minutes after the first car arrived, the final one departed. By eight o'clock the entrance doors to the Amphitheater were locked shut.

Also locked inside were the 100 menacing assassins.

* * *

Loren was at a table of twelve with some of the other organizing executives and a number of lower-status celebrities. It was two-thirds of the way back from the stage and off to the western side, near an exit. Every table had an uninterrupted view of the stage. A thick curtain, resplendent with the logos of various charities, shielded the stage.

Arlia took up a position against the wall near Loren's table. She scanned the arena and counted twelve other angelguards on duty. Some were placed in specific hot spots while others had roving reconnaissance duties.

The dark assassins greatly outnumbered the white knights in the arena. The demons were positioned evenly throughout, with greater concentration at the entrance, the exits and the stage.

A popular talk-show host had commenced his introductory comments as Arlia studied the four demons guarding her escape route. She smiled at them, all four hissing back in response.

The four stationed at her exit did not appear to be anything special, looking like everyday sentinels. Arlia was a veteran, having been involved in hundreds of major battles, and was renowned in white knight folklore for her swordsmanship, courage and athleticism. But experience had taught her never to underestimate the enemy. She studied each of them individually. They were heavily armed: swords, daggers, and two carrying axes.

An enthusiastic applause signaled the end of the introduction and the guests were contemplating the entrées placed in front of them. A hum of good-natured chatter and laughter reverberated around the ballroom.

It was 8:40, twenty minutes to show time.

Athaniel entered with four white knights in tow. The entire enemy contingent immediately stopped what they were doing to follow his progress.

Two demons approached, swords raised.

"There is no need for aggression, sentinels of the dark lord," Athaniel said. "I, and my four guards, come here to seek a better view of the night's proceedings, that's all."

Ten other sentinels took up positions behind their comrades. They stood chests out, ready for action. A handful heckled the angels with expletives.

"Enough!" Slyzor said, stepping forward.

The two groups were four feet apart. Even though they were outnumbered, the angels' extra height made the sentinels a little less threatening.

"What, you don't recognize me, Captain of the Guard?" He walked straight up to Athaniel, black wings extended.

"Slyzor... Hmphh, I didn't realize you were part of this motley gang," Athaniel replied. "It's been a long time."

"Far too long," said Slyzor mockingly, spitting in Athaniel's face.

"Ah yes, Slyzor, the great Falklands Battle. I remember it well. Specifically, you, Slyzor, retreating hastily when I confronted you."

Slyzor hesitated as he recalled that act of cowardice over thirty years ago. He was demoted as a result, never to get beyond his current rank of Sergeant. He had planned for something far greater.

"Oh yesss, Athaniel. I have looked forward with great eagerness to the day when I will avenge that humiliation, when you will bear the pain and suffering that only my sword can evoke. Ha ha ha! Perhaps that day will be—"

Slyzor pointed his crooked, sharp claws at Athaniel, spitting with hatred.

"—*tonight!*"

Athaniel smiled. Despite his previous victory, he knew Slyzor was a worthy opponent. Slyzor had maimed thousands in his time and had just the motivation to hurt Athaniel's cause.

But in his mind Athaniel thought he might be able to use Slyzor's desire for vengeance to his advantage, if not tonight, then later.

Athaniel and his four knights looked away from the band of sentinels and took up positions in front of the sound engineer's station.

Slyzor was seething.

"You dare to mock me, you, you, pompous, righteous—!" he screamed. "I will have my vengeance… if it's the last thing I do… mark my words, oh, sweet Captain of the Guard!"

Athaniel was unconcerned. This confirmed his thoughts: Slyzor's insane rage could well be his undoing.

Slyzor waved his troops away. "To your stations and be ever alert – they're never this obvious unless shielding humans." He stalked off, pushing one of his sentinels out of the way.

* * *

Ten minutes away in a small office on top of a video shop two men were intently focused on the laptop open in front of them.

"Something must be wrong, Max. They were supposed to call us two hours ago," Rick said. He got up and started pacing the floor, whilst wringing his hands.

"Rick, relax, everything is going to be all right," replied Max. "We rigged it all up perfectly this morning. Everything is going to happen as set out in the plan. Poor Vince will have no idea about the two Texans he hired. Our disguises were masterful," he added, nodding to the masks and hairpieces sitting on another table by the window.

"We'll be out of here before you know it, you wait and see." Max turned back to the screen.

"I don't know why we needed to hang around. We've done our bit of the job. We could have been long gone by now." Rick still wasn't satisfied.

"Patience. Now let's start another game of *Words with Friends*."

"All right. I just want to get outta here, and can't stand

the waiting." Rick sat back down and proceeded to bite on his fingernails.

A group of ten demons hovered outside the office, keeping watch over the two humans inside.

In the park directly opposite the video shop, large leafy trees provided a safe haven for two watchers who had followed the agents and their demonic support crew from the Amphitheater earlier in the day.

* * *

It was now hot and steamy inside the arena, not unlike a sauna. Sulfur trails snaked through the rancid atmosphere.

The guests were growing more and more inebriated, encouraged by the sentinels to keep drinking. Expletives were being thrown around; people who had been mild-mannered an hour ago were telling others what they really thought of them. Women were standing in small groups being catty about other women. Lecherous men were working very hard to convince pretty young starlets that they would give them their big break in showbiz, but only if they hopped outside with them for a few moments. Apparent strangers were seen smooching, demons hanging off them, filling their minds with lewd thoughts.

Slyzor sat on top of a row of stage lights contemplating his revenge. He imagined piercing Athaniel's heart with his trusty scimitar and sending him to the heavenly ex-servicemen's club. *Not long now!*

Athaniel was watching all the activity, trying to catch the slightest change in the enemy that might give some clue as to the timing of the attack.

Loren made her way back into the arena. She was engrossed in conversation with the founder of a movie studio.

Arlia returned too, but hung back from looking too interested in Loren.

Another arrived too, unnoticed by all, human or supernatural. Zeldax, a master of disguise and camouflage, was presently assuming the navy-blue wall color of the ballroom. He was able to cover a great distance very quickly, observing all the movements of the white knights. He finally settled on one to watch more closely. The one that appeared to be following a human female. Arlia.

The clock inside the ballroom struck ten.

Simultaneously, underneath the mixing pit, a timer clicked on: 29:59, 29:58…

* * *

A stream of light swooped on the sentinel watch guarding the video shop.

Even though outnumbered two to one, the sentinels leapt into the fray, exploding out of the office, thrashing and hacking straight into the angelic mass. The white knights quickly grabbed the upper hand, drawing the demons away from the video store.

Emur, the white knight leader, seized his chance, shot out of the tree, and entered the now unguarded first-story office through a rear wall. Max and Rick were engrossed in their computer game.

The angel paced the floor, looking outside to see the fight continuing in the park he had just left. The terrific amount of light indicated the angels were still dominant.

The silence was broken by the ringtone of a cell phone.

"Hello," Max answered. And listened.

He put his hand over the mouthpiece and whispered to Rick: "Activation of the timer has occurred, detonation at 10:30." He scanned his watch. "Now fifteen minutes away."

Max listened to the caller.

"Don't worry, Mr. King, it'll be a masterpiece. The fireworks show will be splendid."

The caller interrupted him.

"Yep, you'll be able to read about it tomorrow in the Belgian papers!"

Max listened again.

"Goodbye, Mr. King. Enjoy the celebration!"

He tapped the phone's screen and slipped it into his shirt pocket.

Emur had the information he needed. It was to be 10:30.

He turned, to find he was staring into the sinister red eyes of a sentinel guard.

* * *

The guests were feasting on *fillet mignon*, baked salmon or some vegetarian concoction for the non-carnivores. The noise within the ballroom had increased dramatically as the throng of sentinels continued their harassment.

The white knights were used to this from the enemy. It was important to stand firm unless a human was going to be harmed.

Loren's table was no exception and had become quite rowdy. Four sentinels were teasing and playing with the fast-drinking group. Two large gentlemen, egged on by their sentinels, boxed Loren in. At first she was amused by the men's mischievous behavior, but now they were beginning to get a little out of hand.

One demon was filling the mind of one of the men with filthy thoughts. He placed his hand on Loren's thigh, but she pushed him away. The other man, urged to dwell on his own glories, was regaling her with his tremendous achievements and the wealth he possessed. Loren was polite at first, but soon explicitly told them both to desist.

Zeldax hovered nearby, relishing the scene.

Arlia, a table away, was getting uptight. She moved closer to see if Loren was OK.

Loren's firmness had inflamed the situation further and a man on the other side of the table joined in with some crude comments inspired by the demonic presence standing over him. That served to encourage the two men surrounding Loren. She tried to get up. One of her lecherous dining companions grabbed her arm and stopped her rising.

Arlia had had enough. She moved briskly over to the table and sent one demon flying against the wall. She took three steps and, with lightning speed, flattened the other with a punch to the jaw that would have made a professional boxer proud.

So indeed she is being protected! Zeldax reacted immediately. He escaped through the wall and flew off to report. Agramon would be pleased with him.

Loren's two ogres suddenly stopped misbehaving and apologized profusely.

A gang of five swearing and snarling sentinels surrounded Arlia. She was still pumped with adrenalin, itching for more action. They too wanted a fight. And Arlia's actions were more than enough to start one.

They drew their weapons.

Athaniel watched attentively from his position at the mixing pit as the situation developed.

GLUNK! Slyzor landed between his attackers and Arlia, startling them all.

"Stand down, sentinels – that is an order!" Slyzor demanded.

One, slobbering at the mouth, muttered, "We are not going to let this hag take advantage of us. We must fight back."

"No. Not now!"

"Yes, now," the other said heatedly. He stepped forward, clutching his sword.

"Back down, soldier, or else I'll take you myself," Slyzor snarled, standing almost on top of him. "*Not now!* Your chance will come soon enough."

The gang of five put their weapons away and moved off, muttering.

"Not long now, I'd suggest," Athaniel said to Landen. His shoulders noticeably relaxed with Slyzor's intervention.

* * *

"Yaaagh!" The black beast lashed out, slicing Emur's non-sword arm. Emur stumbled, deflecting a flurry of strikes with his sword. Swiveling to regain balance, he unleashed a ferocious karate kick to his attacker's throat, knocking him backwards. Emur surged in reverse and shot out of the opposite wall of the office, his pursuer right on his tail.

Emur whistled.

The warring angels, still outnumbering the demons, momentarily dropped off, and on seeing Emur's situation, chased after him and his demon pursuer.

A trail of light behind him, Emur had one destination on his mind: the Amphitheater. *Eight minutes to get there. Go, go, go!*

The sentinels quickly realized they had been duped by the white knights. Furious, they raced after them, seeking revenge.

Emur was doing his best, ducking and weaving to get some distance between himself and the sentinel. But his pursuer was not letting up.

* * *

Agramon was flexing his colossal arms and chest as he prepared for war. He was fully clad in his fighting armor.

"Excuse me, sir," Zeldax said meekly. He was now completely visible, cringing like a small child.

"What do you have to report?"

"Good news, sir. I think they do seek to protect a special one! A woman."

"Who is this woman?"

"Summers. Loren Summers is her name."

"Hmmm, Summers…" Agramon's mind clicked over, trying to place the name. "Nothing comes to mind. What's significant about her?"

Zeldax shrugged his shoulders.

"There was only the one engagement whilst I watched, and it involved this Summers woman. Athaniel took an obvious interest in her situation when her guard stepped in against our forces."

"That is interesting. We must act quickly. Go back to the arena and advise Slyzor of your find. Have him ensure she doesn't survive the holocaust!" Agramon grinned unpleasantly.

Zeldax retreated, wondering what his reward would be.

Agramon readied himself, checking his weapons, fixing his armor. He blasted out into the open air like a fighter jet into the midst of the suffocating cover of his demonic army.

* * *

Emur could see the arena half a mile ahead, a hideous blanket of satanic life blocking his path. *How will I get through that?* He had to get the information to Athaniel before it was too late.

Think, Emur, think!

Completing a 180-degree turn, he rejoined his comrades from the rear.

This better work!

The angelguard squadron swooped down in formation, hoping to stay unnoticed by the heaving mass of demons in front of them for as long as possible. The band of trailing sentinels followed, now only three body lengths behind. Emur moved into the centre of the group with only thirty seconds to go before reaching the arena.

It was 10:25.

* * *

Agramon saw it first.

A brilliant flash of light like a giant shooting star in rapid descent headed straight for the arena, with a group of his sentinels in fast pursuit.

He knew exactly what it was.

"White knights at five o'clock!" he bellowed. *"Stop them getting through to the arena!"*

The closest group of eighty sentinels, swords drawn, shot down to cut the knights off.

"Here they come!" Emur yelled, knowing they were hopelessly outnumbered. "Stay tightly grouped, don't slow down, and watch our backs. We only need a few seconds over the arena so I can drop in."

An intense bright light blinded the horde – the impact of the knights simultaneously unleashing their glowing blades.

Chapter 4

Zeldax arrived back in the ballroom, in time to observe Slyzor hurrying out to the foyer with two other demons. They were ushering a man outside, who'd obviously had too much to drink. Attached to his right side was a pretty blonde in an off-white dress who also looked the worse for wear, as evidenced by her staggering gait.

Zeldax followed them out, stopping at the entrance to the foyer. He smiled, seeing the darkness above him. He switched his gaze back to the man and woman, who fell into the back seat of a waiting limousine. It slowly pulled away, accompanied by Slyzor's hounds, who had attached themselves to its roof.

Slyzor swaggered back to the entrance, satisfied that the pair had been safely netted.

"Slyzor," Zeldax yelped. Slyzor ignored him. Zeldax grabbed his arm.

"I don't have time for you, imp," Slyzor snarled.

"Wait, wait. I have news from Agramon!"

Slyzor, simmering, stopped and stepped towards the small chameleon.

"There is a special person the knights are guarding. Agramon has ordered that we ensure she is killed in the attack!"

"What are you saying? You tell me this now?!" Slyzor stood over Zeldax, eyes on fire. "Who is this person... she... you said *she*?"

Zeldax smirked.

"Well, out with it, you sorry little runt!" Slyzor raised his talons threateningly towards the nuisance.

Zeldax smiled, exposing his black teeth. "Her name is—"
CRASH!

They both looked up to see a brilliant flash of light being hit by a freight train of sentinels.

"*Nooo... They've found out!*" Slyzor screamed. "I must get to Athaniel first..."

"—Summers. Loren Summers," Zeldax finished.

Slyzor bolted inside the auditorium, sending the fragile Zeldax into a spin.

* * *

The crash hurt the knights, knocking them back.

THUMP!

Then the smaller chasing group of sentinels smashed into them.

Flashing angelic blades deflected and parried everything thrown at them. Emur and his team ducked, weaved, twisted and turned but still held together.

It was almost too late.

They were locked up in a lopsided vise. The two-pronged attack was actually working in the knights' favor, drawing them closer, whilst Emur remained concealed.

"One huge lunge forward, team!" he yelled. "*Push!*" And with all their combined strength the group shoved forward.

"Almost there ..."

* * *

Slyzor roared into the ballroom, heading straight for the mixing pit.

He spun around, scanning the auditorium. "Where are you?" he screamed. There was no response.

"Where's Athaniel?" he yelled at the demons nearby.

"Ummm, don't know. What's the problem?"

"They know and they are about to tell him!"

And then he saw him, standing on the western wall with two of his troop.

"*Athhhanielll!*" A high-pitched shriek cut the tension within the ethereal domain.

***

SLASH!

A fiery sword opened the lead angel's neck. "Now! Go, Emur! Godspeed!" he cried, and fell earthwards.

Emur dropped down out of the group like a lightning bolt through the roof of the Amphitheater. Four of the sentinels from the rear group took off in pursuit.

Emur was too fast. He had a five-second head start. That was going to have to be enough.

"C'mon, boyo, you can do this. God be praised!" Emur yelled, fists forward, light sparkling off his tunic.

It was 10:28.

***

Emur crashed through into the ballroom, the four snarling sentinels chasing hard. He drove fast and furious towards Athaniel. Out of the corner of his eye he saw a very angry-looking screaming demon heading straight for his leader too.

Gulp! They knew. "Harder, Emur!"

Athaniel turned on hearing Slyzor's scream. He sensed something coming at him from the opposite direction. Emur! Shooting towards him, chased by four bloodthirsty ogres.

His wings burst forth. He grabbed Emur, blazed past the four pursuers and circled the room.

"It'll blow at 10:30!" Emur uttered breathlessly.

"Well done, Emur."

They dropped onto the central speaker panel, Athaniel abruptly pitching two demons to the back of the ballroom with his enormous arms.

His senses were whirling, his mind on overdrive, charged with razor-sharp clarity. He leapt down behind the three panel operators, who were completely oblivious to his presence and the impending doom that was about to rain down on them. He ducked underneath the panel.

He quickly found what he was looking for.

A clock. Counting down: 1:30, 1:29, 1:28…

Slyzor thumped down on the panel. He stood aggressively over Athaniel.

"You're too late, Athaniel!"

WHAM!

Slyzor was sent sprawling by a jaw-breaking punch that he didn't see coming.

Athaniel raced towards Loren and Arlia.

Zeldax helped Slyzor to his feet. Black blood was gushing from his smashed jaw.

"Who did you say they were guarding?" Slyzor mumbled, spitting out a fragment of tooth.

Arlia didn't wait to be told what to do.

Get Loren out!

Loren's cell phone rang.

"Something wrong with the…" Loren struggled to hear over the din of the laser guns on stage. She stood up and moved towards the exit so she could hear better. She felt like she was floating on air.

Arlia was carrying her.

SHOOM!

A flash of light blinded the four sentinels guarding the door. They didn't get a chance to raise their weapons. Athaniel's power was like a bulldozing tank. They didn't know what had hit them.

"Marcie, is that you?" Loren yelled, phone glued to her ear. She sprinted effortlessly away from the arena until she was over 300 feet away.

"Keep going, Arlia!" Athaniel bawled, looking behind him.

Their escape was observed from the black sky above by an extremely annoyed warlord.

Silence.

Everything went still.

Athaniel and Arlia huddled, cocooning Loren, still with the cell phone to her ear.

"Marcie, are you still…?"

BOOM!

The deafening explosion shattered the silence of the late hour.

THUD!

Loren was smashed to the ground with Arlia, the phone ripped out of her hand, flung twenty feet away. Her head hit the lawn, the jolting impact sending her into unconsciousness.

WHACK! CLANG! Athaniel fended off flying shrapnel the size of footballs.

The shrapnel was the least of their worries. Thirty very mad, sword-thrashing killers led by the wounded Slyzor were headed straight for them.

"Arlia!" Athaniel yelled, ducking a flashing red-hot steel rod. He spun around to check where she was. "Arlia, you OK? We've got company. And lots of them!" He helped her to her feet, whistling a sharp signal.

"What about Loren, Athaniel?" Arlia queried as they swung into the air, wings bursting forth, evading the first onslaught.

"She'll be OK so long as we are…"

CRACK! Athaniel slashed at furious speed, cutting through five demons in an instant, his left hand pummeling two others with face-breaking punches.

Four demons had pinned Arlia, but only momentarily. She spun and twisted, swatting them like flies with her powerful swordplay. The two went back to back, Arlia locking her arms into Athaniel's, lifting herself up and side-kicking five others out of the way. But Slyzor's forces kept coming.

Ten surrounded them, frothing and slobbering, multiple weapons drawn… WHAM! Half of them disintegrated as a stream of light broke through their ranks. Hannen, Landen and five other angels charged in, thrashing all in their path.

Arlia broke away, and swooped to the ground to see Loren. She flattened one bat-like demon, but was now off-balance. Another slashed her left arm from behind. It was deep but she'd survive. He didn't get another chance. Electrifyingly fast, she struck the sentinel hard and true through the chest. "Go back to hell!" Her injured arm fell uselessly limp by her side as she scooped Loren up and took her away from the melee.

Hannen and Landen were battling three sentinels each, the clash of silver and black swords creating a deafening chorus of clanging metal.

Slyzor went after the one who had driven him crazy with vengeance all these years. When they had first clashed all those decades ago they had been evenly matched, but the years since had seen Athaniel develop into one of the most feared white knights, while the retribution-filled sergeant had withered, consumed by his desire to punish his arch enemy.

His jaw was broken, but he still tried to speak, spitting black blood: "This is the last time you will make a fool of *meeee*!" His blade flashed in an arc.

Their swords clashed. Athaniel shoved Slyzor away and stared hard at his opponent. "It will be the last time we meet, but not the way you intend."

Slyzor was slashing wildly. Hissing, spitting, flapping. He'd lost control.

Arlia returned to assist Hannen and Landen, who were now struggling against the combined impact of six swords against their two. She turned the tables, forcing the sentinels back. They would not surrender or flee. It was victory or the wasteland.

* * *

The bomb had blown the Amphitheater to pieces, creating a huge fireball that leapt into the air, shooting shrapnel missiles in all directions.

The fireball consumed anyone who survived the blast; Agramon's brood of demonic assassins made sure of it.

A battle royale was taking place around the blaze. The white knights were struggling, outnumbered four to one, against the might of the black horde. The sound of the fierce battle within the supernatural was louder than the destructive force of the inferno raging below.

Sirens were blaring in the distance. The first rescue teams arrived at the scene only to be pushed back by the severity of the flames. Small explosions continued to go off at regular intervals, feeding the fire monster that consumed everything in its path.

* * *

The battle above raged on unabated. The spoils were pretty even after thirty minutes, but Agramon's troops knew their mission had been successful and were beginning to disperse.

Slyzor continued to attack Athaniel with wild jabs of his sword. He knew he was tiring. He had to make a bold move, or Athaniel would just wait till he was too weak and finish him off.

Slyzor circled with renewed speed and drove hard at the white knight leader's heart. The sword penetrated Athaniel's defense and appeared to strike true. Athaniel's head bowed. Slyzor sensed victory, at last.

Athaniel pulled on his attacker's sword with his body, the abrupt jerk snatching it out of Slyzor's grip. His head lifted to stare into his enemy's death-filled red eyes. With a sudden slash of his huge blade he sliced Slyzor's head from the neck that held it up. Black blood gushed up as the now lifeless body twitched for the last time and disintegrated, never to trouble anyone, human or angel, again.

His foe's sword dropped away from under Athaniel's armpit, a small bloodstain emerging on his tunic.

He turned to see his three warriors finishing off six sentinels. He dropped to the ground to inspect Loren. Still no movement. He checked for a pulse. Yes, there was life still.

Arlia, after dispatching two sentinels, settled alongside her leader.

"How is she?"

"Still alive, thank goodness. When one of the others gets free, have them get one of the rescue workers to take care of her. And Arlia: you do not leave her side – ever," Athaniel ordered.

"Yes, sir. I understand perfectly."

"The enemy now knows she is important to us and will do everything to remove her."

He looked at her useless left arm. "Is that alright?"

"Yeah, I'll live!"

Athaniel nodded approvingly and shot off, low to the ground, flying directly into the burning building that, one hour ago, contained a thousand people.

Arlia's heart cried out for Loren. She was hurt but would live. Exhausted, battered and bruised, Arlia had succeeded.

But her job was far from over. It really had just begun.

Chapter 5

Sydney, 26 January

"Dad, look at all the boats in the harbor," said the little blond-haired boy standing on the train seat staring out the window. The train had just pulled away from the station, heading for the Sydney Harbor Bridge, which joined the northern side of Australia's largest city to the east and south.

"Yeah, you're right, Jonah, there are lots of them out there today," Jack Haines, the boy's father, replied, rising to his feet to cross the carriage. He sat down, pulling his son onto his lap. "Hey, buddy, you know you're not supposed to stand on the seats."

Jack Haines was an attractive man in his early forties. Tall and lean with soulful green eyes, he still possessed a full head of thick brown hair, now with distinguished grey streaks.

It was Australia Day. The one day of the year when Australians celebrate the wonderful country they live in. In Sydney, masses of people, just like the Haines family, had converged on the harbor to enjoy the festivities. There was lots to do, lots to see, lots to eat and drink, and the world's two best fireworks shows at 9 p.m. and midnight to finish it all off.

"Hey, Mum, you've got to see all these boats... oh... where've they gone? Dad, I can't see the boats any more." Jonah stood on his Dad's lap.

Jack smiled at Jonah's mother – his wife, Sarah, who sat directly opposite. He was happy. He relaxed back in the seat as he glanced around the carriage, seeing the joy on the faces of Sarah and his eldest daughter, Beth. Sarah was holding tight the tandem pram that carried their infant twin girls, Grace and Catherine.

Jack's sister, Jane, and her three girls were also sharing the day with them, sitting across the carriage.

Thank you, Father, for blessing me with such a wonderful family.

"Daaad!"

"Oh, sorry, buddy," Jack clicked back. "Unfortunately, the bridge got in the way."

"Hey, my little man, you're going to get the chance to see lots of boats very, very soon once we're down at the Quay," Sarah said loud enough to be heard above the noise of the train.

"Cool," Jonah replied, the smile returning to his face. He turned back to the window, eager to take in everything he could.

The train pulled up at the station, the automatic doors opening.

"OK, team, let's all stay together," Jack said. "Especially you three." The older girls were already at the door, ready to hop out. "We've got to go to another platform to catch the train to Circular Quay, so let's all stick tight."

They didn't have to wait long for the new train. They piled on – babies, toddlers and strollers – with a minimum of fuss.

They were in the front standing section of the first carriage of the train. It was full, people shoulder-to-shoulder.

"Dad, when are we getting off?" was a much-repeated whine from one of the older children.

Jack was pleased when he was able to say finally: "At the next stop we hop off!"

This brought forth a united cheer from the children. "Yaaayyy!"

They were speeding along the tunnel on the approach to Circular Quay station when all of a sudden a massive explosion went off somewhere below them.

"What the blazes was that?!" said a man with a strong cockney accent standing next to Jack.

The train jerked forward suddenly. The passengers crashed forward towards the driver's compartment. The strollers toppled over, halting their progress. Jonah flew shoulder first into the driver's door, where he crumpled in a pile on the carriage floor.

Sarah screamed.

"Jack, the babies. Get the babies!"

Jack had been knocked over by the impact and three people had fallen onto him, so he couldn't see what had happened.

The train's wheels screeched as it struggled to slow down. The driver's door opened, pushing Jonah's unconscious body aside. The driver forced his way into the carriage, looking terrified.

"Get back, get back, everyone!" he yelled. "The train's going to crash!"

He didn't get very far with the mass of people, now in a panic, halting his progress.

"Get back, get back, quickly!"

The train rushed out of the tunnel. Someone screamed out an expletive followed by an ominous-sounding "Oh nooo!"

Dear God in heaven, help us, please!

Jack was back on his feet, looking through the open driver's door, out the front of the train. A huge firestorm where the platform once stood, fifty yards away, was rushing towards the train.

Father, pleeease, no!

Fear gripped his heart with greater dread: under the raging fire he could see an enormous hole in the track.

The train was still going too fast.

Jack swiveled, looking for his family.

The five giant angelic beings on the roof of the train could also see what was about to happen.

"Go to work, team!" one shouted.

The children were all crying and the twins were bellowing from underneath their pram.

Jack couldn't see the twins, as the upside-down pram concealed them. He saw Jonah, apparently lifeless, at the driver's door and two of the older girls pressed up against the far wall.

He turned to Sarah, her eyes round with fear. She had just seen the inevitable too.

The screaming intensified as people tried to push their way back from the front of the train. It had slowed, but still not enough. It was going down that hole in the track.

It only took a moment.

Jack grabbed Sarah's hand and squeezed it. He then jumped to cover the two strollers. He thought he felt a body brush his as he landed. He covered his head with his arms.

So too did an eight-foot white knight.

The fireball engulfed the first two carriages in intense, unbearable heat. Within seconds the carriages fell, and fast.

The first carriage crashed into a thick concrete wall at the back of what, moments earlier, had been an Italian restaurant. The combined impact of the sudden jolt from hitting the wall and the second carriage colliding into it caused the rear of the first carriage to flip up. It broke free from the second, crashing down hard on its left side, rear first. The second landed immediately behind it.

The third carriage followed the preceding two, careering straight into the second's roof. That caused it to buckle and slide off at right angles, its head sliding onto the back of the second carriage while its rear settled on the ground.

Carriage four had broken free but was left hanging over the edge of the hole in the track, swinging precariously, having enough weight to keep it on the track. Within an instant, the flames had roared through the carriages, devouring everything in their path.

Screams of helplessness and panic could be heard coming from within as the inferno incinerated its innocent victims.

Circular Quay was now ablaze, thick black smoke reducing visibility to almost zero.

Emergency rescue teams had arrived on the scene and the first firefighters were attacking the blaze where the wharves had stood only minutes ago. Police, ambulances and fire-and-rescue services charged into action.

One of the emergency crews reached the train carriages lying on the forecourt. Firemen, with no thoughts of self-preservation, threw themselves into the battle against the fire demon that had spread its tentacles around the three fallen carriages.

There were dead people everywhere. The boardwalk to the nearby Opera House, packed with people, had collapsed into the water.

The rescue crew in the rear of the carriage was working

furiously and bodies were now being hauled out. Most were charred beyond recognition, making the job that much harder for the brave workers.

Three hours later, a Gulfstream Jet flying over Western Europe

"What a horrible mess," said a male voice with a mixed European accent – part French, part Finnish. The speaker was watching an up-to-the-minute television broadcast on a wall-mounted plasma screen.

"Indeed, sir, it's truly horrible... hahaha!" Another man broke into a laugh.

"Ssh, let me hear the reporter!" said the first.

"As you can see, there is carnage everywhere. It is still far too early to know the possible death toll. Besides those passengers on the train, the causeway was packed with people – no one has any idea how many. Plus there are at least five ferries impacted by the explosion. This is just an absolute disaster of the grandest scale. Ummm..." The lady reporter pulled away as she sought to control her emotions. "Rescue workers continue to work tirelessly to save as many people as they can. All we can do at this time is hope and pray..."

"Yes, hope and pray, that's right," interrupted the second man, muting the sound on the plasma. "What a magnificent success, sir!"

"My son, London, Los Angeles, and now Sydney – all three have been simply outstanding. Never in my wildest dreams did I think they would all go so well. So much loss of life, so much destruction, and so much fear. I congratulate you on a job very well done."

He raised an almost empty scotch glass to the other, who was sitting behind him.

"Thank you, sir," replied the second man, getting up to refill the first man's glass. "This would not have been possible without your inspirational leadership and planning."

Neither of them was aware of the demonic presence that slipped away from the jet, similarly pleased with his significant role in creating the wave of global panic. He had an appointment to attend.

"However, we have the final piece of the puzzle to land yet. Only then will we have accomplished our goal. Ahhh…" He savored his replenished drink, turning back to face the plasma screen, watching as two strollers, one single and one double, were maneuvered out of a train carriage. Three babies were lifted out, all three alive. Then the body of a man was stretchered out. He was unconscious but still breathing. He would be the final one.

* * *

The crystal-clear water lapped lightly onto the virginal, white, soft sand of the shore. The untouched beach went on for miles, far beyond what the human eye could see. The sun was hot, very hot. The sand was baking under its intense gaze, cooled occasionally by a gentle sea breeze.

A large school of multicolored reef fish scuttled through the idyllic waters just a few yards from the shore. The dorsal fin of a shark unexpectedly broke the smooth surface twenty yards to their rear. The sight of a mallet-head gracefully slicing through the sheer swells confirmed that the predator was a hammerhead, raising panic within the now fleeing school of fish.

The peace of the blue desolate setting was disturbed by a mad thrashing as the killer reached the back of the school, snapping up the slowest.

Then there was silence. The lapping of the small waves on the shore was the only sound. It was like nothing had changed. The circle of life, the survival of the fittest, could not be halted.

The shoreline was narrow, backing onto a dense forest. Large trees reaching 150 feet into the air merged at their tops, their expansive branches forming a solid roof inhibiting the sun's rays from reaching the forest floor. Streaks of light did filter through, but generally the temperature within the forest was a good ten degrees less than that out on the beach, a few yards away.

A set of dark brooding clouds was swarming over the empty ocean and would reach the uninhabited atoll in a matter of minutes. The afternoon thunderstorm would bring relief from the harsh sun while providing nourishment to the jungle life until the next storm the same time the following day.

Lightning bolts exploded out of the clouds. Their electric rays shot erratically over white-capped waves breaking on the outer reef.

The echo of thunder brought the jungle's animal and bird inhabitants to life, erupting in agitated chatter as the late-afternoon ritual commenced.

A large bat-like creature shot out from behind the rainclouds and descended into the middle of the jungle. The chorus of chatter rose to a screeching fever pitch. It landed amongst some ruins, heading to the largest, which had a twelve-foot-tall entrance. As it entered the familiar hideaway, the first heavy drops of rain broke through the clouds, making large splashing pockmarks in the dusty brick pavement of the hidden ancient village.

Two similar huge creatures were awaiting its arrival, turning to greet the sinister interloper.

"You're late, Agramon! I am not pleased!" The smallest of the three spoke with a deep growl.

"Sorry, your Excellency. I was delayed overseeing the final touches to the Sydney disaster," Agramon grated in response, his red eyes burning with fire.

"Sydney was a catastrophe of epic proportions. Congratulations." The smaller one had stepped forward, dwarfed by the third member of the party, an eight-foot-tall gorilla of a demon, Lord Bacchazar.

"Thank you, sir. Yes, it was outstanding, greater carnage and death than even I had envisaged."

The heavy downpour of the afternoon thunderstorm infiltrated the partly destroyed roof, forcing the three occupants to speak up to be heard. Darkness had descended; sporadic flashes of lightning through the hole in the roof provided an eerie glow within the demonic headquarters.

The three huge leathery creatures stood around making idle conversation. There was a familiarity between them all but also tension: they would not relax in such company.

General Thrasos, though a good eighteen inches shorter than his two lieutenants, wasn't intimidated by their bulk. His over-developed muscular physique couldn't distract attention from his gruesome face. An enormous scar ran the length of his right cheek, a permanent reminder of one particularly savage battle. His thick black hair had streaks of grey, showing that he was an elder soldier. It ran the length of his back in a ponytail meticulously tied every couple of inches. His lifeless black eyes bore into his subordinates, filling them with instant fear.

He had known many battles in his time as chief warlord of the Fallen Angel. Much of his time was spent in the inner sanctum of the Most Evil. But judging by the heavy traditional armor he wore, he also frequently engaged in combat. Unfortunately for the demonic armies of Hades, the majority of his battles didn't involve the enemy. Infighting within the evil ranks was all too common.

His two lieutenants were seasoned campaigners in the ongoing vicious war for the hearts of mankind. Lord Bacchazar had responsibility for the old world of the northern hemisphere: greater Europe, the Middle East, plus Africa. Agramon's responsibilities lay with the new world: the Americas and Asia.

The General was justifiably cautious. Suspicion was a dominant trait in the demonic psyche; the capacity for trust had been lost thousands of years ago when the Most Evil left his birthplace. These two were famous for their treachery and were quite capable of turning on their superiors. He knew they both coveted his position.

"I must commend you both for the manner in which you have poisoned the minds of the humans responsible for the carnage. It is a tremendous example of the power of subtle influence at an early age."

"Indeed, General," smirked Agramon. "Once sin becomes habitual, it is very difficult for the human heart to recover."

The General stepped closer, sinister intent boring into his subordinates.

"Let's not get ahead of ourselves." His patronizing tone irritated the pair. "Stay fiercely focused on maintaining the violent rage in these men."

"General, your utmost Excellency, when will the celebrations start?" Bacchazar said derisively, eager to get away.

"Ah, Bacchazar, always impatient, even when it comes to being commended. A few more moments," the General replied mockingly.

The ground behind them shook violently, causing the three demonic leaders to turn their heads towards the sound.

"Thunder, no doubt," Lord Bacchazar offered.

"No doubt, Lieutenant," the General hissed, belittling him by using his formal title.

The air within the hideout began to thicken. The two regional leaders began to feel uneasy. They were both skilled at creating an atmosphere of fear and tension, but this was something they had never experienced. Sweat covered their faces, dripping over their leathery muscular torsos.

The air was now so thick, they could barely breathe, their hands grabbing for their throats, somehow hoping that it would open their airways. The duo dropped to their knees, their heads bowed, fighting for every last breath.

The General stood to one side, calmly staring at the two incapacitated demon lords, a sinister grin adorning his face.

What happened next completely surprised the two stricken beasts. From out of the shadows of the murky haze appeared a nine-foot creature of androgynous beauty. Its features couldn't be clearly discerned, masked somewhat by the cloud that surrounded its large frame. But they saw enough to be able to see that the one they most feared and adored was in fact completely different in appearance to the ugly demonic vision they had anticipated.

The Fallen Angel stopped a few yards away from the kneeling pair. The giant had long, flowing, midnight-black hair but, in complete contrast, a face that was pale, albino-like. A shadow cast darkness over its eyes and nose. Unexpectedly, it smiled, somewhat haughtily, revealing a mouth full of bright white teeth.

"You have served me well!" The voice was chilling, and would haunt the two miscreants for the rest of their lives.

"General, give them their reward!"

"Yes, your Highness! Consider it done!" The General responded, bowing to his master.

With that, the beast rocketed out into the sky and was gone. The thick haze disappeared, the tightness round the lords' throats cleared. Unnerved by the experience, the Fallen Angel's shrill tone still echoing in their ears, they both rose to their feet uneasily.

"Well, my two Lieutenants, you heard it first from the one himself! A very rare honor indeed." The General sniggered, silently rejoicing, witnessing their squeamish response.

"And what is our reward… your Excellency?" Lord Bacchazar asked, trying hard to disguise the shock and lingering fear that coursed through his body.

"Why does it not surprise me to hear that from you, Lieutenant? Impatient for acknowledgment, eh?"

He went over to a fire where two branding irons were resting. He grabbed one out of the fire and turned, snarling.

"And who wishes to be first?"

They recoiled in shock as they saw the General holding up the red-hot branding iron.

"The mark of our glorious leader is only given to those who are most deserving and who are *Most Evil*!" he cackled, pulling his hair aside, revealing the upside-down cross branded to his forehead. "You should feel truly honored our King has bestowed this mark upon you!"

Agramon stepped forward to receive his reward first, screaming in pain as the branding iron burnt the reminder of his leader into his forehead. Lord Bacchazar then knelt before his superior, biting down on the scabbard he had placed in his mouth. He almost fainted, the pain was so excruciating. He stumbled to his feet, his bulging red eyes shooting daggers at his tormentor.

"Now away, the two of you. Get back to your mischief and mayhem," the General ordered.

Bacchazar and Agramon didn't need to be told twice. They stormed out of the ruin together and into the heavy rain, feeling deflated, dispersing to their respective homes without saying a word. Anger welled up inside them both as they sped off, hissing all manner of obscenities as the rain smashed into their faces.

Someone would suffer tonight!

Chapter 6

Four weeks later

"Are you in there, dear?" the silver-haired mature lady asked as she popped her head through the half-open door.

"Yes, Mum, I'm here, just been dozing," Jack replied as he swiveled around on the recliner.

Mum entered the lounge, the walls of which were adorned with photos. Photos of the family devastated by that fateful train trip. Louise Haines was a spritely sixty-seven, short, with olive sun-tanned skin and striking sapphire-blue eyes.

"I'm off to grab Jane and the girls, so we can all have dinner together tonight," she announced moving closer. "Won't be long, half-hour or so."

"Okay, Mum. Anything I can do in the meantime?"

"No, Jack, you just rest. Oh, and perhaps pray that Jane's spirits lift." Jack smiled weakly. "Prayer. You do remember what that is, don't you, son?" She was standing over him now.

"Uh, not sure, Mum. Been pretty dry since the attack. God seems far away at the moment."

"I know, dear, but He's here, always, even when we don't think He is. Try it. You might be surprised what He says." She gently rubbed the back of her hand against his cheek. "I must fly. Jane will get anxious if I'm late." She squeezed his hand, letting go as she strode out of the room, tears welling up in her eyes as she turned from her son.

Soften his heart, Lord.

Jack reached out for the crutches nearby. His broken left femur was healing well but the eight-inch scar on his thigh where the bone pierced the skin would always remind him of the injury.

Not that he would ever forget it. How could he?

Sarah, Beth, and Jonah had all perished whilst his twin girls, Grace and Catherine, had survived. He stood shakily on his crutches in his lounge, staring at the wall where numerous photos hung. He was pensive. Sadness enveloped him. And anger.

Jack wanted revenge. The hate in his heart was growing every day. It was as intense an emotion as he thought he'd ever felt. It was like a raging inferno deep within his stomach that couldn't be sated. He hated those responsible.

The long-taloned hands continued massaging his shoulders, as an impish snigger came from the mouth of the grotesque amphibian-like creature pressing tightly to Jack.

"That is enough!" came the cry as a flash of light erupted in the supernatural. A quick succession of sword strokes banished the creature before it knew what hit it.

"You've had your playtime," said the strongly built white knight. "It's now time for healing. And I'll smash any of you who try to get in the way." The angel's wings were still extended as he strode purposefully around the room, sword drawn, daring two demons that stood at a distance. They lowered their weapons and watched.

Jack fell back into his chair, dropping the crutches and grabbing the armrests till his knuckles were white.

"Why, Jesus, why?" he yelled out. "Why did you let this happen? Why did they have to die?" He fell forward, hands covering his face, as the tears burst forth.

The white knight felt Jack's pain, the hurt and grief. He stood over the recliner, wings spread, cocooning the wounded man.

You blame me for their deaths.

Jack heard it in his mind.

It's OK, Jack. Please tell me how you feel.

He heard it again. His fingers clenched into a fist as he rocked rhythmically in the recliner.

Tell me, Jack.

"Yesss! I do!" he screamed, stretching forward his torso. His ears were fiery red.

No response.

He flopped back, exhaling loudly. Calm flowed into his heart.

Two large hands rested on his shoulders.

Looking to the ceiling, he said, "Jesus, I need you." His whisper was shallow.

I've never left you and never will.

Jack was right where he was meant to be.

* * *

The three horrendous bomb attacks in January had changed the world irreparably. The people living in London, Los Angeles, and Sydney had become more suspicious, more careful about what they did and whom they talked to. It would be like this for a while.

A group of ten men and women were meeting quietly in Pat and Lucy McCarthy's house in the city of Cork in Southern Ireland. Since the attack in London these ten people had started meeting daily for thirty minutes to pray for peace in the world, praying that God's army of angels might reign over the demonic hordes of Satan.

A similar group met at the McAllisters' house in Glasgow, the Evans's house in Cardiff, the Framptons' house in Norwich, the Smyths' in Liverpool, the Perezes' in Madrid, the Mullers' in Frankfurt, the Kims' in Seoul, the Osbornes' in Nashville, the N'Konos' in Bulawayo, the Connellans' in Melbourne, and so on and on. Hundreds of thousands of these groups had sprung up all around the globe with one purpose: to seek God's intervention in ridding the world of this spirit of terror and restoring peace to this war-torn planet.

People from all nations were praying vehemently and vigorously for peace. People who hadn't prayed for a long time or ever, were now doing so.

Their prayers were being heard.

By the heavenly host. The prayers were then passed on to those in the thick of the battle, providing strength and encouragement.

To the angelguard.

* * *

Jack had just returned home from his day at the university and was sitting down with his mother having dinner. He'd been back at work for a few weeks now. The twins were already in bed but would wake around ten that night for a feed and to spend a little time with their dad. Jack loved that special time with Catherine and Grace.

"Mum, remember I mentioned last week that my annual trip to Insead is coming in a couple of weeks?" Jack opened the conversation.

"Hmmm, yes, vaguely."

"Well, I need to make a decision now if I'm going to pull out, so they can prepare another professor to lead the class."

"Oh really? Where are your thoughts leading you at the moment?"

"My initial thought was to say no, but I had a long chat about it with the Dean today. He's keen for me to complete the program. This would be the third year I've participated and for the first time, I'll be involved in a program that is dedicated to one corporate organization, which would be great. He also told me this will be the first of a four-stage process, requiring me to make three other trips over the course of the next year. And the client is FJ Caille, which happens to be one of the world's largest advertising businesses."

"Jack, do you think you would be up to it so soon after the accident?"

"Mum, I'm definitely feeling better. I'm now getting through all my classes without any trouble. My focus and concentration are back. The leg isn't too far away from being right. I should be able to ditch the walking-stick before I leave. My biggest concern is leaving the girls. I feel strange thinking about leaving you all for a few weeks."

He paused.

"Ah… I don't know, Mum, I really don't know. This is a great opportunity and I always love getting back to Insead."

"You really love that place, don't you, Jack?"

"Yeah, it has such fond memories. It was so special to Sarah and me. It will be strange going back, knowing we'll never be there together again. But that's also kinda one of the reasons I'm drawn to go. We had a magical three years there together."

Silence. They both looked at the table, caught in their own thoughts. Jack pushed his food around on his plate.

"You know, it might be really good for you," she offered, surprising Jack. "A bit like a holiday. You know what they say about a change! Going back to where you and Sarah spent your first years of marriage may help the healing process. Don't worry about the girls, I can look after them, and Jane is getting on pretty well now."

Jack nodded his head pensively, taking a mouthful of food.

"So you wouldn't mind looking after the girls for a couple of weeks while I take the program?"

His mother paused, reflecting. "I can't really see any reason why you shouldn't go. Sure, the threat of another attack will always be there, but we've got to live our lives and not be in hiding. We can't let these terrible people take over our lives. And Jack, we gotta live by faith. God's in charge, not Satan, even though there are all these bad things happening around the world."

He smiled. He loved his mum's undying faith. Nothing ever appeared to budge it. Losing three of her grandchildren and her daughter-in-law had devastated her, perhaps even more so than losing Patrick, Jack's father, suddenly, sixteen years ago. She responded in the only way she could: she camped out at church, spent even more time on her knees in prayer and got busy supporting her loved ones.

"OK, thanks, Mum." Jack gave her a kiss on the cheek as he rose to take the dishes to the kitchen. "Let's see how we both feel about it in the morning."

* * *

"Good, he's warming to the idea," said an angel sitting cross-legged in the roof of Jack's house, watching the conversation below.

A second came from out of the shadows, his shoulders hunched, as he was too tall for the enclosed area. He was strikingly blond.

"Yes, Darius, that's very good. But it's time to help Jack come to the right decision, time to send a clear message."

"Aye, aye, sir," responded Darius, getting to his feet. "We will then need to go into action to ensure Jack's safety on his travels."

"Darius, is there any word yet whether the enemy is aware of Jack's role?" the other asked.

"No, Tagan, we are confident they know nothing."

"No other skirmishes like the one a few weeks ago?"

"Tagan, that was a mischievous imp cashing in on Jack's broken heart. We see it all the time when a human's defenses are down. None have dared approach since that day."

"Good, Darius. Let's get Jack out and into action." Tagan grabbed Darius' shoulder in a friendly embrace as they headed down into the house, unseen by Jack and his mother.

* * *

Louise Haines was on her knees beside her bed, as was her usual practice before retiring for the night.

"Gracious Lord, thank you that Jack's physical wounds continue to heal. You know the state of his broken heart. You too weep for our loss and the pain he in particular is suffering. Please, Jesus, heal his heart. Renew his desire to know you; pour fresh faith and hope into his heart."

The white giant smiled and walked through her bedroom door.

* * *

Jack woke startled.

His room was bathed in a brilliant white aura. He wondered if he had died during his sleep and was entering the gates of heaven. He felt a wonderful peacefulness. In particular, he no longer felt afraid. He hadn't felt that since the attack.

From somewhere, he couldn't tell where, he heard a soft male voice, a beautiful harmonious baritone.

"Go to Insead, Jack. Everything will be alright."

"Who are you?" Jack called out, now fully alert.

"Be strong and of good courage. We will be with you!"

"Who are you?" Jack called out again.

As suddenly as the room had lit up, it went totally dark, his digital alarm clock providing the only light. It was 2:50. All was silent in the house. He heard a possum scampering over the roof tiles.

He was confused, unsure whether he'd actually heard what he'd heard or whether it had all been a dream. He put his head back on his pillow. It only took a few moments for him to fall asleep, whispering, "Come back, come back."

* * *

A cry from the twins woke Jack at 6:30. He got out of bed with a renewed step. His leg was stiff, as was normal each morning, but felt stronger. As he headed off to their bedroom next door he recalled the dream he had had last night.

"Hello, my sweet, beautiful girls!" he greeted them.

They were both standing up in their cots, leaning against the side to keep their balance, both arms outstretched, waiting to greet their daddy.

Jack grabbed Catherine first and took her over to the changing table, playing with her little feet and hands as he removed her pink jumpsuit and nappy.

"Only wees," he said playfully, Catherine giggling in response.

He changed her nappy and put on a fresh singlet and jumpsuit before putting her back in her cot. He then repeated the exercise with Grace.

Now ten months old, the twins were fraternal. Catherine was the blonder of the two while Grace had more hair. Both had bright-blue eyes while Grace was slightly taller.

His mother greeted the three of them a few minutes later as they were playing on the lounge floor.

"Good morning, my sweet angels. How are you both this morning?"

The two girls giggled and chortled as their grandmother pulled them both up and held them while Jack continued to lie on the floor.

Grandma played a little with the girls and then gave them back to Jack. She knew this was an important time for him and didn't want to disturb his morning ritual with his girls. She left them as they rolled around on the floor.

"You know, Mum, I really want to do this Insead gig," Jack said fifteen minutes later as he wandered into the kitchen. His Mum was tucking into some toast with marmalade whilst reading a newspaper.

"What's that, Jack?" she said, without taking her eyes away from the morning news.

"I'd like to do that corporate program at Insead."

"Oh yes, dear. Didn't we agree that last night?" She was still more interested in the paper.

Jack rolled his eyes, a smile forming. He went over to the refrigerator, pulling out the girls' breakfast.

"When would you have to leave?" she asked.

"The program starts May 15th, and I'll need to be there a good week beforehand. So that means I'll be leaving the weekend after next."

"OK, dear. Let me finish this page and I'll be all ears."

Jack retreated to the lounge and reappeared a few moments later, a bright chirpy girl in each arm.

"Two girls ready for breakfast," he said, marching into the kitchen in the direction of their high chairs.

"Well, we best start getting you organized for your trip, then, dear." His mother had dispensed with the paper and was coming over to help with the girls.

"Your daddy is going off on an airplane," she said, pretending to be one herself. The girls laughed at their silly granny.

Chapter 7

London, early May

The plane landed at Heathrow Airport on schedule at 9 a.m. Sunday morning.

Jack had slept fitfully. He didn't enjoy flying any more, having loved it early in his career. One really bad flight eight years ago late at night, Chicago to Seattle in a snowstorm, had freaked him out. He'd been thrown from his seat whilst asleep and spent the rest of the flight furiously gripping the armrests whilst nursing a bump on his head.

"Can't wait to see you again Jack. Remember Danny doesn't know yr coming! Jo" was one of many text messages he'd received whilst in the air. He responded: "Just landed, on way thru customs now. C u soon." Then he sent another one to his mum: "Landed safe. Had great flight. Miss you all, big kiss to G&C. Call soon."

Security had been significantly beefed up since Jack's last trip a year ago, due to the January terrorist attack at the football match. Army personnel were conspicuously on patrol throughout various parts of the airport. The intimidating patrol teams of two were dressed in their full battle uniforms, M4 carbine rifles equipped with bayonets held close to their chests, as they surveyed all passers-by.

Jack exited the airport to be met by a typically dull, chill London morning, thankful his mother had reminded him to take his brown leather jacket. He had a noticeable limp, his injured left leg particularly stiff after the long flight. He was still glad to have discarded the walking-stick last week.

He didn't have to wait long in the rank for a London black cab that would take him the twenty-odd miles east to Croydon.

He was looking forward to seeing his old friends, Danny and Joanna Connolly. When Joanna heard he was heading to Insead, she insisted he pop in en route.

Traffic was light at that time of the morning, enabling him to arrive well before midday.

The Connollys lived in a five-bedroom period detached residence arranged over three floors. He followed a couple through the open front door, conscious of wanting to surprise Danny. The home was full of activity and people; it appeared the church had reconvened at the Connollys'.

"Welcome, Michael and Cheryl." Jack heard the familiar voice of Danny coming from the front room. "Just head on through the kitchen and out the back. Jo's preparing lunch." Jack snuck down the hallway; nothing had changed since he'd been here last year.

Jack entered the kitchen, and with his finger to his mouth encouraging another couple to stay silent, he crept up behind a lady busy over the stove.

"'Allo, Jack!" said a boy about ten, before Jack could pull off his surprise.

Instantly Joanna spun around and, on seeing Jack, squealed with delight. She wrapped her arms around his neck, giving him a big smooch on the cheek. Her petite body melded into Jack's lean physique and he returned her warm cuddle.

"Hello, Jo, lovely to see you again," Jack said, a little overwhelmed by Joanna's welcome. "And you too, Jack," he said to the boy, scuffing his hair up.

"Ohhh, Jack, it's so good to see you!" Joanna replied in a thick southern Irish accent.

"Has Danny seen you yet?"

"No, I heard his voice in the front room and figured I'd sneak around to find you first."

"Well, let's go find him. He'll be so pleased to see you." They walked off arm in arm, the boy Jack holding big Jack's hand. "How's my favorite godson, Jack?"

"Great, thanks, Uncle Jack!"

They entered the front room; Danny had his back to them as he chatted to a striking, tall French-African couple with a toddler.

"Look who's here, Daddy!" said little Jack, causing Joanna

to give her son a look of feigned disappointment. He ignored her. "It's Uncle Jack, Daddy – he's come to see us!" He was jumping up and down with excitement, still holding onto Jack's hand.

Danny turned mid-sentence, a huge teeth-filled smile lighting up his face.

"Good-daay, mate!" Danny said, doing a terrible impression of an Australian accent, as he hugged Jack.

"G'day, Danny," Jack responded in a wholly authentic Australian accent.

"What are you doing here? Why didn't you tell me you were coming?" Danny queried.

"He wanted to surprise you, dear," Joanna piped up.

"What a great surprise, my old friend. It's so good to see you, mate. How long you here for?"

"Literally, just today, Danny. I'm booked on a seven o'clock flight tonight to Paris en route to Insead. I'm helping run a corporate program that starts Monday week."

Danny became conscious of the other couple, now standing a little lost amongst the joy of his family. "Oh, Jack, can I introduce you to a new couple to our church: Thierry and Ruth Le Bon and their son, Mikey." Danny reached over to the Le Bons, encouraging them to join the group. "Thierry and Ruth, as you probably can see, a dear old friend of ours has unexpectedly popped in to see us, all the way from Australia: Jack Haines."

"How do you do," Thierry offered, extending his hand, which Jack accepted. Mikey stood sheepishly gripping his father's leg.

"Very well, thank you, Thierry, good to meet you both." Jack took Ruth's open hand, "Hello, Ruth." He couldn't but notice Ruth's stunning natural beauty. Her finely textured face required little makeup to complement her dark skin tones.

"And hello to you – Mikey, is it?" Jack got down on his haunches and put one hand up. "High-five?" Mikey, seeing the friendliness of Jack's smile, smacked the open hand. "Got it, good one, Mikey! Good to meet you."

Mikey had been blessed with the fine dark textures of his mother, with a rounded jaw. His mop of hair was full of tight little curls.

"How old's Mikey?" Jack asked, getting back to his feet.

"Twenty months, Jack," Ruth responded. "He doesn't usually respond to strangers that well."

"Uh—"

"Uncle Jack," it was little Jack, interrupting Jack's response, "will you sit next to me at lunch?"

"Now, Jack," Joanna had overheard, "you know there's a special kids' table. You'll be able to spend time with your godfather after lunch, once all the guests have left. But you can show Jack and the Le Bons the way outside. How 'bout that?"

"OK, Mum." He grabbed Jack's hand and led the way back towards the kitchen, ignoring the Le Bons, who followed.

* * *

Darius and two other heavenly winged beings watched from one of the children's bedrooms upstairs as their charges left the front room.

"Good to see the introductions are over," Darius offered.

"They'll get on well, I think," said Hannen, the classic blond Scandinavian. He stood over seven feet tall and possessed a lean and lithe physique. His large, piercing, crystal-blue eyes immediately stood out in contrast to his pale complexion. "Whatya think, Elijah?"

Elijah was shorter and dark-skinned, similar to the Le Bons, with jet-black hair and an unruly beard.

"Yeah, no worries. They'll all get on fine."

The ebony-and-ivory angelguard team had been together for well over 500 years, and had seen many gruesome battles in their time. They were a dynamic pair who had been responsible for reducing the demonic ranks in large numbers.

"Let's see how the friendship develops over lunch," Darius suggested, heading out to the balcony outside to get a better view. "You going to join me?"

"Absolutely," Hannen and Elijah said in unison, joining their southern-hemisphere comrade outside, overlooking the lunch below.

* * *

Jack was seated opposite Thierry and Ruth, who sat on the two-person wooden garden bench, all three gingerly supporting hot plates of curry on their laps.

"How long have you been attending Croydon City Church, then?" Jack asked, trying to get some conversation going.

"We only joined two months ago," Thierry replied. "We understand Danny and Joanna hold these new members' lunches quite regularly, so that's why we're here today."

"What made you come to this particular church, if you don't mind me asking?" Jack felt a little awkward probing, but then, did it matter? He'd probably never see these people again after today.

"We hadn't been to church for a very long time but after the January terrorist attack we thought we'd try to find a church that appealed to us," Ruth responded.

Thierry took it one step further. "We are not really quite sure why we chose Croydon CC, and in fact we wonder if it chose us, if you know what I mean?"

"You believe you were led to it?" Jack knew what Thierry meant.

They both nodded their heads.

"That attack was absolutely terrible. I read something only the other day saying the death toll is now almost 13,000. Just horrendous," Jack said.

"The latest number was reported in the papers this morning – 12,617. But they are still digging through the rubble and expect to find more," Thierry replied.

"Ah, that's just incredible. And insane. The worst terrorist disaster ever!" Jack exclaimed, exasperated.

"And Jack, you had one in Australia only a few weeks later!" Ruth piped up.

Jack nodded.

"Jack, do you come from Sydney?" Ruth asked.

"Yep, born and bred!"

"Did you know anyone affected by the attack on the harbor?" she asked.

"Yes, in fact. I lost my wife and two eldest children. My sister lost her two eldest as well." Jack had found that the best way to handle the information was to tell it straight, but that didn't make it easy.

"What?! Ohhh… we're *so* sorry, Jack! It must be terrible for you," Ruth said, reaching her hand out, tenderly touching his forearm.

"Yes, it was a horrible day. My one blessing was that my twin girls survived the attack."

"And you obviously did too!" Ruth added.

"Something of a miracle that I still can't comprehend," Jack replied.

The three simultaneously took mouthfuls of curry.

"You know, I still can't get over the sheer madness and insanity of these attacks, and also that one in LA," Jack said, sadness in his eyes. "Why would anyone murder so many innocent people, especially children?"

"I know, we think the same about the football stadium attack," Ruth replied. "Losing Thierry's nephew Jerome was just so unnecessary and, frankly, just vile."

"So you lost someone close too?"

"It was his first football match," said Ruth. "Thierry had given him the tickets for Christmas."

Jack held up his hand.

"Hold on. So, Thierry, you were at the match also?"

Thierry nodded.

"And you survived too. This is amazing!"

Ruth smiled. "Who would have thought that two surviving victims from attacks thousands of miles apart would meet at such an innocuous event as this: a church new members' lunch!"

"If you don't mind me asking, is that scar on your forehead a souvenir of the attack, Thierry?" Jack asked, noticing its darkness, deducing it was a recent addition.

"It sure is!" Thierry responded, touching the five-inch healed wound. "Every time I look in a mirror I am reminded of that despicable day. It's not as if I need the physical reminder, as it's never far from my thoughts. I'm just thankful for God's mercy in healing my wounds. Without Him I wouldn't have been much good to anyone these past few months."

"I couldn't have expressed it any better myself, Thierry," Jack said, his green eyes fixed firmly on his comrade in survival.

"To this day it still amazes me how I managed to survive when Jerome died. I shouldn't have survived. The blast happened only a few feet away from me. It was like the hand of God pushed me out of the way," Thierry said, caught between the wonder of his survival and the sadness of his loss.

"Me too. I was at the front of the carriage and shouldn't have lived. It was like someone stood over me, protecting me from the impact."

There was a moment's silence, all struck by the chance wonderment of their meeting and the similarity in their survival stories.

Danny and Joanna were doing the rounds of the guests, finally reaching Thierry and Ruth. Jack sank into the background as he helped himself to some more of Joanna's curry. He made some pleasant conversation with another couple before heading back inside the house.

The guests soon took their leave.

Thierry and Ruth were the first to leave and on their way out found Jack in the front room studying some family photographs on the mantelpiece above the fireplace.

"It was good meeting you, Jack," Thierry said as he approached from behind.

Jack turned around instantly. "Oh, are you off, then?"

"Yes, some things to do this afternoon."

Ruth had an idea.

"You'll pass our place on the way to Heathrow. Perhaps you could pop in and have supper with us before you catch your flight? We could then take you the rest of the way to Heathrow."

Jack thought for a moment.

An invisible hand touched him on the shoulder.

"Yes, I'd like that very much. It would be good to hear some more about your healing since the accident."

Ruth provided him with their address details and they agreed to meet around four that afternoon.

Hannen and Elijah left with the Le Bon family. Darius stood at the front window watching them as the humans got into their car while the angelic twosome hopped on the roof for the short trip to East Putney.

The first part of the plan had been successfully achieved.

Los Angeles

"How's she doing, Arlia?" Landen asked, having just arrived in a leafy elm tree that sat prominently at the back of a well-manicured garden, full of spring blooms.

"She's looking really well this morning," Arlia replied. "She awoke early with the sunrise. Those headaches continue to play havoc with her sleep. She's lucky to get four hours in a stretch."

"The head must be OK now, judging by the way she's throwing herself into this kick-around with Taylor and Luke."

"The wonders of modern medicine and headache tablets, Landen, I'd suggest."

"Yaaayyy... what a goal!" screamed Taylor, having shot the ball past Luke into the toy goal, complete with netting. She ran a little jig, high-fiving her mother as she ran past.

"You're still two goals behind me," Luke exclaimed, dropping the ball at his feet, ready to take the mother-and-daughter team on.

"Oh, I'm beat, kids!" Loren slumped, hands to knees. "Why don't you two keep playing whilst I rustle up some breakfast for us all?"

"Orrrghhh, Mum," Taylor protested, "we can't stop yet, we can beat Luke this time."

Luke, ignoring the two girls, dribbled past them both and smashed the ball at the other goal, but missed. "Darn... should have got that... yep, Mom, good idea, let's have some breakfast. Pancakes?"

Taylor stood, hands on hips, cranky.

"Ohhh, don't worry, Tayls, we'll beat him next time," Loren said with a cuddle. She got the brush-off with a shrug of the shoulders. "I want to keep playing!" Taylor walked off towards the elm tree, sulking. She ran up the step-ladder that led to a very flash two-room cubby-house and plonked herself down in the first room, cross-legged and cross-armed.

"That sure ends the soccer game," said Arlia.

"Any activity from our invisible friend, Zeldax, overnight, Arlia?"

"Oh, Landen, we had an unexpected visitor last night," Arlia said enthusiastically.

"Really, who?"

"None other than Agramon himself!"

"You're not serious?" Arlia nodded. "Why didn't you call me?" Landen said, with disappointment in his voice.

"He was only here a short time. Arrived about two in the morning, chatted with Zeldax over in the club-house and then shot out of the roof, straight up into the night air at a furious pace. He then stopped at about 10,000 feet and hung there for sixty seconds or so with the glow of a full moon at his back. It was quite a sight to behold. He laughed – well, cackled – before shooting off into the distance, headed for the hills."

"Sounds creepy."

"That it was, Landen."

"Why would he show up? Golly, Arlia, they're really onto Loren, if the head honcho pays a visit!"

"Athaniel said it was very unusual."

"Gee whiz."

"Athaniel wants extra protection for Loren, and so is sending over reinforcements this morning. We've been ordered to keep ten guards around Loren at all times. Also there'll be an additional ten to track her children, as the enemy may try to take them out."

"Wow. It's about to get pretty crowded around here. Lucky for us Loren has a big backyard."

The two sets of eyes followed Taylor. Finding herself ignored by mother and brother, she hopped out of the cubby and rushed back into the house.

"Loren leaves for Insead in a week," Arlia piped up. "Athaniel believes they'll try to stop her going."

"Great – some action for us, then. I'm pleased she's decided to go. With all the confusion at her work, it must have been very hard for Loren to agree to attend. Her girlfriends are sure working wonders with their persistent prayer."

"The Father loves nothing more than prayerful disciples."

"Kiiids, pancakes are ready!" Loren came out into the outdoor lounge area holding a tray of pancakes and glasses of juice. She set it all down at a solid wooden table, and both children eagerly plonked themselves in their designated seats.

* * *

"He wants me to make sure she doesn't get on the plane! How do I do that? Think, Zeldax, think. You gotta get this right or else you're a gonner."

Zeldax was talking to himself as he hobbled to and fro, his trusty crooked walking-stick supporting him. He'd been in this fitful, agitated state for hours since Agramon had left.

Since the Universal Studios atrocity, he had based himself in the clubhouse of the park, conveniently located directly across the street from Loren's two-story colonial house. Zeldax's ability to meld into all backgrounds enabled him to move quite freely, unobserved most of the time. He now knew Loren's standard routine as well as that of her two children.

"What to do, what to do? Should I get the children? Uhhh, nope, better to get her."

He stopped.

The concrete floor was covered with markings. He now scratched something out, adding to the mess of lines, stick-figure drawings and maps. A smirk grew across his deformed face.

"I got it, I got, *I got it!*"

Chapter 8

London

Jack was in a London black cab approaching Wandsworth Borough on his way to the Le Bons' house. After all the guests had left the Connollys', he told Danny and Joanna the amazing coincidence that Thierry and he had discovered about each other. They too thought it miraculous and encouraged him to make the most of his time with the Le Bons.

On saying goodbye to Jack, they immediately went to their knees in prayer. They committed him to Jesus, seeking God's blessing upon him as he journeyed to Paris. They sought divine inspiration in drawing Jack together with their new church members, Thierry and Ruth Le Bon.

The cab soon pulled up outside a block of four similar two-story Victorian brick houses. The Le Bons' house was the second.

Jack walked to the front door past a small, well-manicured garden featuring a collection of mixed fragrant flowers splendid in lilac and virgin white.

"Hey, Jack, good you could drop by." Thierry welcomed him at the front door and escorted Jack through a narrow hallway to a recently refurbished kitchen.

The kettle was on the boil as Ruth joined the two men.

"A cup of tea, Jack?" she asked.

"That would be lovely, Ruth."

"Why don't we have tea outside?" She led them outside through the elegant French windows that opened out from the breakfast room. A football in desperate need of some air sat in the centre of the empty courtyard. The well-maintained garden beds carried the same lilac-and-white theme that Jack had noticed in the front.

"At least one of you must have a green thumb, judging by the look of your garden," Jack said.

"Yes, the garden is Ruthie's domain…" Thierry replied. "I don't really have any great fondness for gardening."

"It's something I've taken on since Mikey was born," Ruth said while she offered round the cookies. "Being at home a lot, it gave me something to do, and Mikey spends a lot of time out here playing, so we can both be out here together doing something useful. I do enjoy pottering in the garden. I can quietly contemplate life as I clear the weeds or prune the shrubs."

"So how have you coped during the past three months?" Jack asked.

"As you can imagine, it was very difficult at first," Thierry started. "The day I left hospital, I went straight to another hospital – a psychiatric one."

Jack raised his eyebrows in surprise.

"No, it wasn't me – it was my sister, Charlotte. She had tried to take her life the night before, and fortunately didn't succeed. She's a sensitive, highly strung person, so losing her only child, Jerome, pushed her over the edge."

Jack was listening intently as he sipped his hot tea. Ruth was holding Thierry's hand while she looked on, absorbed in his words.

"Her progress has been slow. She stayed in the hospital for over two months. They feared she would do it again, and were treating her for severe depression. It was probably a good thing she stayed in the hospital, as it meant she was never alone through that first intense period of grieving."

"She must have been through a horrible time," Jack said with kind sensitivity. "Jane, my sister, and I have experienced some real troughs coping with the loss of our loved ones. For a number of weeks after the tragedy I wondered if I would get out of the depths of despair…" Jack paused as his throat tightened. He was holding his mug firmly, head bowed as he composed himself.

Thierry and Ruth looked on compassionately, willing him on with their eyes.

"… But… at some point I was able to assess whether I was going to let this… destroy my life…" Jack regained his composure, "… or live a fulfilling one. I chose the latter. I'm sure that's what Sarah and the kids would have wanted." He finished, holding his head high, to find both of his listeners teary eyed.

Jack managed a weak smile, and gulped down some more tea.

"I hear no one has claimed responsibility for the Sydney attack?" Ruth asked. "We still don't know any more about the one here, either."

"Nor the LA one," Thierry added.

"No," Jack agreed. "The usual Middle Eastern Muslim extremist suspects are always mentioned in the press but none of them have owned up to it."

"All has gone quiet here now on who the police are chasing. It's all speculation. Perhaps we'll never know," Ruth suggested.

"And tell me what led you back to church," asked Jack, changing the topic of conversation.

"I became a Christian as a teenager, but through my twenties I got absorbed in my work and getting ahead in life – so much so, that my faith waned. My first marriage ended sixteen years or so ago, and I fell away further," Thierry began.

"Uh huh," Jack said, nodding his head.

Ruth heard Mikey cry from the baby monitor in the kitchen and popped back inside to check on him.

***

"Thanks for meeting me here," said Hannen. "I didn't want to risk the enemy getting wind of Thierry and Jack's connection."

"Yeah, good idea, Hannen," Darius responded. "It could place the entire mission in jeopardy. Where's your mate, Elijah?"

The two white knights were holed up in an old vacant house a few doors down from the Le Bons.

"He's at Thierry's on watch duty."

"I understand Thierry's had a renewal of his faith since the attack a few months back."

"That's correct. About six months before the stadium tragedy we'd become aware of the enemy's sinister plans. The archangels got wind of the ultimate objective and had seen how the enemy was poisoning the minds of a connected group of powerful and wealthy men from different nationalities to bring about some serious carnage. They'd been sucked into a thirst for even more power and money and were prepared to do anything to get it, even sacrifice innocent people. They had made a choice, one that pleased the dark lords from hell. Tagan, on instruction from the archangels, established a plan to stop them. Thierry was at a particular stage of life where he'd be able to clearly recognize the Father's intervention and desire for him to come back to the faith. A large team of people have been praying for Thierry and Ruth ever since."

"And what's occurred since the stadium attack?"

"Thierry's faith was reignited. He and Ruth started attending church where they got reacquainted with Jesus. It's been lovely to watch. But we realized Thierry was being constantly monitored by the enemy. And by a particular demon that had much history with me. I had seen him at the stadium that day but was too busy protecting Thierry from the blast to be able to confront him. He obviously also noticed me, and has been tracking me ever since."

"Yep, know that feeling," Darius stated, fascinated. "What's this demon's claim to fame?"

"Unfortunately for me, this gangster happens to be one of hell's meanest. A demon that bears a striking resemblance to a Viking warlord and goes by the name Drakkin."

"Never heard of him."

"Drakkin stands over eight feet tall and weighs, I guess, in excess of 450 pounds."

"A bruiser!"

"Yep, he's a monster of enormous proportions. The heavy Viking helmet exacerbates his already oversized head. It covers his face completely, with holes for the eyes, mouth and nostrils. His crimson-colored eyes are permanently locked in a death-like trance, similar to a shark's eyes. Being caught in that stare usually means death isn't far away."

"He's really something. What weapons does he carry?"

"He doesn't carry the typical demon sword, rather what the Vikings used in their day: an oversized axe that can slice through thick steel, and a heavy, round shield big enough to cover his massive torso. He's also been known to use it as a battering ram."

"And the two of you have been chasing each other for centuries?"

"Afraid so. Through all the great religious historical battles waged in Europe over the centuries we've fought. You name it: the Spanish Inquisition, the Reformation, the two World Wars of the twentieth century, and the continual conflict in the Holy Land. Each time either of us was knocked down, the other hasn't been able to inflict the final killer blow that would end it, for some reason or other."

"And now, this conflict between you two that has prevailed for over 1,200 years is once again to be renewed," Darius announced ominously. Hannen nodded in affirmation, revealing no fear – rather, excitement was igniting in his eyes.

***

It was time for Jack to head off to the airport for his flight to Paris and then on to the picturesque mountains and lush forest surrounding the world-renowned Insead campus.

Jack bade his new friends a warm farewell, swapping contact details as he headed out the door.

Jack, Thierry and Ruth knew their meeting was more than just chance. It was meant to be. For what purpose, they knew not.

But all three were anxious to find out.

Little did they know they were about to be thrown into a battle that would have an incredible impact on the entire world.

Chapter 9

Los Angeles, a week later

The black Lincoln pulled up to the curb in front of the heavy oak door of the restaurant that served as the entry for members of the Royal Cuban Club. The car stopped just long enough for Ray Malone to alight.

The hostess on reception advised Malone that Tom Mayer had already arrived. He came out of the first-floor elevator to see Mayer seated at their usual table on the balcony, smoking a particularly large cigar.

Two dark, huge and ugly forms followed close behind Ray. As they approached they made eye contact with Mayer's keeper, Grazag, who gave them a dismissive shrug of the shoulders, beefy arms folded across his imposing chest.

"You got something to celebrate tonight, Tom?" Malone asked as he approached the mahogany table, his eyes registering the size of Mayer's cigar.

"I might, my friend!" Mayer replied enthusiastically, pointing to the vacant black chesterfield chair, encouraging Malone to sit in it. "Quickly, your ice has almost melted in your Chivas."

"Thank you," Ray replied.

Mayer began to fidget with his glass. "So what did you so urgently want to discuss with me?"

"I wanted to get a better understanding as to the progress of the takeover and, particularly, the current timing for executing it."

"Takeover?" a quizzical look came over Mayer's face. "Oh, yes, the takeover! The big takeover."

"Yes, you know, the thing we've been discussing for the past nine months," Malone said with heavy irony. "As I understand it, the original plan was to have a completed proposal ready for discussion with Giresse and his team in Paris in the next few weeks. Is that still the case?"

"Ah... no, Ray. I've just spent the last three weeks with some of the European backers, and a combination of factors, namely the global financial crisis and the troubles the European Union is experiencing at the moment, has meant they're not interested in doing this deal now."

"So that's it?" Malone said tersely. "Why wasn't this discussed with me? I am only the planned CEO of the new venture!" His anger was beginning to rise. "And by the way, don't you think it's about time I met some of these backers so I can make appropriate representations to Giresse?"

"Ray, we fully intended to engage you in this decision, but it's only been in the last forty-eight hours that it was agreed that now wasn't the right time to proceed," Mayer said nonchalantly. "As you know, I only flew in last night, so haven't had the chance to update you."

"Right. So who are these backers, then? And shouldn't we plan to pull them all together so that I can meet them?"

"Ray, you know they are just the consortium we've discussed previously. Some wealthy industrialists and their banks passionate about the advertising industry. As you well know, the ad industry has taken a real hit in the past two years. The values of the Big Three global agencies are down almost 70 per cent on their peaks. The consortium still sees real value in combining the US assets of FJ Caille with those of Graves Advertising – trust me, Ray!"

"Tom, it's strange. I bumped into Sir Edward the other day and, after some general chitchat, I alluded to the change in ownership. He didn't appear to know anything about it, even when I pressed him more explicitly a second time. At one point he said in his usual pompous New England accent, 'I don't know what it is you're talking about, Malone!'"

While listening to the conversation, Grazag had encouraged Malone's minders to take a walk down the end of the balcony. Naively, they left Malone alone.

"That old toad! You know, Ray, he's just being cagey with you," Mayer quipped, trying to reassure Malone as he gulped down the remaining dark-amber liquid. "He won't give anything away until the deal is almost done. He's got too much too lose, considering he's providing over 40 per cent of the cash for the proposed deal."

Grazag moved behind Malone, ready to assist his human stooge in what was becoming a sticky situation.

"I don't know. I used to be able to read Sir Edward pretty well, and it looked to me like he knew absolutely nothing about any deal. Or he's become a very good liar." Malone drew back on his cigar. "Anyway, why would he hide it from the guy who's going to lead the new group? I don't like it Tom, one little bit!"

"Ray, don't worry. You're getting agitated about nothing," Mayer said forcefully. "I tell you what I'll do. I'll have a talk to Sir Edward and have him call you to discuss it further. I've been in constant communication with him and his people over the past few days. He's in full agreement with our new plan."

"That would be good," Malone said as his agitation with Mayer began to recede. Grazag filled him with positive statements reinforcing the impression of Mayer's desire to do the right thing by Malone. They were all lies, just like all the other statements Grazag had filled Malone's head with over the past nine months.

A wave of relief washed over Malone, realizing his good friend was still going to help coordinate his ascension to being president of the biggest new agency in North America.

Malone's keepers returned from their short jaunt around the balcony, eyeing Grazag suspiciously, completely oblivious to his role in taking the initiative away from their human.

Malone continued, "Anyway, I'm actually pleased it will be delayed a little, as I don't think it's the right time for me to leave the company just yet, with all that's gone on. I need another couple of months to get it back on track and have the new hires settled before handing over to someone else."

"Any idea who the Board will appoint to replace you?" Mayer asked, hiding his relief at being able to change topics.

"It's funny that, literally the afternoon of the attack, Roger

McDowall – may he rest in peace – and I were just discussing that very matter. At the time I was leaning to McHutchison. Casey McHutchison, my creative head. He unfortunately also died in the attack. Now my recommendation really boils down to one of two people. Gary Jordan, my new acting Creative Director who's come over from Darlings in New York, or…"

"… or Loren!" Mayer completed the sentence for Malone. "You really think she's ready for it?"

"It will be a *big* stretch for her to start with but… yes… I reckon she's up to it."

"Right. Well, you should know. She's worked with you for so many years. At least I wouldn't have to pay any more child maintenance," Mayer said in a throwaway manner, chuckling to himself.

Malone ignored Mayer's silly remark.

Malone got up, informing Mayer he was off to the bathroom.

Mayer lounged back into his chesterfield and smiled at his good fortune. Once again, he'd managed to keep Malone toeing the line. A warm rush came over him with the thought that he didn't need to bother with Malone for much longer. He had what he wanted: 50 million of Swain & Peters' greenbacks transferred by Malone to three shell companies based in Bermuda. Unknown to Malone, Mayer had since wired the money to an untraceable Swiss bank account and closed the shell companies, all records of which had now been destroyed. It looked like 50 million dollars of Swain & Peters' money had just vanished.

It was time the authorities learnt of Malone's misdeeds, Mayer pondered.

"Not just yet, Tom… A little while longer… Malone's time can wait." The deep baritone of Grazag's voice whispered in Mayer's ear. The dark sentinel knew Agramon hadn't given the OK yet for Malone to be sacrificed.

Mayer decided that giving Malone up could wait a little while longer.

"Did I tell you I'm off to Insead as well?" Malone said, returning from the bathroom.

"What, really? Why?"

ANGELGUARD

"The course involves the senior managers making presentations to the executive group. I convinced Giresse that I should give him a personal update on our progress in rebuilding the business and, in the process, attend the final two days of the workshop."

"Very smart of you."

"Haven't been to France for over a year," said Malone. "Candice is coming with me. It'll be good for us to have a break, especially with all that's happened these past few months."

"Keep you out of your secretary's pants for a week or so," Mayer said smugly.

"Cheap shot."

"But it hit you right between the eyes. Come off it, Ray. I still can't believe you got caught, literally, with your pants down, on the night of the tragedy. And with your secretary, no less."

"Yes, not my proudest moment," Malone grimaced. "Having the hotel night manager barge in, catching Trish and me in a compromising position, was a bit awkward."

"You're lucky it didn't derail your career. And if anyone on the consortium finds out before the deal is consummated, I reckon you'll be history."

"I hear you. Fortunately, the night manager and I are old buddies, and with a little financial encouragement, that episode won't get dragged up again."

Mayer raised his glass. "Here's to Ray managing to keep his pants on!"

"Hear, hear," Malone responded disinterestedly, conscious that his friend had something else to hold over him. He knew too well that Mayer was a ruthless businessman who would sell his best friend down the river if it furthered his pursuits.

Malone stood up and announced, "It's time I moved downstairs. Candice and I are having dinner and she'll be waiting for me."

A distinctive ringtone interrupted them, the famous Queen song, "Another one bites the dust". Mayer answered his BlackBerry.

"We are just finishing up now," he said as he looked at his watch.

He listened to the response while he waved Malone off.

Grazag leant back on the balcony railing, watching Malone and his two sentinel keepers depart, a small mischievous smile growing into a wide, haughty grin.

"Silly, incompetent fools," he said to himself. "It'll be sad when the two of you are cast out to the abyss. I'll have to find some new idiots to mock and mislead."

He laughed a hideous, arrogant laugh unheard by human ears. But it generated an invisible current that raised the hackles on Mayer's neck, sending a chill up his spine.

Mayer pulled his suit jacket from the back of the chair and put it over his shoulders, feeling a sudden drop in the early evening temperature.

***

Loren's house was a buzz of activity.

"Mum, watch me slide. Yipppeee," Luke said as he slid down the staircase handrail, reaching the base of the stairs in a matter of seconds.

Loren and Taylor descended the stairs on foot. By the time they reached the bottom, Marcie was coming in the front door, ready to take them to the airport.

"Right on time," Loren said, as Marcie, dressed casually, entered. Her dark-brown cowboy boots made a sharp noise on the maple floorboards.

"Good morning all," Marcie greeted them. "We all ready, then?" She gave Loren a hug and a kiss on the check.

"I think we are, Marce," Loren replied, looking at the four bags now sitting in an organized position at the base of the stairs.

They all got into Marcie's SUV. Arlia watched it pull out of the drive as Grindor and Mylee rode on top of it. She had marshaled her troops to all be prepared for the conflict she felt was inevitable this morning.

"You reckon they're going to try hitting us this morning?" asked Landen.

"Yes. Zeldax left earlier than usual last night and hasn't returned. He's always come back the three months he's been here. And Athaniel reported there was a significant build-up of demons at the studio which Agramon uses as his lair, around three this morning."

"I've received word the knights you dispatched to the airport are in position. The plane Loren is flying on is now fully protected," Landen reported.

"Good. You know what you have to do?"

"Yes, Arlia. They're in for a big surprise if they try something en route to the airport."

"Great, Landen, that's what I want to hear! I'll see you at the airport." Arlia rose up into the bright sunlight, bristling with nervous energy and confidence as she sensed the imminent battle. She lived for these days. Her golden blood raced through her veins with excitement while a stern look of concentration came across the strong contours of her smooth, pale face. She lightly touched the hilt of her sword as she visualized foiling her enemy's plans once again.

She sped south-east to where an army of 100 white knights awaited her, ready for her instructions that would let them loose against the enemy.

* * *

The trip to the airport had so far been uneventful. Luke and Taylor were squabbling in the back seat over the tablet computer while Loren and Marcie discussed nothing in particular while some southern gospel music was playing in the background.

Grindor and Mylee were ever watchful as they flew above the SUV travelling along the eight-lane south-bound Interstate 405. Traffic was unusually light for a Saturday morning, while overcast threatening clouds hovered overhead.

Grindor saw it first. What looked to the human eye like a dark cloud sitting lower than the other rain-filled clouds, was moving a lot faster and coming closer to the car. It was also alive and seething with murderous intent.

Mylee now saw it too, approaching from the north-west.

"I'd estimate no more than fifty of them. What do you think, Grindor?"

"I'd reckon you were right on the money. But if we don't get to the exit ramp in less than about five minutes, the lynching mob may well get their prize before Arlia's army can stop them." As he said it, he put his hand through the roof of the SUV and leant on Marcie's shoulder. Almost instantly, the speedometer moved steadily up through sixty-five and then to pushing seventy.

"Exit ramp one mile ahead," Mylee announced as Marcie drew the vehicle into the right-hand lane, ready to make the turn.

"Go, Marcie, go!" Grindor encouraged her as the black mass to their left started to break up, revealing its true composition.

The demon sentinels, black heavy swords now drawn from their scabbards, were swooping down to execute their plan: overwhelm the two angel guards and force the SUV over the exit-ramp barrier, crashing forty feet below on South Sepulveda Boulevard. If they were fortunate, they would take out a couple of other vehicles, adding to the likely disaster, but most importantly, they would have caused the death of Loren Summers.

"How long now, Aunty Marcie?" an impatient Luke asked.

"Not too much further, Luke. Probably another five minutes," Marcie replied, "See over there, a plane's just now taking off." They all looked to their right in the direction of the airport just as a big United Airlines 747 took to the air as gracefully as a swan.

It was smart thinking of Marcie, as both children's attention was now drawn to the plane.

The SUV was slowing as Marcie prepared to take the sharp corkscrew turn of the exit ramp onto South Sepulveda Boulevard, which would lead them onto the approach to LAX.

The first group of ten sentinels swooped down to hit Grindor and Mylee. The two angelguards were ready, swords drawn.

Just as the ten sentinels were fifty feet from the car, out from below the exit ramp shot thirty white knights led by Landen. They crashed through the outnumbered and shocked demonic crew, their bright silver swords hitting true and sentencing all ten to oblivion.

The instant the first group was swept away, another thirty white knights led by Arlia approached the rear of the sentinel troop, while two teams of twenty each hit them from either side. The remaining murderous villains, numb from the shock of the ambush, didn't stand a chance as 100 white knights quickly surrounded them, slashing through their pitiful resistance. Within five minutes not a trace of the sentinels could be found. All had been disposed of, mercilessly and speedily. It had been a complete wipeout.

"Great victory, Arlia!" Landen said, rushing up to her in mid-air. "Congratulations. You picked just the spot where they would attack. Super strategizing."

"Ah, thanks! Athaniel deserves a lot of the credit in picking the kill zone." Arlia looked frustrated as she swung around in each direction, looking for somebody.

"What's up? You should be ecstatic!"

"Zeldax. I didn't see him go down."

"I wouldn't worry about him. He's history now, if Agramon stays true to form. Failure is never tolerated. He'll be dead before we know it."

"No doubt you're right, but I wanted his scalp."

"Let him go. You're going to have plenty on your hands making sure Loren arrives safely at Insead."

The satisfied angelic leader observed Marcie's Ford SUV as it approached the ramp to the departure drop-off zone, none of the occupants aware of how close they all came to losing their lives only a few moments previously.

"Yeah, Agramon will be appalled at their feeble showing today. He'll be embarrassed knowing this failure will be heavily broadcast. He'll want to strike back, and quickly, or else he too will soon know what lies within the abyss of Satan's wastelands."

Arlia and Landen watched as Loren and family got out of the SUV, knowing full well this morning was merely a minor skirmish.

Loren had a target on her back. And they knew the enemy would not lie down so easily next time.

Chapter 10

Brussels, the same day

Leopold Grosch was running late for his breakfast meeting.

It was a typically dull grey day in the Belgian and EU capital. Grosch was a solid, some would say overweight, fifty-five year-old, with receding black hair revealing a very prominent forehead. He was bundled up in a heavy charcoal overcoat protecting him from the early morning chill.

Grosch entered the large ballroom of a five-star hotel. The guests were milling around, seeking their allocated tables. Grosch knew his would be the one at the front, the one where his close friend and confidant, the prime minister, would eventually take his seat, last of all the guests.

Another political fundraiser, the third that month. The prime minister was doing all he could to ensure he received as much of the corporate vote as possible. He knew he could count on the financial support of one of the country's biggest companies: the Grosch Group.

The Grosch Group was a conglomerate of diversified companies. It had started out thirty years ago when Grosch bought a small printing-press business. The young founder struggled in his first five years to keep the business afloat, but through some favorable connections with a certain parliamentary member, his father, the now late Guy Grosch, managed to sign a ten-year contract to sell presses to the biggest newspaper company in Belgium. This company had also spread its wings into the Netherlands and by the mid eighties was responsible for generating over 60 per cent of the newspapers sold in the two countries. This contract gave Leopold Grosch, then in his late twenties, sufficient cash to fund the acquisitions of a series of companies across different industries.

Soon the Grosch Printing Press became the Grosch Industrial Group, producing everything from sheet metal-working machines to power control systems and laser beam systems. These businesses led Grosch into the extremely lucrative defense and security industries, supplying control and electronic systems to the major defense companies in the world. Terrorism fueled enormous demand, providing the Grosch Group with significant cash-flows. As the Belgian government commenced its privatization strategy, Grosch acquired the country's electricity and gas distribution business, which now supplied over 80 per cent of all the country's electricity and gas needs.

Grosch was a keen admirer of the US way of doing business and modeled the Grosch Group on some of the prominent Fortune 500 industrial conglomerates. However, unlike some of the celebrity CEOs that ran those mega-businesses, he shunned the spotlight, rather focusing his energies on tightening his relationships with the powerful men and women who dominated European and global politics.

His hunger for acquisitions grew feverishly in the mid to late nineties. He wasn't seduced by the dotcom craze, instead sticking to businesses that were either defense related or recession proof, providing essential products for consumers and companies. He moved into textiles, transport and logistics as well as diamonds, as a result of some South African connections he had fostered during the eighties. Grosch Diamonds was now the world's biggest producer of diamonds and precious jewels.

Grosch watched as the youthful-looking fifty-year-old prime minister made his way to his seat, all in attendance now on their feet, applauding the man who had almost completed his first term in office. Under his reign, and during the global financial crisis, Belgium had secured a more solid influential seat amongst the traditional European powers of France, Germany, and Britain. Investment dollars had poured into the country, enhancing the standard of living for all Belgians.

These dollars had aided Grosch and his group of companies significantly, fueling his continued acquisition drive and enhancing his own personal fortune, now estimated at somewhere close to 10 billion euros.

Grosch pumped the PM's hand as he finally arrived at the table, a big smile on his face. The ten other people seated at the head table, all from various local businesses, sat in awe of their two distinguished guests.

Grosch sat down and engaged in some idle chatter with the guests seated around him. A distinctive vibration from his suit chest pocket distracted his thoughts. He reached inside to his BlackBerry and unwound an attached earpiece, putting it in his ear.

He deleted the message as his mouth broadened into a warm smile.

* * *

"Right on time, my good friend," Grosch said. He was in his silver Mercedes-Benz SLR McLaren, heading home. His garage housed over twenty rare cars at a combined value in excess of 10 million euros. Besides the Formula One SLR McLaren, there were an original Ferrari F40 and a Jaguar XJ220, each of which would now command in excess of 1 million euros. His major sponsorship of one of the Formula One teams also helped fuel his passion for very fast cars.

"You know me, Leopold – always punctual," an American accent replied.

"How did you get on with Malone last night?" Grosch asked.

"No problems," the caller responded. "He's under control for now but is getting a little on edge about the whole situation. He's very keen to speak to Sir Edward, so I committed to set up a conversation between the two of them."

"Tom, I'd be happy to speak to Malone personally. I do a very good Maine accent." Grosch was fluent in French, Flemish, Arabic, and English, and adept at adopting the dialects of various countries.

"That would work out well. It should keep him happy for a week or so. He is heading over to Paris the week after next to catch up with Giresse and others in the group," Mayer advised.

"He wouldn't be stupid enough to raise the possible buyout with Giresse, would he?"

"No, I don't think so. Ray will use the meeting to assess where Giresse is headed. We all know Giresse has no choice – he has to sell the group."

"Yes, but to whom?" Grosch interjected. "The fact we have no intention of buying it will come out sooner or later." He paused. "I think it's time we removed Malone – he's served his purpose. We've got the money."

"You're right, but…?"

"But what, Tom? He's disposable. Let's get it over and done with before he becomes a problem."

"Yes, but he's an old—"

"Don't go soft on me, Tom. I realize you've known him for many years but he can only become a hindrance now. We've come this far. Just let him go."

He didn't leave time for Tom to argue. "I'll call Malone tomorrow and put on my best Sir Edward voice and dazzle him with our plans for him when we eventually proceed with the buyout. I'll make him feel like he's king of the world."

"What if he happens to bump into Sir Edward before he heads for Paris?" Mayer's voice was petulant.

"That's unlikely. Sir Edward is on his boat cruising the Mediterranean as we speak and will be for the next ten days."

"Nothing beats your attention, does it?"

"Tom, you know me, I always like to lead from the front. In order to do that you need to know what all the key players are up to, all the time.

"I don't think Malone should get to France," Grosch continued. "Arrange for him to disappear before he lands, please."

"What? Disappear? Do you mean kill him?"

"Better we just remove him altogether."

"Leopold, that's a rather drastic course of action, don't you think? Having his extortion brought to the attention of the SEC was more along the lines of how I saw it. He's sure to get twenty years for his criminal act. That should be sufficient for our purposes, don't you think?"

"Killing him would be a lot simpler. Also, how do you know the SEC won't find the embezzled monies and trace them back to you? If that happens your life won't be worth living."

Mayer felt his windpipe tighten as he realized for the first time that Grosch would also have him killed at a moment's notice.

"Hmmm… let me think on it a little further and get back to you," Mayer suggested, doing his best to conceal his nerves.

"I expect to hear of your plan within the week."

Mayer covered his mouthpiece as he released a large sigh. Droplets of sweat were beginning to slide down his hairless chest.

"Leopold, you will have it. I notice you have removed the money from the account. Why is that?"

"Moved it to another account that attracts greater interest," came the laconic response.

"And when can I expect my commission?"

"You will get your commission when you dispose of Malone."

Mayer didn't respond. *What have I got myself into?*

Grosch broke the silence. "Don't worry, you'll get your money, my friend." It was like he could read Mayer's thoughts. "All in good time."

"Uh…" A sudden urge to flee raced through Mayer's mind.

"Goodbye. I have some important business to attend to."

Grosch pressed the red hang-up button on his steering wheel, cutting Mayer off. The Mercedes had been sitting on the large cobbled driveway of his massive property for the past five minutes. He noticed he had received a message. He read it:

"Thank you for a delicious breakfast. Till next time. x"

He smiled, recalling his eight o'clock meeting after the fundraiser. It had been immensely satisfying for him too.

Grosch was unmarried, having been too consumed with his businesses and being unwilling to commit himself to the one woman. His father had married young but had maintained a steady number of mistresses, of which his mother had been miserably aware. Grosch followed his father's example, and he too had steady, long-term relationships with three women.

One short-lived relationship in his early twenties had produced a child. A son. An heir. He didn't need any more than the one to ensure his desires and plans continued long after he was in his grave.

Lord Bacchazar sat on the car's roof, content with the outcome of that phone call. He yelled mockingly while raising a defiant fist: "All praise to King Leopold! Long live King Leopold!"

Los Angeles

Mayer got to his feet a little gingerly and looked around his expansive study, his eyes finally settling on an antique wooden photo frame sitting on the top of a cedar filing cabinet. He wandered over to the cabinet and picked up the frame and studied the two photos, of his children: Luke and Taylor.

His shoulders slouched as he whispered to no one: "What have I done?"

Grazag watched Mayer, initially at a distance. Then the demon moved over to him and pierced Mayer's heart with one of his black talons, expunging the sentiment and self-pity.

His other claw then reached into the back of Mayer's head.

Mayer put the frame down and quickly went for the door. He had never intended to personally kill anyone, but if that was what needed to be done, then so be it. Working for Leopold Grosch would be significantly beneficial, financially speaking.

He left the room. Grazag's bellowed laughter sent a chill through the corridors of Mayer's apartment building.

Chapter 11

Paris, that afternoon

It was madness at Paris-Charles de Gaulle – a typical day for one of the world's ten busiest airports.

The well-dressed man of Eastern European appearance noted the attractive brunette exiting immigration, pushing a luggage trolley. His black suit looked expensive, as did his polished shoes. He whispered something in a mouthpiece as he nodded to a similarly dressed man of darker complexion standing near the terminal exit. This one pulled a small sign from under his jacket and moved towards the brunette.

Loren's face was pale, the hustle and bustle of the over-crowded airport draining her usually bright complexion. On leaving the plane she had been overcome by the seething mass of people. The effort to work her way through the press of bodies had taken its toll, reminding her of the small amount of sleep she had on the flight.

"Be alert, everyone," Arlia said to no one, more a prayer. She was nervous. The enemy had not revealed itself during the flight and Arlia's reconnaissance team in Paris had found no evidence of their whereabouts. Her fifty-strong company had spread themselves around the airport and the nearby streets, scouting for signs.

Arlia saw the sign "Summers" first, being held by a thirtyish-looking man of North African descent. Loren was almost right on top of the man when she noticed her name written in bold black letters on a small white noticeboard. He was immaculately dressed in a black two-piece suit and a white business shirt with a perfectly knotted black tie.

"Hello, I'm Loren Summers," she said, extending her hand.

"Hello, Ms. Summers," the man replied, his French accent quite prominent as he shook her hand. But his copper eyes were immediately intoxicating.

Loren smiled. His handshake was gentle but firm. The cologne he was wearing gave off a pleasant aroma.

"My name is Anan," he said, smiling back with perfect teeth. "I take your bags, Madam." He took the handle of the trolley, being careful not to bump Loren in the process.

"Thank you, Anan." Loren was pleased to hand that job over.

"Vehicle this way, please," Anan said, pointing across the street at a late-model black Peugeot 607 that shone in the midday sun revealing a recent polish.

Anan opened the rear door. Loren climbed in, not needing any encouragement to shelter from the wind. While Anan was putting her bags in the boot she grabbed her travel mirror and hairbrush so that she could rescue her tousled hair.

The inside of the Peugeot was cozy and very black. The tinted windows and black upholstery made Loren think she was in a hearse for a moment. But the car smelt of the driver's pleasing cologne.

By the time the car pulled out of the airport grounds and onto the Route Du Noyer-Au-Chat, Loren had already dozed off. Anan noticed the slumping of her body via the rear-view mirror, and smiled.

He reached for the hands-free phone sitting in a cradle in front of the dashboard. He dialed a number.

The peace within the car was broken by the gruff voice of an English-speaking male with a strong Eastern European accent on the other end of the line. Loren stirred momentarily and then fell back into her state of slumber.

"Hello?"

"*Oui*, sir… hello… it is Anan. I have Ms. Summers in the car now. We are headed for Fontainebleau now. Be there in one hour."

"Good," the other man replied. "Call when you have dropped her off."

"*Oui*, sir. *Au revoir*," Anan said, hanging up.

Arlia was atop the roof of the Peugeot.

"Grindor." Arlia waved him over from the group of twenty angelguards following nearby. "Something doesn't feel right. I'm not sure what it is, but I've got a sense the enemy is playing with us. Take ten guards and trace the path to Fontainebleau. Look out for anything suspicious – vehicles, people…"

"And…?" Grindor asked in response.

"If you find any, distract them from their mission."

"Yes, Arlia, on our way." Grindor marshaled ten of the angel guards, and with a strong flap of their wings they rocketed off ahead.

Loren was continuing to drift in and out of sleep as her driver fumbled his way through the Paris back streets. They finally reached the A104 motorway that would take them to the outskirts of the Forêt de Fontainebleau.

They were now on open road, pushing seventy miles per hour. The motorway was surprisingly quiet, except for a number of buses full mostly of Asian tourists who were madly snapping every passing tree or boulder.

Before long the car had reached the northern end of the forest. The road was now bordered on either side by rows of enormous trees, mostly oak and Scots pine. The light became dull as the imposing trees blocked the sun's rays.

The temperature in the car soon dropped, waking Loren from her precious sleep.

She looked out the window and was surprised to see trees as far as her eyes could see. A thick mist curled in and around the large trunks.

"Excuse me, er… Anan… are we nearly there?" she asked.

"Still some distance to go, Ms Summers," he replied.

Loren was fully awake now. She didn't fancy starting up conversation with Anan so reached into her handbag, pulling out her stylish cell phone. It only took a few moments for it to find a France Telecom signal. Soon after she heard the "beep beep" informing her she had received a text message.

It was from Marcie's phone but the message was from Luke and Taylor:

"Hi mom. Hope u had a good flight. Miss u. Luv u lots. L&T."

It would only be around 5 a.m. in LA, so she shot back a text message rather than waking them.

***

Marcie didn't hear the text message arrive.

She was on her knees praying, her husband's contented breathing adding to the calm of the pre-dawn.

"Father, you woke me with Loren on my mind. Something is going down – I sense it, O Father. Surround my dear friend with your mighty warriors. May no harm come to her, O God. Please, please. May no weapon forged against her prevail… May no weapon forged against her prevail… May no weapon forged against her prevail…"

***

Anan was keenly focused on the road as he kept his foot firmly on the accelerator on a constant speed of sixty miles per hour.

Arlia saw the dark shadow hanging above the forest about five miles to her right. She'd seen enough of those shadows to know they meant only one thing: a pack of demons. Arlia judged that it was probably more than 100 strong.

Grindor and his party had returned. They too had noticed the pack.

"I can see it, Grindor," she said before he could inform her. "How close did you get?"

"We got to within half a mile. The forest is very dense."

"So how many?"

"At least 150."

"Anyone important that you could see?"

"No, just sentinels under the leadership of some sergeant who's hoping to big himself up."

"So what do you think is their plan?"

"There is another car waiting about three miles away in a clearing in the forest. Two men are inside it. They appear to be similar in nationality to our driver friend here." Grindor stopped and then added gravely, "Arlia, it looks like a classic abduction."

Arlia's large eyes narrowed with intensity. "Well, today is not going to be the day they outsmart us and have their way with one of our people. We'll make sure of that!"

The car had increased its speed so much that Loren was feeling a little concerned.

"Hey, Anan, slow down. We don't have to break the speed record for the Paris-to-Insead rally, you know!"

Anan ignored her.

She leant forward and put her head between the front seats.

"Anan, didn't you hear me?"

He turned, glaring at her, then swung his right arm, backhanding Loren across the face. The abruptness of the strike knocked her back into her seat. She touched her throbbing right cheek. On drawing her hand away, she saw that blood had started trickling from her nose.

"I heard you, American *whore*!"

Oh no! Help me, someone!

A chill ran up Loren's back. This couldn't be happening to her. A million things shot through her mind: she should have checked his ID before getting in the car, but he looked the part of a proper limousine driver. What was he going to do to her? Was she going to be raped, beaten, murdered? Held for ransom? She'd read an article about this happening, Americans kidnapped for ransom. Her mind quickly jumped to various options: call someone on her mobile, open the door and jump out of the car, jump him and force him off the road? Thoughts of Luke and Taylor flashed in her mind. The article featured a woman who survived such an episode. What did she do? She couldn't remember.

Her heart surged as adrenaline roared through her veins. Every inch of her body was on high alert, all her senses working overtime. She clenched her fists, her raw white knuckles reflecting her panic and fear as the blood drained from her face. *Breathe, girl, breathe, you gotta stay alert!*

She took some deep breaths as the blood stopped running out of her nose.

The car took a sudden sharp turn to the right and sped off into the forest along a fire trail. The trail was bumpy, causing Loren to bob around in her seat. She tried the door. Locked.

Anan kept one eye on her through the rear-view mirror and one on the trail.

The car was still doing sixty and bouncing wildly. The mist limited visibility to a few feet, making the trip more hair-raising. She remembered his phone call. He'd done it before. There must be others – *oh, help me, God, please!* A pack rape. Her stomach was churning and her hands and face were clammy. *Breathe, Loren, keep it together.*

Incredibly, the car abruptly stopped, jerking Loren violently forward. Safety air-bags exploded out of either side of the dashboard, breaking Anan's impact with the steering wheel.

Dazed and dizzy, Loren heard the safety lock come off the doors. She quickly unbuckled her seatbelt, opened her door and flung herself out, all in one motion. She landed roughly on the rocky trail but got to her feet easily, as if an invisible someone had helped her. She ran off back down the trail, surprising herself with how quickly she was making good distance from the car.

Anan was struggling in his seat. Somehow the air-bag had not deflated and he was caught in a vise-like grip. He wasn't going anywhere fast as Grindor applied the pressure.

Arlia had Loren back to the edge of the motorway within moments. She sank to the grassy verge. Already a black Mercedes had pulled over to offer assistance as Arlia made her visible to the driver.

Shaking his head to clear what he thought must have been a hallucination, the driver saw Loren lying by the side of the road and approached her.

"Excuse me, *madame*," he said in perfect English but with a beautiful soothing French accent, "you wouldn't be Loren Summers, by any chance?"

Loren looked up at the stranger, gingerly got to her feet and then immediately collapsed into his arms.

* * *

Landen appeared at the entrance to the trail that Loren, moments before, had followed.

"Mission accomplished!" he said.

"How so, Landen?" asked Arlia.

"Grindor had advised me of the situation prior to returning to report to you. We set up a decoy run throughout the forest that drew the majority of the sentinels away from the clearing where they were hiding in ambush. We led them on a merry chase down the Seine and managed to lose them thirty miles on. We took an alternative route back here so they wouldn't trace us back to you."

"We polished off those who stayed behind here," Arlia responded.

"Another great victory!" Landen chortled.

"Too easy, my friend. What do they take us for? Sending inexperienced imps to fight us? It's almost insulting, Landen."

"Let's enjoy it, Arlia, as it won't be long before they send their heavyweights to tackle us head on."

"Yes, that we can surely count on. And let's be thankful Loren is now safe."

Arlia jumped atop the Mercedes as it took off down the motorway, twenty other angels regrouping behind to escort it the rest of the way to Fontainebleau.

"I'll finish up here with Grindor and meet you later," Landen called out.

"Thank you for your great job. Go in peace!" She waved, leaving Landen at the fire-trail entrance. She turned her attention to Loren, sitting fitfully in the front passenger seat below.

The Chateau de Fontainebleau

"WHAAAT?!"

The deafening roar of disgust caused the enormous creature to step back, standing to attention mechanically.

"Again?!" snarled the bigger of the two creatures within the ornate mahogany double doors. *"Who* did you assign the job to?" it growled, turning to reveal a hideously disfigured face.

"To the same team that successfully completed the kidnap and rape of the two French ladies in the Riviera last month," said the other. He looked up with a trace of defiance. "They came highly recommended, my Lord!"

"Really? Who do you get your news from, you fool? Cartoon Network? That incident in the Riviera was an absolute fiasco – the two humans got away with barely a finger being laid on them!"

"Sir, Lord, sir... um... really... I wasn't aware! Sergeant Major Hedrag suggested them to me," he replied, taking a few steps back.

"You *cretin*!" The larger one grabbed the other around the neck, lifting him off his feet with one hand, eyeballing him.

"I now have to inform Agramon that we failed to get his human!" His forehead bore a mark resembling an upside-down cross, badly inflamed. "How do *you* propose we should explain our *failure*?" he continued, still holding the smaller one at eye level.

"I... I... I... um... I... um..."

"Yes?"

"um—"

THUMP!

The creature hit the solid-oak floor-to-ceiling bookshelves and crumpled to the ground.

SWISH!

The larger demon whipped out his black, barbaric, fifty-inch sword and sliced his subordinate's head off.

"You won't fail *me* again, Colonel! Go and join your failed comrades in Hades!"

Lord Bacchazar turned and swung his midnight-black cloak across his colossal torso, disappearing through the library window.

Chapter 12

Forêt de Fontainebleau, early evening

Deep within the forest sat a derelict bench on top of a rocky hill. Large pools of fresh rainwater covered half of the rocky outcrop. The early evening air was unusually still.

Arlia was the last to arrive for this impromptu brief meeting. After the earlier events of the day, she couldn't be too careful with Loren's protection.

She landed effortlessly and silently on the rock, approaching the small group of supernatural beings whose radiance shimmered in the dim light of sundown. A three-quarter moon was making itself known in the fast-descending night air.

The two with their backs to her turned slightly inward, allowing Arlia a full view of the one she had never had the good fortune to meet. For centuries she had longed for this honor.

On entering the group, she immediately fell to one knee in respect and adoration. Her head bowed, she could feel his piercing, deep, ocean-blue eyes gently exploring her heart, in loving concern and mutual respect. She remembered stories about him: supposedly he was blessed with the ability to read the hearts and minds of all supernatural beings. Could he, she now wondered? Was that why he was such a formidable warrior? He always knew what the opposition was likely to do next.

He was one of a handful of angels given divine authority by the Father himself. The majority of the angels within the Kingdom regarded Tagan with almost the same esteem as the archangels that surrounded the Holy Throne. He had been the leader of the European region for centuries and never tired of his mission to guard and protect the Father's creation.

He arose from the bench and momentarily stood over his respectful liege. He gently placed his hand under her chin and with his eyes motioned for her to stand.

"That is not necessary, Arlia, but I appreciate your courtesy."

"It is an honor to finally meet you, my Lord!"

"Thank you. But please do not call me 'Lord'. 'Tagan' is more appropriate. There is only one Lord, the risen Christ, whose servants are we all."

"Yes, yes, of course… Tagan…" Arlia said nervously.

He stood straight and tall with one hand resting on the hilt of his sword as he prepared to address the brave angelguard threesome that stood in front of him.

"Arlia… you know Athaniel…" Tagan said, gesturing to the dark-haired angel who stood to her left.

Arlia nodded an acknowledgment.

"Good to see you made it safely here," Athaniel said. Arlia was a good six inches taller than Athaniel but that didn't bother him in the slightest.

"… and this is Darius, from Australia!" Tagan said as Arlia turned to see an angel of raw beauty. His long, flowing hair was unkempt, adding to his rugged appearance. He had walnut-brown eyes that glistened as he smiled and a perfectly shaped mouth that revealed brilliant white teeth.

"Hello," she said matter-of-factly, shaking his hand.

"Hello… it is good to meet the one whose daring feats of the past few days have been heralded across the Kingdom."

"I will be brief, as you all need to get back to your charges," Tagan said. "Lord Bacchazar is holed up at the Chateau with an army of 500 sentinels. We expect that to double by the week's end, as we understand another battalion is due from Paris any day."

The three angelguards showed no emotion nor did they comment at the announcement.

"After the botched effort today, Bacchazar will seek vengeance sooner rather than later. Athaniel has also confirmed we will enjoy the exalted presence of Agramon in the next few days. He didn't take kindly to today's news and has decided he should get personally involved."

"Tagan, are they aware of Jack's role yet?" asked Darius.

"No, Darius. We are confident they aren't and it's vital we keep it that way. They would have taken some interest in the fact that Jack met up with Thierry and Ruth last week, but that could easily be explained away as coincidence, nothing else."

"So that means Loren will be under attack again?" Arlia said with a tone of concern.

"We expect so, yes, Arlia. They are convinced Loren is critical to our mission as a result of our strongly armed intervention in her life. So they will try again to dispose of her or at least minimize her impact."

"That's just great!" Arlia said, exasperated. "She's taken so much and now is set to be hit again." She started pacing in front of the other three, waving her arms around in frustration and anger. "Sorry, but I'm just not sure how much more of this she can take."

"I know, Arlia," Tagan said, placing a reassuring hand on her shoulder. "That's why I have decided to stay here. I will assist Athaniel and his team who are watching over the Chateau. His squad is 100 strong, all very senior white knights who have successfully fought Bacchazar's battalions previously."

"It was very clever of the enemy to use the kidnapping ring to grab Loren. It's amazing how that ring has infiltrated the official hire services," Arlia said.

"Yes, it's a ring that has very wide tentacles across many European airports," Athaniel advised. "They used to focus on younger women to sell off as sex slaves but now are also chasing older executive-types for extortion. These rings epitomize Satan's maliciousness in playing with people's souls."

Darius and Arlia shook their heads, downcast expressions on their faces.

"I hate to think what would have happened if Loren didn't have such wonderful girlfriends who are so relentless in their prayer for her," Arlia interjected.

"Yes, Arlia, and we need them to keep it up," Tagan agreed. "Darius, you keep doing what you're doing with Jack. But I'd like you also to keep your eyes on Arlia's troop. Even though they are greatly experienced, having a warrior like you nearby will be a big help."

"Yes, sir, consider it done," Darius responded. "Ouch!" He recoiled from a whack to the shoulder.

"C'mon, Darius, toughen up! I don't have time for soft touches," Arlia smiled warmly.

"We will meet here each night at this time for a brief roundup of the day," Tagan announced. "Let's close in prayer before we head off!"

They grouped into a huddle, arms around each other's shoulders.

* * *

"Let me sleep on it, Marce," Loren said quietly into her phone. She was sitting in a fluffy white bathrobe supplied by the campus, as evidenced by the Insead inscription on the left breast.

"Oh, the facilities? Pretty basic, babe, but they're designed like that, as you don't get to spend much time in them. Sleep and shower, that's probably all I'll be using it for, I imagine.

"Bye, babe, thanks for listening… and praying for me… I feel much better now. I was a bit of a mess. The bath and then hearing your voice have been really soothing… I love you… Give Lukey and Tayls a big kiss from me… Bye, bye."

She put the phone down and sighed. Tears rolled down her cheeks. She reached for the empty wine glass as she got to her feet to refill it.

Arlia stood behind the sofa, her heart aching for Loren. "Yes, Marcie, thanks for praying and please, please, keep it up, tenfold."

* * *

She awoke startled. Looking around, she saw nothing familiar. The malevolence of darkness gripped her heart and mind. She pulled the covers up closer to her chin as she sat upright in bed, her knees to her chest. The luminescent glow of the alarm clock beside her bed read 1:16. *What?! Just four hours of sleep?!*

The fear was now dissipating as she recognized her new lodgings, aided by the pale glow of the moon invading her room.

Loren hopped out of bed. The impulse to sleep had now left her and the fear that woke her brought back memories of that horrible car ride. She grabbed her bathrobe, to shield her from the frostiness of the room. *Oh, for my Ugg boots back home! Socks will have to do.*

She wandered out of the bedroom to the kitchenette, putting the kettle on. As she waited for it to boil, she sat on the worn sofa and reviewed the selection of magazines on the coffee table: French *Living* magazine, French *Vogue*, and a book on the history of Fontainebleau. None appealed, so she switched the TV on, flicking through the twenty or so channels, but nothing grabbed her.

She headed back to the bedroom, tea in hand, deliberately leaving the main room's light on. On hopping back under the still warm covers of her bed, she reflected on recent events.

The tea was pleasant but her nerves were still frayed at the edges. A whole jumble of thoughts went through her mind: the charming face of her abductor – she wondered if she'd ever forget it; disbelief that she survived that 'ride to hell', as Marcie had dubbed it; waking up in the ambulance after the bomb attack a few months earlier; the hundreds of funerals she attended for weeks afterward.

Why, oh why are these horrible things happening to me? Are these signs I should just enjoy every moment of every day, as my time is about up? What am I doing here? I should be with Luke and Taylor, Mom and Dad, Marcie, Rebecca.

The tears began slowly but it didn't take long before she was openly weeping. She looked heavenward with outstretched arms and then fell face first onto the duvet cover, resting there like a ragdoll while the tears continued to flow.

Arlia knelt by her bedside. She stroked Loren's shoulder-length hair that lay sprawled over her head. It pained Arlia to see Loren so distraught. Loving concern for Loren was mixed with anger towards the minions of darkness. Arlia would not rest until the one responsible for this suffered under her blade.

Loren slipped into a fitful doze.

The next thing she knew, the ringing of the hotel phone next to her bed was waking her up.

"Hello," she said, half asleep. All she heard in response was an automated wake-up call message.

It was 7 a.m.

* * *

Hostilities in the Middle East continued unabated.

The spate of natural disasters kept occurring. One month a horrifying earthquake and accompanying tsunami; the next month wild tornados reaping mass destruction; a landslide killing thousands the month after.

The European Union was imploding as its member countries reeled from one financial calamity to another.

The spirit of terror was taking a greater grip on the world's people. An act of terror was committed somewhere in the world almost every day. Prayer groups across the world had grown a hundredfold. They sought God's almighty interference in bringing peace to a world overwhelmed by enmity.

Many reflected on these words from Matthew 24:

> Watch out that no one deceives you. For many will
> come in my name, claiming, "I am the Messiah",
> and will deceive many. You will hear of wars and
> rumors of wars, but see to it that you are not
> alarmed. Such things must happen, but the end is
> still to come. Nation will rise up against nation, and
> kingdom against kingdom. There will be famines
> and earthquakes in various places. All these are the
> beginning of birth pains.

Believers continued to pray for all people, Christian and non-Christian alike. Those prayers served to invigorate the army of angelguards commissioned to fight for the souls of all the people of the world.

Chapter 13

Insead, Fontainebleau

The twenty FJ Caille Group executives participating in the program were enjoying a short break for lunch. They were seated in the campus café. It would be a demanding two-week program running to nine o'clock most nights, so such breaks were essential to recharge and replenish the mind. Sunday was to be the only day the delegates would receive respite, with a half-day off to explore the forest or venture into the town center.

A multinational academic team of four professors were leading the program: one Dutchman, one American, one Frenchman and one Australian: Jack Haines. The four had spread themselves across the four tables occupied by the executives.

Jack was at the servery when Loren came up alongside him. She was dressed casually in jeans, a sky-blue long-sleeved linen shirt and a pullover draped over her shoulders.

"Excuse me, Professor Haines, I thought I'd introduce myself. I'm with the Caille program." Jack had been introduced to the group but was yet to lead them.

Jack turned to face her. "Oh, hello, Jack Haines. Please, none of this 'Professor' stuff." His green eyes were particularly striking, Loren noticed as she shook his hand.

"Loren Summers from LA."

"Ah, Loren, how are you feeling today? I was so sorry to hear of that incident yesterday!"

"How do you know, may I ask?"

"Monsieur Rocheteau informed the four of us, considering it best we be aware of the ordeal. How are you feeling?"

"Weary." Jack noted Loren's paleness. "I went for a run this morning around the campus to clear the cobwebs, but I feel like I didn't get rid of them all."

"It will take a bit of time, I expect. So don't push yourself these next few days. The four of us are conscious that you're likely to be somewhat... uh, how do I say this – fragile? – after that experience. We half expected you not to attend today. Take the day to rest up."

"I did seriously contemplate staying away but figured the mental stimulation would be good for me. Also, I didn't fancy playing catch-up with the rest of the team, starting a day later. And it has been good so far; I've got stronger during the morning. The others have all been very supportive too."

"That's great, Loren." Jack made a move back to the tables. Loren, coffee in hand, walked with him. "I look forward to our time together over the next two weeks and hope you find it an immensely satisfying program."

"Likewise, Professor Haines. And thank you for your concern."

"Don't mention it. And it's *Jack*. Professors are at least sixty years old with a head of grey hair, if they have any at all, and a bright-red nose from drinking too much red wine while marking essays!" Jack grinned, and was pleased to see an answering smile.

They parted, heading for their respective tables.

The Chateau de Fontainebleau

The famous castle had hundreds of rooms, as diverse in style as the thirty-four sovereigns who had occupied it over a 600-year period.

One large room in the basement, now for the most part ignored by the thousands of tourists who visit the enchanted but mysterious castle each year, contained abandoned oak barrels that gave off a stale odor of fermented grapes. The disused cellar still held wall-to-wall racks of solid oak, now empty, that would have stored at one time somewhere in the vicinity of 5,000 bottles of wine.

Two sinister protagonists of the sentinel armies taking residence in the famous Chateau stood at opposite ends of the dark cellar.

"So when should we attack your American lass?" asked one of the eight-foot-tall creatures in a very gruff voice.

"So you wish me to determine the date and time of our victory?" the other said, stepping forward into the shard of moonlight that shone through the one very small window. His massive bulk was covered in thick black hair.

"No, no, no, Agramon, you misunderstand me. I only asked *when* you think we *should* attack. Not when we *will* attack!" the other stated emphatically and menacingly.

"Bacchazar…" Agramon swung over in a flash and stood eyeball to eyeball in front of his comrade. "Don't fool around with me, or else I'll have you sucking out of a straw for the rest of your horrible little existence!" he hissed, mouthing each word very deliberately.

"Ah, hah hah…" Bacchazar took a step back. "You are so easily baited, Agramon," he said condescendingly. "Better be careful, as it might be your undoing one day."

Agramon swung away, growling, and smashed his right fist into the concrete wall. The room shook.

"Now, let's get back to work before our mutual disrespect for each other ruins any chance of us prevailing. Otherwise both of us will lose any chance at succeeding The General," Bacchazar observed, "which is what we both want more than anything else, don't we?"

"Absolutely… my snake-oil salesman of a rival!" Agramon breathed heavily, then smiled, exposing black teeth. "I think we should wait a few days and see if anything transpires on the program. I'd also like to see how she takes the news of her boss's passing. She may well return to Los Angeles as a result and then I can deal with her myself in my own good time."

"I would be much happier if you dealt with your own problems rather than passing them off to me," Bacchazar added snidely.

Agramon interjected, "What, so you can mess them up like your flock did the other day? Your cronies didn't even get to have some fun with her, let alone finish her off!"

"And whose unit also failed miserably on the way to LAX? She didn't even know there had *been* any attempt on her life, it was so pitiful!" Bacchazar roared back in protest.

Agramon spun around in disgust, seething with rage. That slimy Zeldax had made him look a fool. Killing him still hadn't sated his anger.

Bacchazar looked out the small, high window. Sunday's failure still cut him deeply.

He turned to face Agramon, whose black leather straps only served to make his huge muscular shoulders look even more imposing.

"We will need to be more involved this time," Bacchazar offered.

Agramon turned to stare down his rival. They were six feet apart.

"I will kill her myself if I have to," he growled through gritted teeth and stormed out the door.

Bacchazar only smiled as he wondered how his rival would release his simmering rage.

***

The rain fell steadily that night in Fontainebleau. The temperature gauge fell into the mid forties, ensuring residents needed their electric blankets and hot-water bottles.

An eerie grey haze fell over the village which, together with the continual rain, made visibility difficult. Bats flapped over the village, playing havoc with the hectares of grape seedlings planted in the vineyards surrounding it.

The howling of dogs soon pierced the quiet of night. Their shrill barking didn't let up, even though many owners soon rescued their four-legged friends from the cold.

The state of agitation wasn't only limited to those with four legs. Screaming arguments broke out in house after house as husbands and wives started shouting obscenities at each other for no apparent reason. Sibling rivalry took on a new dimension as brother and brother, brother and sister, sister and sister started laying into each other, verbally or physically.

Soon the sirens of the police, ambulance and fire services could be heard racing through the small streets as scuffles broke out in bars and restaurants. A group of teenagers torched an empty car near the hospital. By nine o'clock reports of burglaries started coming in, one by one and then two by two, stretching the small police unit to the max. Some of the domestic arguments soon turned nasty as wives hit husbands and more husbands hit their wives.

The teenagers who had torched the car had made their way to the town center where they smashed the window of the local corner store and made merry with its contents.

And then, just as the craziness was reaching its peak and the constabulary had almost given up hope of being able to cope… it just stopped.

The dogs stopped howling. The bats went back to the forest. Husbands and wives started kissing and hugging. The scuffles in the bars and restaurants ceased. The teenagers turned themselves in to the police, giving everything back they had stolen from the corner shop.

Tagan and Athaniel had seen elements of the mayhem from their secluded hideaway in the forest directly behind the Chateau. They knew there was only one explanation for it.

Demons. Demons playing havoc with humans. They saw the troop of over 500 shoot out of the castle. And then return one hour later.

"Someone's not happy would be my guess, Athaniel," said Tagan.

"Agramon was at the head. He was moving so fast, he must have been incandescent with rage," Athaniel responded.

"Hmmm… perhaps Lord Bacchazar and Agramon had a tiff," Tagan offered.

"Let's hope so."

"Yes, my old friend. Over the years we've seen many sentinel troops self-destruct, haven't we?"

Athaniel chuckled. "Let's hope it happens again here in this pretty village. It would sure make our stay a little more pleasant."

* * *

The first three days of the program had been intense and tiring. The professors were all stretching the twenty executives and stirring them to learn and develop. Much time had been spent in self-analysis and in groups working on personal change management.

On finishing dinner at a quaint traditional French restaurant in the village, the group was boarding the school's minibus for the short trip back to the campus. It was almost eleven o'clock.

Jack Haines was the last to board. He eyed one of three spare seats, the one nearest to him.

"Would you mind if I take this seat?" he asked in his now familiar Australian accent.

Loren looked up and said enthusiastically, "Absolutely!"

"So you would mind... if I sat here?"

"Oh... I'm sorry!" Loren realized her response wasn't the one she intended. "Absolutely... please sit down, Professor Haines."

"I won't if you keep calling me Professor."

"Please... Jack, I'd like you to have this seat."

They immediately fell into conversation, initially covering the progress of the course but soon moving on to other subjects.

"How does your family find living in France?" Loren asked.

"My family is back home in Australia. I am only here on secondment specifically for this program."

"They do that, do they?"

"Who does what?"

"Insead... invites professors from other universities... even... even... all the way from *down under*?"

"No. It's actually quite unusual. They only do it when they want the services of an exceptional academic," he paused, smiling.

"Really, so why did they invite you, then?"

"Touché!"

116

Loren continued to play along. "Professor Jack from Australia… what makes you such an exceptional academic, do you think?" she said, holding her clenched hand up close to her face, mimicking a microphone.

"Why, I just happen to be the leading authority on the mating calls of the now extinct Tasmanian tiger."

"Really, Professor Jack? That sounds like a particularly important subject." She still held her microphone-hand up. "Why would twenty executives of one of the world's largest advertising agencies have any interest in such a topic?"

"I didn't say they did!" he responded with a large grin on his face. "I didn't plan to teach those executives 'from one of the world's largest advertising agencies' on that subject." He paused. "But now I think about it, they most likely would find it very useful in running such a *biiigg* company!"

They both laughed.

He felt very relaxed in Loren's company. Their banter was something he hadn't experienced with a woman for a while. He always had more female friends than male. Growing up with Jane always having girlfriends around helped him develop an enthusiasm for friendships with women.

Loren dealt with men all day, every day, in her office. But there was something different about Jack. His eyes were caring and calming. He was confident, but not conceited, quite charming and playful.

He yawned.

"Keeping you up are we, Professor?" Loren asked, even though she too was beginning to feel the first seeds of tiredness.

"Oh, you know, it's been a long day. I hope you all bounce back well tomorrow for the other professors."

"You're not leading us tomorrow, then?"

"Nope. Got the day off."

"Lucky you. So what will you do on your day off?"

"Play some golf in the morning. Then have an extremely long lunch well into the afternoon, and then perhaps have a spa and sauna before preparing for dinner."

Loren looked incredulous.

Jack smiled, sensing her confusion in not knowing how to take him.

"No... actually, Didier Rocheteau and I are heading to Paris to meet with some of your senior executives in Head Office who will be participating in the program next week. It'll be a good opportunity for me to walk around and get an idea of the culture and work ethic. I'll be talking to some of the other staff to get their views on the organization – what works, what could be improved, and so on."

"I'd imagine you'll find Head Office different from the operational offices, though," said Loren. "Shouldn't you really see both?"

"Absolutely. But Head Office will still give me a strong indication of how the senior brass views the world. I hope to visit some of the other offices later in the year to assess what's similar, what's different and what impacts they have on the people."

"Hmmm... sounds interesting," Loren summed up. "I'd suggest it's even more interesting than the mating calls of the Tasmanian... what was it again?"

"... tiger!" Jack helped her out.

"... that's right... the Tasmanian tiger," she chuckled as she said it.

Jack smiled warmly.

Those seeds of tiredness were now growing fast, enveloping Loren in a sleepy haze. She couldn't resist the urge to yawn a long "My head is crying out for a pillow"-type yawn.

"Oops, I'm sorry," she said, removing her hand from her mouth.

The bus had now pulled up in the car park nearest the campus accommodation. Jack, being close to the door, jumped to his feet.

"Well, good night, Loren. Rest up and have a good day tomorrow."

"You too, Jack. Hope you find your trip to Head Office beneficial," she replied, feeling slightly disappointed the trip had ended.

Jack skipped down the stairs and immediately started chatting to one of the other delegates.

Arlia and Darius were nearby, pleased their two charges had now made decent contact.

Jack picked up the pace as he branched off away from the group, whistling a tune.

Chapter 14

Outskirts of Brussels, the following day

Grosch stood at the large window staring at the sweeping, lush, green countryside that surrounded the head office of his conglomerate of companies. He had this sprawling campus-like office complex built five years ago, having been inspired by those in America, especially the high-tech companies such as Microsoft, Google and Apple. A series of five low-lying three-tiered pods were connected via a hub-and-spoke arrangement, all joining the main pod that sat at its core. The main pod was smaller than the others but was slightly raised, allowing Grosch an uninterrupted view of his empire.

One of the three phones on his desk rang. His private one. Only a few people knew the number.

"Yes?" he answered by pushing a remote control that he had in his shirt pocket.

"Have you heard?" a rich Californian accent came through the surround-sound speakers of his lavishly decorated office, the size of a standard tennis court.

"Nice of you to call. Why have you not returned my calls sooner?"

"Leopold, just very busy... you know how it gets," the Californian replied.

"Out spending that huge commission check you believe you are going to receive?"

"No... actually. Trying to arrange matters so that I *can* receive it!"

"Tom, you haven't completed the final task I set you in order to receive the commission. Malone's in France as we *speak*!"

"Oh… yes… you obviously have heard. He snuck out of the country unannounced, even surprising his secretary."

"Ah hah," Grosch said, unimpressed.

"… something to do with celebrating his twenty-fifth wedding anniversary with Candice, his wife."

"Really? Funny way to spend your anniversary, by arranging meetings with your bosses in head office."

No response from the other end of the line.

After a few moments of silence Mayer finally responded. "I… I wasn't aware of that. Trish, his secretary, showed me his itinerary. I presumed the Thursday in Paris meant sight-seeing before heading off to the Riviera for a five-day weekend, then on to Insead next Wednesday, when he'd also catch up with Giresse, as planned."

"Hmmm… never become a private investigator or contract killer – you'd be hopeless at it!"

"Neither of those careers particularly appeals to me."

A slight pause. Grosch was pondering his next move. He stood in front of a glass-framed black-and-blue-striped football jersey of the club he owned, the number "6" emblazoned on its back together with "GROSCH" stamped above it.

"Is there anything else?"

"Ah… what are your plans, then?"

"Yes… that's right. They are now *my* plans, aren't they, as you failed in your mission? In fact, it's now really none of your business."

The click as the phone hung up could be clearly heard through the speakers, Grosch having touched a button on the remote in his hand.

The phone rang immediately.

Grosch ignored it, throwing the remote onto his oversized desk and heading out through the door of his office.

It shut behind him, as the phone continued to ring.

As he walked briskly down the corridor flanked by a series of five original Monets, Grosch called a number on his BlackBerry.

"Be ready to leave in ten," he demanded.

A pause.

"Paris."

* * *

"I'm doing great, Mum," Jack told his mother over Skype. They'd covered the status of the twins, Jane and others. "The exec group is outstanding and particularly bright."

"That's good, dear," Louise Haines replied, trying to show interest. "How's the leg?"

"Great. Well, much better. The limp is less noticeable and I've dropped the painkillers, which I'm really happy about. I better go, Mum."

"OK, dear. Lovely talking to you. And remember to keep holding tight to the Lord."

"Absolutely. But please keep praying for me."

"Always."

"Love you. See ya."

"Bye bye, dear."

Jack's face disappeared from the laptop screen. "Heavenly Father," Louise started praying at her desk, "please keep protecting Jack. Bless him with wisdom and discernment as he goes about his day. May you shine brightly through him as he teaches and guides the class. And please, Father, put a hunger in his heart to keep pursuing you with a passion. In Jesus' name, Amen."

FJ Caille Group Headquarters, Paris, the same day

Jack and Didier Rocheteau entered the training room to find five men standing around the coffee machine making idle chatter. These were the senior executives who would participate in the program in the second half of next week.

Jack introduced himself to the five – four Frenchmen and one American. Darius stood at the back, smiling; he knew what he needed to do.

After a brief introduction from Didier, Jack led the group through a detailed presentation about the full year's program, giving particular focus to the first two-week session that was now well under way.

The meeting lasted for two hours. It was lively, just as Jack had wanted and expected from a group of high achievers. The five were all a little dismissive at first but after thirty or so minutes, Jack had them lapping it up. He saw their energy levels crank up a gear when he got them to believe in the program.

All except one. The American, Ray Malone. Throughout Jack's presentation Malone had been quite distracted. Jack had often caught him looking at anywhere but him or the screen. He also spent a lot of time doodling or writing notes to himself.

Jack caught him before he left the room.

"Ah… Ray… excuse me, Ray. You got a minute?"

"It better be quick, son. I've got another meeting to go to," Malone replied. Jack didn't believe him.

"What do you think of the program?" Jack asked.

"It looks spot on, Haines. Hmmm… can't really see how it could be improved upon."

"Really? All programs like these can be improved."

"Oh… sure… give me a few days and I'll get back to you."

Jack decided to change tack.

"Loren Summers is an impressive executive."

"You're absolutely right there. Loren's worked for me her entire career."

"I wasn't aware of that."

"Listen, Haines, I really must fly. Good to meet you," he said, shaking Jack's hand firmly. "I'll see you next week. Looking forward to it."

He rushed out the door.

Hmmm, that went well. Not! It bothered Jack that Malone appeared disinterested. *Wonder what Loren thinks of him.*

Darius nudged Jack's thoughts to follow Ray's path to the door.

As Jack headed for the door, his attention was drawn to a solitary scrunched-up piece of paper that lay on the ground next to a rubbish bin.

He picked it up and for some reason opened it.

The piece of paper was a basic fax header page addressed simply to a "Ray", handwritten. No surname. *Must be Ray Malone.*

Funny, didn't think anyone used faxes any more. Guess Ray's from the old school.

It was "from", again simply in handwriting, a "Tom". It was dated a few weeks ago and had "5" pages following.

What was most interesting about the piece of paper was that it was full of what Jack figured were Ray's doodles. The doodles he had spent the best part of the last two hours constructing.

He looked closer, soon realizing they weren't doodles at all. To call them that would have been very impolite. What Jack had in his hands was quite clear, even though it was a little messy.

He was looking at an organization chart, which Ray had dubbed "Newco".

The top box of this scrawled chart had "Ray" written in it. Jack read this to mean Ray was CEO or head of this "Newco". There were three large boxes of similar size underneath: the one on the left had "S&P" in it, the one in the middle "APA", and the right one "GA". Jack worked the first two out easily from his knowledge of the US subsidiaries of the Caille America group: "S&P" was obviously Swain & Peters, "APA" was Akers Prestwidge Advertising, the Chicago-based sister company. "GA" wasn't what he was expecting in the third box, rather something abbreviating Darling Partners.

He thought for a moment. The only "GA" he knew in the US advertising industry was the second biggest agency: Graves Advertising. *Could that be what GA represents?*

To his surprise, he saw another name he knew. It was under the "S&P" box: "L. Summers – CEO".

"Loren, CEO?" he said under his breath.

The fax header was one of those blank pro forma ones that Microsoft Word created. There was no company logo or reference to the sender, except for "Tom".

And then he saw it. At the very top of the page, the thin header the sending fax machine prints, informing you where it had been sent from: "Maple, Mayer and Masters."

Incredible!

Stephen's investment bank.

Darius smiled, knowing Jack wouldn't let this go.

***

The Hotel Ritz was regarded as one of Paris's finest. It was the standard residence for all visiting royalty, world leaders and celebrities.

Leopold Grosch entered the main bedroom of the Imperiale Suite from the en suite bathroom wearing a silk bathrobe. The jacuzzi had been just what he needed.

A plain brown envelope sat on the king-sized bed ready for delivery.

His BlackBerry on the bedside table rang.

"Hello," he answered.

"Two this time." A pause as he listened. "Yes." Another pause. "All the instructions will be in the envelope." Pause. "Fifty now, fifty when complete." Pause. "There'll be a man wearing a black-and-blue striped football jersey at the west end of the Eiffel Tower in exactly one hour. He will wait for ten minutes. If you have not shown up he will leave. Code word is Incredible Hulk."

He waited for the response.

"I know. You have never failed me before. I have every confidence in you."

Grosch headed over to the wardrobe and picked himself out a black Zegna suit for his dinner engagement with the French president.

***

On returning to his room, Jack called Stephen. He tried his office number first. New York was six hours behind Paris, so Jack figured his brother would have a few hours in the office left.

No answer, so he left a message on his voicemail.

While he waited for Stephen to return his call, he went on the net to do some research of his own.

Maple, Mayer and Masters was easy to find. Google took him straight to their home page. The "three Ms of investment banking", as they referred to themselves – in the business of "*m*aking *m*agic *m*oments for their clients."

Jack recalled Stephen telling him he was headhunted from his lucrative job at one of the biggest investment banks in the world to join this new boutique firm that, by all accounts, had a client list second to none. Judging by the website, that was how they wanted it to stay: small but extremely wealthy. In fact, no one with less than $100 million need apply as the 3Ms weren't interested in anything less.

The phone in Jack's room rang and he picked up the hand-set. It was Stephen returning his call. They chatted for a few minutes, catching up, until Jack brought the conversation around to what he was after. He still had his eyes on the website.

"Hey, Stephen, I'm just going to put you on speaker for a moment, if you don't mind." Jack pressed a button on the phone and put the hand-set down.

"Can you hear me all right?"

"Coming through loud and clear," was the response from a voice with a strong Australian accent. "What, can't give your little brother your undivided attention for a few minutes? I bet you're marking some paper while we talk?"

"Oh, no, mate, I'm actually looking at your company's website," replied Jack "… and that's what I wanted to talk to you about."

"Finally, you've decided to spread your theories on organizational behavior to the most important industry: investment banking."

"Oh sure, after the penalties the SEC has just handed out to the big guys, your industry could sure do with some help – one that keeps you all out of jail!"

"You got me there," Stephen responded with a hearty laugh.

"This may sound like a strange question, but I came across a document that referred to a 'Tom' from your company. Is there a Tom that works there?"

Stephen thought for a moment.

At the same time Jack found what he was looking for on the website.

Simultaneously they both said, "Tom Mayer!"

Jack was now looking at a picture on the webpage of a very

good-looking man with dark hair, showing no trace of grey, and a great tan. Probably in his early forties, Jack thought.

"He's the only Tom we have working here," said Stephen. "We only have thirty-odd employees, so I know every one of them."

"Would he be doing any work with the Caille advertising group, by any chance?"

"You know I couldn't tell you if it wasn't public, but I'm not aware of anything we are doing. Why? Why do you ask?"

"Oh, it's nothing. I came across something addressed from Tom to one of the senior executives, that's all."

"And what did it say?"

"Nothing. Absolutely nothing. It was a blank fax header that was sent from one of your fax machines. The five accompanying pages were not attached."

"So, then, why the interest?"

Before Jack could respond, Stephen spoke. "You said a blank fax header, no corporate logo, nothing?"

"That's right. One of those standard template fax headers."

"That's odd. What was the number on it?"

"+1 212 310 3999."

"Yep, that's our prefix. Just hang on a sec. I'll see if it's in our directory."

Almost immediately Stephen was back.

"It's Tom Mayer's personal fax number."

Silence, as the brothers were distracted by their own thoughts.

"You might have yourself a little mystery, brother," Stephen said. "But more than likely they are just old buddies."

"Yeah, you're probably right."

"Tom works out of two offices. The other's in LA," Stephen offered.

"Oh, well, there you go. They're probably members at the same country club."

"He's only been working out of the office here for the past year or so," Stephen outlined. "Before that he was almost entirely based out of LA. He travels an awful lot. He does a lot of business out of Europe and the Middle East. That was, I believe, the main reason for spending more of his time out of New York, closer to the Continent, you know."

Stephen reflected briefly. "He has some kids, I think, that live in LA. I remember he told me once. His ex-wife is some high-flying exec herself and they have two kids. That's why he doesn't move here permanently, so that he can see the kids. Now what's his wife's name, I'm sure he told me?"

Silence again as Stephen thought for a moment.

"Loren, that's her name."

"She wouldn't by any chance work with Swain & Peters, would she?" asked Jack.

"I don't know, mate – she might. I can't remember if he told me who she worked for. Why, do you know a Loren at Swains?"

"Sure do. Loren Summers. EVP of Strategy and Planning. She's attending this program I'm leading."

"Wow, small world."

"Well, that's if it's the same one. But the interesting point, Stephen, is that Loren's boss is a guy by the name of Ray. Ray Malone. The fax header was addressed to a 'Ray'. And I'm absolutely certain it's this guy, as I was in a meeting with him this afternoon."

"Wow. Hmmm… it's getting more interesting by the second," offered Stephen.

"Now get this. On the fax header was scribbled an organization chart. An organization called 'Newco' that had Ray at the top and three companies – S&P, APA and GA – grouped below the CEO's box. And Stephen: Loren's name was written down as head of the S&P box."

"Gee, sounds like some coup or takeover."

"Just what I was thinking."

"Listen mate, I'll do some scratching around here and see what I can uncover. Probably nothing, if Tom's done a good job. But you never know. In the meantime I'd suggest you don't say anything to anyone. Sounds like you've come across something that's most likely highly confidential. A deal might be going down and it's in the early days of it. Perhaps Ray Malone or Caille has engaged the 3Ms to lead it."

"Sure, no probs, bro. I don't have any plans on telling anyone anything. And thanks for doing some hunting around. I'd sure be interested to see if you uncover anything."

"Listen, I better go. The market's closing and I must get back to it," Stephen said. "I might just place an order for a big swag of FJ Caille shares. Only kidding! See ya, mate. Talk to you soon."

"Yeah, great, Stephen. Talk soon. Bye."

Chapter 15

Jack found Loren in the bar.

The campus bar featured dark-leather lounges and stools together with a full-sized pool table. Glass doors led out to a well-lit balcony but the cool night made that a non-option for the guests.

Jack strolled over to her group of five. Judging by their relaxed body language, they had finished for the night.

"G'day, team," he said cheerily.

"Pull up a pew, Jack," one of the men said.

Jack grabbed a wooden chair with leather upholstery and placed it in the gap next to Loren.

"A fruitful session tonight, then?" he asked.

A few nodding heads and then Joe, one of the male participants from Chicago, offered: "Absolutely. We actually need more group time so that we can pull together the plan and prepare our presentation."

"You'll get a lot of time next week to prepare, don't worry. Half of Tuesday and most of Wednesday will be given to you working in your groups so that you can be ready to give your presentations on Thursday."

"Oh good," Joe said, while others in the group murmured in the affirmative.

"It's 10:30, I think I might go to bed," Joe proposed as he got to his feet. "I've got a few calls to make to home."

"I might join you," said another man.

"Me too," said another.

"Yeah, I'm about done for the night," said the other woman in the group.

After saying good night, the four headed out of the bar, leaving Jack and Loren alone.

A group of four men were playing what looked like a very serious game of pool. There were a few other people scattered around the bar.

"How was your trip to Paris today, *Professor* Jack?"

"It was very informative," replied Jack, ignoring her jibe. "Do you want a top-up?" he asked, getting up to go to the bar.

"A glass of Chablis," she replied, as their eyes locked momentarily.

He went up to the bar.

She watched him walk and then confidently order the drinks from the barman with the handlebar moustache. She liked the way his casual approach blended with a healthy self-confidence. To add to the mix, he was also highly intelligent – and attractive.

He came back with the drinks.

"One Chablis for you."

"Why, thank you, sir."

"Didier and I had a very productive day in head office," Jack picked up from where he left off.

"That's good. We had a long day with Professor Jordan on business case preparation and financial statement analysis."

"Pretty dry, huh?"

"You betcha."

"Listen, I met your boss this afternoon. Well, I presume he's your boss. Ray Malone?"

"Ray? Is he in town? I thought he wasn't coming till next week."

"Yep, he attended our debrief this afternoon."

"He must be catching up with some of his colleagues over here," Loren suggested.

"Uh, huh," Jack nodded.

"It's been a rough time for Ray and… well, all of us," Loren said as she took a long mouthful of her drink. "After the blast, we had a really tough few weeks trying to pull together everyone who was left."

"Oh, of course, the January bomb attack!" he suddenly recalled the horrific incident. "It must have been absolutely terrible for you all."

"You wouldn't believe it. Words can't describe what it's like to… to come back to an office that's like… like… a morgue. That's what it felt like at first," she said as her throat tightened from the recollection, still very vivid.

"Would you like to talk about it?"

"Ah, it's… quite amazing. I… I'm sorry… you must think of me as some overly fragile female…" As she struggled to express herself, her eyes began to go misty.

"Please, don't be sorry. You experienced something that no one should ever have to face. And I certainly don't think of you as overly fragile. Especially after all you've been through. I would have been surprised if you hadn't gotten emotional."

He paused, the green in his eyes prominent as they fixed on hers.

"And… um… I can sort of understand what it must have been like."

"How do you mean?"

"Did you hear about the terrorist attack in Sydney in late January? I think it was a few weeks after your one."

"Ah, yes, I did hear about it. A wharf was destroyed, and a train wreck, wasn't it?"

"That's right. Well, my family was on that particular train."

"Nooo, really?! Wha… what happened?"

"I lost my wife and my two eldest children. And my sister, who was traveling with us, lost her two daughters too," Jack said, sadness enveloping him.

Loren was too stunned to reply. She could feel the self-control she had just momentarily managed to regain slipping away, and fast.

"Oh, Jack. I didn't know. Oh… that's horrific…" she said, almost in a whisper, tears welling up in her eyes. She took a long breath.

Jack bowed his head, his mouth now dry.

Time passed, but neither of them took any notice.

Loren lifted her head to see those calm green eyes looking straight into her own.

Jack started to grin one of those awkward grins, reflecting

his discomfort. Loren smiled slowly at first, then leant over and put her hand on his forearm.

Neither of them paid any attention to the winning pairing at the pool table cheering their victory. It was almost like they didn't hear it.

For those few tender moments the rest of the world didn't exist.

It dawned on them both in that silence that they were two survivors. Survivors of the worst possible experience.

And, strangely, they had been brought together.

Loren pulled back and looked away.

"Thanks," Jack murmured and then sat back in his seat, holding his Heineken. *Hold it together, Jack.*

A few more moments of silence, both lost in their own thoughts.

Loren moved to get up, disrupting the peaceful serenity.

"I'm just going to powder my nose. I must look terrible," she said.

"Oh... ah... alright, then," Jack said, a little caught out, but pleased for the few moments he'd have to collect himself.

Sarah, I miss you.

Relax, mate, it's all good, no harm done.

"It's going well, don't you think?" Darius suggested as he and Arlia stood nearby.

"Perfect," Arlia replied, following Loren as she entered the ladies' bathroom.

Loren returned a few minutes later looking a whole lot brighter with more color in her face, her hair now brushed back into place.

"Do you have a family back home, Loren?" He noticed she wore no wedding band and, after his discussion with his brother tonight, presumed she was no longer married.

She smiled a little out of awkwardness. "I'm currently single and... and unattached. My marriage ended over four years ago. I have two gorgeous children: Luke, who's seven and Taylor, five. My parents live only twenty minutes away from us, which is very handy, especially when I need babysitting."

"Yes, where would we be without the help of our parents?

My mother is living with me at the moment while I get back into a routine with work."

"So you have other children, then?"

"Yes, two daughters. Twins, in fact. Catherine and Grace."

"Twins! Oh, how wonderful. How old?"

"They're almost ten months old." Jack paused as his mind turned to his daughters.

He pulled out his phone, revealing a photo of the two girls on his screen. "They're just so beautiful. They take after their mother," he said, feeling his throat tighten.

Loren smiled, recognizing that that last comment would have been difficult for Jack.

"Mum's been a great help. I couldn't have done it without her," he said. "What about you? How have you managed since the attack?"

"I was fortunate that I really didn't have any physical injuries of any substance. I was thrown away from the blast somehow, I'm still not sure how. Marcie, my dear friend, is convinced God intervened and saved me. But I'm not so sure about that. I had some concussion and a few bruises, but that was it. Naturally, I was in shock for a while but I went back to work after two weeks. I couldn't stay away, considering how many people we lost and how much work needed to be done to get the company back on its feet."

She paused for a moment, glancing behind her as she noticed the racket coming from the pool table for the first time.

"Ray and I spent the first few weeks just attending funerals and memorial services and comforting those employees who had lost colleagues and friends. We lost count of how many services we went to — it would have been over a hundred. Ah... I'll never forget it, never. It was just shocking and so surreal. You know... there were a lot of times when I thought I would wake up and realize it was all a horribly sick nightmare, but... nope, it was real."

Jack leant forward, listening.

"I feel very blessed having a couple of wonderful girlfriends. Marcie, who I mentioned before, and Rebecca. I call them my guardian angels, as they are always there for me when I need them. They have this incredible capacity to give of themselves.

They're the most selfless people I've ever met." She smiled as she spoke of her two dearest friends.

"They are both born-again Christians who are always encouraging me to attend their church and sharing their thoughts on what God is doing in their lives and… also what they think He might be doing in mine. Hahaha!…" she stopped momentarily. "They believe God is seeking me out, and the car kidnapping on Sunday only reinforced that view in their minds. Once again, I escaped… quite miraculously, you could say."

"And what do you think about the idea of 'God seeking you out'?"

"I don't know. I believe in God and… you know… I sort of hope He is seeking me out. I guess I'm just too busy to give it the time to think it through and I'm also… quite selfish and want to do what I want to do. I'm not sure I want to be as giving as Marce and Rebecca are."

A pause.

"What do you think?" she asked.

"About what? God?"

Loren nodded.

"Well, I'm a believer in Jesus. Born again, if that's the expression you're familiar with. I'm convinced that God directly intervened in the attack, saving my life, Jane's life and the three littlies… Why didn't He save Sarah, Beth, Jonah, Rachel and Claire's lives? I dunno. I don't think we're meant to know all the answers. Some, we'll just have to wait until we meet Him in heaven. But I do know they are in a much better place and one day I'm going to join them." He paused, reflecting. "Do I hope that will be soon? Probably not. I've got Catherine and Gracey to look after."

"But aren't you angry at God that your wife and children died?"

"Sure, I was furious at Him at first and it took me some time to come to terms with it. But I also believe that there is real evil in this world. And it all stems from one source – Satan. He and his armies are always waging war on us. He wants us dead and wants us to not know Jesus. It's a vicious war. God's angels versus Satan's demons.

"Throughout history there have always been battles between good and evil and, you know, we invent our own stories about it – superheroes, X-men, you name it – we are all fascinated by it. And I believe the fascination stems from the conflict within our innate makeup: God made us, but Satan infiltrated, broke us and now wants to keep us away from Jesus and the truth."

He paused.

"Sorry, this is probably getting a bit heavy."

"No, no, go on. It's very similar to what Marcie keeps telling me. She'd love to meet you."

"As a result of that internal conflict, we always have a choice: to choose God's ways or our own ways. God became man through Jesus so that we could make that choice, and as He defeated Satan, in choosing Jesus we've defeated Satan too. So I choose Jesus. That doesn't mean I don't struggle. Every day I have to make a conscious decision to follow Jesus. Sometimes, and probably too often, I fail, but other days it works out."

He stopped.

"So does that answer your question?" he asked.

"Yep, it sure does. Thanks for being so honest."

Loren looked at her watch. It was now close to 11:30.

"I think it's about my bed time."

Jack looked at his watch too. "Yeah, I think it's about that time for me too." He felt a little deflated. *Did I say too much? A bit too preachy? God, did I do OK?*

"Would you walk me back to my room, Jack?"

"It would be my pleasure."

They grabbed their jackets and headed past the bar, Jack giving the barman a wave.

It was bitterly cold outside. A chilly wind had come up and was biting at any exposed skin.

They walked briskly, steam coming out of their mouths.

"Loren, what's your ex-husband do?"

"He's an investment banker."

"Out of LA?"

"Um, he works out of LA most of the time, I think, but also out of New York. He set up a boutique firm with two partners who were based out of there about two years ago."

"What's his name? My brother Stephen is an investment banker, working out of New York."

"Oh, right. Tom Mayer's his name."

"As in Maple, Mayer and Masters?"

"Yeah, that's the one. The 3Ms, they're called."

"You wouldn't believe it, Loren... but... that's who my brother works for."

"Really?"

They were now standing outside her door.

"Wow, that's amazing," she said. "What a night for incredible coincidences!"

They stood facing each other, both uncertain as to how to end the night.

"Goodnight, Loren."

"Night night, Jack. After tonight I might just have to think a bit more about God."

"You do that, Loren." Jack grinned. "Sleep well and I'll see you in class bright and early."

Jack turned and was out the front door of her block before she'd even managed to find her room key.

Chapter 16

Fontainebleau, Friday

Arlia was leading her delegation of angelguards as they hovered above the fast-moving Mercedes. She had deployed her standard formation: four groups of equal size at the front, back and both sides. She alone rode atop the car, having complete faith in her squadron.

She anticipated the enemy would now be well aware of their movements and were likely to be in the vicinity, monitoring their progress.

The turnoff to the airport was now within sight. All was going just as they wanted.

A group of demons were observing every movement of Arlia's troop at the perfect vantage-point of 10,000 feet above the angelguard squadron.

"Reconnaissance, bah!" said the leader of the motley crew to another flying alongside.

"Bacchazar expressly forbade any attack, if you recall," the other responded.

"Yeah, but how pleased would he be if we did away with this Amazonian goddess, Arlia – can you imagine? And Agramon would all of a sudden become my new best friend. I'd enjoy a stint in the Americas for a change. Sure beats the cold of Scandinavia, which is all I've known for the past 2,000 years."

"You'd be a fool! Besides the fact that they outnumber us two to one, if you managed to survive, Bacchazar would have your head."

"Have more confidence, Chonnggi! We could become overnight heroes."

"You'll be on your own, Tetak. No one here will back you."

"Come off it, wouldn't you love to get your teeth into that white knight hide?" Tetak was almost frothing at the month with excitement, like a ravenous dog.

"She'd take your head off before you got your mouth anywhere near her. Haven't you seen the length of her sword?"

"Chicken!"

"If you don't believe me, you're a fool." With that Chonnggi fell back into the group. He'd had enough.

* * *

The Mercedes arrived at the airport and the back-seat passenger disembarked, surrounded by a six-pack of white knights, completely disguising her identity to supernatural eyes.

Eighty others were all on alert, watching very closely for any sign of the enemy.

They headed straight for the departure gate.

"Great, the board says 'Go to gate'," Arlia announced as she led the pack with their human cargo. "Perfect timing."

Landen, from his position above the Air France Airbus jet, watched the group of sentinels as they completed a circuit of the airport. He counted forty. He was surprised at how obvious they were. He was also amazed how haggard and disheveled a bunch they looked. Even from afar he could see they struggled to hold any kind of formation.

He could clearly see some sort of disagreement between the leading demons. *What a bunch of misfits.*

"Any sign of action, Landen?" Arlia asked as she joined him atop the plane.

"Just a bunch of inexperienced goons not appearing to know what to do," Landen replied as the demon flock flew on by. "Looks like they're breaking up, figuring the job is complete. I don't think we'll be seeing any action now."

"Well, we're all aboard, doors are shut, and we're ready for takeoff," Arlia announced. "We've got five on the plane, and no sign of any danger inside."

The two rode the plane as it took off, headed for Madrid, Spain, content in the knowledge they had completed their task. They now had to hope the enemy in fact believed Loren was on the flight, and not Elsie van Buyten, one of Insead's finest academics, who had chosen to spend the weekend in Spain's capital.

* * *

"So the Summers woman has elected to leave the program, has she?" Bacchazar queried. He was holed up in their usual bunker within the Chateau.

"Indeed, yes," Agramon replied. "Your sources are correct – they're better than your fighters," he sniggered.

"Well, there's no longer any need for you and your bunch of hacks to hang around, is there?"

Agramon smirked. He wasn't going to take the bait. "I thought you enjoyed my company."

The two demon warlords locked eyes. They only stood in each other's presence for as long as they needed to.

"She's unlikely to cause us any harm from Spain," Agramon suggested, "but I am still curious as to what she's up to, and more importantly, what Athaniel is plotting. The signs were clearly evident that she had been chosen to play a role in the white knights' game plan."

"They do like to use decoys, you should know that."

"Huh… Madrid, what's in Madrid?" Agramon was thoughtful, rubbing his imposing bearded chin.

"Perhaps it's time you went and found out!"

"What?" Agramon's mind had already left and wasn't interested in sparring with his rival. "See you later, Bacchazar."

The demon lord nodded. "And you."

Agramon disappeared through the paneled external wall, leaving Bacchazar grinning ear to ear.

* * *

Twelve minutes later Tagan and Athaniel watched from their forest vantage-point as a large cloud of simmering evil rose into the air above Fontainebleau.

"They've split up," said Athaniel.

"My hunch is the bigger group, led by Agramon, is returning to the US, whilst the smaller group of twenty is on its way to Madrid. They'll struggle to even find our decoy. She will have already landed and, knowing Arlia and Landen, they will have hidden Professor van Buyten so well, the demons will have no trail to follow."

"Our plan is working."

"Yes, it's going well so far," replied Tagan. "But we now need Bacchazar's company to also leave, or else our ruse will be discovered too soon."

"I think that black mass surrounding the Chateau is our answer, Tagan."

"Yes, right on time, Athaniel. Malone's plane should be taking off just about now from Orly Airport for the flight to Marseilles."

Brussels

Marie Verheyen parked her silver 5-series BMW in the hotel car park.

She was early for her appointment, knowing that Grosch, who was flying back from Paris, was still an hour or so away.

Marie was tall and slender, maintaining her shapely body through three intense personal trainer-led sessions each week and a daily early morning walk with her golden retriever. She was self-assured, extremely intelligent – she had topped her MBA class at the London Business School – and was driven to succeed. Grosch and Marie were ideally suited in that respect.

Their four-year affair had been advantageous for them both. The passion was good but the pillow talk was of far greater interest to the power-hungry couple. Grosch, in initiating the liaison, had particularly benefited. Ms. Verheyen was one of the four deputy prime ministers and Minister for the Budget, Social Integration and Social Economy. She was married to another member of parliament, with four teenage children, but had been seduced by Grosch's power and influence.

As she rode the private lift to the penthouse on the hotel's top floor, she thought how increasingly distant he had become in recent weeks. They were spending less time together and when they did meet it was mostly just physical. Their relationship never used to be just about that. For her, at least, there had been something more. She admired him greatly, and early in the relationship she could have even fallen in love with him, but now it was too business-like. Their relationship had become transactional, as each provided the other mostly with information.

She was still stirred by his power and would gladly sacrifice much, including her marriage, to get access to it, but she wanted some more emotion in their relationship and less transaction. She knew she could never tame him, and doubted he would ever love her, but she wanted more than what she was now getting.

She entered the suite that was permanently leased to Grosch. She knew he'd be especially happy with her tonight. She had secured the funds the Grosch Group had sought from the government to build a new gas pipeline that would run from Charleroi in the south through Brussels and then on to Antwerp in the north. She had phoned with the news earlier. The official announcement of the project would be made early next week.

While she waited for him to arrive she busied herself with reviewing a number of proposals that her assistant had given her as she left her office. Judging by the size of the pile, she would be spending most of the weekend reviewing them.

Room service soon arrived with a bottle of Krug Clos du Menil as well as some caviar, cheese and baguettes. Being the mistress to one of Europe's wealthiest men certainly had its privileges. Grosch insisted on the finest of everything: from the Renaissance furniture in this suite, to his Abraham-Louise Bregeut eighteen-carat gold watch, to the best French champagne and Beluga caviar. Nothing but the best. She always ensured she wore nothing but designer clothing when she was meeting him. The Lagerfeld black woolen suit accompanied by a silk Versace blouse that he had bought her was today's selection.

The porter had also brought a parcel addressed to Grosch. She didn't give it a second thought as she left it on his dressing table.

* * *

Grosch hadn't been in the mood for idle conversation. He entered the suite looking agitated and flustered, quickly announcing he didn't want to talk until they had had sex.

Tonight he was rougher than usual, and less caring. Fifteen minutes later it was all over, leaving her unsatisfied and feeling used.

He returned from having his shower a lot more relaxed and attentive. He leant down gently, kissing her tenderly on the lips. It was the first time he had kissed her on the mouth since arriving.

"What's that on the dresser?" he asked, looking past her, noticing the parcel for the first time.

"The porter dropped it off for you."

He picked it up. His back was facing her, which masked the boyish grin that formed on his face as he studied the parcel's markings.

"Could you give me a few minutes, Marie, to read its contents?" His tone was such, she knew she had to obey.

"Ah... all right, then," Marie said, put out. She slid out of bed, still wearing only her black stockings, and headed for the walk-in wardrobe, grabbing a robe hanging just inside the opening.

"Thank you, my dear," he said, watching Marie walk out of the bedroom. "Please shut the doors behind you."

It was almost 8:30 when he surfaced from the bedroom, two hours since he had made her leave it. She was silently fuming. She had helped relieve him of his tension and then had been left to her own devices while he studied some letter. He had the rest of the weekend to study it, she thought, feeling miserable.

"I'm so sorry, my dear," he said as he opened the bedroom doors. "It was rude of me to leave you alone for such a time. But it was quite imperative that I study the contents of that parcel immediately. Those were the final plans for the new gas pipeline and Patrik, my head of the operation, wants a response from me first thing tomorrow morning."

"Do you never stop working, Leopold?"

"You know what these big projects are like, always running behind schedule."

He walked up behind her, kissing the back of her neck, giving her goosebumps. His warm lips moved from caressing the back of her neck, to the side, and then to the front until locking on her lips, intoxicating her. They kissed passionately as he slid the robe off her shoulders.

She knew what he was doing but she wouldn't let him, she was still too angry.

She drew away from him, pulling the robe up around her shoulders as she stood up. "Some champagne, my darling?" She drew the chilled bottle out of the elegant silver wine cooler.

"Um... yes... that would be lovely," he replied, put off by her response.

"And what would you like for dinner, Leopold?"

"Are you not having to be home for your children?"

"I thought I was staying the night. You forgot, didn't you?"

"Ah, yes. I did. But, I would like you to stay the night. Who is looking after the children?"

"Niels is taking them all camping for the weekend, remember?"

"No, I don't," Grosch smiled, recovering quickly. "That doesn't matter. You are here now and don't have to leave. I'll have Johann organize something nice for us."

He headed for the phone and was soon talking to his personal butler.

"Thirty minutes. A feast fit for a king and queen!"

Those plans for the new pipeline must be particularly good, she thought. She couldn't recall ever seeing such a change in his mood before. Her frustration and anger were completely forgotten when Johann and his two assistants served the appetizer – wild Burgundy escargots, one of her favorite dishes.

Los Angeles

"The decision has been made. Mayer has served his purpose. He can be disposed of now." The deep, booming voice of Agramon echoed around the cavernous sound studio.

"You'll get no arguments from me," Grazag replied.

"Grosch assigned one of his killers to the case. You know, one of those private-army mercenary types. He knows a few of them,"

Agramon advised. "So the job will be done well, and done soon. I need you to make sure nothing gets in the way of the mission."

"Certainly, sir! No problem. Any angelic interference will be dealt with by my trusty blade here," Grazag said as he caressed the long black blade that hung by his side.

"Now get out of here and make sure it's successful. The underworld will enjoy receiving this particular soul!"

Grazag didn't need to be told twice. He shot up out of the studio into the dawn.

The early risers of LA were just starting to stir on what was going to be a very warm spring day.

Brussels, the next day

The demonic odd couple watched as Grosch made his way down the elegant, carpeted staircase of the brightly lit, opulent hotel foyer.

"He looks a very happy, contented man this morning, sire," Volkyre offered in his croaky monotone.

"He should be, my old friend. In his briefcase, he carries the duly signed letter of intent confirming the multimillion-dollar deal will go through. All that is left now is for the lawyers to sort through the final contractual matters." At in excess of 300 million US dollars, this was far and away the biggest deal in Grosch's company's history. "It pushes our man into the real big league in the business world. Goes to show – expanding the business into defense and security was a great plan."

"You did a good job influencing the Americans to favor his proposal against one of their own."

Bacchazar nodded, flattered. "I must admit, Volkyre, for a long time I was convinced they would buy local, but seeding the committee with that bribery scandal worked a treat."

"He likes the greenbacks, doesn't he?"

"Grosch is so power hungry, he'd take anyone's money, but the fact that he despises the Yanks makes it even more rewarding."

"Some would suggest, ironical."

"Too true," Bacchazar slapped his smaller sidekick on the shoulder. "What a twenty-four hours our man has had: first, the commitment from the Belgian government to assist in the building of the new gas pipeline, and now landing this huge electronics deal."

"And both deals will help him continue our campaign," Volkyre added. "How pleasing that such acts of terror were financed by either corporate or government monies."

"Now that's irony, my friend. Thanks to Marie Verheyen, the gas pipeline project is flush with funds. Just as he planned it. Now he won't be personally out of pocket to fund the final assignment. In addition, his prospective acquirer will be doubly pleased. Won't be long now before that deal gets consummated too."

"Yee-ha!" Volkyre screeched, as they watched Grosch hop into his already running vehicle, accelerating out of the driveway, into the now busy main street of downtown Brussels.

The two demons took to the air, following him. Like their client, they carried the smirk of arrogant contentment.

* * *

She woke feeling particularly rested. She turned over to find the bed empty. She was surprised, even disappointed. *It doesn't matter,* she thought as she rolled back, pulling the bedclothes over her shoulders. Her body caressed the fine cotton sheets as that wonderful feeling of security and warmth one gets from an especially comfortable bed oozed through her veins.

She looked at the digital clock on her bedside table and was taken aback: 8:57. *Wow, almost nine!* It was time to get up and get moving.

On returning from the shower, she headed out into the living area to find Leopold. The dining table had been set up for breakfast, copies of the *De Standaard* newspaper sitting at either end.

Leopold was nowhere to be seen.

She phoned Grosch's butler.

"Johann, did you see Mr. Grosch earlier, by any chance?" She listened to his response. He spoke like he had expected her call. "So he mentioned he'd be back by 11. All right then, thank you… yes, breakfast would be lovely, thank you, Johann."

She remembered his comment last night about discussing the plans of the new gas pipeline with his operations manager, but didn't think that meant he would go out, rather than doing it over the phone.

Life was always full of surprises with Leopold, she thought. It's all part of the excitement of having an affair with such a powerful man. He had his hand in so many different pies; she wondered how he kept on top of it all.

Breakfast arrived, which she picked at before getting dressed. She headed for his dressing table to write him a note and noticed the parcel from last night. *Hmmm, strange that he didn't take this to his meeting.*

"Beijing?" she said aloud on noticing the postal markings.

As she turned the parcel over, its contents accidentally slipped out, falling to the floor. She picked them up, turning them over. A memo document was on top:

MEMO
TO: King
FROM: Vincent
DATE: 10 May
RE: Project Trojan Horse

Please find enclosed the final detailed term sheet for your review and approval.

I believe you'll be very pleased with the progress we've made in negotiations with the Chinese and in particular the revised pricing and termination clauses.

All is now in readiness to move to contract and we await your final approval to proceed.

Rgds
Vincent

She merely glanced at the enclosures.

Negotiations? Chinese? Are they buying into Grosch? But he said last night it was to do with the pipeline.

Trojan Horse? To invade? Who or what?

She carefully put the papers together and slid them back into the envelope as the anger and frustration started to well up inside her. She couldn't understand why he would lie about it to her. He had gone to great lengths over dinner last night to explain the intricacies of the state-of-the-art gas pipeline. She began to wonder how many other lies he had told her.

The more she contemplated how many lies he might have told, the more she could feel anger and resentment well up inside her again. She wanted to scream.

Get out of this place! Get out of this relationship!

She quickly packed her belongings. Before she left, she carefully photographed the documents in the envelope.

Chapter 17

Fontainebleau, Sunday

After enjoying a well-earned sleep in, Loren had spent the morning pottering around the eclectic collection of boutiques and small shops that Fontainebleau was renowned for. She had passed the very impressive Chateau but didn't have any great desire to explore it. She only had a few hours before heading back for a group session at four o'clock.

Grindor and two other white knights escorted Loren everywhere. Arlia's other duties had held her back when Loren went out in public, much to the angel's frustration. She had every confidence in her comrades but had such a deep love for Loren that she would never forgive herself if something did happen.

Loren had stumbled upon the Sunday markets where locals who fancied themselves as amateur artists or craftsmen displayed their wares, hoping to sell them and perhaps be "discovered". Loren loved such places. She was always taking the kids and even her girlfriends, if they'd oblige her, to the beachside markets back home which set up every second Sunday.

She turned the corner blindly and walked straight into Jack!

He saw her first and avoided a collision.

"Found anything of interest?"

"Oh! Hello, Jack. Professor Haines, I mean," she replied, caught off guard.

"I thought we'd lost the Professor prefix."

"Sorry, Jack... There's some great stuff here. Much better than the local markets back home. I could spend hours here without any trouble."

"Got time for a coffee?"

"Hmmm… you give me a half day off and now you want to have coffee? Sure, I'd like that. My stomach's rumbling, so I could do with some lunch."

"I've already eaten but I'd be happy to watch you eat!"

Jack, knowing the village well, led them away from the markets and down a cobbled alley that had a number of small, quaint cafés to choose from.

"Ah, this one looks alright," he said, glancing at the blackboard menu, all in French.

A matronly looking woman led them to a small table.

"Lucky I have you, or else I wouldn't have any idea what to order."

Jack talked her through the menu. They gave their selections to the waitress.

"Funny we bumped into each other," he said.

"You sure you're not stalking me, by any chance?"

He just laughed.

"How have you occupied yourself on your day off?" she asked.

"Hired a bike and went for a ride in the forest. I used to go riding there a lot when I was studying here."

She encouraged him with her eyes to continue.

"There are hundreds of tracks to explore, most of which can lead you nowhere or worse, down a creek without a paddle, but I find it so enchanting. There are these huge oak trees, some that stand a hundred feet high with massive trunks… it's quite spectacular."

The matronly woman served them.

"I was thinking whilst riding how strange a coincidence it is we met here, especially in light of our common experience of surviving terrorist attacks," he said.

She was too busy with a mouthful of salad to respond, so just urged him on with a nod of her head.

"When I was in London on my way over here I visited my old church and happened to meet a couple there. Thierry, the husband, miraculously survived the London football stadium attack. It was a week or so before the LA one."

"Yep, I remember it," she replied. "Wow, that's quite amazing!"

"I'm going to catch up with them both on my way home before flying back to Australia."

"What do you make of it?" she asked, still enjoying her salad.

He looked directly at her. "What, the fact that in two weeks I've met, out of the blue, two people, like myself, who have probably experienced the Hand of God in saving their lives when others they love perished?"

"Well, I might not have described it as eloquently as that, but… yes," she chuckled.

"To be honest, I've got no idea what it means!"

Loren said nothing, but raised an eyebrow, inviting him to continue.

"Yeah, it sure is strange, but I get some sense that God has drawn you and Thierry to me for some purpose."

"What sort of purpose?"

"I don't know. It may be as simple as me being a link in the chain that helps you come to know God personally, perhaps, or… " he paused.

"Or what?"

"That I'm not sure about. If I knew I'd gladly tell you. God can work in pretty mysterious ways sometimes. That's why faith is so important," he finished, simply.

"Hmmm… well, do let me know when you get any firmer ideas. I'd be most interested in knowing," she said as her eyes sparkled through the gloomy setting of the café.

"Count on it."

New York

He was in luck.

As he suspected, Mayer's attention to security and filing wasn't as good as it should have been. Judging by the number of unsecured files sitting on their shared drive, it appeared his two partners weren't any better. He had always felt there would come a time when knowing the office network security administrator would come in handy.

There wasn't much but it was enough. Jack would find it all very interesting. So would the SEC, he thought, as he copied the final documents to his hard drive.

He felt very uncomfortable playing the snoop, but he had always thought Mayer wasn't as straight as he came across. He noticed some correspondence regarding a couple of other recent deals, the contents of which also made for interesting reading.

The copying was complete. He drafted a brief email from a personal account attaching the zip file of documents. On receiving the "message sent" confirmation, he deleted the email.

"Well done, Stephen," Athaniel said in the supernatural as he watched from the back of the office. "Now the pieces are starting to come together."

Stephen opened another document he had drafted a couple of months ago. He made a couple of minor modifications. He printed it and signed it.

He knew he was making the right decision. This firm would get caught once the SEC had finished with the big guns. It was just a matter of time and he didn't want to be around to see it.

He turned the light out, taking his business card holder with him as he walked out. They might not let him go back to his desk after he broke the news to them tomorrow. He knew he'd find another job soon enough. Perhaps he'd head back home and help Jack out for a while.

The burly, black security man nodded as Stephen headed for the glass doors that would take him out into the glorious sunshine of a New York Sunday afternoon.

* * *

The navy Jaguar XK8 convertible raced along the narrow road heading up the lower hills of the Alpes-Maritimes.

There were no streetlights. The expensive cruiser's headlights and a three-quarter moon that hovered over the serene bay at Antibes provided the only illumination.

A cool sea breeze cascaded its way up the mountains after a sultry late spring day.

The roof was down. Ray and Candice Malone were

headed back to the exclusive hideaway of Tourrettes-sur-Loup, a charming medieval village located a thirty-minute drive from the Mediterranean coastline.

Having set off early that morning, they'd had a full day in the old town of Antibes exploring the Provençal markets and the various world-renowned museums, including the Picasso. Having tired legs, wearied minds and full stomachs, they were both ready to flop into bed.

"How much longer, darling?" Candice asked, turning down the symphony blaring out of the stereo.

"Five, ten minutes at the most," Ray replied.

He handled the car in the limited visibility with aplomb, caressing the rugged mountainside with treacherous blind corners, as though he drove it every night.

"I'm looking forward to a glass of that seventy-five-year-old Hennessy we opened last night," Candice said.

"Yes, that, with one of my Machado cigars, will be the perfect nightcap."

SMASH!

As he took a tight bend, a yellow bulldozer came out of nowhere, its large lights momentarily blinding him and Candice. The force of the impact knocked them sideways.

Both airbags shot out of their restraints, slamming into their heads. Now they couldn't see what was in front of them.

Fear and panic struck and overwhelmed them, as the huge mechanical beast didn't stop.

Candice looked to her right and started screaming.

"*Ray*, it's pushing us closer to the edge of the road. Make it stop, Ray, make them *stop!*" she shouted hysterically.

Ray was powerless to stop the hulking machine. He struggled frantically with the wheel but the steering had been switched off when the airbag was activated.

"Hang on, Candice, hang on!" he said, grappling with his airbag.

With one last powerful lunge, the dozer's driver lifted the arm on the shovel blade. It took the convertible saloon right to the edge of the road's shoulder, beyond which was a sheer drop into a chasm of darkness.

It was too late. There was nothing Ray could do. It was inevitable.

Candice fainted in shock as the horror overwhelmed her.

Ray resigned himself to their doom.

Time stood still for the few seconds it took for the Pirelli tires to lose their grip on the road and break through the flimsy wire fencing. He saw flashes of his childhood, his parents, winning the inter-collegiate football championship, their wedding day, meeting George Bush Senior.

He looked up at the machine that was about to end his life, managing to get his head above the airbag to see… him… the man, or thing, responsible for sending him to his death.

The car toppled over the edge just as Ray saw the evil smile and the deadpan eyes. That look of pure, unadulterated evil would be the last thing he would remember, ever. He would take it with him to the other side.

Their seatbelts held them tightly in their seats even though gravity was trying to pull them out. The breeze grabbed Candice's scarf from her head.

The car sailed straight down, smacking into the rocky hillside. It tumbled into a roll until finally its progress was stopped by one of the many concrete ramparts that were a feature of the Côte d'Azur.

The fuel tank exploded, destroying the car. A ball of fire rose twenty feet, momentarily lighting up the countryside.

A while later the police arrived. They found the bulldozer, but no sign of the driver.

On inspection of the blackened shell of a car, the police were stumped by what they saw.

Or, more precisely, what they didn't see.

There were no bodies. No sign of any human fragment, bone or tissue.

All they found was a black handbag.

The police were dumbfounded.

* * *

The assassin stood atop the rocky spur, overlooking the night-lights that flickered along the enchanting coastline. A sadistic grin could be seen through the open visor of his dark, intimidating helmet.

A group of seven black forms stood facing their evil master.

"Good work, demons," he bellowed. "Now away with you all. Go find some more souls to taunt!"

As the group of seven took flight, Drakkin stared out into the night, watching his ugly gang climb high, silhouetted against the moon's radiance.

With one leap he too became airborne, but headed due north. He was looking forward to gloating over his success.

* * *

It was after midnight.

A small middle-aged woman dressed in a traditional nun's habit was gently bathing the head of someone lying, eyes closed, in a single bed. The only light was that which the stars and moon provided through the window. Its tranquility conflicted with the disturbed state of the patient.

"Will she be all right, sister?" A man's voice asked from the shadows. He was American.

"Oui, monsieur," responded the nun in a sweet, calm voice. "Ah…. how do you say it?… shock?… *oui*, shock."

"The pill should help her sleep," she said. "You rest too… over there… " She pointed to another single bed in the far corner of the room.

"Sister, I'm not sure I can sleep," said the man. "The whole incident was so sudden… I was sure we were dead… and about to meet our maker!"

A second nun entered the room carrying a tray with two steaming bowls and a baguette, sliced.

"Some chicken broth and bread for our guests," she announced in perfect English but with a hint of a Canadian accent.

"Thank you so very much, Sister Christine, we are indebted to you and Marianne here," said the man as he walked out of the shadows. His dark hair was unkempt, and the left shoulder of his white silk shirt was badly torn.

"How is your wife doing, Mr. Malone?" Sister Christine asked.

"I think she's going to be alright," Malone said. "She's drifting off to sleep now. That sleeping tablet looks like it has finally kicked in."

"Oh, I am pleased. We should probably have the local doctor check her out in the morning. Just to make sure there's nothing serious."

Marianne rose from the bed and modestly dropped her head as she passed Malone.

"Thank you, Sister Marianne," Malone said as she passed him.

Marianne turned and nodded demurely.

"Marianne is just next door if you get worried during the night," Sister Christine said. "She's a fully trained nurse as well as a nun."

She made for the door. "Goodnight, Mr. Malone. Rest well. You will be safe here. God is our protector!"

"One last question, sister, before you go."

"Yes?" She turned to face Malone.

"Do you have any idea how we got here? All I can recall is waking, seeing your face when I came to, lying on your front doorstep. We should both be dead now. But somehow we survived. Somehow we were delivered here. To a hospice run by the Sisters of St. Etienne, ten miles from where our car went off the road."

"There can be only one explanation Mr. Malone," she offered.

"And that is?"

"God's angels delivered you here," she answered reverently.

"Oh, really? Delivered by angels?" he said, laughing. "You are very sweet, Sister Christine, but perhaps you have been in the church for too long now."

"Oh, Mr. Malone. You limit our God. He can do all things," she said smiling, her eyes sparkling in the moonlight. "You should be thankful that He has chosen to spare you and your wife's lives.

Forever thankful."

Ray suppressed a chuckle. It seemed somehow inappropriate.

"Good night, sir," Sister Christine said, turning to leave.

She closed the door behind her.

Malone sat at the small table. He sampled the soup after blowing on it gently.

It was very good, he thought. He sat down and polished off both bowls quickly. It revitalized him and calmed his still fragile nerves.

He looked over to his now soundly sleeping wife. The night was so still that he could hear the soft whistling noise emanating from her mouth as she slept.

He wandered over to the other bed, shaking his head as he recalled the sister's words. The quiet resonance of his wife's breathing soon sent him into the most peaceful sleep he'd had for a long, long time.

* * *

"Gee, it feels good!" Athaniel announced triumphantly as he danced around the room, punching the air with his huge fists.

"Yes, my friend. It does."

"Come on, Tagan, get excited! It's exhilarating! Beating the enemy like that, and them not realizing they've been beaten! Yowwweee…"

Tagan and Athaniel had timed it to perfection. They swooped just before the convertible hit the side of the mountain and snatched the Malones out of the toppling wreck. They knew that at that exact moment the free-falling luxury saloon was hidden by the cliff's overhang and out of sight of the vultures prematurely celebrating above. Once again, their planning had been perfect to the very second.

"Let's not get cocky, Athaniel. They will know soon enough," Tagan said with a tone of caution.

Chapter 18

Fontainebleau, Monday

"Hello, you must be Marie Verheyen. I'm Jack Haines, one of the leaders of the program."

Jack was standing in the foyer of the central administration building on campus.

He extended his right hand, which Ms. Verheyen took firmly, returning his warm smile.

"Yes, hello, Jack. Good to meet you. I was expecting Professor Luscombe."

"Alain's currently taking the group and asked me to meet you. Your session isn't scheduled to commence till after eleven, so we still have a little bit of time. How was your flight?"

"Fine. No problems. Getting out of Paris took longer than expected but once we were on the motorway it was all smooth sailing." Ms. Verheyen's English was musical and idiomatic.

They walked outside into the dull morning, overcast cloud as far as the eye could see. Her two bodyguards accompanied them.

She looked immaculate in a black business suit and cream blouse. She carried a black leather briefcase in her right hand while nursing a Burberry overcoat on her left forearm. She looked closer to forty when in fact she was almost fifty.

"I read in this morning's paper your government's plans to modernize the gas pipeline from Antwerp to Charleroi," Jack offered idly as they marched across the main courtyard.

"Ah, yes. The system is in real need of modernization after too many years of inefficiency and waste."

"So do you consider privatization to have been a success?"

"Yes… we do," she replied a little distractedly.

"So successful that the government is putting up h. money for the project!" Jack said a little flippantly.

"Jack… this upgrade or overhaul was always anticipated when we completed the privatization back in the early nineties. But it's…" She paused.

"It's overdue, huh?" Jack said, raising his eyebrows.

"No, not at all. The timing of the upgrade was always in Grosch's hands. It has always been their responsibility to determine the right time to commence and complete the upgrade within the first ten years of taking it over."

"While Belgians struggle with an inefficient and ineffective gas supply?"

"Always one of the issues of privatizing public utilities. What can I say?"

"Indeed it is. The profit-mongering of private enterprise versus what's right for the people. Interesting that that was the thrust of the article in this morning's *Le Monde*!"

"I haven't seen that one. I've only read the Belgian press on the flight over. You wouldn't have it handy, by any chance?"

"I left it in my room but we will be passing some of the professor's rooms, so no doubt they'll have a copy handy." Jack paused. "It was a nice picture of you and Leopold Grosch, in fact," he said jovially.

"Oh, I can just imagine."

"How well do you know Grosch?"

"Oh, you know… not that well…" She paused again. "He's obviously a very important man and very well connected, so I run into him fairly frequently."

"Yeah, for someone so powerful and wealthy, by all accounts, there is very little written about him. He does a very good job keeping his affairs private and out of the press. Judging by this morning's article, he appears to be well connected within your government."

"Mr. Haines, it's common practice for the wealthy and powerful to be well connected in government circles. Surely it's also common in Australia."

"Oh, of course, yes. And please call me Jack." Her statement could be interpreted a few different ways, he thought, some not befitting a senior government minister.

They walked a little further without saying anything.

"What's his background, like where was he born? Is he Belgian by birth?" Jack suddenly asked.

"Who... Grosch?" she said, as Jack nodded his confirmation.

"I don't know it all. His father, Guy, was a member of parliament for a number of years, so he's Belgian as far as I know."

"Hmmm... there's always been some suspicion that he's been involved in a number of shady deals."

"Jack, you do ask a lot of questions," she said, wishing they'd change topics.

"I'm sorry. Being a disciple of big business, I'm always keen to understand what makes the leaders of big corporations tick. I'm interested in knowing more about him and his conglomeration of businesses. The Grosch Group is very like GE, with its many disparate companies. Obviously GE is significantly larger but also, interestingly, has a far more public face to it. Perhaps that's because it's a public company while Grosch is still predominantly privately owned."

"Yes, well, Jack, I guess you might just have to ask the man himself one day."

Oh well, Jack thought, he'd bite his tongue for now.

They entered the small lecture room, which was empty. The group had broken for morning tea.

* * *

Jack was back in his room, catching up on his emails, having left Ms. Verheyen in Professor Luscombe's care.

It didn't take him long to see Stephen's email. He noticed it had an attachment enclosed. It read:

Jack, you may be right about Mayer. A couple of
the documents enclosed indicate that he was up to
something with Ray Malone. Looks like it may have

involved some transfer of funds from Swains to us, or at least to Tom, on a regular basis. Could simply be monies Mayer is investing for Swains. But I couldn't see any obvious investment strategy nor are Swains listed as a major client, which is standard practice when we start acting for a company. Made me wonder what Mayer was doing with the money?

Then I stumbled across a sub-folder called "Bryggja" that contained some memos and emails addressed to a "King". They also mentioned monies being transferred to a series of offshore accounts based in Switzerland.

It looks suspiciously like the money he got from Malone went into those Swiss accounts for "Bryggja", no doubt a code name or something or other.

Jack, it's all very suspicious and frankly the SEC would love to see these documents. It would get Mayer and probably the firm into a lot of trouble. So much so that I've decided to quit. I might even come home and spend some time with you and Jane, what do you reckon?

I've been thinking the Lord is leading me home. I've come to realize there's more to life than doing deals!

So, brother, I hope this helps.

Talk soon.

Stephen.

Encl. Winzip file: Stephen

Jack downloaded the zip file. It contained four documents: two relating to Malone, the other two to Project "Bryggja".

He read all four quickly and then re-read them.

The two Malone documents stated what Stephen referred to: the transfer, on a regular basis, of a certain sum of money to an account Mayer had specified. It made reference to a "new future when the American companies would run their own race untangled from the behemoth that threatened to bring it all crashing down!" So that supported the organization chart that Jack found the other day with the three companies' initials on it.

Perhaps GA is in fact Graves Advertising? Why transfer the money, though? Reduce the asset value of the business to make it look cheaper, perhaps? Assist the acquirer with funds? Now, that's really strange. Or could it be simply a pre-paid commission to Mayer and his buddies in doing the deal?

Then he set his mind to the "Bryggja" documents – a memo and an email. This email contained a sequence of emails and responses from a party titled "King". It was pretty clear to Jack that: (1) Mayer received the monies from Swains; (2) money was transferred to Swiss accounts; (3) the money was used for some major "investment"; (4) Mayer expected a hefty commission check from "King" for obtaining the monies.

He knew he should just let it go but it intrigued him, especially since he knew some of the players. He went back to the string of "King" emails. The final sentence from this "King" person really fascinated him: "We now only require the final contribution from MV to complete the pot of gold that will give us sufficient ammunition to shake up the world!"

A whole myriad of thoughts raced through Jack's mind. Two bits of the email bothered him: "MV" – who were they? Was it one person? And "ammunition to shake up the world" seemed overly dramatic for a corporate takeover. Could it have something to do with a war?

He let it lie in his mind as he tackled some of the other emails, including one from his mum, before calling Stephen.

Outskirts of Brussels

Grosch's sparkling SLR McLaren looked incongruous parked in front of the dilapidated farmhouse about fifty miles south of the Belgian capital. A fine layer of dust from a mile of dirt road coated the luxury car.

The farmhouse was concealed from the country lane by a seven-foot-high unkempt bush. The front windows were boarded up and its wooden balcony was missing many planks.

He knew the place well. He should do. He had spent his youth here. He bought it from his parents thirty years ago when they had decided to make the capital their home. From that day he had let it run down.

He still loved being out in the open air, away from the hustle of city living. Even though he thrived in the city, he would one day return to the country and see out his days. He hoped that day was not too far away.

Three other men, all dressed impeccably in dark suits, greeted Grosch as he entered through the front door. The interior of the house was still fully furnished. Three lounges were protected by dust-encrusted sheets.

Stale hot air filled the room. Grosch immediately discarded his jacket. Volkyre snarled at the three demon interlopers attendant on each of the men, putting them in their place as he hobbled to a position behind his human victim.

All four men hugged each other enthusiastically. It had been over six months since they last met. They always gathered here before a job.

The three others were an odd mix of nationalities: a Russian, a Saudi and an American. All had been schooled in Switzerland, where their friendship began over forty years ago. From those early days, the foursome learnt the power of money, fuelling insatiable greed that had driven their future education and employment decisions.

Four powerful and wealthy men. All were men of influence. All wanted to leave their marks on the world. They had been planning their strikes for the best part of a decade. They had watched as the extremists and militants had conducted their own deadly missions and marveled at the continued vigor with which those groups persisted.

They weren't interested in the so-called faith-based battles. Their religion was money.

But the world had seen nothing like the three merciless strikes of January past, which had shown such unbridled hatred towards humankind, such lack of remorse.

A champagne cork popped, signaling a celebration.

"Vintage Krug, Leopold, just as you like it!" said the man holding the bottle, his accent thick and throaty.

"Excellent, Sami, excellent!" Grosch replied.

Sami poured the champagne, handing a glass to each of the men.

"To victory, my friends!" Grosch said loudly, holding his glass high.

The others raised their glasses in salute to their leader.

"Now to business, gentlemen," Grosch said, inviting them to sit on the dust-covered sheeted lounges.

From his carryall, Sami brought out two new blue sheets and covered the loungers. An unlit brick fireplace still full of wood sat at the end of the room.

One of the others pulled out a small notepad from his breast pocket. "We have received confirmation that all members of the Security Council will be in attendance, together with the leaders of the G8 countries."

"Ah ha… just what we wanted!" said Grosch in delight. "Where better to send our message than to the G8 summit?" The focus of the summit would be on world terrorism, and would be attended by all those responsible for creating security infrastructures.

"Yes, surely Congress will have no alternative than to loosen the budget constraints and approve increased spending on security," said the American.

"Such an attack will lead to an international outcry that will force the administration to start spending again, just like it did post-9/11," Grosch added, raising his glass for the second time.

"Hear, hear," the other three concurred, raising their glasses too.

"Have we finalized all the arrangements for the plane and the time of impact?" Grosch asked.

"Yes, Leopold. The Gulfstream will leave Stansted Airport, just outside of London. Flight time is estimated at just under two hours. As you previously advised, the plane should be in position by no later than 7 p.m., giving you sufficient time to get out of the hotel for your dinner engagement," said one of the others. "And our pilot and co-pilot are devout Islamic militants who will gladly surrender their lives for their greater cause. They are experienced pilots, having trained with the al-Qaeda network for a number of years."

Grosch nodded in approval.

"Two of our men have been employed by the Berlin control tower for the last six months and they will be able to ensure the detour goes unchecked by any others," Sami continued, his sunglasses an affectation in the dim room. "Therefore, we estimate the plane will be almost on top of the hotel before anyone can do anything about stopping it."

"And the bomb?" Grosch asked.

"Now we have the final installment – thank you, Belgian government – we can make our final payment to the Koreans."

"And getting it on the plane has all been organized?" Grosch asked

"Yes, yes," said the Russian. "It is housed in a specially designed box that fits within the propulsion system of the jet. I have overseen its manufacture. It will detonate on impact."

The others laughed.

"Yes, the beauty of having good relations with your vendors," Grosch said, "All right, then. Sounds like we are all ready." Grosch stood, ready to leave. "Ensure our Korean friends do not live to tell anyone of their sale, won't you, Igor?"

"Leopold, that is under control. If anyone gets their hands on the transaction, it will look like the Koreans sold it to the Iraqis, and they will not be able to trace it back to us."

"Kill them anyway, for extra insurance, Igor," said Grosch.

"Yes, sir!" He would have no qualms carrying out the order.

"Goodbye, all," Grosch said, hugging Sami, then the others. "By this time next week our mission will be complete, a message will have been firmly sent, and our careers as terrorists will be over! I might even choose to retire and become a farmer!" he said, wiping his hands with a handkerchief and dropping it in a wastebasket inside the kitchen door.

He opened the front door, and stopped briefly to take in the country air while pulling his sunglasses from his suit breast pocket. He felt a strange sense of relief that it was almost over. It had distracted him for long enough. This latest deal with the Americans had ensured his preferred vendor status that should enable him to capture a good share of defense contracts in response to the attack, making Grosch Industries one of the top five defense contractors in the world. The Chinese purchaser would be pleased.

He climbed into his elegant car, pulled out his BlackBerry, and dialed a number.

"All in readiness for Sunday?... Good. Just make certain that the plane doesn't take off and that the police find the bomb with the two men... And what about the three amigos?... Outstanding! Goodbye."

Grosch hit the "off" button, dropping the phone on the passenger seat as he started the engine.

"Goodbye, gentlemen," Grosch said quietly to himself as Volkyre stroked his back. "I've enjoyed our friendship. Enjoy your last days."

The McLaren sped off down the dirt road.

* * *

Jack was walking from the campus restaurant to the classroom to take the afternoon session, Darius striding ever watchful by his side.

Jack's mind kept going over the bits and pieces of information. Alain Luscombe's comment just now, about the rumors of a longstanding affair between Marie Verheyen and Grosch, had come in from left field. Surely it was just that, a distraction, nothing to do with the Caille deal and money laundering possibilities that Stephen had uncovered.

His enquiring, analytical mind wouldn't let up. Jack loved those criminal forensic shows where the good guys have to piece together a bunch of obscure facts to get the bad guy. The evidence always told a story. Where was the story here?

It bothered him that he was even contemplating this. It had nothing to do with him and was now becoming a distraction from what he was paid to do: teach. But he couldn't get over the fact that these individuals were all connected in some way: Loren, Ray Malone, Mayer, Marie Verheyen, Leopold Grosch. But how? As had been his custom over many years, when faced with a puzzle or a decision: as he walked, he prayed.

"Dear Jesus, I praise you for being Lord over all things and all people. You are the King of this world. For some strange reason, all these events and people have come into my world. I don't know why but sense that I'm supposed to get involved. You know the mystery excites me but, Lord, I don't have time for wildgoose chases. Please, Lord God, provide me with confirmation that you wish me to continue unraveling this mystery – something, Lord God. Please also protect the others involved, especially Loren and Stephen, and please bring forward any others who may be able to provide insight.

"I love you and need you. Protect me, I pray, and may I inspire and challenge the group in this next session.

"Thank you for loving me. Amen."

Chapter 19

Berlin

The two maintenance men, wearing royal-blue overalls, were just completing their check of the central unit, discreetly located on the roof, that managed the air conditioning for the entire hotel.

The hotel supervisor greeted the pair: he knew them well. He reviewed the maintenance checklist, confirming all tests were successful. All was in order and nothing unusual or non-standard had been found during the checkup.

"Great work, gents. All ready now for the big G8 event next week. See you in three months."

Unfortunately, as the supervisor didn't check their work, he failed to notice the large non-standard water tank and separate piping the two men had installed on one of the air-handling units. They had counted on his slovenly approach: they, too, knew him well.

***

An hour later Grosch was toweling himself down after a warm shower, standing in his usual city hotel room. A chime from a mobile phone invaded the silence in the room.

He opened his briefcase. Three mobile phones were sitting on top of a wad of papers. Only one indicated receipt of a message. He picked up the silver Nokia and clicked on the message.

"Package in place and secure."

He thumbed in a reply.

"Excellent. Will initiate your payment."

He picked up a second phone and searched for a number. It answered almost instantly.

Grosch said in perfect English: "Package in place and secure. Please arrange for the depositor to be removed."

He listened to the response, then hung up.

* * *

A young man of Asian descent put down his mobile phone. He turned to the laptop sitting open on the desk. Strange his employer had used his voice, rather than a text message. Was the old man slipping? He saved the recording.

The room was drab and sparse, in complete contrast to the view outside the window. The North Sea waves crashing on the cliffs below highlighted the majestic wonder of the ocean, and its power.

The man clicked on an icon on his laptop to reveal a grid of some description, a red dot flashing as it moved. Then he clicked on a second icon to open another program. He typed in a simple two-letter command: "GO", followed by what appeared to be a phone number.

Five hundred miles away outside Berlin, two air-conditioning maintenance men in their van never knew what hit them. The van exploded as they turned onto the motorway that would take them back to Brussels.

The young Asian turned back to the grid on his laptop. The red dot stopped moving and then disappeared.

He picked up his mobile phone and thumbed in a text message: "Depositor eliminated."

He put the phone down and wondered if a similar fate was soon to befall him. He packed up his laptop, his cell phone and a small overnight case and headed outside. A green 3-series BMW sat in the driveway. His tenth hire car of the last six months. He reversed out of the drive of his sixth rental house of the same period. He figured if he always kept mobile, the employer he had never met and only knew as "King" couldn't locate him.

He slipped the car into fifth as he let down the roof, the early evening breeze sending shivers down his spine. All he owned and cared about sat in the back seat: a laptop, a cell phone and a bag containing a few old clothes.

* * *

"Got Zhou Chau's location, sir!" a male voice said.

"Well done," Grosch responded, standing over his cell phone, now on speaker. "Follow him, catch him and bring him to me."

"Will do, sir."

Grosch ended the call. He smiled, cockily.

* * *

The view from the summit of one of the world's most prominent landmarks was breathtaking. However, it was all wasted on the sinister, bloodshot eyes of the duo that sat on its very peak. The Eiffel Tower was lit up, as it is every night, while the guests below in the lavish restaurant were delighting in the atmosphere of a mild spring evening in the city of lovers.

"Grosch's plans are looking solid, Bacchazar," said the General.

"Yes. All is now ready. My only concern is whether Tagan tries to intervene."

"Be assured they will try to," responded the General.

"Yes, yes, of that I am sure. I hope the diversion plan may also fool him. Alternatively, I will just have to confront him myself and do what I should have done so many years ago: finish him off!"

"Bacchazar, I don't need to tell you that he is a mighty foe. Indeed, one of heaven's finest!" The General smirked at his companion's discomfort.

"I know," growled Bacchazar.

"How are your sentinel numbers?"

"Fine!"

"Will you request Agramon's assistance?"

"Absolutely not!"

"Please yourself. Let's face it, you could probably do with their assistance…" the General paused mid-sentence, "…judging by some of the recent *failures* of your sentinel squadron."

"Have you come to judge me?" Bacchazar jutted his ugly, oversized head straight into the General's equally hideous features.

The General pulled away calmly.

"Not at all, Bacchazar. Your performance in outwitting and defeating the enemy, together with the tally of souls claimed for the Most High is how you will be judged." He paused. "And frankly, *he* is not pleased with your recent failures."

Bacchazar's flaring wings twitched.

"My dear, egomaniacal fool! He is informed of all activity. And he will not accept any further failures. Do you *hear me*?"

"Loud and clear!" Bacchazar said, gritting his teeth.

The General didn't want an apology. Just results. Otherwise there were plenty of other good soldiers ready for a tilt at his role.

"What are your plans regarding Malone?"

Bacchazar instantly felt a stabbing surge of rage inside him. Drakkin had let him down badly, being too cocky to carry the attack through to its bloody end.

"Drakkin has been reprimanded!" Bacchazar responded. "But he is too good a warrior not to use in Berlin."

"All right, then," replied the General. "I will trust your judgment on this one. Drakkin is usually very good… even if he was stupid to give the enemy an opportunity to rescue the Malones. He won't let it happen again, I'm sure of that."

"We will attack Ray Malone subtly this time. Once he knows he's been conned by Mayer, he'll be terrified about being caught and going to jail. We'll use that to drive him over the edge. Grosch has already dealt with the failure of the assigned hit man in his usual efficient way." There was a slight emphasis on "efficient".

"Let's meet again the night before the attack," the General demanded. "Five days from tonight. Berlin. Till then!"

The General leapt off the tower, instantly disappearing into the dark evening sky.

Left alone, Bacchazar took a deep breath, then screamed, "Tagan, your time is up!"

Patrons in the Tower's upper restaurant were momentarily startled as a cold chill suddenly descended, causing many to reach for their coats.

* * *

Zhou Chau was dozing in the first-class section of the high-speed train as it sped through the French countryside towards Paris.

Zhou figured he could get lost in France's capital for the few days before his final act.

He felt confident he knew who the "King" was. Especially after receiving that phone call last night. Having taped it and then having matched it to 99.5 per cent compatibility, he was now very confident. He had traced the various numbers "King" had used to send him text messages over the past few months back to the network carriers. Zhou had been smart enough to decipher the combination of different numbers that he'd used. Then by asking the right questions, combined with some fairly shoddy security on the customer service helpline, he had got the information he required. Zhou knew he didn't need to use that information, yet, and perhaps never at all, but he had a hunch that one day it would come in useful.

His sloppy dark-blue pullover and scrappy jeans were in direct contrast to the suits worn by the men and women who were setting off for a week of work in the French capital. His unwashed, black, straight, shoulder-length hair added to his bedraggled appearance.

Zhou was unaware of the huge angelic presence standing nearby.

As of a few hours ago, Andola had been frustrated, minding a still-recuperating Charlotte Le Bon in London. But Tagan realized he needed a heavy hitter for this assignment. Andola, with her supermodel looks, was summoned.

Andola had picked up Zhou on the motorway to Brussels. She surprised the three urchin-like demonic sentinels that had attached themselves to him with a head-on confrontation that had them backpedaling immediately. Never before had they seen such a magnificent angelguard. And they would never get a second chance, as Andola had promptly disposed of them.

In the short time she had been alongside Zhou she had searched his heart and mind. She found a young man very much confused and lost with a heart full of anger and bitterness. The fatal attack on his family last year by a gang of youths had sent him spiraling down into depression for a number of months. Revenge on the world had appeared to be a good way of appeasing the pain that was bolted vise-like to his heart.

Considered a child prodigy in his homeland for his abilities in mathematics and computer science, three years ago he had left home at eighteen to embark on a PhD. His achievements at home led to many attractive scholarship offers from all around the world, culminating in him choosing a prominent university in Sydney, Australia. The eldest of four, he had high expectations heaped upon his narrow shoulders.

On hearing the news of his family's demise in such a sinister and callous attack, he returned to China, deferring his final year of studies.

As he looked out the window, the diminishing lush green countryside was being replaced by suburbia. *Not long now,* he thought.

He felt tense and noticed his hands were shaking. He couldn't recall the last time he had a decent night's sleep. When he did sleep he woke from horrible dreams, which only increased his agitated state. He considered what options he had to escape his edgy state as he grabbed his worldly belongings together.

It's working, Andola thought, as she watched Zhou stand up and head for the doors even though the station was still five minutes away. She could see the intense trauma working through his mind: just one final act or walk away now!

She also watched the two men, both dressed in smart business suits, who had been tracking Zhou since leaving Brussels. They stood in preparation for beating the rush to the doors. They were accompanied by two demons, who snarled as she stepped through the train's wall.

Hmmm… won't be long till they make their move.

The train pulled into Paris Nord station.

***

Jack was getting anxious. He had woken unusually early at 5:30, his mind full of various conspiracy theories. As each day passed, his feeling of homesickness increased as he thought more about the twins. He was ready to go home.

Only three days to go, he thought.

He turned CNN on to see what was going on around the world. The first story featured the history of the G8 summits, the next of which was due to he held in Berlin next week. He flicked through the channels looking for something a little more interesting. He settled on the NBA playoffs.

A muffled ringing disturbed his thoughts. He got up, headed for the bedroom and rustled through his soft leather briefcase, while a standard cell phone ringtone broke the silence of the early dawn.

"Hello," Jack said, a bit agitated.

He listened to the response. It was familiar, strangely so. A voice he hadn't heard for a while. But he couldn't place it.

And then a faint crackle as his battery cut out! The phone went dead.

***

It had been a hot, humid day with temperatures reaching the high eighties.

Jack had spent most of the day in his room. All the windows were open to allow some circulation of air. He had spent the morning preparing the sessions for the last two days of the program.

He now turned to his personal investigation. He still wasn't sure what he was doing nor why he had the elements of some sort of puzzle. So long as it didn't intrude on his teaching, he would persevere with it until he hit a roadblock or God specifically led him away from it. But his instincts were telling him that God was leading him deeper and deeper, into what, he knew not.

Two words from the documents Stephen had provided kept going through his mind: the project name "Bryggja" and the recipient, "King", who by all accounts looked like the mastermind behind it all.

His search on the internet helped him with the project name. "Bryggja" was the original Old Norse word for what is now the city of Bruges, located in the north of Belgium. He had no idea what that meant. He knew from experience that project names were often meaningless, reflecting some point of interest or even a hobby of the person who created it.

Now "King" could mean anything. *Highly unoriginal alias,* Jack thought, *but sufficiently anonymous.*

He had tried a number of routes on Google. Kings of England: nothing grabbed him from the Henrys and Georges of yesteryear. Elvis, the King – was the person an Elvis fan? That just narrowed down the possibilities to many millions around the world.

No, he doubted that idea.

Bruges, Belgium, King. The Kings of Belgium? Did Belgium have kings, he wondered? He knew a number of European countries did have kings – Spain, Denmark, for example – but he wasn't sure about Belgium.

He googled "Kings of Belgium", and over 129,000 possible entries came back. He scrolled down the first page. The first entry was in a foreign language he didn't recognize. The second didn't say much. But the third caught his eye:

Rulers of Belgium – Belgian Kings
This is a chronological list of the people who have ruled Belgium; the dates given are the periods of said rule. House of Saxe-Coburg-Gotha (Kings) 1831–1865...

That looked good. He clicked on it. He scrolled down the page and there it was: the list of Belgian kings. A total of seven since 1831 to the present. Albert II was the current King of Belgium. Jack had never heard of him.

But interestingly, three of the seven had the name Leopold. Leopold I, II and III.

"Huh."

He sifted through some papers on his desk but couldn't find what he was after. He got up out of his chair and looked around the room. Then he saw what he was looking for. He walked over to the coffee table, picking up the Monday edition of *Le Monde* that had the article announcing the Belgian gas pipeline project. It included a picture of Minister Marie Verheyen and the president and founder of the Grosch group of companies, one Leopold Grosch.

"Leopold. Coincidence? Hmmm…"

He went back on the net and looked up the Grosch Group. Head office was Brussels, that was no good. He searched to see if the site had any information about its founder. Nothing. Just the corporate photo of him dressed in a dark suit.

Jack went back to the newspaper article. Nothing more there. He looked again at the accompanying picture. It looked like it was taken in an office, perhaps Grosch's office. In the background he noticed what looked like a football jersey framed in glass. It was framed with the back showing, with a large white number "6" in the middle. Above that was printed "Grosch", also in white.

"So, Mr. Grosch, perhaps you are a supporter of a particular Belgian football team? But which one?"

It didn't help that the back of the jersey was what was framed. The long-sleeved jersey was striped, with two colors, one darker than the other. Pity it wasn't in color. The sleeves were in the darker color, which Jack presumed was black, with piping similar to the Adidas three-stripe running the full length of the sleeve.

Jack knew a bit about English football but not too much about European. He knew of the big teams in Spain, Italy and Germany but not much about any of the smaller countries.

He went back to Google and entered "Belgian football teams". 98,300 entries came back. He clicked on the first one, which took him through to the official club site of Club Brugge. Unfortunately, it was all written in Flemish and French.

But there it was! The jersey. Blue-and-black striped with black sleeves and three white stripes.

He looked back at the newspaper. A match.

He then flicked back to the Grosch website. The official company colors of the Grosch group were black and blue. The colors of Club Brugge.

He was sure this was it.

Leopold Grosch was a keen supporter of Club Brugge.

That linkage was enough for Jack.

Somehow Ray Malone was involved directly or indirectly in some "project" with Leopold Grosch. Jack wondered if Malone knew the funds he had been supplying Tom Mayer with over the past twelve months had made their way to Belgium. And into the hands of one of the wealthiest men in the world.

"Yes, yes, yes," Jack pumped the air with his fists. He'd cracked it. Some deal going down between Grosch and FJ Caille?

Or was it?

He rushed back to his seat and opened up the email from Stephen.

He quickly scanned the series of emails between Mayer and "King". He stopped at the final sentence. He highlighted it with the cursor, bolding it.

We now only require the final contribution from MV
to complete the pot of gold that will give us sufficient
ammunition to shake up the world!

Grosch buying an advertising agency or agencies would hardly constitute shaking up the world. It might create a new global powerhouse, but that was about all. The French would probably prefer a Belgian ally to buy the business rather than have it get into the hands of the Yanks, he thought.

And who's "MV"? He raised his head from the computer screen and looked at the newspaper article.

!!!

MV was Marie Verheyen!

Grosch was using the funds from the Belgian government to "shake up the world".

This wasn't about a business deal or a gas pipeline. This was something more.

He couldn't stop thinking about those final four words. They sounded ominous. Was Grosch up to something far more sinister?

Chapter 20

The Insead campus

The bar on campus had been booked out for the night's "cocktail party". There were no invitations or decorations, no requirement to wear suits or cocktail dresses, nothing. Just turn up at 6:30 for some refreshments and nibbles.

The event had been set up to allow the delegates to meet the five executive team members who would actively participate in the final two days of the program, including Ray Malone.

Soon after 6:30, the group of executives arrived together, led in by Didier Rocheteau, who had collected them from the village hotel where they were housed. Malone came in last, locked in a serious discussion with one of the other executives.

It was closer to 7:00 before the first students began to arrive. The six women had all taken the opportunity to dress a little more elegantly, having swapped their standard day attire of jeans and shirts for smart casual summer dresses. The men too had spruced up their appearance: dress pants and jacket. No ties, but everyone was suitably and fashionably respectable.

Jack, wearing a black suit with a dark-blue open-collared shirt, ran his eyes over the student group.

One was missing. The one he most wanted to see.

The waiter, dressed in the standard waiter penguin suit, stepped up to Jack, offering him a selection of beverages, alcoholic and not. Jack selected a glass of red wine. He turned towards the group that was now milling around the centre of the room.

And there she was. Standing in the doorway. No one else appeared to notice. Only Jack. It was like time stood still. She was resplendent in a black cocktail dress with spaghetti straps that showed off her athletic body, holding a small handbag in her left hand.

Jack had to stop his jaw from dropping. Her elegant beauty overwhelmed him.

Time went back to normal speed when a waiter approached Loren, offering her a drink. She selected a flute of champagne. Jack watched her make some idle chatter with the waiter, who had served them a number of times in the bar over the past ten days.

As the waiter drew away from Loren, Ray Malone left the main group, having spotted his star protégée. He hugged her and they chatted for a few moments.

Jack caught Loren's eye. She smiled, encouraging him to join them.

"Hello, Loren. You look lovely this evening."

"Thank you, Jack," she replied, not taking her eyes off his. "The course instructions said to bring attire appropriate for a cocktail party, so here's my little party dress."

She paused, allowing him time to catch his breath, pleased with the effect she had had. "You know Ray, don't you, Jack?"

"Sure do. Hello, Ray. Good to see you again." Jack extended his hand towards Ray. "Trust you've had a good time in France this past week."

Ray took his hand and shook it a little warily, as if he wasn't sure whom he was meeting. "Ah, yes. We met last week at the introductory session, didn't we?"

"That's right. I'm Jack Haines," Jack said, a little disappointed in not being remembered but also recalling how distracted and disinterested Ray had been at their first meeting.

"Do excuse me, Jack and Loren, but I need to catch Rocheteau to chat about the night's proceedings. I'm sure I'll see you both later."

Malone moved away, leaving Jack and Loren alone. There was electricity between them. Loren moved closer to Jack while looking around the room.

The balcony was almost full, angelic beings busily feasting their eyes on the cautious proceedings inside. This was business as usual. They watched intently, monitored, spoke amongst themselves, always reaching out in love for their human charges.

Darius wandered in and out of the main room, carefully taking in Jack's movements.

"Good to have you out of hiding, Arlia," Darius said as he approached her.

"Miss me, huh?"

"Well, I wouldn't go that far. Tagan must consider it safe for you to come out of confinement."

"Yes, after I badgered him. But I have strict orders to continue to lie low for the next two days, not to raise any suspicions amongst the local heathen."

She moved gracefully between her warrior friends but at the same time tried to lighten up the atmosphere with playful remarks and word games.

Tonight Athaniel led them. Tagan was meeting with the archangels, getting a better view of the threat that was now only a few days away, one that would have serious consequences for the entire world.

* * *

The night had passed quickly.

It was now past eleven and it was really dragging on for Jack. He wanted to head back to his room, make some calls and then go to bed. But he also wanted to spend some time with Malone.

Malone was sitting with three of the delegates, two women and a man, in the comfortable leather chairs and lounge beside the unlit fireplace. Their conversation concluded, the three delegates all got to their feet simultaneously and headed for the exit, leaving Malone by himself.

Now was his chance, Jack thought.

"Mind if I join you, Ray?"

"No, not at all, Haines."

Silence.

Malone soon broke it. "It's been a good night. I've enjoyed meeting the team. There are some very smart people amongst this group."

"Yes, absolutely. They're excellent. You'd find it hard to find a better group of twenty executives-in-waiting."

Darius and Landen left the balcony and were joined by Athaniel as they took up positions standing around the sofas, forming an invisible barrier to the rest of the room.

The group around the pool table was getting rowdier as the game got further along. Loren and her team were leading, with only two balls to sink.

"And how's all the merger activity going, Ray?" Jack asked.

"What merger activity are you referring to, Jack?"

"The one that involves Caille America merging with Graves, with you becoming CEO of the new combined organization," Jack said, staring straight into Ray's eyes.

"I'm still unsure as to what you are talking about," came the uneasy reply.

Jack reached into his jacket pocket and pulled out the fax header he had picked up at last week's meeting. He leant over and showed it to Ray.

"The one that you scribbled down at last week's introduction."

"Oh, that!" Ray looked at the piece of paper, recognizing his handwriting. *Funny,* he thought to himself, *I wasn't aware I had lost it.* "Jack, I was just doodling. It's common knowledge that the group is looking for more acquisition opportunities. I had planned to meet with Giresse here today to discuss the matter with him further. Unfortunately, he had to cancel our appointment at the last moment."

"So why engage Maple, Mayer and Masters?"

Ray paused, not taking his eyes off Jack. He wondered how long this game would continue. How much did Jack actually know? Ray realized the investment bank's name was on the top of the fax, so Jack hadn't said anything more than the obvious.

"As I understand it, the finance guys over here have engaged a number of companies to explore various scenarios. I happen to know Tom Mayer well – we're close friends – and I asked him to provide me with some informal advice regarding pricing the businesses."

"Oh, right!" Jack said matter-of-factly, nodding his head. "So how do you explain the moneys that you have transferred to your friend, Tom Mayer?"

Ray didn't flinch. He gave nothing away, but his heart was racing. *How could he know that?*

If Jack mentioned that to anybody, Ray was out of a job and what's more, likely facing a jail sentence for embezzlement. And then it struck him. Could Jack perhaps have some knowledge of the attack the other night? Perhaps he was even responsible for it. His mind started to wander off onto crazy tangents. He knew he would have to find out how much Jack knew and who else he had told.

"What money are you referring to?"

"Come on, Ray, you know what money I'm talking about."

"Haines, I have no idea what you are talking about. And if you persist in taking this any further, then I will up and leave you and join the pool players."

"Are you aware it's been transferred to a series of European bank accounts?"

Malone chose a different tack. "Haines, why these questions? I feel I'm being interrogated. Are you secretly an undercover agent or something?"

"Would you be worried if I told you I was?"

"I'm almost certain you're not. Merely a nosy academic who's asking too many questions for his own good."

"Sounds like I've hit a nerve."

"Not at all, Haines. But you're beginning to annoy me with your line of questioning!" Malone said, almost growling at Jack. The urge to rip Jack's head off was building fast.

Darius was standing over Jack, whispering, "Go easy on him, or you might lose him."

Athaniel and Landen were around Malone, encouraging him to hold it together.

None of the angelguards were sure where this would lead.

"So, are you going to tell me where you're coming from?"

"Hey, Ray, I'm just an academic with a real interest in business and organizational behavior. Change is my specialty and that's what takeovers and mergers are all about – *change*."

"So you're looking for a job, then? Is that your angle?"

Jack chuckled, causing Ray to smile for the first time.

"That's right. I want to be involved if a takeover or merger does indeed take place."

"You know, we can probably arrange that, *if*, and I repeat, *if* a takeover or merger does in fact take place," Malone said, hoping this might sufficiently satisfy Jack and bring an end to this tricky conversation.

Jack paused. "Ray, what if the money you provided Mayer wasn't being used for the purpose you intended? What if it was being used for something else, something a little more sinister?"

There it was. He'd said it. He was fishing now, hoping Malone might take the bait.

Jack's heart was beating fast. But nowhere near as fast as Malone's. That final question stunned Malone. He was convinced Jack must know something. He needed to think about a response, or else he could give himself away, and then what would stop Haines from telling the board, or even the police or the SEC? He had to stop this and now!

Fortunately someone else did it for him.

"Mind if I join you chaps?" Loren sat down between the two adversaries.

She immediately sensed the tension in the air.

"I haven't interrupted something important, have I, gentlemen?"

"Not at all, Loren," Malone offered. "Haines and I were just sharing stories of corporate takeovers, that's all."

"Good. My team got beaten at pool and then all the others decided to retire for the evening. Leaving just the three of us to the bitter end."

"Well, my trusted friend," Malone rose slowly from his chair, "I must leave you with Haines here. I've got a bit further to go than you both and it's past my bedtime."

He reached over, taking Loren's right hand, kissing it tenderly.

"Good night, Haines. I enjoyed our little chat," Malone said, lying. He had to force himself to shake Jack's hand. But he did so, giving him a deathly stare.

"Likewise, Ray. I hope we can continue our discussion over the next couple of days."

That thought stung Malone back into reality. He vowed silently to avoid Jack at all costs.

"Goodnight," Malone said, his shoulders slumping as fatigue struck him, due to the late hour and the intensity of the conversation with Jack. He pulled his coat from off the hook next to the door and promptly exited.

Athaniel and Darius looked at each other as Arlia drew close.

"Your boy sure is a feisty one," Athaniel said to Darius.

"Yes, Athaniel. That was a real battle of wills, wasn't it?" Darius replied.

"I'm not sure where that's going to end up," Athaniel said, a frown forming on his brow. "Malone left a worried man. He doesn't really have many options, does he?"

"If he confides in Jack, he's giving himself away to a complete stranger," Darius said.

"But, Darius, why would he do that?" asked Arlia. "What's he to gain?"

Darius shrugged his shoulders in reply.

"Peace of mind!" Athaniel stated directly. "He sure doesn't have any of that at the moment."

The three angelguards turned to Jack and Loren, who were both sitting peacefully, Jack still on his chair, Loren on the lounge.

"And what of these two?" Arlia asked, noting the magnetism between the two humans.

"Their attraction to each other is obvious," Athaniel replied. "But what is most important is that Loren's desire for Jesus grows, and no romantic entanglement distracts them until Grosch is stopped."

Darius and Arlia both nodded, fully aware of what needed to be done.

New York

Grazag followed Mayer out of his apartment, heading for the elevator. It was 6:46 and Mayer was dressed in shorts and an LA

Lakers yellow-and-purple tee-shirt, set to take a run. His first in a few weeks.

He hopped into the open elevator and pressed the ground-floor button. The hairs on the back of his neck rose while goose-bumps attacked his arms as he shivered in the unusually cold and dark elevator. He thought he could see a foggy haze encircling the fluorescent light in the ceiling. A strange invasive odor stung his nose, reminding him of school chemistry experiments gone wrong. Nausea rose to the back of his throat as pangs of anxiety attacked his mind.

He got out of the elevator and went through the rarely used back door into the deserted back alley. He wished Loren had answered her phone when he had called earlier.

Mayer chose his usual course down the southeastern edge of Central Park. He wasn't sure he could reach the zoo before turning back, but he would give it his best shot.

He started running up the alley. He turned left into the main street that would take him across to the park—

WHAM!

He bounced backwards off the thick black bull-bar of a dark-green SUV of indistinguishable make, somersaulting uncontrollably, breaking his back and neck.

The unmarked assassin on wheels continued on its eighty-mile-an-hour journey, as if it had struck nothing more than a stray dog. It turned right when it reached the end of the alley, never to be seen again.

Mayer's body lay contorted in an unnatural position. His head was at right angles to his body. An expression of absolute anguish was fixed on his face. A pool of deep-red liquid was now running steadily from under his head, his life flowing freely out of him. A scruffy brown tabby cat put its nose to the rapidly growing puddle, but quickly rejected it.

Mayer felt no pain now. He wondered where he was. Had he only been dreaming of going for a run this morning?

Everything was pitch black and silent. He thought he opened his eyes, but nothing changed. Just endless darkness – no light, no stars, no moon. Nothing.

He wondered if he was blind.

He couldn't feel his body, his arms or legs.

Nothing.

Smothering blackness swallowed him.

And then it hit him.

He was… alone.

He knew he would always be… alone.

He wanted to scream but couldn't.

Again something told him no one would hear him anyway.

No one! Ever!

Grazag smiled wickedly as he saw what was left of Tom Mayer slip away…

His sinister grin turned into a deep raucous cackle that followed Mayer's soul on his endless terrifying journey.

Chapter 21

Insead, a few hours later

It was almost 2 a.m. when Jack left her at her doorstep. They had walked and talked, talked and walked some more.

She felt sure he felt the same way she did. The energy between them was magnetic, drawing them both together. When he tenderly touched her arm, or her side, or flicked a stray hair off her brow, heat radiated in her heart.

Loren was beaming as she entered her room.

Her heart jumped when she heard the familiar ringtone of her cell phone.

Jack?

Blast, where's my phone?!

She found it, under a pile of papers, just as it stopped ringing.

"Rats!" she said under her breath.

No incoming phone number was on her screen, indicating it was most likely a call from overseas. To her utter amazement, she noticed she had missed twenty-six calls. Someone wanted her bad.

Please don't be something wrong at home.

Ah, eleven texts? Darn!

She clicked on the first one. It was from her mom: "Call home ASAP."

No, no, no, pleeease!

After deleting the message she ignored the other ten messages for the time being and dialed her mother, the phone on loudspeaker. It would be about five o'clock in the afternoon in LA.

After a couple of rings the phone answered.

"Hello," she heard the soft gentle tone of her mother.

"Hi, Mom, it's me, Loren."

"Hello, darling. Thank you for calling back," Mom said calmly but matter of factly. "Have you not had your phone with you? I've called you about twenty times."

"No, Mom, I've been out tonight and forgot to take it with me."

"I even called Marcie to see if she could help track you down. She gave me the university number, but they had closed for the night, as every time I rang I just got the voicemail. Well, I think it was their voicemail, as it was mostly in French."

"What's up, Mom?" Loren asked impatiently.

"We got a call about an hour ago from Tom's parents," she paused.

"And...?"

"And they, um, told us that... Tom was involved in an accident today. A hit and run, they believe." Loren could hear the sadness in her mother's voice.

"And is he all right? Is he in hospital?" Loren asked anxiously.

"Um... darling, he... er... passed away. I'm so sorry, my darling!"

"*Whaaat?*" Loren whispered, her mouth stuck open, eyes drooped, brow furrowed, as a wave of disbelief collapsed over her.

Her legs buckled, forcing her to her knees. She started rocking slowly backwards and forwards, a dazed look on her face.

Thoughts rushed freefall through her mind: the first day they met, their wedding day, Luke's birth, Taylor's birth, messing about on Malibu beach late one warm summer night, before making love and then being interrupted by a pesky Alsatian that had run free from its owner. She could only think of good times, not the bad times, not the wretched horrible times before they separated.

"Are you there, darling? Can you hear me? Loren, please say something!"

"I'm here," Loren said mechanically, her body shaking.

Even though she'd stared death in the face a lot over the past few months, it still hadn't prepared her for this. She thought of Luke and Taylor. How would they cope? A knot hung in her throat like a swallowed bone. Her mouth had gone dry.

The tears fell silently at first, small sobs escaping from her mouth.

Her mom heard this and made a suggestion.

"Perhaps you should call me back in a few minutes?"

"Er… OK, OK… thanks, Mom," Loren said between sobs that were now getting louder.

She collapsed onto the bed and just bellowed. The knot in her throat was constricting her breathing. A shooting pain hit her stomach as grief gripped her hard. Her black mascara and eye-shadow began to run as tears broke the dam within her eyes.

Arlia sat on the bed, her invisible hand stroking Loren's hair.

All the pain, sadness and grief she had experienced and worked through three months ago just came flooding back. She couldn't move a muscle.

Arlia too was grief-stricken to see her charge so devastated, and so apparently helpless. She spread her wings to their fullest extent over Loren.

"Let it all out, Loren, let it all go," she whispered gently and soothingly.

Loren continued to wail as she lay motionless on the bed.

"God, why, oh why, God, is this happening?" she bawled out, thumping her clenched right hand on the bed.

After ten minutes she felt some semblance of control coming back. The tears had subsided and the anguished howls had now become a small whimpering. She sat up, and then stood up. She wiped her eyes, spreading her mascara even further around her now puffy red eyes.

She was headed into the bathroom when she heard what she thought sounded like knocking at her door. She walked out of her bedroom. It *was* someone knocking – actually banging on her door. She heard a male voice calling her name but wasn't in any state to be able to put a name to the voice.

"Hang on, hang on, I'm coming!"

She opened the door halfway, seeing two piercing green eyes through the darkness, and then a pained expression on the face she'd only moments ago seen laughing.

Seeing him made all her fears and grief rise to the surface once again.

Jack pushed the door open and stepped in just as Loren collapsed into his arms.

He picked her up and carried her to the lounge.

"Tom's dead… Tom's dead…. he's dead," she said through her sobs.

"I know. I know, Loren," Jack whispered in her ear.

"Just rest here while I get you some water." He made her comfortable, placing her head on two cushions on the lounge.

Within moments he was back with a bottle of Evian and a thin blanket. He placed it gently over her body and legs.

She propped herself up and received the water from him. "Thank you…"

"Sssshhh… there's no need to talk… for now… just rest."

But she wanted to talk.

"I… I… I… can't believe he's dead! Luke and Taylor will be beside themselves," she said quietly through sniffles.

Jack pulled out a tissue from his jacket pocket, handing it to her. She took it gratefully.

They sat silently in the dark, the only light coming from her bedroom.

She reached out to Jack with open arms.

"Please hug me, Jack."

He complied. She gripped him tightly and he reciprocated. She let out an audible sigh as the security and comfort of Jack's strength renewed her.

The ring of her cell phone interrupted the peace of the moment.

She drew away and got to her feet.

"Oh, that's Mom. She's probably worrying about me," she said, heading to the bedroom.

She soon returned, phone to her ear, talking quietly. Her strength was returning quickly but the lateness of the night and the tiredness of her mind and body were impacting her thinking.

Jack sat on the lounge as he heard Loren sign off from her mother, promising to call her first thing in the morning.

She held the phone in her right hand as she sat down next to Jack on the lounge.

"When you opened the door you said something like you knew."

"Stephen, my brother, had left some messages on my phone. I called him when I got back to my room."

Loren still had a look of surprise on her face.

"Remember, I told you Stephen worked for Tom."

"Ah, yes, that's right, you did tell me that… What do I do, Jack?" A long sigh accompanied the question.

"The first course of action is to get some rest," Jack proposed. "Then work out what to do in the morning."

"I must call Marcie. She'll be beside herself with worry." Loren accessed her phone's messages section. She clicked on the first one: "Call Mom ASAP". Exactly the same as the one she'd read earlier. Then another, exactly the same. Then another. And another.

Then a new one: "Phone your Mom urgently, Marce."

"Would you like me to stay a little while?" Jack asked.

"I'd like that… thank you."

She dialed Marcie's number as she got to her feet. She slowly paced the room as she talked to her. She stopped as her head sank, the tears starting to flow again.

Arlia wrapped her huge invisible arms around Loren, trying to soothe her. Darius sat off to the side, head bowed. *How many more will die before this is all over?*

Jack was making a pot of tea as he looked in Loren's direction. She was weeping into the handset. His heart cried out for her. She had suffered so much already, and now this…

"Oh, Father in heaven," he prayed quietly under his breath, "please wrap your loving arms around Loren. Hold her tight. Keep the enemy away, please, dear Lord."

Jack had no idea that his prayers were being answered that very moment. God had already provided a response through the beautiful angel, Arlia.

Her majestic form appeared to take on greater radiance

as the prayers of Jack, Marcie, Rebecca and many unknown to Loren sought God's intervention in her life. It was like an invisible relay baton. The Holy Spirit received the requests from the prayerful; He passed them on to the Son, who then gave them to the Father, who then passed them to Arlia, who used them to touch Loren's heart.

Loren hung up, walking dejectedly over to the small dining table where Jack had placed a pot of tea, two cups and saucers, a jug of milk and a sugar bowl.

"I made some tea. How do you take it?"

Loren smiled for the first time since the news broke. At that very instant she thought she could very easily fall in love with this Aussie, the man from the Great Southern Land. Perhaps she already had.

"Just milk, thanks, Professor."

"Coming right up."

She took a seat, her heart full of conflicting emotions, as he poured from the pot using a strainer he'd found under the sink.

"My mum makes the best cup of tea in the world..." he said, "always only with tea leaves. I can never make it taste as good as she does."

"Probably because someone else made it," Loren suggested. He looked at her quizzically. "You know everything always tastes better when someone else makes it."

"Well, not always," he replied. "No one makes better coffee than I do!"

"One day you'll have to prove that to me," she said, a spark trying, but without success, to work its way through her sad red eyes.

"Absolutely! It'll be my pleasure."

They sat and sipped their tea in a comfortable silence.

* * *

Jack left Loren's apartment in the early morning light, feeling light-headed, having not had enough sleep. He knew that by missing his four-hour minimum he had made himself susceptible to a migraine during the day.

He felt the vibration of his cell phone in his jeans pocket.

"Jack Haines speaking."

"Professor Haines, hello," said the caller.

"Yeah, this is Jack Haines. Who's this?"

"Professor, it's Zhou. Zhou Chau."

"Zhou?" Jack said with surprise. "How come you're calling me after all this time?"

Zhou was one of Jack's top students who had left suddenly without any explanation last year. One day he was in class, the next he was gone. And now here he was, out of nowhere calling one of his professors.

"Professor, ah, I'm not sure how to say this, but I need someone to talk to."

"Yeah, sure," Jack responded tentatively. "Now's probably not a great time for me, though. Is there any chance you could call me back tonight?"

"Ah, yeah, I guess I could. I just really need to talk to someone."

"Where are you, Zhou? China? Sydney?"

"You won't believe this, Professor, but I'm actually in Paris!"

"Wow, really," Jack replied with a tone of disbelief. "And you won't believe that I'm also in France, about forty minutes away from Paris. In Fontainebleau, at my old alma mater, Insead."

"Oh, that's amazing!" Zhou said excitedly. "I could drive down to meet you so we could talk in person rather than over the phone."

"Yeah. Um, yeah, I guess you could," Jack said, lacking enthusiasm. The last thing he needed right now was another person in need. He really wanted to use any spare time he had caring for Loren.

"Professor, I really need to talk to you. Ah... I'm caught up in something I'm not sure I can get out of."

"OK, say nine o'clock tonight?" Jack said, resigning himself to the situation. He thought it must be reasonably serious if Zhou had decided to call him after all this time.

"Great... thanks, Professor Haines," Zhou said, feeling some relief already.

"Hey Zhou, do you know how to get to Fontainebleau?"

"Don't you worry, Professor, I've got a whole day to figure it out."

"All right then, see you at nine tonight. Call me when you're nearby and I'll meet you outside the main administration building. You can't miss it."

"Sure thing, Professor. Thanks a lot."

"Not a problem. See you tonight."

"Goodbye, Professor Haines."

Jack continued on his way back to his room. *Wow,* he thought to himself, *what a bolt out of the blue!* Zhou Chau, the super-smart student from China, who he never expected to see again... He recalled Zhou shared little of his family or his upbringing, being something of an enigma who had made few friends at university, not because he wasn't a nice kid but because, for some reason, he chose to be solitary.

Coffee. I need coffee badly.

Jack did a U-turn to get himself onto the path that led to the campus café. Thank heaven it opened early!

Chapter 22

The derelict wooden bench within the Forêt de Fontainebleau

The five arrived together, resplendent in their bright armor and tunics. This meeting couldn't wait until sunset, as had been the routine since their arrival in this small quaint village.

"Thank you for coming at such short notice," Tagan said. "It has been confirmed by the heavenly host that an attempt will be made to assassinate the leaders of the largest countries of the world…"

He paused.

There was no response – just grim, focused expressions on his companions' faces.

"… in four days' time," Tagan concluded.

Athaniel spoke: "This is no real surprise. We knew Grosch was planning something big. Fortunately, we have enough time to stop it!"

"What is happening in four days' time that has the leaders all together in one place?" Landen asked.

"It's called the Group of Eight summit," Tagan replied. "The leaders of the eight most powerful nations get together every two years or so to attempt to resolve some of the world's big issues: poverty, disease, inequality, terrorism."

"The eight countries are France, Russia, Canada, the United Kingdom, Germany, Japan, Italy, and the United States," Athaniel added.

"In addition," Tagan interjected, "various other prominent leaders attend for certain meetings. So, for example, leaders from China, India and various African states get invitations."

"So how many leaders will be there altogether?" Darius asked.

"There will be over twenty national leaders," Tagan replied, "plus others, including the heads of the European Union, the United Nations and suchlike."

"Wow, this is really big!" Arlia stated the obvious.

"It certainly is, Arlia, and we're going to ensure Grosch's plan doesn't succeed!" Tagan said defiantly. "But it's going to take some work, and a lot of coordination between us and your charges."

"You can count on us, Tagan," Landen said.

Darius and Arlia nodded in agreement.

"What would you have us do, Tagan?" Darius asked.

"Well, Darius, your man Jack is the key. He is the one who must prevail and stop it."

"Really? Wow! What an honor," Darius said, a little surprised. "And how is he going to do it? He's only a regular guy."

Tagan nodded. "Certainly, he is only a regular guy, but a very brave one, and one who loves the Lord Jesus dearly. Remember, Darius, all things are possible to those who believe."

"I can't knock that," said Darius.

Athaniel walked up on his other side and stood beside him. "And you're going to be with him all the way."

"I wouldn't miss it for the world," Darius said, baring his teeth in anticipation.

"Now, listen up, team," Tagan said, encouraging Landen and Arlia to draw close. "Darius and Jack are going to need a lot of support."

Landen and Arlia nodded.

Tagan continued, "Jack has arranged to meet an old student of his tonight, who happens to be one of Grosch's assassins."

Darius nodded, aware of the phone conversation Jack had had an hour or so ago.

"Gee, how does a student go from studying organizational theory to killing the leaders of the world?" Arlia asked.

"It's a long story, Arlia, and we don't have time at the moment to tell you all of it, but it involves Satan poisoning his heart with revenge and hatred as a result of his family being massacred."

Darius, Arlia and Landen shook their heads, not out of amazement or surprise, but with disgust. They were used to dealing with the aftermath of Satan's evil deeds, all perpetrated in order to deny people their birthright – that is, to know their Creator.

"What's this student's name, Tagan?" Arlia asked.

"Zhou Chau."

"He's twenty-one years old, super smart and understands computers and wireless technology extremely well," Athaniel explained. "He's baby faced, but don't be fooled – he's a killer."

"What is his weapon of choice?" Arlia asked.

"Explosives activated by cell-phone text messages," Athaniel replied.

"That's how the three bomb attacks in January were activated, wasn't it?" Landen asked.

"Yep, sure was. He had a part to play in all three of the attacks!" Tagan noted the grim expressions on Arlia and Landen's faces. "Yes, that's right. He was responsible for the biggest terrorist attacks in history."

"So why's he coming to see Jack, then?" Landen asked.

"We've been working on him for the past few weeks," Athaniel said. "And now he's found his conscience. He's also convinced Grosch will take him out after Sunday."

"Why so?" Darius, this time.

"Because he's ridding himself of all potential turncoats before returning to a normal life," Athaniel said.

"What Athaniel's referring to," Tagan added, "is that Grosch has demonstrated a tendency to dispense with those who have successfully completed their assignments – or unsuccessfully, for that matter."

"Mayer!" Arlia said aloud.

"Yes, that's right. Mayer had served his purpose. Grosch disposed of him."

"How can he keep doing this?" Arlia asked in exasperation.

"Too easily, unfortunately," Tagan replied. "He is too powerful, too wealthy and has far too many tentacles spread around the world. He pays very handsomely for jobs and then, before anyone has the chance of reporting him to the authorities, he does away with them."

"Satan can't keep doing this. He can't! We can't let him get away with this any longer!" Arlia said, now getting worked up and angry. "Let me at his crew!" she spat out.

"Arlia, we know how you feel," Tagan said soothingly. "Trust me, we all do. And we all want Grosch caught and Satan's plans foiled. But the most important outcome of our mission on Sunday is to protect all those leaders. It's needless violence and will only rock the world even more, creating more havoc and unrest."

"Who's keeping guard over this Zhou man?" Landen asked.

"Andola," Tagan replied.

"Ah, I don't know him," Landen said in surprise.

"Her," Athaniel corrected him. "And she's one of the best, don't you worry! She's a veteran of many generations and some of the biggest battles in the northern hemisphere."

"I look forward to meeting her," Landen said.

Tagan interrupted, "So let's see how tonight pans out between Jack and our assassin with a conscience. We should regroup as soon as possible after that to determine our next steps."

"Yes, Tagan," they all said in unison.

"Darius, we need a lot more prayer from Jack's church and family if we are to succeed," Tagan added.

"I'll get onto it immediately."

"Let's close in prayer, team!" Tagan said.

The five came together into a huddle, arms around each other, and prayed ardently, praising God in heaven for His love for their charges. Their fervent prayer soon moved into a time of worship. They sang loudly and passionately in praise, gaining renewed strength and replenishment for the battle ahead.

* * *

They had agreed to meet in an open place in the sunshine.

Jack, in his eagerness, had arrived at the rendezvous in the grassy amphitheate a few minutes early. They would only have thirty minutes till the group was to reassemble.

He saw her coming over the top of the grassy hill while he waited down in the "stage" area of the ancient and well-worn auditorium. She was casually dressed in jeans and a black sleeveless cotton top. Her long slender arms already bore the first fruits of summer, being a nice shade of pale brown. Her long dark hair hung loosely over her shoulders, giving her a rugged rock-chick look.

"Hi ya," said Jack. "How are you feeling this morning?"

She walked up to him and embraced him tenderly.

"Hi, Jack. Pretty good, considering!"

They sat down, Loren almost on top of Jack. He moved along the grassy step to give them both some room. He was particularly conscious of being in the open. He was also aware of mixing up his feelings for Loren with her sorrow. Her loss was what was most paramount now, not a possible entanglement between them.

"It's such a strange thing," she said tentatively. "Even though we were in a relationship for ten years and I really loved him, I feel quite numb about him dying."

Jack nodded, encouraging her to continue.

"He was the love of my life. I'd never fallen for someone so strongly before. We were so good for each other – well, to start with. I didn't think anything would split us apart." She paused. "And now he's gone." She sighed, her eyes watering.

Jack pulled out some tissues from his pocket. His face showed real concern as he handed one to her.

She took it, tapping the corners of her eyes gently. "Thank you… I'm not sure how to feel, you know. We had some great times, but also some really awful ones. They sort of balance each other up. I really hated him for a while there, when he just left us high and dry, as he went after one busty bimbo after another."

She took a breath.

"He just ignored us for years. I could have killed him," she exclaimed, raising her fists in the air. "It wasn't me so much that I was worried about, but Luke and Taylor. You know, Taylor didn't really have anything to do with him until a couple of years ago." She paused momentarily. "Poor sweetheart, she grew up thinking her poppa was her father!"

She stopped, shaking her head. It soon dropped gently on his shoulder. She didn't want to move from this position. She was safe by this man's side, his gentle and tender concern for her warming her heart.

Two tiny pied flycatchers barely five inches long popped down a few feet away from them, chirping happily, pecking at the ground.

Loren and Jack sat for a few minutes, saying nothing, her head still on his shoulder. Jack was boiling over inside, wanting to let his heart go, but conscious of his responsibilities, and still painfully aware of his years with Sarah. He took her hand in his and rested them on her thigh. His hands were a strange mixture of strength and suppleness, not rough at all, revealing that he exposed them to little physical work.

"What do you think I should do regarding the children?" she asked.

"That's a hard one," Jack started tentatively. "I think it would be best you told them in person and not over the phone. Wouldn't you think so?"

"Yes. Absolutely. I want to see their reactions and be there for them."

"So that really leads to the next question. When should you leave for home?"

"Yes. The big question!" she said firmly but distractedly. She looked out across the grass towards the campus, conflicted.

"Where are your thoughts going with that?"

She turned her face, their eyes meeting. Both felt the spark between them.

'Oh, I don't know, Jack," she started hesitantly. "I know I should probably catch the first plane home, but…" She paused, not sure how to proceed. "But I've found that I feel really strongly for you." She'd said it! Her head dived into the recess of his shoulder, seeking reassurance.

Jack's heart started racing, hearing words he wanted to hear. But also didn't.

"Hmmm… that's a problem then, isn't it?" he said with a pensive smile as he gently lifted her head up.

He continued, "I too feel something for you, Loren." Her

heart skipped a beat. "But we're talking about your kids here, and they are entitled to be told about the death of their father as soon as possible."

"I know, I know. Always so logical and practical, aren't you, Professor Jack?" she said, knocking her right shoulder against his left.

"It's not about logic and practicality," he said, smiling, acknowledging her playfulness. "It's more about what's best for your two kids. They're going to grieve too and need the time to do that."

"I know." She looked away as she said it, knowing Jack was talking sense.

"Do you know anything about the funeral arrangements yet?" he asked.

"No, Mom didn't know anything about that. I presume they'll ship the body back to LA, as that's where all Tom's family is based. That may take a few days," she said, more out of hopefulness than with any degree of certainty.

He smiled back, knowing where her thoughts were heading, "Yeah, it probably will. So the funeral's not going to happen before Monday or Tuesday, then – perhaps later," Jack suggested.

"Yes, that's right. I'm booked to fly out lunchtime Saturday, I think, and I arrive back in LA sometime early evening. So I could tell Luke and Taylor when I get home then."

"I guess that's one option!"

"And the other one is to go home now, right?"

Jack nodded his head in affirmation.

Jack looked at his watch. Ten to twelve. He knew he needed to make his way to the lecture theatre.

"Loren, I must go to the group," he said, turning to face her. "I will understand perfectly if you don't join us, and I will let the group know you had a death in the family overnight."

"No, I wanna come to the group," she said. "My team's up second to present. I'd like to at least see what the first group is like and what we are up against. It will also help me switch back into work mode."

"Remember, there's a thirty-minute break between presentations."

"Good. A last-minute chance to prepare my final sales hook," she said, laughing.

"So this means you're not going home this afternoon, then?"

"I guess not. I'll phone Mom and Marcie after my group is finished and discuss it with them."

"Sure. Good idea." Jack got to his feet. "I'd be happy to discuss the pros and cons of your options after you've made those calls, if you like?"

"Yes, I would like that very much," she said as she joined him standing.

They stood barely an inch apart. He looked into her blue eyes and then down at her supple lips. He was so tempted to kiss her. But he resisted the urge and stepped back.

"I must fly," he said, walking past her. "I'll see you in class shortly."

He started running up the dirt steps of the auditorium before she could respond.

She watched him scale the steps two at a time, and then turned back. The two birds were now only five feet away from her, nuzzling into each other. She smiled, thinking how cute they looked.

She turned and started walking up the stepped path, leaving the lovebirds the quiet of the stage all to themselves.

Sydney

"Heavenly Father, we bring before you Louise's son, Jack," a lady prayed. She was sitting on a couch, eyes closed, head bowed, holding Louise Haines' hand, whilst six other women sat nearby joining in prayer. "Thank you that Jack knows you, and thank you that you continue to heal his heart since the January disaster. It rocked his faith, but you are faithful, Father, continuing to answer our prayers for him."

She smiled and raised her head. "Protect him, oh God, and lead him not into temptation and deliver him from the evil one. This we ask in Jesus' name."

"Amen," the ladies all said in unison.

"He's going to be all right, Louise," said the one who'd prayed, giving Louise a tight squeeze.

"Thank you, Sheila, and all of you, for joining me in this vigil," Louise replied.

"So, same time tomorrow night, then?" said another, standing to her feet, looking ready to leave.

"Yes, if it's still not inconvenient?" Louise replied.

"Don't be silly, Louise! You've always been the first to start the prayer chain for the rest of us when something goes wrong," the one standing said. "Well then, be blessed, ladies, till tomorrow night."

Chapter 23

Paris, same day

Zhou was headed out of the city of lovers, having rented another car. This time, something really flash: a silver 3.2-liter Porsche Boxster. The roof was down, the air rushing through his ebony unkempt locks added to the exhilaration as he pushed the car past 100 miles per hour on the motorway. He'd recently come to love fast cars; the thrill of speed helped him relax, if only momentarily. All the murder and destruction that he had been responsible for never left him. It bubbled under the surface constantly. Sometimes he could put a lid on it, but not for long.

It would haunt him forever, he knew.

At his current rate he would make Fontainebleau by six, leaving three hours before he met up with Jack Haines at Insead. As he reduced his speed, he noted in his rear-vision mirror the black SUV that had been trailing him since he left Paris. It had managed to keep up with him even when he was racing at his current speed, but had never gotten closer than a couple of hundred yards or so.

He was naturally suspicious. He had to be now. He'd killed three of his employer's hired hands and figured it was only a matter of time before it was his turn.

Thick forest now appeared on either side of the two-lane motorway. The road straightened, so he took the car into fifth and took it beyond 120 miles per hour.

The SUV had picked up speed too and was staying within the 200-yard gap that it had maintained throughout the entire journey. Zhou was surprised that it was able to keep up. He pushed the Porsche to 140 and then on to 150 as it hummed down the straight road.

After five miles he noticed the SUV was no longer in his rear vision.

"Huh, not fast enough to keep up, hey?" he said aloud.

Andola saw it first.

A roadblock.

Three cars – two marked police cars and one other. A black SUV, not unlike the one that had been following Zhou.

Of greater interest was the demonic cloud that hovered over the cars.

She dropped onto the passenger seat and spoke into Zhou's mind: *Time to turn around.*

Zhou soon saw it too. On the horizon. Something on the road.

"Time to turn around," he said, smashing down through the gears into second, sweeping left, frantically bumping across the grass median strip dividing the motorway. He floored the accelerator as he set off in the opposite direction.

"Blast, they've seen me!" he said, scanning his mirrors. "Go, baby, go!"

He pushed the speedster to maximum revs as the two police cars shot off after him.

Exit just ahead, Andola said, having scanned ahead.

Zhou saw it too, adjacent to the motorway – a large industrial park running alongside the exit road.

"Think, Zhou, think!" he said as he immediately came to a divide in the exit road.

Right! said Andola.

He veered right, the first pursuing police vehicle coming into view in his rear-vision mirror, quickly followed by the second, both with sirens blaring.

Hard right, nowww!

His right tires screamed in protest as he flew around the corner heading south again, on a main road that ran parallel to the motorway.

He knew going to Fontainebleau was no longer an option, as they would be waiting there for him.

"Got to get off these main roads, or else they'll haul me down."

Andola had one hand on his shoulder. *Stay calm, Zhou.*

He kept one eye on his mirrors, whilst overtaking three cars in one stretch.

"Yesss!" he yelled as a semi-trailer passed going north, momentarily stopping the pursuers from overtaking.

"Oh, blast!" He saw the lead vehicle come past the last car, all three having pulled onto the shoulder of the road on hearing the sirens.

He then rapidly approached a large roundabout.

Third exit, Zhou!

"Oh, thank you, Lord!" Zhou whispered, seeing a sign for the Seine River crossing.

He didn't slow, roaring through the roundabout, ignoring the honking horns, and jumped into the exit.

But the pursuers didn't slow down either.

He charged over the bridge.

Hard right, again! Andola encouraged Zhou, leaping into the air, her wings unfurled as she darted ahead of the Porsche, looking for an escape route.

"Ahhh!" He clipped the curb, bouncing back onto the road, as he raced south down a country-style road, the Seine a few feet to his right and forest on his left.

"Now this is looking better." The road ahead was clear of cars. He floored the accelerator, scanning left, looking for an opening of some description.

The lead pursuit car was hot on his heels. He caught sight of the passenger reaching out of the window, a pistol aimed directly at him.

PING!

"Blast!" Zhou yelped, ducking as a bullet ricocheted off the back of his headrest, a second crashing through his passenger windscreen.

One bend, a second bend, and then a third slowed the police cars slightly, giving him a fifty-yard lead.

Then he saw it.

He flew left onto a narrow paved road, then did a hard right, and then a left, the roofs of country estates bursting out of the thick forest on either side of the rural lanes.

Left, Zhou, quickly! Andola said, hovering directly above him.

An electronic gate closing, tall thick hedges either side of a driveway. Instinctively he shot diagonally across the road, slipped through the gap where the gate was going and stopped abruptly behind the hedge.

Andola stood at the driveway entrance, wings fully extended, shining brilliantly, reflecting off the now closed metallic gate.

The two police cars shot past, oblivious to the fact that they had just passed the driveway entrance to the most desired country estate in the area.

"Phhhewww!" Zhou's heart was beating fast as he listened to the sirens wail past his hiding spot. "Thank you, Lord, thank you." He closed his eyes and leant his head on the steering wheel.

Time to go, he heard in his mind. *They'll be back soon enough.*

He stretched as he got out of the car. He was in a hidden alcove, not able to see the house, which he hoped meant any of its occupants couldn't see him. He grabbed his bag and set off at a run alongside the hedge. He knew he needed to get as far away from the house as possible so he wouldn't be seen. He crossed the extensive garden and jumped into the forest, and hoped to find somewhere he could lie low and work out what to do.

Brussels, that night

"What do you mean, he escaped?" Grosch yelled through his cell phone.

He was in his office, scanning the news channels on the large wall-mounted television. He listened to the caller for a few moments, then cut them short.

"I don't care for any of your limp excuses. I'll have a chopper sent over to help in the search… Yeah, I know it's getting dark. It's almost dark here in Brussels too, but we can't wait till tomorrow to find him. He could be halfway round the world by then… The chopper has spotlights which will light up the countryside… Just tell them you're looking for your prized cow that's gone missing… Do I have to do all the thinking for you? Call me as soon as you have him!"

Grosch snapped the phone off. He stood a moment, composing himself.

The Insead campus

It was all very quiet around the administration building. The majority of the workers had left for the day, leaving just three night-shift cleaners.

Zhou was thirty minutes late.

Jack was sitting on the front steps leading up to the building. The sun had been replaced by a half-moon and a large mass of stars.

He pulled his phone out of his pocket. No missed calls, no messages, nothing.

I should've gotten his number!

Perhaps he'd changed his mind. Or got lost?

Darius nudged his spirit: *He's in trouble, Jack.*

Jack sensed a need to pray:

"Almighty and loving Father, for some reason you've put Zhou on my heart. Protect him, oh God, surround him with your angels and keep him safe from all the wiles of the enemy. I also pray that you may soften his heart towards you. May Zhou recall some of those great chats we had about you and faith. Please give him a revelation of who you are – his great loving Creator – and may he choose to turn to you. In Jesus' name I pray. Amen."

Jack made a call. It was busy, so he left a message.

"Loren, Jack. Hey, great job this afternoon. I was very proud of you. Call me when you're free!"

He got up and walked off into the night.

The forest north of Fontainebleau

Andola and her colleagues heard it at the same time. Many sets of wings, fast approaching.

Zhou was hunched over, his hands on his knees. He was contemplating entering a stretch of thick deciduous forest. He was exhausted, having been on the run for well over four hours.

Andola and another angelguard shot down from the sky, directly for the gap between two large beech trees. Their incredible speed swept away the mass of leaves and other forest debris that sat dormant on the ground.

Zhou scanned the forest wall and then saw a small opening that might give him a hiding place, at least so he could rest for a bit.

He made his way between two large thick trees but found the trail only went in ten feet or so. Then it was a solid maze of twisted vines and thick underbrush.

He turned to go back but heard a sound. He froze. He held his breath.

What was that? Footsteps? It sure sounded like it.

THUMP-THUMP-THUMP!

Andola knew exactly what that meant: demons directly overhead.

Zhou squinted through the darkness, trying to catch any movement.

The sound stopped. All was quiet and very still. Incredibly still.

He pushed through the foliage, ignoring the scratches of the branches attacking his face and upper body.

One of the thick beech trees had a large opening in its trunk, providing a form of shelter for him. He knelt down and crawled into its girth, finding it completely concealed him.

And just in time.

* * *

The last demon sentinel had seen a flash of light coming from a small opening in the forest below. He fell off from the rest of the company to investigate.

He landed on the trail where Zhou had stood moments before. He noticed the gap in the hedge.

A scraping sound, leaves being moved.

There it was again. Very close, through that gap.

And then he smelt it. The distinct smell of a human. There was someone in there.

And who'd be the hero, who'd get all the credit for finding the fugitive?

He crouched, putting his head forward between the two large trees.

He didn't see it coming. A brilliant flash of light blinded him as the razor-sharp edge of Andola's mighty sword came down on the back of his neck. He disintegrated before hitting the ground.

* * *

Zhou, completely unaware of what had just taken place in the supernatural, thought to himself what a good spot he'd found. He could rest for the next hour while the sun finished its descent, allowing him to go into the night and somehow find his way back to the French capital.

He sat hunched, his knees up to his chest, arms around his shins. He noticed the coolness of the forest for the first time.

His heartbeat was slowing after the frenetic pace of the past few hours. His eyes closed as his head leant into the bowels of the tree that was his hiding place.

Sleep came over him.

* * *

Loren was in her room. She'd just finished a forty-minute conversation with her mom.

Huh, a missed call.

She put the phone to her ear to listen to the message.

Her heart jumped as she heard Jack's voice.

"Loren, Jack. Hey, great job this afternoon. I was very proud of you. Call me when you're free!"

She immediately called him.

"Jack Haines."

"Hello, Jack Haines. Loren Summers here."

"Hello, Loren Summers. Just wanted to see how you were doing and to tell you you did a great job today, especially considering all the emotional turmoil you're going through."

"Thanks, Jack, appreciate it. I'm doing OK right at this moment. Had a good long chat with my mom and I'm just about to call Marcie. Um, I haven't eaten. Have you, by any chance?"

"Ah, no, I was just going to get some room service back in my room. I'm a sucker for a good BLT and have wanted to try the one on the menu since I've been here."

"Um, you wouldn't want some company?" Loren asked with a large dollop of hope in her voice.

Jack didn't immediately know how to respond. His heart was yelling at him to say yes, while his head was gently warning him against it. He surprised himself when he finally responded: "Ah, Loren, I'd really love to, but tomorrow's going to be a big day and I'm pretty tired after last night. I think I need to have an early night. Sorry."

Her heart sank a little. "I understand, Professor." She paused. "Probably best I do likewise. An early night would do me good too!" That final comment didn't make her feel any better. She didn't want to be alone; she could feel her positiveness ebbing away.

There was an awkward silence, neither knowing what else to say, both disappointed with the outcome.

"Loren, call me if you need someone to talk to. Please, anytime, even if it's two in the morning."

She smiled. He's not rejecting me; he's got a job to do.

"OK, thanks. I appreciate that, Jack."

"Well, good night. I hope you have a good night's sleep."

"Yeah, you too. Nighty-night."

The frown on her forehead confirmed her disappointment. Sadness pricked her heart. She felt alone. Her stomach shrank, her chest tightened, her breathing quickened.

"No, no, no, I don't want this any more, I want some answers," Loren said aloud as she gripped her cell phone, looking for Marcie's number, completely oblivious to Arlia standing over her, wings outstretched.

She found Marcie's number and clicked on it.

"Hello, Marcie speaking."

"Hi, Marce. Loz here."

"Hey kiddo, how ya doin'?"

"Um… I'm… ah…" Her lips were quivering as she tried to hold it all in. "Oh, Marce…" The first tears broke through.

"Oh, sweetheart, it's OK, I'm here," Marcie said, hearing Loren weeping. "Tell me what's going on."

"Ah, Marce… tell me about Jesus," Loren said firmly, wiping the tears away as she regained some control.

That wasn't what Marcie was expecting. She'd been waiting for her best friend to ask her that for more years than she could remember, and now here they were, on different continents. It brought tears to her eyes. And to Arlia's.

Thank you, Jesus. Please fill my mouth with the words you want me to say.

They chatted for the next hour, Marcie doing most of the talking while Loren asked a lot of questions. They had covered most of it a number of times before, but it was different now. Loren now had a yearning, a desire to know Jesus. She wasn't sure why, but now was the time.

"How do I let Jesus into my life, Marce?"

"You just ask him."

"It's that simple?"

"Yep, sure is."

"What do I say?"

"How about I say a prayer for you. And you repeat it after me?"

"I'd like that, Marce."

Both of them were trembling with anticipation. Marcie was excited about seeing Loren accept Jesus into her life, knowing how incredible her new life was going to be. Loren was fearful about stepping out into the unknown, but was ready and willing to see what lay ahead. Arlia stood calmly over Loren, her eyes and giant arms pointed heavenward.

"You ready, Loz?"

"Sure am, let's do it!"

"Dear God in heaven," Marcie said, and Loren repeated it quietly.

"I confess Jesus is the Son of God." Marcie paused while Loren repeated the statement. "I ask Jesus to come into my life.

Jesus, I choose to surrender my life to you. Cleanse me from all my sin. Help me to follow you. Fill me with the Holy Spirit. I renounce Satan and his evil ways." Loren repeated each of these statements.

"Thank you, Jesus, for loving me." Arlia heard Loren say these words, tears streaming down both of their faces. "Thank you that tonight I am saved."

Marcie could hear Loren quietly crying.

"That's it, Loz! Jesus is now your Lord and the Holy Spirit is in your heart."

Loren couldn't speak. The emotion within her heart was so overwhelming. But this was different to anything she'd felt recently. She was exhilarated, excited, happy. A burden had just been lifted from her shoulders.

"Are you still with me, Loz?"

"Yes, Marce, I'm right here. Wow, that feels good," Loren replied, wiping her tears away whilst Arlia was dancing a little jig in the kitchenette. "If I'd known it would be this good I would have done it years ago," she chuckled.

"Oh, Loz, I'm so proud of you, and so excited! Come home immediately so Bec and I can start sharing everything with you."

"Yeah, maybe I should."

"Um, what's stopping you, Loz? I expected you'd be halfway home by now."

"Ah, there's only the one day of the program left and according to Mom, the funeral's been set for Tuesday afternoon, so I can come home as scheduled. What do you think?"

"Makes sense, I guess," Marcie pondered.

"So you don't think I'm being a terrible mother not rushing home to tell Tayls and Luke their father has died?"

"Under the circumstances, Loren, no, I don't think so."

"Thanks, Marce. Mom had similar thoughts."

Loren's phone beeped in her ear.

"Marce, I've got very little battery left. I better go."

"No wonder, we've been talking for almost ninety minutes. Hey babe, I'm really proud of you and I love you very much.

And more importantly, Jesus loves you. Be strong and let's talk tomorrow."

"OK, thanks for being there for me tonight. It means so much to me, how much you love and care for me."

Her phone beeped again.

"Love you, Marce. Give the kids a big hug..." The phone died. "Blast!"

Chapter 24

Zhou awoke startled, surrounded by darkness.

Where am I?

He quickly remembered.

5:30. Wow, I slept a long time. Too long.

THWOCK-THWOCK-THWOCK.

Helicopter. He knew that sound.

He gingerly stepped out of his hiding place within the tree-trunk, stretching his thin frame before inclining his head towards the track he'd been on last night. On hearing nothing, he pushed through the undergrowth, leaping onto the track.

He gathered by the chirping of birds that it was near daybreak. The forest floor was still shrouded in sepia light.

"Which way?" he said aloud. "Left or right?"

I need my GPS.

He turned his phone on.

Blast! No coverage.

"Lucky, that," said Andola to her colleague as they stood either side of Zhou. "We don't need Grosch's people to identify your location just yet, young man."

The other angel simply nodded in acknowledgment.

"The helicopter will make its next pass shortly. So we need to stay off the beaten track for a little while longer."

"What's the plan for the day, Andola?" the other asked.

"To get to a small town called Melun by nightfall. It's a bit over six miles from here, so he'll do it easily, but we need to guide him so he stays unnoticed. That's going to be the hard part."

Andola put a hand on Zhou's shoulder, encouraging him to move forward.

"What about the enemy, Andola?"

"Well, our little diversion should keep them busy for a while, but they'll be back. Grindor's marshaling a troop above us and will keep watch."

Straight ahead, then, I guess. Zhou started off.

Brussels. Friday morning. a few hours later

"He'll turn up," Grosch said over the speaker of his office phone. He was always in the office early.

"Sir, you sound in good spirits this morning, may I say?" The youthful voice had a Flemish accent similar to Grosch's.

Grosch ignored him. "I had a good look at the satellite map last night, and with those reinforcements landing this morning, he won't be able to break through our grasp. These men have never failed us before."

"Good, sir. Can he cause us any real trouble, anyway?"

"How do you mean, son?"

"Well, we know the code, and he doesn't know you're in charge, does he?"

"Certainly, we have that in our favor. Zhou's a very, very smart young man and I'm not sure what he does and doesn't know. That's what concerns me most. I always prefer to eliminate any unknowns. Particularly when there is so much at stake. Take that as a lesson."

"I will, sir."

"Keep me posted, son. Goodbye."

Fontainebleau. Friday

"Mayer did a great job convincing me there was a deal going." Malone and Jack were having breakfast at a café on Rue Royale, fifteen minutes from the university.

"He indicated he'd been employed by the acquirer to make it happen and furnished me with quite explicit details of who the parties were. But he swore me to secrecy, and as part of my reward for staying silent, I would be made CEO of the new venture. About six months ago he indicated the deal had hit a hitch in that the acquirer was short on funds. That got us thinking that I could help make the deal possible. I know how stupid and foolish it all sounds now, and I can't believe that my absolute lust for power overrode any semblance of sanity. I know it was madness." He sighed unhappily. "I will have to accept the consequences of my actions."

Jack was looking across the table at a man now so different to the one he had met a little over a week ago. Then he was cocksure, arrogant, proud and boastful, his demeanor fitting perfectly into the black Zegna power suit he wore. All he saw now was a broken man. Here was a man who had seen his future flash before his eyes and then, just as suddenly, vanish.

"Have the NYPD called you yet?" Jack asked.

"No, why would they?"

"Mayer's death. I would imagine they would want to talk with any close friends and business associates, of which you are one."

"Yes, yes, of course!" Malone sounded a little frightened.

He changed the subject as he polished off his final mouthful of bacon.

"A strange thing happened to Candice and me last Sunday…" He stopped, wanting to see if Jack was interested in listening to it.

"When you were in the French Riviera?"

"Yes. We were driving back to our guest-house up in the lower Alps around ten at night, when a bulldozer came out of nowhere and promptly pushed our rental car, with us in it, off the road and down the escarpment!"

"Wow! How did you survive?"

"Well, that's one of many unanswered questions. We just don't know. We woke up outside the front door of… of all places, an old-fashioned convent!"

"Gee, this story is getting better and better!"

"Sister Christine, who cared for us, after hearing our story, explained our miraculous survival as the work of angels! Can you imagine that, angels?"

"As a matter of fact I can imagine that, and believe it to be very possible."

"Really?" Malone said, almost under his breath. "So you think that such things exist, then?"

"Absolutely. They are God's warriors in the never-ending battle against the hordes of demons."

Darius and Landen both smiled.

"Right. Each to their own, I guess," Malone said, looking bemused.

"What do you mean by that, Ray?"

"I believe in God, absolutely, fate and all that. Candice is still having trouble coming to grips with it all. She can't get out of bed. The doctors say she is suffering from a deep traumatic shock."

"I'm sorry, Ray. Is there anything the university can do to help?"

"No, thank you. Just make sure she gets home safely."

"What, won't she be going home with you?" Jack caught Malone's strange comment.

"Yes, yes, we're leaving tomorrow around lunchtime."

Malone had finished his large breakfast, looked at his watch and got to his feet. "I must get back to check on Candice before this morning's class."

"Oh, all right then," Jack said, surprised at Malone's abruptness.

"Let me get the check, Ray."

"No, no, I'll get it on my way out. Thank you. And thank you for listening."

"Pleasure." Jack stood to shake Ray's hand. "See you in an hour or so."

Malone appeared to be in some sort of daze.

"Are you all right, Ray?"

"Yes, yes, never been better."

"OK, see you shortly."

Ray acknowledged Jack with a slight smile.

Jack sat, flagging one of the waitresses down.

"*Oui, monsieur,* how can I assist you?"

"Another espresso, thank you."

"Certainly, sir, I'll arrange that for you straight away."

Jack looked to his right and saw Malone walking past the café, dragging his feet. There was no vibrancy or spark in his step, no urgency. He looked forlorn, completely lost and defeated.

Jack quietly prayed for Malone as he waited for his coffee.

* * *

Malone didn't return to his hotel. He never had any intention of doing so. Prior to leaving Candice, he had kissed her goodbye whilst she slept.

He was surprised how easy it had been for him to purchase what he wanted. Even in this tiny village. Amazing how, in every town, there was some low-life that could fulfill your every need, no matter how right or wrong it may be.

And all for a lousy thousand bucks.

He set off south down Rue Royale in the direction of the Chateau, his demon watchers now reunited with him. They were going to really enjoy this – the moment of triumph, their victory. Agramon would be pleased.

If he did this right, Malone reasoned, it would take them days, even weeks to find him.

* * *

"Everything in place for Zhou's chance meeting tonight?" Tagan asked.

"Yes, sir, all in readiness," Athaniel replied.

They had taken refuge in a vacant country house not far from Zhou's present location.

"So we need Andola and her troop to keep him out of Grosch's hands for twelve hours or so," Athaniel continued.

"Easier said than done, I suggest," Tagan replied. "Bacchazar's cronies won't give an inch."

"Andola's crew is large enough to provide sufficient protection."

"Let's pray they do, Athaniel."

* * *

Zhou knelt away from the open track, forehead resting on the trunk of one of the thick beech trees common to this forest.

Andola and her partner had led Zhou stealthily through the

heart of the forest, staying well away from all roads, lanes, and houses. The chopper had hovered close on a few occasions, but they were able to find a place to hide each time. In the short time she had spent with him, Andola had seen innate goodness in him. Yes, he had suffered much and he had allowed himself to become consumed with evil thoughts, succumbing to the basest of all human natural tendencies. She knew he could be won back, won for good. And she intended to make it happen.

He thought about his future. He ignored the fact it might be cut short in a matter of hours. He knew Grosch wouldn't let him go. Zhou couldn't imagine how such a man could live without trusting anybody.

He imagined living in the rolling hills of New Zealand. The Otago basin in the south or the Bay of Islands in the far north – he couldn't decide. He would buy a farm and raise some cattle, sheep and perhaps goats. Grow organic vegetables as well. Become part of a small community. Join the community progress association or council or whatever they called it. He now wanted to do something with his life, help people for a change rather than kill innocents.

If he could avoid prison, of course. How, he wasn't sure, but he would do everything he could. First, he had to survive Grosch.

He could feel the emotion rising within his heart. He didn't know where it was coming from. Since the day he buried his family he had only felt pure rage, pure hatred, seeking revenge for those he had lost. But this feeling wasn't new – he recognized it. It had been growing with every job. He could give it a name now: remorse.

His phone vibrated in his pocket.

Coverage… finally.

The number was blocked from showing on the screen. *What the heck?*

"Hello."

"Hello, Zhou," the caller replied.

"Who is this?"

"You don't need to know my name. Think of me as someone concerned for your welfare."

"Ah, my employer, I take it," Zhou replied. He'd heard the voice before.

"Employer – indeed, yes, that I am. But I'm not used to insubordination from my employees."

"A road block, then shot at? Is that any way to treat an employee… sir?"

"You know I've done far worse. In fact, you've even helped me in some of my… how you would say… reprimands?"

"'Punishments' is a more appropriate word, I'd suggest."

"Yes." There was a short pause. "I'm tired of having my resources tied up trying to find you in that blasted forest. So here's my one-time offer. I call the men off your trail and we meet tonight in Fontainebleau."

"What, so you can kill me yourself?" Zhou said, aghast.

"Why would I want to do that? You are a valuable employee. I'm sure I will continue to be able to find good use for your skills in the future."

"And what future may that be, sir?"

"We don't have time for that now, but I would be delighted to share some of my plans with you tonight."

The two angels looked on suspiciously.

"You do realize that in a forest like this the cell-phone base station triangulation won't give you any greater clarity as to my present location, if that's the true purpose of this call?"

"Ah, yes, I do appreciate that, Zhou. I am sincere in my offer."

"Why, Mr. Grosch…" Zhou gulped. "I hope you don't mind if I address you by your name?"

"'Sir' will do fine," the caller stung back without a pause.

Hmmm. Zhou wasn't convinced.

"So, last chance. Fontainebleau tonight, or I'll send in the dogs." More menace now.

"I'll take my chances with your dogs, Mr. Grosch," Zhou replied and promptly hung up.

"Great response, Zhou," Andola cheered, giving her partner a friendly thump on the back.

"And so what do you think the enemy will do next, Andola?"

"Not sure, but we're definitely going to have our hands full."

***

"Silly, silly boy!" Grosch fumed, smashing his hand on his expensive desk. "I was tempted to let you off, but no longer. You will die along with all the others."

Two other beings, unseen by Grosch, were similarly unimpressed by Zhou's response.

"Volkyre, get the message out to unleash all the local demons in the vicinity of Melun and to engage any of the heavenly host on sight," Bacchazar demanded.

"It shall be done, sir!" The smaller demon walked through the wall, his wings unfurling.

Bacchazar stood behind Grosch, sneering. "It's time to die, Zhou Chau."

Grosch sniggered as he contemplated his next move.

***

Jack rushed out the door of his apartment, arms full of luggage. He was heading home. To his girls.

For some reason he thought of Zhou.

He was in trouble. He knew it. And God was calling Jack to pray for him. Right now.

He stopped in his tracks, leant face first against the wall next to his door and started to pray.

"Father, please protect Zhou. He's in trouble and you've put him on my heart. I ask for your protective hand to come over him. Please protect him from his pursuers, whoever they may be, natural and/or supernatural. May you cover him with your breastplate of righteousness, keeping him safe from the arrows of the evil one. And please – put a desire in Zhou to know you. Amen."

Darius stood nearby, watching in admiration.

***

Zhou heard the barking.

Blast! Didn't think he meant real dogs!

"Four of them, Andola." It was Grindor, who'd dropped from the tops of the trees. "No more than a mile in front of you. Two headed east and two coming straight for you."

"Thanks, Grindor. You handle the two going east. Jolane and I will deal with the two coming this way."

Grindor shot back up to the treetops.

"Jolane, you know what to do when they arrive."

"Sure do, no problem. Love dogs, especially big ones."

Zhou was panicking. *Think, think!*

He looked up. His only chance. They'd have his scent. He knew he couldn't outrun a police dog.

Great, a tree with low branches!

He leapt onto the lowest branch, only four feet off the ground, and started climbing. He'd done a lot of gymnastics as a kid and fortunately still had the nimbleness and flexibility to move rapidly up the tree.

Andola followed him, whilst Jolane went straight for the bend in the track seventy feet ahead.

Two muscular German shepherds came racing around the bend, baring their teeth menacingly. They had the scent.

Stop, Zhou, Andola said.

Zhou stopped climbing. He saw the two dogs charging for the tree.

They suddenly stopped in their tracks, twenty feet away. They both sat obediently, heads raised, waiting for instruction.

Their handlers soon arrived, confused, seeing the dogs sitting. Commands were spoken firmly in French, but the two dogs didn't respond.

The handlers, puzzled, conversed animatedly.

The dogs suddenly bolted off, straight past Zhou's tree, and the surprised handlers ran off after them.

Moments later, Jolane arrived in the tree.

"Told you I love dogs. They're so obedient – especially to high-pitched instructions the human ear can't hear."

Andola simply chuckled.

That's sure weird! Zhou thought, a perplexed expression on his face.

Time to go, my friend, Andola spoke to his heart.

Zhou commenced the downward climb.

Chapter 25

Paris, Charles de Gaulle Airport

Jack hung up the phone and put it in his jacket pocket.

"That was Thierry," he announced to Loren, who was sitting opposite him in the airport club lounge. "Confirming it's all OK for us to stay at their place tonight."

Loren didn't immediately respond. Her mind was distracted. What was she doing, going to London, with this man she hardly knew? He had surprised her, and himself, by inviting her, out of the blue, to join him in London. But she so wanted to spend time with him.

"It's not alright, then?"

"Yep, it's great, Jack," she said finally.

"They're going out tonight, to their Bible study group, and won't be back till late. We'll head out, find a nice little restaurant and have a great time."

"That sounds lovely."

"Now tell me more about last night," Jack said eagerly.

* * *

"He's still definitely in the forest, sir," said the voice on the speakerphone. It was the same one as earlier that morning.

"Thanks, Vincent. How can you be sure?" Grosch replied.

"He just made a phone call in the vicinity."

"And?"

"Looks like he called the same number as he did the other night. The one in Fontainebleau," Vincent said.

"A call for help, I expect."

"The terminating cell was in Paris, Charles de Gaull Airport."

"Hmmm. Trace his calls, get transcripts if you can. Time we found out a little more about this Jack Haines."

"Will do, sir. Haines just received a call from London. Perhaps that's where he's headed?"

"Find out. He isn't going to be much good to our Chinese friend there, is he?" Grosch smiled. "Get to it, Vincent. I want to know everything I can about Haines."

***

"Hey, Stephen, I can't talk now. I'm on a plane and it's about to take off. I'll call you when I land."

"Hang on, Jack, I've spoken to the NYPD about Mayer. They're going to call you!"

"OK," he said, pausing in thought. "How'd it go with the po—"

"Excuse me, sir, we are about to take off. Please switch your phone off," said a female flight steward, leaning over Loren to pick up his empty pre-flight drink glass.

Jack nodded in her direction.

"Bro', I've got to go. Sorry. Are you OK?"

"Yes… I think," came the reply.

"Talk to you later."

Jack hung up and switched his phone off.

"Is there a problem, Jack?" Loren asked.

"No… just my brother from New York," he said distractedly.

Jack sat back in his roomy business-class seat, his chest tightening as a wave of nausea threatened to rise in his throat.

He closed his eyes as he assumed his standard breathing-exercise regime that brought relief to his anxiety. He prayed quietly as the 737 taxied to the runway.

God, please keep Stephen safe from any injustice or harm. Please also keep me safe. May I not fear what lies ahead but just be open and honest with the police. Amen.

Jack so wanted to tell Loren everything, but knew he couldn't just yet, especially now that he was going to be questioned by the NYPD. The last thing he wanted was for her to get caught up in all this Malone and Mayer mess.

"I had a call from the NYPD this afternoon," Loren announced out of the blue.

"Really? What did they say?"

"It was a very courteous discussion. A Detective Tony Saba-something or other, I've forgotten, called to inform me that no one has come forward with any information regarding Tom's accident, nor have there been any witnesses, so they are treating his death as suspicious. He doesn't have any evidence yet, but suggested Tom may have been murdered."

"Really? *Murdered?*"

"Yes," she said, frowning. "He asked me if I knew of anyone who didn't like Tom or if any deals he'd been involved in may have gone bad."

"And what did you say?"

"I told him the truth. I explained we had had little to do with each other since our divorce and didn't discuss his business. I wasn't aware of any enemies he had while we were still married. He seemed satisfied with my response."

"That's good."

Neither said anything for a few moments.

"Amazing to think that Tom may have been murdered!" she said, still shocked. "Who would want to do that?!"

Jack touched her forearm tenderly.

"I know this is hard. The last thing you need at this time is a murder investigation. But they'll find the culprit and he'll get put behind bars for many, many years."

"Yes, I hope they find them soon," she said with an awkward smile.

"It's going to be OK, Loren."

Melun, north of Fontainebleau, Friday night

A storm was brewing in the sky above. The chill that typically ushers in rain was penetrating Zhou's sweat-soaked shirt.

He had made his way into a small town. He steered clear of its center, rather focusing on the adjoining side streets.

Nightfall had arrived. It would be easier to conceal himself.
Wow, a bustling metropolis!

The narrow two-way street he entered was only three small blocks long and completely without life. Everything appeared shut for the day. After-hours trading hadn't reached here yet, he figured.

Four street-lamps, two on either side, dimly lit the street, giving him sufficient visibility to explore his surroundings. All the buildings were very old but still in relatively good condition. The first building he passed had been converted into what looked like the local delicatessen, with a small bank (no ATM) next door, and then an even smaller post office.

SWAT! SLASH!

Andola disposed of two dark urchins following Zhou. She then joined Jolane on a rooftop across the street. Jolane was scanning the horizon for any more of Bacchazar's henchmen. Fast approaching from the north-west was a flying creature, not of the supernatural kind, but of the mechanized man-made kind: a helicopter. A fog light illuminated a large area in front of it.

Zhou heard it too. The THWOCK-THWOCK-THWOCK of chopper blades. He saw the bright light first. He couldn't see any obvious places to hide, no doorways to escape into, nor alleyways. The hairs on the back of his neck rose abruptly as a feeling of dread hit him deep within his stomach. He couldn't see any escape, any way of avoiding the fast-approaching light that would reveal him to his pursuers.

The angelic duo saw his predicament.

Zhou ran through the shadows of the building fronts to make some distance between himself and the chopper, but he knew he couldn't outrun it. He came to the third and last block, the edge of the light moving closer and closer to him.

It's useless! Zhou thought. *I'm a goner!*

His heart was beating so rapidly. Every breath he took burnt the back of his throat.

He leant up against a solid wooden door on the last building, resigned to his fate. The chopper hovered at the top end of the street with a high-beam spotlight stretching half a mile, canvassing every square foot of the area.

The beam was only ten feet away from him. *Should I make a run for it, as they've still gotta land the chopper?*

Blast! Following the chopper on the ground was a police car. It was moving very slowly, very deliberately, its strong flashlights invading the shadows of each building.

His heart sank. He didn't know what to do.

Oh no! A second police car approached from the opposite end of the street. He was surrounded; the hopelessness of his situation enveloped him. Sweat dripped off his forehead.

Please, God of heaven, save me!

He was violently grabbed from behind... and yanked through the door he was leaning against.

* * *

Dark storm clouds appeared almost out of nowhere, blocking the moon and the few stars in the night sky. Streaks of lightning and cracks of thunder rolled in over the valley, followed immediately by torrents of rain.

The temperature had mysteriously dropped to almost freezing, unheard of in summertime in this neck of the woods.

"He's about to arrive," Tagan announced, watching from the vacant country house.

A sharp lightning-bolt cracked through the forest, illuminating the nearby park momentarily.

"He's just landed!" Tagan's voice had taken on a very somber tone.

* * *

"Shushshsh..." the strange voice said.

The pursuing lights beamed through the windows but sailed over Zhou's body as he sprawled on the floor. His rescuer knelt over him, with one hand over his mouth.

The light passed and darkness returned to the room. Zhou was helped to his feet. He was drenched with sweat and his heart was beating like it was now in his throat. He edged his way to the window.

"Be careful there, my wanted friend," a voice said in good English but with a very heavy French accent.

Zhou turned his head to see who the voice belonged to and in the darkness all he could see was a shock of silver hair, a long beard and sideburns. He wondered if his savior was, indeed, Santa Claus.

He looked back onto the street. The two cars were now facing each other, bumper to bumper, with engines still running. The drivers were out talking to each other and smoking. Light rain could be seen through the glare of headlights. One waved to the chopper idling in the air above. On receiving the signal, it shot off into the night. The drivers climbed back into their respective cars. The one facing away from Zhou reversed, making way for the other to pass, and then completed a U-turn, screeching its tires on the bitumen, to accelerate after its companion.

His heartbeat slowed. He sighed very loudly and dropped to his haunches with relief. They'd gone. He was safe, again. For now, at least.

"Phew, that was close," Andola said to Jolane as they looked in the window from outside.

"Praise be to God, the Lord of all creation. Thank you!" Jolane said in admiration.

They zipped through the walls, curious to meet Zhou's savior.

"Won't be long, Beny," came a man's voice from the shadows.

"No rush, Etienne, but I have a little surprise for you," the silver-bearded one said softly.

Zhou, hearing the voices, got to his feet to greet the man who might well have just saved his life.

"Hello. Thank you so much. I am in your debt!" Zhou said, extending his hand.

The silver-bearded one took it. He too was short, meeting Zhou eye to eye. As they took a moment to measure each other up, Zhou changed his mind as to who the man in front resembled: he was a cross between Santa Claus and one of the guitarists from ZZ Top. His silvery hair was pulled back into a single long ponytail that extended down to the middle of his back. His similarly colored bushy beard extended to his chest. A prominent scar ran across his right cheek while the shape of his nose revealed he had been involved in fights in his past.

"Glad I could be of assistance," the man said.

"I'm Zhou."

"And I am Benoit, or Beny, as my friends, like Etienne here, like to call me."

"Really glad to make your acquaintance, Benoit."

"And who is your new friend here, Beny?" came the voice of Etienne as he appeared out of the shadows. He was holding a candelabra with three tall lit candles that provided an eerie glow in the dark. Through the dim light Zhou could make out he was standing in a bar.

"Etienne, this is Zhou. I pulled him from the street where he looked like he was in some trouble."

"He doesn't look like a troublemaker to me," Etienne replied, shaking Zhou's hand whilst noticing his disheveled appearance.

"Nor to me," Beny said.

Zhou studied the new arrival. Etienne too was a man who looked well into his seventies. He sported long grey hair with small streaks of brown still visible.

"Who were those people chasing you, Zhou?" Beny asked.

"It's a long story and one that, if I told you, you probably wouldn't believe," Zhou responded.

The two elderly gentlemen looked at each other and shrugged their shoulders.

"We are glad to have been of service to you," Beny concluded, seeming resigned to the fact he wouldn't be hearing Zhou's story.

"Are you hungry by any chance, my friend?" Etienne asked.

"You bet! I haven't eaten much these past twenty-four hours."

* * *

"Still no news, huh?" Grosch demanded through his cell phone.

He was standing in the bedroom of his usual Brussels hotel

suite, dressed in a navy-blue silk robe, brown loafers on his feet. His black suit and white business shirt were lying in a heap on the floor at the end of the four-poster king-sized unmade bed. Violet lingerie was on the floor nearby, indicating he had company.

"Time to use my contacts in the Belgian police to get French Special Forces involved," he announced. "Keep at it, Vincent. Goodbye."

There was a firm knock at the slightly open door, and then the face of Marie Verheyen popped through it. Her short ebony hair was freshly brushed.

"Is anything the matter, Leopold?"

"No, everything is just fine," he replied brusquely.

She recoiled slightly but then stepped into the room, wearing a cream silk robe.

"Please… I'll be out soon," Grosch said, calmer and a little more caring. "I just need to make one more call."

"All right, then. I brought you your champagne," she said, a glass in her left hand. She glided up to him, gave him the glass and a peck on the cheek.

"Thank you. Honestly, I won't be long, just a few minutes more."

Ms. Verheyen turned and glided back out of the room, leaving the door as she found it, open slightly. She resumed her position on the other side of the door, listening.

She smiled. Revenge would be very sweet indeed!

* * *

Torrential driving rain battered the modern community hall in the park just outside Melun as a cluster of pitch-black clouds deposited their heavy loads.

Assembled inside was wall-to-wall evil.

The General didn't come alone. He was accompanied by at least 100 sentinels, all baying for the blood of the European Head, Lord Bacchazar.

Bacchazar, supported by only ten, extended his huge frame. All his muscles were tensed, ready for combat.

"Welcome, General," he said almost reverently.

"It pleases me not at all to be here, Bacchazar. I had hoped my presence wouldn't be required until after our victory on Sunday. What news of the fugitive?"

"The search continues unabated. It is only a matter of time before Grosch's men have captured him."

"Really? Do you think the white knights of heaven will give him up so easily?"

"Grosch is a resourceful man," Bacchazar replied with a nonchalant shrug of his shoulders.

"I do recognize your extreme confidence but also wonder if it's just more of your arrogant bravado…" The General was prowling the room, a murmuring of loathing from his army slowly rising. "In fact, I suspect the situation is indeed lost!"

SMACK!

One of Bacchazar's men fell flat to the ground, sending a shudder through the room. A chorus of laughter broke out.

"Silence!" commanded Bacchazar. He was unafraid. He stood tall and confident. "General, it is far from lost. I have a squadron headed north into Paris and one still based in Fontainebleau – the only likely destinations in which Zhou would head. Grosch has now involved the Paris police, which will add weight to the numbers of humans now searching for the fugitive."

"That all sounds very good. And you will be pleased that I have brought some extra assistance for you, as well. All of these that stand with me are here to help in the search. They will be led by another…"

Bacchazar cut him off. "There is no need for additional leadership, General. As I have indicated, all is under my firm control!"

"Well, that's where I beg to differ, and so I have asked… someone… whom you know well to assist our cause."

Bacchazar looked in dismay as one of the General's troops made his way forward to stand alongside him.

"Hello, Bacchazar, I didn't expect to see you again so soon," Agramon said menacingly, his distinctive black eyes, tinged with red, boring into his foe.

Chapter 26

London

Jack awoke from a deep sleep to the "You'll never walk alone" ringtone on his cell phone.

"Stephen, what's up?" he said groggily.

"Ah, Professor Haines, it's not Stephen… it's Zhou Chau!"

"Zhou! Why are you calling me so late? It's…" Jack looked at his watch, "… it's one o'clock in the morning!"

"I know, Professor, and I'm very sorry for calling you at this time, but I need your help." Jack heard the panic in his voice.

"Hang on, Zhou, just a minute. First I'd like to know why you didn't make our appointment on Thursday night."

"It's a long story, Professor, but to cut to the chase – I'm in some serious trouble. They're going to kill me, sir, unless I can get away. Honestly, they will. I'm really scared and I didn't know who to turn to but you."

"Whoa! Wow! Hey, Zhou, slow down there, mate. Perhaps we should start at the beginning. You've got my attention."

For the next hour Zhou offloaded his incredible story, giving Jack a full rundown since he'd left Sydney last year to attend to his massacred family. A warring Chinese triad had mistaken Zhou's family for another and killed them in error.

Zhou had vowed to avenge his family's deaths and joined his friend's triad. It was a particularly powerful triad that had spread its tentacles far and wide, not just within China, but also around the world. They introduced him to a group in North Korea who had strong political affiliations, even as high up as key ministers of the communist government. This North Korean cell had strong ties in supplying weapons and bomb-making technology to several other countries including Libya, Egypt, Pakistan and Iran.

The Iranians had led Zhou to a chance meeting with a respected Saudi businessman who had discreet ties to an anonymous but very well-connected and well-financed group, who were in the market for Zhou's particular skills: sequence code derivation and activation.

Jack felt the anger rise up inside him as Zhou made reference to the three January attacks. Images of Sarah, Beth, and Jonah filled his mind. He felt a sudden urge to drag Zhou off to the police. Finally, after all those months, here was someone who had some priceless information about those responsible for those heinous crimes.

"Excuse me, Zhou." Jack was on his feet, pacing the small bedroom. "It's best you know that I lost my wife and two of my children, as well as my sister's two daughters, in the Sydney attack!"

There was silence on the end of the phone.

Zhou's heart sank.

"Zhou, did you hear what I just said? *Zhou?*" Jack became conscious of raising his voice and waking others in the house. The fiery spear that had struck his heart could easily send him off into a rage. He had to stop himself from yelling down the phone. *Jesus, give me patience, pleeease!*

"Zhou… are you still there?"

Another few moments passed.

"Professor Haines… I'm… so… sooo… sorry!" Zhou whispered, struggling to get the words out between sobs. "I… don't know… what else to say." His voice was cracking up; a bullet of utter grief had pierced his soul. He felt like he was sinking, a huge weight tied to his feet, while he was thrashing to stay alive, the one person who could rescue him having now left him for dead.

Darius had both hands on Jack's shoulders.

Find it in your heart to forgive him, Jack! Zhou needs you now. Love him, Jack. Dig deep. I know it's really hard, but dig deep into that heart of yours, please, Jack.

Jack heard all these statements flash through his mind as hot

ANGELGUARD

tears stung his eyes. The conflict raged within his head. He didn't want to let Zhou off that easily. But God was telling him to.

"Professor Haines, I'm so sorry, I had no idea about your family…" Zhou managed to say quietly.

"I know…" Jack squeezed out.

"Please forgive me!"

Those three words flooded Jack's veins like an antibiotic, dousing the cancer in his heart. It didn't heal it completely; a residual ache still lingered. He sucked back the knot in his throat, letting out a loud sigh.

He immediately felt an unexpected calm course through his body.

"Perhaps you should continue your story, Zhou," he said, wiping his wet eyes on his shirtsleeve.

Zhou proceeded to pick up where he'd left off. He described the way he'd received the instruction to extinguish the lives of more people the other night. He didn't know who they were, or what they did.

That was the final straw.

And there was no way he was going to do it again. He gave Jack a brief outline about Sunday's planned attack.

Even though he was still struggling with Zhou's confession, Jack was fascinated by his story. Appalled, absolutely, but he found it somewhat intriguing.

"Zhou, what an incredible story!" Jack said, summing it up. "And I'm very glad you're still alive to tell it. I'm touched you called me for help, but I'm not sure how I can."

"Professor Haines, what I remember most about you is your belief in God, and maybe that's all you can do to help me. Teach me some more about the great God of heaven!"

"Sure, would love to." It was getting easier for Jack, the longer they spoke. "And, Zhou, there's no need to call me Professor. Jack will do just fine."

"OK, then… Jack."

"Just one thing about your story. Do you know who's in charge? Have you met them?" Jack wasn't sure why he asked.

"No, I haven't met them, but I've got a very strong suspicion who it is."

"Ahhh…" Jack sighed in frustration.

"I'm almost certain it's… Leopold Grosch, the founder and chairman of the Grosch Group!"

Jack's heart raced as he heard Zhou say that name. He was dumbstruck.

This can't be!

"I spoke to him on the phone this morning. He didn't confirm or deny it when I suggested he was Grosch. But I'm very, very confident, based on some checking I've done and his Flemish accent."

"Wow!" Jack's mind was racing. *Grosch, a murderer?*

Jack recalled the final paragraph of the email that mentioned "shaking up the world". That had troubled him. But was Grosch a terrorist? He couldn't believe it.

"Jack? Professor Haines… are you still there?"

"Oh, yeah, Zhou, just deep in thought." Jack continued: "Now this next event that you've provided the code for, you say it's on Sunday. This Sunday, the day after tomorrow?"

"That's right."

"And do you know anything about what the event is?"

"No, nothing. All I know is the bomb – I'm assuming that's what it is, just like the other three – is to be detonated at 6:30 p.m. It's quite simple. The bomb is activated by a text message carrying an encrypted code that I've written. The message sets off a timer that counts down to the time of detonation. Typically, I would receive an instruction to send the text message thirty minutes prior to detonation. So in this case I would be sending a message at 6 p.m."

"And you're positively certain that you don't have any idea as to where the bomb may be?"

"Nope, no idea. I wish I did, so I could let the police know."

"So you're prepared to give yourself up to the police, then?"

"No, I didn't say that. There are other ways of getting information to the police without giving yourself up, if you get my meaning?"

"Hmmm… sure, I get your meaning," Jack said, thoughts continuing to race through his head. He had all the pieces of a giant jigsaw puzzle, bar a few key ones. It frustrated him that he couldn't finish it.

"But it can't go off without you, is that right?"

"No, they have the code and cell phone number and can activate it themselves. He always has a fallback option."

"So they don't need you? Why would they be chasing you, then?"

"It's strange. For the previous three big hits I've been required to be present in the city. So I was in London, LA and Sydney when each of the blasts occurred. I did my bit and whammo! A bomb went off thirty minutes later. This time I'm not required, which seems odd. Why change the formula that has worked so successfully? That's also why I don't know where this one is going down. But he wants me primarily because I know too much, and I expect he's concerned I might report him."

"Ahhh… yeah. So you didn't set the bomb and the activation device in place?"

"No, that's never my job."

"Well, Zhou, I'm not sure what's the next best thing to do. But may I suggest you try to get some sleep, and then let's talk again in the morning. Are you somewhere safe now?"

"Yes… I think so. I met an old truckie in a town not far from Fontainebleau who seems to have taken a liking to me and has taken me in for the night. I'm at his home on the outskirts of Paris now."

"Great. Try to get some rest, then."

"Jack, are you still in Fontainebleau?"

"No, I left this afternoon and am now in London. I'm flying home to Sydney midnight Saturday, around twenty-two hours from now."

"Oh, OK."

"Let's see what the morning brings. Our heads will be fresher and we can devise a plan then. That reasonable?"

"What time will you call?"

"Ah… how's 9 a.m. Paris time sound? I'm an hour behind you. Best if you call me, Zhou. But give me your number, just in case."

Zhou recited the number slowly, then added, "The name of the truckie is Beny."

"Good. Sleep well and we'll talk again in a few hours."

"Good night, Jack, and thank you."

"No problem. Goodnight, Zhou."

Jack hung up, burdened by Zhou's dilemma. He felt a real pulling on his heart, an intense desire to protect this young man. It was like God was telling Jack to protect him, to go to his aid. Even though he was responsible for the deaths of thousands, including Jack's own beloved family.

"Dear God of heaven, why, oh why have you placed this man on my heart? You know he's responsible for killing Sarah, Jonah, and Beth, not to mention all those other thousands of people. I don't understand. Please, God, explain it to me, I beseech you!"

Jack was pleading with God, wanting an answer. He sat on the end of the bed, expectant. He knew God would respond.

Pray for Zhou, Jack. Intercede for him. Pray for Zhou. Trust me. I won't fail you!

Those words floated through Jack's mind. It wasn't the answer he wanted. But it was an answer. His Father was calling him. Jack didn't want to fail Him.

"Father, I praise you for your great love and your great mercy. Thank you for the life of Zhou Chau, thank you that you love him… dearly, even though he has been responsible for taking life away from those you have created. I seek your merciful pardon for his soul. Forgive him, Lord, for his actions – his murderous, revengeful actions. But Lord, he now has a heavy heart. He knows the crimes he has committed are wrong, not just in man's eyes, but more importantly, in your eyes. Please forgive him, gracious and loving Father. Yes, he doesn't deserve your gracious forgiveness. Nor do I, nor do the rest of us, but through the blood of your Son Jesus we are forgiven through your loving grace! Thank you, Father, and I praise your mighty and holy name!

"God, I don't know what it is you want me to do. For some reason I have this information. I sense I'm supposed to know it for some purpose, a purpose that only you know. Please, dear

God, guide me, direct me, lead me, as to what to do with it all. Grant me the wisdom to draw it all together into a complete picture that I can then take to the police. At the same time, Lord, please protect me. Keep me safe from the enemy. Please also keep Zhou safe from the enemy and from those men who are chasing him. Bind them all.

"Lord, loving God, most of all, protect Zhou's soul, his heart and mind. Tonight, please touch his heart. May he feel your loving presence and may he recognize that it is you, his great and loving God, who wants a relationship with him. Even after all he has done!"

Jack slumped back onto his pillow. His mind was too distracted to sleep. He kept going over this new information in his mind. Could it really be Grosch? Was the reclusive billionaire really a killer, a mass murderer? Was he responsible for murdering Sarah and the kids? If he was responsible, Jack wanted him locked up. A tidal wave of anger and revenge gripped his heart and mind again. He clenched his fists, punching them into his pillow repeatedly.

"Oh, God!" Jack cried out as tears began to flow. The horror of the past few months exploded back into his mind. "I don't want to feel this hatred, this anger, this desire to hurt, to maim, to gain revenge for my loss. I want to be able to turn the other cheek, but at this moment I can't! Forgive me, dear and loving Father. Heal my aching heart, mind and soul, Lord God. And Lord God, may you lead the authorities to those responsible for murdering my loved ones – please, Lord God!"

You're going to be the one who does that!

Jack heard a silent voice in his mind. Did he imagine it? Was it just his own mind desiring to be the hero, or was it really the Holy Spirit talking to him, or maybe it was Satan? Once again he felt confident in believing what he heard in his mind. He had been given this riddle to solve so the police could catch those responsible.

The thought intimidated him but at the same time thrilled and excited him.

He jumped out of bed wideawake with adrenalin pumping through his mind and body. He couldn't sleep now.

"This is excellent!" Tagan said to Athaniel as they stood over Jack. "Jack and Zhou are connecting the dots. One final piece should confirm it. We need to ensure that the two meet up and that Jack can get sufficient confirmation from the third source in the morning."

"I'll make sure Zhou is heavily guarded for his trip from Paris," Athaniel replied.

"Good. Jack knows whom to call. Now we need that person to deliver the goods."

* * *

Grosch couldn't sleep, even though it was well past three in the morning. The police had uncovered nothing; Zhou Chau had just vanished. All of his lieutenants were quick to share their own theories about where he'd got to, but Grosch didn't care – he just wanted the fugitive caught.

It would be better in the morning, he thought. Daylight should make it easier. A fugitive on the run can last only so long with law enforcement, Interpol, and the like chasing him. Sunday wasn't at risk so long as the decoy plan was executed well. Fortunately, he'd put that in very capable hands.

But he still didn't feel reassured. A police tip-off would put him behind bars.

His phone rang for the umpteenth time that evening.

"Yep?… Interesting… The call was from Paris?… My thoughts exactly. Who's going to call him at two in the morning and have a twenty-minute chat? That's gotta be our man… Agreed, get a car there now and have the place watched. Grab him when he moves… This is great news, Vincent. I think I'll be able to sleep now… What's that? Ah, no, keep with the plan for the decoy for Sunday. I'll manage the message for Berlin… Gooooodnight!"

"Yeeeesss!" He punched the air.

Grosch wasn't the only happy one. Volkyre, who had taken up a position near the balcony doors, laughed smugly.

"Lord Bacchazar will be redeemed!" he said grandly, waving his walking-stick in the air.

* * *

Marie Verheyen's ears pricked up at the name "Vincent". Wasn't that the name on the memo she'd accidently stumbled across recently? She strained to hear everything Grosch was saying:

"… plan for the decoy for Sunday… message for Berlin…"

What's all this about? she wondered.

Chapter 27

Jack almost jumped out of bed on hearing the alarm of his cell phone. He wasn't sure when he'd finally dropped off to sleep. Even though he'd only had a few hours of sleep, he felt surprisingly fresh and alert. It reminded him of his student days when he'd rise at three or four in the morning to cram for the final few hours before an exam.

After speaking to Zhou he had gone back over the material Stephen had provided. He had everything he needed except for the most critical piece: where was this major event to take place?

He needed some coffee and made his way out to the kitchen. Thierry was sitting quietly reading, while Mikey played on the floor in front of him.

"Morning, Thierry. You get the early morning shift, huh?" Jack said in a whisper.

"Hey Jack, didn't expect you to be up so early, especially after getting in so late last night."

"We didn't wake you, I hope?"

"Well, not exactly. Let's just say I hadn't dropped off to sleep when you walked in the door!"

"You're beginning to sound like my mother," Jack said, chuckling, giving Thierry a friendly punch on the shoulder.

"Ah ha, coffee just brewed?" he asked, spotting an almost full percolator sitting on the bench.

"Yeah, help yourself!"

Jack poured himself a cup.

"Chelsea fan, I see," Jack said as he noticed the mug he was drinking out of.

"Absolutely. Have followed them all my life. What about you?"

"Liverpool has always been my team. I grew up watching the great team of the seventies and eighties on *Match of the Day* and have followed them ever since. Unfortunately the last twenty years have been pretty lean in terms of trophies.

"Listen, Thierry, I've just got to make a phone call and then I'd love to chat some more about soccer – sorry, football!" Jack said, edging his way towards the kitchen door.

"Yeah, sure, no problem." Thierry returned to his book.

* * *

Marie Verheyen was toweling herself off in the opulent Roman-styled bathroom when she heard her cell phone ring. Her first thought was that one of the children was sick or in trouble, so she quickly put on her robe and rushed out to the bedroom.

She got to it just before it diverted to voicemail.

"Hello."

"Hello, is that Marie Verheyen?" the strangely familiar male voice asked.

"Yes, it is she, and who am I speaking to?" she replied stiffly.

"Ah, Ms. Verheyen, it's Jack Haines, we met last Monday at Insead."

"Yes, I remember, the Australian professor."

"That's right. Ms. Verheyen, I do apologize for disturbing you so early on a Saturday morning."

"Yes, it is highly irregular. And how did you get my private number, may I ask?"

"Alain Luscombe gave it to me. Once again, I apologize for the intrusion, but I was wondering if I could talk to you about a… sensitive matter that I think you may be particularly interested in."

"Ah, yes, what sort of sensitive matter?" She frowned.

Jack took a deep breath. "I believe the gas pipeline that your government is so generously providing the capital for is a front for another project, one that is significantly more sinister."

"Go on." Marie raised an eyebrow.

"I know this might sound crazy, but I have sufficient information that leads me to believe… a certain Belgian

industrialist whom you know very well is planning a large…
attack."

He'd said it. He was marching a circular track in the confined
space of the bedroom.

"What sort of attack?" she asked, walking over to close the
door to the living-room.

"A bomb attack of some description, I believe." Jack winced.

"This sounds preposterous! What sort of information do
you possess?" she demanded, quickly lowering her voice.

"It's difficult to tell you that at this time, but let's say I have
spoken to someone who has a pivotal role in the assignment and
who is employed by this particular industrialist. In addition, I
have copies of correspondence that corroborates this person's
information and also makes specific reference to, and I quote:
'the final contribution from MV to complete the pot of gold that
will give us sufficient ammunition to shake up the world' – end
quote."

She covered the mouthpiece of the phone and swore
quietly.

"It's difficult for me to believe what you are saying without
seeing this information you have!"

"Ms. Verheyen, I understand perfectly. My only concern is
there is not much time. I understand the attack will take place
tomorrow, Sunday, in the early evening!"

Jack was going out on a limb, giving away almost all he knew.

That last comment made Ms. Verheyen think back to the
notes she had taken last night. She moved briskly over to the bed
and pulled out her small notebook, scanning them.

She recalled Grosch's complete change in demeanor. One
minute, extreme agitation; the next, complete relief on receiving
that phone call. She hadn't seen him like that before.

"Professor Haines, the allegations you make are hard to
believe, and at this time I wonder what is really driving you to
make such startling and damaging claims. You could be putting
your career in jeopardy. Do you realize that?"

"I know, and that's why I'm speaking to you first to assess
whether you may indeed be able to corroborate any of what
I'm saying. Yes, it does sound startling. However, I am of the

firm belief that these claims I make are absolutely true and that, indeed, some attack of catastrophic proportions will take place around dusk tomorrow evening."

He sounded very convincing. She thought of the conversations they had last week. He had caught her off guard with his blunt honesty. She recalled Alain Luscombe speaking extremely highly of Professor Haines. He was well regarded in the business world, particularly in the US. Why would he make such accusations if they were not true, or at least partly true?

His comments also helped explain Grosch's edginess during the night and filled in some of the blanks of the half phone conversations she had managed to listen in to. But could her lover be responsible for murdering people? She didn't want to believe it.

"Are you still there, Ms. Verheyen?"

"We need to meet," she said, surprising Jack. "And you can show me what information you have. That is the only way I could possibly believe what you are saying!"

"Once again, I appreciate where you are coming from but I don't think there is time." Jack was pleading this time.

"But what would you have me do with this information? I don't know why you would call me. Why not just take it to the police?" Ms. Verheyen said, getting a little excited. Her instincts were telling her this might be consistent with the information she herself had gained. But she wasn't prepared to risk public scrutiny without having enough information at hand.

"I've thought of that and may well do that. I had perhaps hoped that you might be able to assist me. Perhaps he let something slip that at the time didn't mean much, but now, with this information, it may make a lot of sense." Jack paused. He hoped that final comment might have struck home. In fact, a lot was making sense to Ms. Verheyen now.

Jack went on. "I've taken enough of your time," he said, sounding defeated but in fact hoping this would get her to offer assistance. "I'll let you get back to your Saturday and I apologize for this intrusion."

Marie Verheyen could make quick decisions.

"We should meet," she said. "I can have a plane come and get you. It's less than an hour to Paris and we could meet early this afternoon here in Brussels. If you are able to convince me, we can take it to the Chief of Police."

"I'm no longer in Paris, Ms. Verheyen, I'm now in London," Jack said. "Ms. Verheyen, your suggestion may work but I must make a call first. Let me make this call and then I'll call you back in… say, no more than ten minutes."

"All right. I look forward to your call."

Ms. Verheyen put her notebook back under the mattress. She made a mental note not to forget it before she left.

* * *

"Good morning, Professor," said a friendly voice from behind the door. A familiar face with pillow-sculpted hair appeared through the open door.

"Hey there, sleepy head," Jack replied with a huge grin.

"Oh, do I look that bad?"

"Absolutely terrible. I couldn't imagine asking you out on a second date!"

"You're supposed to say I'm always beautiful in your eyes, or something to that effect."

Jack chuckled as he hugged her.

"Didn't you know we Aussie blokes are hopeless when it comes to the romantic stuff?"

"Well, in fact you've done very well disproving that… up until now, that is," she said, feigning a backhanded slap.

He drew away from her, a look of disappointment forming on her face.

"Listen, Loren, I've got to make a couple of phone calls and then we can sit down and have some breakfast. Thierry tells me he's super in the kitchen, especially with hot breakfasts, and he's dying to cook us up a storm."

"Sounds great… I'll go have myself a shower and meet you in the breakfast room shortly."

"Done. Enjoy your shower."

He closed the door behind Loren. He didn't know how he was going to explain this to her, especially if he was going to have to go to Brussels.

"Ms. Verheyen, Jack Haines," he said, the Minister answering after only one ring.

"So what's the verdict?"

"Change of plan, Ms. Verheyen. Let's meet in London and I'll introduce you to the particular individual I mentioned previously."

"No, Professor, that's not going to work. Remember you're the one trying to convince me of some issue with the project my government is financing. I didn't bring this to you."

"Ms. Verheyen, I understand that, but it wouldn't look so good for you or your government to be implicated in providing funding for some maniac who blows up and kills a bunch of people, now would it?"

"Is this extortion now?"

"Of course not. I haven't made any demands, nor do I plan to."

"All right," she decided to change tack. "How can we make this easier for you, Professor? I've already offered my airplane, and that's obviously not enough!"

"As I said, you come to London and meet me here."

"But if you are so convinced this Berlin attack is going to happen, then we are going to have to take it to the police. I can make one phone call and have the Belgian Chief of Police all over it."

"What did you say?" Jack heard it. The reason he called her in the first place.

"What, about calling the Belgian Chief of Police?"

"No, before that, you said '*Berlin* attack', didn't you?"

"Um, I might have, yes!" Ms. Verheyen said, unsure of the importance of that remark.

"Ms. Verheyen, I didn't say anything about where the attack was going to be."

"Yes, you did, I'm sure you did in our earlier conversation," she said defensively as she went back over that conversation.

"No, Ms. Verheyen, you're wrong. I didn't say 'Berlin', because that was the one piece of the puzzle I didn't have. I didn't know where the attack was going to take place."

"Umm…" was all Ms. Verheyen could muster.

"So you do know something about this, don't you, Ms. Verheyen? You're in on it, aren't you? That's why you pushed through the financing, wasn't it? I've got all I need to go to the police now!" Jack was exhilarated from the adrenalin rush in solving the puzzle, but a talon of fear suddenly struck. He may have just told one of Grosch's co-conspirators all he knew. The last thing he needed was Grosch after him.

"No, no, I'm not in on it at all, Jack! You've got to believe me," she said, struggling to keep it together.

"So how do you know this, then? And how certain are you that in fact it is Berlin?"

"That's just it, I'm not sure of anything and that's why I was so intrigued about what you knew. Mr. Grosch has been acting quite suspiciously of late and last night, over dinner, he was particularly agitated about something, more agitated than I've ever seen him. Someone important had gotten away or something like that. I overheard a couple of his phone conversations and he made reference to getting to Berlin, amongst other things. That's all I know and you've got to believe me!"

She was suddenly very anxious not to reveal her personal relationship with Grosch.

"So it mightn't be Berlin, then?" Jack asked.

"Maybe not," she said, sounding more composed.

Suddenly Grosch walked in the bedroom door.

"Are you ready yet, Marie?" Jack heard clearly.

"Just a minute – I'm just finishing up a phone call," she said, very composed, while fear stung her from the inside.

She removed her hand from the phone.

"Darling, I must go. Call me in about an hour when it's more convenient," she said and promptly hung up.

Jack was stunned. He didn't know where they stood now. All he knew was he should call her again in an hour.

"Lord, I really need your guidance!"

Darius appeared from the shadows in the corner of the bedroom, coming alongside Jack:

It's going to be OK, Jack. Trust your instincts, trust what you hear in your mind! the angelguard whispered into Jack's ear.

He left the bedroom, a troubled look on his face. The

alluring aroma of bacon cooking reminded his stomach it needed sustenance.

"Gee, something smells good!" Jack said, entering the kitchen. Thierry was standing by the stove.

Jack fidgeted, unsure what to do or say.

"So is that the last of the calls? What are you up to, Jack?"

"Probably not, Thierry. It's a complicated story."

"Sounds mysterious! I like a good mystery, you know."

"Mysterious it is, but unfortunately I don't know how it's going to end," Jack said. "Now what's for breakfast? I'm famished."

"So am I." Loren's voice could be heard before she appeared.

Ruth immediately arrived too, Mikey in her arms. "All clean now and ready for some breakfast too, aren't you, Mikey?" she cooed, carefully placing him in his highchair.

"Jack, I think that's your phone I can hear," Loren said, still standing inside the doorway. "I'll grab it for you!" She disappeared, soon reappearing, the phone to her ear.

She handed it to Jack. "Zhou for you."

"Oh thanks," he said, walking out into the back yard.

"Loren, do you know what all these calls are about?" Thierry asked. "Jack seems on edge. He's worried about something, by the looks of it."

"He's made a few calls this morning?" Loren asked.

"That's all he's been doing since he got up!" Thierry replied.

"He's probably just telling those at home that he's going to be back soon, creating havoc in their lives," Loren said with an uncertain expression on her face. It just hit her that in a few hours her holiday romance could be over.

Ruth noticed it.

"You really like him, don't you?" she asked, coming up alongside Loren, putting her hand on her arm.

"Yes, very much, Ruth," Loren said, gladly receiving Ruth's show of affection.

"He's quite a guy! We don't know him very well at all, but Danny and Joanna, two of the pastors at our church, just rave about him."

"I wasn't expecting to meet a man so special, perhaps ever. He's just the complete package: good looks, intelligent, funny and with a big heart that really cares."

Ruth gripped Loren harder.

"Everything is going to be fine, Loren – you just wait."

"Hmmm, I haven't had a long-distance relationship before," Loren said, drawing her forefingers under her eyes to remove any tears that may have gathered there.

"Right, how's that bacon doing?" Jack said, breezing into the room.

Mikey stole Jack's thunder and the attention of the three others as he started banging on his table, also impatient for breakfast.

Ruth tended to him while Loren grabbed some plates and started setting the table.

Soon all four were seated and eating. Mikey was devouring a cheese stick and an assortment of dried fruits and sultanas, a look of contentment on his face.

"I need to share a story with you all," Jack announced, as Darius joined Arlia, Hannen and Elijah in the room.

The others invited him with their eyes to commence.

"This is something I stumbled on about ten days ago and then last night, various new pieces of information came to my attention, adding to its intrigue. But I must also point out before I go on that this is really quite incredible and, I believe, is something very close to us all. In telling you this, I may be drawing you into a web, that I guess has the potential to be quite dangerous." He stopped, waiting for comments, a look of concern etched across his face.

The others didn't say anything, slightly surprised and unsure of how to react.

"Are you happy for me to go on? Because if you are concerned about being 'involved', then stop me now!" He still wasn't sure if he should start, but his instincts told him it was a positive thing to do.

"Yes, count the two of us in," Thierry said, looking at Ruth.

She nodded: "Sounds mysterious and quite exciting."

"Exciting it very well could be, but also *dangerous*!" Jack added.

"Jack, I think Thierry and Ruth would agree with me when I say we trust you and know that you wouldn't lead us into something dangerous, intentionally," said Loren. "But also, we're all adults and can stand up for ourselves."

"Here we go, then," Jack said, and took a deep breath.

For the next forty minutes, the three sat largely in silence. Their turbulent emotions gradually surfaced as the enormity of what Jack was telling them struck home. Soon they were all showing signs of real tension as anger began to tug at their hearts.

"So you believe this person was responsible for the three attacks that hit us all?" Thierry asked, amazed. He was struggling to keep a lid on the rage building inside him.

"How can you, Jack, know this when police forces around the world and the best intelligence agencies haven't been able to find them?" Ruth asked incredulously. "Jack, I can't believe what you're telling us is true!"

Thierry reached over the table and took her hand, saying nothing.

"Ruth, I understand. It sounds unbelievable − I know it does. But for some reason I've been given the dubious honor of finding bits of information piece by piece till the final piece was handed to me this morning, by accident. I don't have any idea why I've been the one to receive it all. I don't really want to spend much time reflecting on that just now, not because I don't want to, but because I don't think I've got the time to!"

"So, Jack," said Ruth, still in disbelief, "you're really convinced, aren't you?"

"Absolutely, Ruth! Until I spoke to this ex-student early this morning I'd dismissed it as some corporate scheming, but now I'm absolutely certain there is going to be an attack tomorrow. And Berlin is the city that's going to be hit!"

Loren hadn't said anything. She appeared to be in shock. The two most influential men in her life in the past ten years − one had been her husband, the other her boss − had been caught up in this plot in some way. A plot that had devastated her business, had murdered all those innocent friends and work colleagues. She didn't want to believe it.

Jack saw her dismay and pain. He got up from the table and came alongside her, reaching his arm towards her.

"No, Jack, please don't," she said, pushing him away while still in her chair. She was struggling to keep it all together.

She pushed the chair back and abruptly got to her feet. Her chair tipped over onto the floor, making Mikey cry.

She rushed out the door, not really knowing where to go.

"Tee, look after Mikey." Ruth jumped up and went after Loren.

"Oh, blast!" Jack said, pacing the room, his arms wrapped across his chest.

"Thierry, I've gotta call this Belgian politician to sort out what we do next!" he said.

"Jack, make the call!" said Thierry, leaving Mikey to hug Jack. "I believe you! I can see that God is at work in all of this. He has wanted you to be the detective, and now He wants us all to work out what to do next!"

"Yeah, Thierry, that's what I was thinking too. I just wish this wasn't so hard for Loren."

"We know that, Jack – and so, I think, does she."

"I guess," Jack said, drawing away from Thierry. "Thanks, mate."

"Best make that call, then."

"Ta… back soon, I hope," Jack said, walking out into the back yard.

He returned shortly afterwards.

"No answer – went straight to voicemail. Must be switched off. I'll try again in a few minutes."

"Hey, Jack, you said Berlin was where the next attack was going to be, right?" Thierry asked, studying the front page of the *Guardian* newspaper.

"Yes, Berlin."

"Well, if you're right, then the world's going to be in a big mess!"

"Why's that?" Jack asked.

Thierry pushed the paper over to Jack. The headline leapt out at him: "US to exhort G8 to share the poverty burden".

"G8 starts tomorrow… in Berlin!' Jack said, aghast.

The two men stood staring at each other, both not daring to speak first, both recognizing the incredible enormity of the information they possessed.

Chapter 28

Marie sat in Grosch's speeding black vehicle, frustrated and frightened. Frustrated, because she knew Jack would have called her. Frightened, because of who she was sitting next to and what could become of her. She wondered if he knew she now knew.

For the entire trip, Grosch had been on the phone. She listened intently for any clues or words that bore resemblance to last night's calls. But nothing was forthcoming as she struggled to understand the context of his conversation.

They were about to arrive. Another blasted corporate fundraiser for the government. A polo tournament on the southern outskirts of Brussels, organized by Grosch's company. In part, it was a show of appreciation to the government for their significant contribution to the gas pipeline project. In addition, it was an opportunity for the other wealthy members of the Brussels elite to contribute to the election coffers.

Grosch ended his call.

"You seem a little tense this morning, my dear," he remarked.

"Oh, do I? Just a bit tired and wanting some time with my children," she lied.

"Are they all right?"

"Ah, yes… just missing their mother, that's all. Leopold, you too seem on edge. Is something the matter?"

"It's just business, you know. Trying to get this gas pipeline project off and running. We had some unfortunate news last night. One of the key engineers on the project has gone AWOL for some unexplained reason. My project manager ascertained his whereabouts early this morning and now he's attempting to make contact."

She was amazed how he distorted the facts.

"He's probably just gone away for a while?" she offered.

"Perhaps, but we doubt it. He's been behaving strangely for the last few days, making everyone suspicious."

"So sack him and replace him."

"Unfortunately, it's not that simple. I wish it were. This particular engineer is quite brilliant and knows too much about the project for us to let him just leave."

"And what would happen if your manager doesn't make contact with him?"

"Oh, we've already built redundancy into the project, but at the moment we are more concerned he'll go to the opposition and take our plans with him."

"There are contractual ways of stopping that."

"Yes, my man is working on that as we speak. I may have to manage the situation from Berlin when I go there tomorrow for the G8."

She couldn't believe it – he even confirmed the venue.

"Why Berlin?" she asked the obvious.

"Oh, part of the redundancy plan, that's all. I'll use one of my people who'll be with me to fill the hole. But either way, I need to sort this troublemaker out and ensure he can't cause me, and the project for that matter, any problems."

She caught the menace in his voice.

"Well, let's hope he turns up, then," she said sheepishly, fear snatching at her heart.

"Yes, let's hope so, indeed." They pulled up in the graveled VIP parking area behind a series of white marquees, on the other side of which stood the polo field.

An outer suburb of Paris

"There's movement. Get ready!" said a voice from the back seat of the black late-model Renault. It was parked on a narrow Paris suburban street lined either side with modest single- and double-story homes. Cars were parked on both sides, reducing the street to a single lane.

"That's him," said the driver as he started the engine. Two houses down on the opposite side of the street, an Asian man stood inside an open front door with his back turned. He was chatting to an older bearded man.

"This is going to be interesting," Grindor said to Andola. The two angels stood at the closed gate, five steps away from Zhou. "Good job we dealt with the enemy during the night," she said, looking towards the roof of the house where twenty white knights sat, waiting for any instruction from their leaders.

"Yes, at least now we only have to deal with the human element here, if required," Andola replied. She moved into position, standing in front of the gate as Zhou and Beny started making their way towards it.

"Keep alert, boys," said the driver, putting the car into gear, the engine purring with anticipation.

"Thank you once again, Beny, for all your help," Zhou said, stopping, allowing Beny to pass.

"Salut, Cedric!" Beny waved to a man who had appeared from the house directly opposite. This man hopped into his car and re-parked one car spot down from his house.

"Bonjour, Beny!" said another man walking through the front gate of the house one up from Beny's. He was considerably younger and extremely large.

"Merci beaucoup, François," Beny replied. He watched François get into his car, which was parked directly in front of the house he had just left.

Zhou still stood at the open gate, watching very attentively. Beny stepped out towards his very old-model Citroën parked directly in front.

"Farewell, my good friend. Be careful." Beny unlocked the driver's door, got in and promptly drove it diagonally across the road, making it impossible for any car to pass.

Simultaneously, Cedric's car pulled up, Zhou jumped in the back seat and the sporty Fiat shot off down the street, Andola and Grindor shadowing it closely.

The black Renault surged forward, horn honking, as it drew up to Beny's Citroën. François pulled his car out from the curb and parked it straight behind the Renault. It was boxed in.

"Get your car out of the way!" yelled the man from the back seat as he leapt out, remonstrating towards Beny, who was grappling with the column-mounted gearstick, giving the impression it was stuck.

Beny paid him no attention until the man banged on his passenger-door window, yelling expletives in English. Beny threw his hands up, confusion all over his face.

François stepped out of his car and went to Beny's aid, gesturing with his hands whilst saying something in French. Neither was listening, but both gesticulated enthusiastically.

Many of the angels were now at street level with large smiles on their faces, enjoying Beny's acting prowess.

François opened Beny's driver door, offering his assistance. Beny looked straight down the road and saw the Fiat turn at the nearest intersection. Zhou's escape was complete.

The front-seat passenger of the Renault now got out and thumped the Citroën's bonnet with his fist whilst shouting an expletive-filled demand that Beny move the car, and quick.

François shut the door and stepped away as the Citroën reversed slowly, the issue with the stuck gearshift seemingly resolved.

The Citroën headed down the street, slowly, the Renault close behind, blasting its horn.

***

Grosch was seated on a plush beige leather three-seater lounge in his own personal marquee, which was just as large as all the others.

He was alone in the marquee.

"And what about this Haines person? What do we know about him?" he asked into his cell phone.

"By all accounts he's an acclaimed professor of business, based out of Sydney, Australia," said the person on the other end of the line. "When I typed his name into the search engine, over 1.3 million entries came back. Looks like he's written a number of books and articles, all on new-age business mumbo-jumbo – you know."

"What was he doing in Fontainebleau, then?" Grosch asked.

"Attending Insead, the school where he received his MBA in the early nineties," was the response.

"And he obviously taught our fugitive friend Zhou Chau in Sydney before Chau departed on his mercy mission to save his parents," Grosch added.

"Yes, that's right, judging by the transcripts of their phone conversation."

"And our friend was calling out to his old professor in his hour of need, then?"

"It looks like it, sir."

"It's strange this Haines character was at Insead the same time that Ray Malone was there too. I wonder if they met. Hmmm…"

"Insead's a large university. It's unlikely they would have met."

"Check any other calls he makes, just in case. Chau will try to contact Haines again."

"Yes, sir. Just doing it now. Should have the results in the next few minutes."

"Good. Call me back."

Grosch shut his phone as he got to his feet and walked out of the marquee.

***

"Listen, Jack, I'm stuck at this event till early afternoon. I can't just up and leave!" Ms. Verheyen was saying as she paced around the gravel car park.

"So what do you propose as a new plan, then?"

"I think we should go back to my original proposal of picking you up in London and then bringing you here to Brussels. That way we don't lose any time. You won't get here till mid afternoon and by that time I'll be finished at this fundraiser and can meet you somewhere near the airport."

"Ms. Verheyen, I'm still not sure I can trust you," said Jack frankly.

"In that case, you'll just have to wait until I can get to London this evening," Marie Verheyen responded. "I thought you considered this an urgent matter?"

Jack thought for a minute. He wasn't sure what to do, but Zhou's words rang in his ears: "She's probably told Grosch and he's on his way now to get us…"

"Well, that's going to have to do. It's running it tight, but if we are able to convince you, then we should still have time to stop the tragedy, assuming it is to take place tomorrow evening. I'd suggest you put your police chief on notice."

* * *

"Hello," Grosch answered his phone, drawing himself away from the attractive blonde he was talking to.

"Mr. Grosch, sir?"

"Yes?" Grosch was pleased with Vincent's swift response, but not about to say so. He did not use praise as a motivator.

"Mr. Grosch, some bad news about this Haines fellow."

"What is it?" Grosch had little patience with temporizing language.

"It looks like he may have been talking to someone in the Belgian government."

"Really? Do you know who?"

"Yes, it's a Ms. Verheyen, sir!" Grosch's stomach leapt into his throat as he heard the name.

He didn't say a word.

"Mr. Grosch, sir, he's talking to her now!" the caller said excitedly.

"What?"

"They are talking to each other right this very minute!"

Grosch looked around but couldn't immediately see her.

"Good. Please get me a list of all calls between the two of them and details of all other calls she has received and made over the past forty-eight hours. Have them emailed to me at once." Grosch strode around to the back of the marquees.

Then he saw her pacing in the car park and yes, she was on her cell phone.

"Yes, sir. It will take a few minutes to get all that information but I will get it to you as soon as possible."

No response.

"Mr. Grosch…"

"Yes, son, do it – fast!"

He started to move quickly, closing the gap between them.

* * *

"Yes, I'll contact him before I leave," Marie Verheyen responded.

"In the meantime, I'll have my associate get to London so he can tell you what he knows," said Jack.

"That's good. I'll let you know later what my likely ETA will be." She turned and walked straight into Grosch.

She froze, not knowing what to do, still holding the phone to her ear.

"Oh, sweetie… Mummy's gotta go now," she said, fumbling, trying to remain calm and collected. "Bye, bye, I'll be home this afternoon. Love you. Kiss kiss."

She hung up.

"Is she alright?" Grosch asked abruptly.

"I think so, a bit of a fever, but yes, she'll be OK."

"The presentations are going to be held shortly. You can't miss those, especially when you are one of the special people we are honoring today," he said brusquely, taking her elbow. He locked it tightly against his side, directing her back to the main group.

Chapter 29

Paris

Jolane saw them first. Six demons charging down the street. They stopped outside the bank where Zhou had just been.

"They've tracked him to the bank," she said to the others.

"How do you mean?" Landen asked, turning to face her.

"See our friends at the bank," she said, gesturing towards it. "Four burly men just hopped out of that Mercedes and went in."

"We best get outta sight, then," Landen said. "The last thing we want to do is lead them to him."

The two of them quickly dashed into the small menswear shop that Zhou had, surprisingly, entered. Locating Andola and Zhou wasn't a problem, as the shop was tiny and there were no customers other than Zhou, with one overly attentive elderly shop proprietor. Zhou disappeared into the solitary changing room with a selection of shirts and trousers.

"Andola, six sentinels accompanying four henchmen half a mile up the road at the bank we just left!" announced Landen.

"Landen, keep watch," ordered Andola. "Zhou will be busy for a little while, trying on all these clothes."

The two angels saw him take his cell phone out of his pocket to answer a call.

"Jack, we got a decision?… Great!… I'll make my way to the Eurostar station and grab a train to London… Three hours, you say? Any idea how frequently the trains run?… Good, well, I should be there about four, then… Talk soon… Bye…"

Zhou now picked up the pace, trying on only one shirt and one pair of trousers. They fitted well, so he went to the cash register without bothering to remove them.

"Phew, that was close!" Landen exclaimed with relief as the three angelguards watched the black Mercedes, accompanied by its team of enemy sentinels, flash past the menswear shop.

Zhou was now dressed in dark linen trousers with a white linen long-sleeved shirt and loafers, looking like any well-dressed tourist. As he stepped out of the shop he realized he was missing something. Before the angelguards were out of the shop, Zhou had gone into the one next door. It was a typical tourist shop selling postcards and all manner of knick-knacks. He saw what he was after immediately: a navy-blue baseball cap with the initials "ND" plastered on its front, and a pair of cheap sunglasses.

***

"Missed him, Vincent," said Miroslav, a stout hairy-armed Russian with a particularly gruff voice.

"He's catching the Eurostar from the Gare du Nord," replied Vincent.

"What's Garr doo Norr?"

"Gare du Nord! It's the main train station in Paris. You won't be far from it."

The driver of the Mercedes punched the name into the GPS system on the dashboard between them.

"Got it, Slav, no problem," the driver said in a deep monotone.

"Hey, Vincent, we got it on the GPS, so we'll be there in no time," Miroslav said through the mouthpiece of his phone.

"Go, then. Don't let him get away!"

"We'll do our best, but it's a bit like looking for a needle in a haystack, especially at a major train station."

"The French police will be on lookout too. There's an all-points bulletin out on him."

"That's what I like to hear," Miroslav said, pleased that he wasn't working alone.

"Goodbye, Slav," Vincent said, signing off.

***

Grosch now sat at the makeshift desk in his private marquee, his laptop open, his contorted facial expression confirming his angst and complete shock.

His phone rattled on the desk. He snapped it up.

"Yes?!"

"Sir, we're back in the game with Chau. He's about ten minutes away from the central railway station. I've got some men headed there now."

"Excellent!" Grosch slammed his fist on the table, sending his laptop toppling to the ground. He got to his feet, ignoring the cracking plastic.

"I have other news that will please you even more," Vincent announced.

"Yes, what is it?"

"We've been tracing all of Haines' phone calls and have made some interesting observations."

"Spit it out."

"There were some incoming and outgoing calls to some numbers in New York. One of the numbers is to a cell phone used by a Stephen Haines – a relative, I presume."

"So, he talks to his brother."

"No, but get this, one of the calls came from the offices of Maple, Mayer and Masters."

"Hmmm… now that's very interesting. And do you think it was his brother he was speaking with on that particular line?"

"Hang on, there's more. Another set of calls we've been able to trace back to the NYPD, Central Park precinct!"

"Ahhh… Why would the NYPD want to talk to our professor?"

"We're still looking into it. Also, we've got a new cell phone number that Haines called about an hour ago. We're confident our fugitive friend was in that location at the time Haines called."

"So the two are talking again. Our professor is becoming a nuisance."

"My hunch is that Zhou's told Haines what he knows. Somehow Haines' brother got wind of Mayer's role, which is very dangerous. I'm guessing that's why the NYPD are calling

Haines. But why Haines is talking to the Minister baffles me. How do they know each other, for starters? And did he meet Malone at Insead and Malone blabbed?"

"Too many questions and not answers, Vincent." Grosch paused to remove his tie. Volkyre was hovering. He thrust his walking-stick threateningly towards Grosch.

"This is very worrying, especially if the NYPD have discovered the money transfers," Vincent interjected.

"That will be OK. We did such a good job setting up the bank accounts, it will take a long time to trace the laundering back to me or anyone else connected with the Grosch Group. How are you doing with those transcripts of the Haines and Verheyen calls?"

"Not long now, sir!"

"That will be what ties the three together. We need them urgently!"

"How will you manage her, do you think?"

Grosch was very tempted to take her for a stroll in the surrounding countryside, slit her throat and leave her for the forest birds and insects to feast on. "Nothing to concern you. Anything on any of her other calls?"

Volkyre sniggered.

"She called her pilot this morning."

"So she's taking a little trip, is she? To where, I wonder?" Grosch was pacing whilst constantly flicking his hand through his hair.

"I'll go and hurry up those transcripts, sir!" Vincent said, but Grosch had gone.

* * *

He'd walked briskly, almost running some of the way.

Zhou could see the opening to the French capital's central railway station a mile ahead. It was close to 12:30. He had no idea when the next train to London would be, but Jack had mentioned they ran frequently, so he didn't think he'd have to wait long.

The lunchtime crowd was out and this main street was

full of people, locals knowing exactly where they were headed and just as many tourists struggling to find their way around. He was glad of the crowd, helping him maintain his anonymity. With baseball cap pulled down low on his forehead and the dark sunglasses, it was difficult to recognize he was of Asian descent.

"What's he up to, going into another menswear shop?" Landen asked, watching Zhou suddenly change course.

"Beats me," Andola said.

The six demons they had spotted before were now holding court above the train station at the top of the street.

"Funny how they don't try to conceal themselves," Landen said.

"Yeah, it always beats me how so many of them must have not been paying attention in the 'Basics of the Art of War' class. They do some of the dumbest things sometimes," Grindor said mockingly.

Landen laughed at her comment.

"You two stop joking around," Andola said firmly. "I think it's more to do with their arrogance. They believe they can take anybody on, at any time, and win. I think they're daring us to hit them head on!"

"So shall we?" Landen asked.

Andola didn't respond immediately. She then turned to her two comrades, fixing them with her steely gaze. "Absolutely, Landen. We'll give 'em exactly what they want."

* * *

Zhou left the Armani shop dressed in a black two-piece suit, a white business shirt with French cuffs, a silver silk tie and black ankle-high leather boots so shiny they sparkled in the sunlight.

In his right hand he carried a black briefcase large enough to hold his small carry bag. He'd discarded both the baseball cap and the cheap sunglasses, replacing the latter with the latest designer number.

To the angels' surprise again, he jaywalked across the street. He proceeded through the door of an old-fashioned barbershop.

"What's he doing now? He's got a train to catch!" Landen shook his head. He, Andola, and Grindor sat and waited, keeping one eye on the entrance to the station.

Twenty minutes later Zhou left the barbershop and headed for the station. Well, the three angels took it to be Zhou.

"Wow," Grindor offered.

"Good on ya, Zhou," Landen said.

Andola shook her head and grimaced. "I just hope the demons and the humans waiting for him are as surprised as we are. They're probably not watching for a bald-headed Asian executive. Let's hope Zhou's disguise passes the test."

The three had determined their plan. A very simple one, one they felt confident would work.

Two large black forms descended from the left. Andola saw them from out of the corner of her eye. Grindor and Landen had left her to check the super-fast train that Zhou would soon board.

"What is your business here, white crawler?" one of the demons said, stopping Andola's progress, spitting his disgusting bile in her face.

"Just minding my own business," Andola replied, meeting their gaze straight on.

The other demon came around, locking her in.

"We don't like seeing the likes of you round here!" he said, pushing his forefinger into her chest. She didn't budge.

"Hey, Tweedledee and Tweedledum, as I said, I'm just minding my own business." Andola resisted the urge to take them out.

Neither reacted to the names she had used, appearing not to understand the implied insult.

"You white knights never 'just mind your own business'. You're always minding some human's business! So which one is it?"

"Never you mind," Andola replied, a disapproving look on her face. She saw the bald head of Zhou through the crowd up ahead. He was approaching the security gates. This would be his sternest test. Andola noticed two big bodyguard-types leaning against the wall beside the gates. Their eyes had zeroed in on Zhou.

So too had the red bulbous eyes of her two intimidators.

***

So far so good.

Zhou approached the security gates. His stomach was churning, doing cartwheels as fear gripped him.

"Excuse me, sir," a strong and demanding voice said from behind. His heart leapt into his throat. He feared the worst and froze.

Blast! What do I do now?

A hand clutched his shoulder. He went to push it away with his free hand, ready to bolt.

"Hey, mister." A teenager's face suddenly appeared at his side. "You left your briefcase at the ticket counter!"

Zhou sighed. His body instantly relaxed.

"Oh… thank you very much. I'm a klutz!"

Zhou took the case. He saw for the first time the two large unshaven henchmen leaning against the wall. They had seen everything.

Zhou's heart began to race again. *Grosch's hit men!*

"Nice day, Mr. Chau," he thought he heard one of them say in his direction. He didn't flinch. It was his turn to step through the metal detector. He placed his briefcase on the conveyor belt, emptied his pockets and walked through the detector.

Clean. No beeps, no nothing.

He picked up his belongings and headed straight for Immigration.

One more gate to go.

***

"What brings six of you out to play on this wonderful summer's day?" Andola asked, trying to deflect their attention.

"Oh, just looking to create some havoc amongst these weak humans – you know, the usual," one replied. "Might even have some fun with that blonde babe with the long legs over by the counter. Whatya reckon? We could have a couple of the men over there frisk her at the gates. She looks like she could do with a good once over! Hey whitey, whatya think?" he hissed, soaking

Andola with his foul-smelling saliva.

"There'll be none of that today – not with any human, thanks very much!" Andola said, pushing her way through the two, having had enough of their banter. She felt confident they didn't suspect her.

The second sentinel reached out to stop Andola but the first one knocked his hand away.

"Wendeck, no! We have more important things to do than continue harassing this bitch! Her time will come, one day, and when it does, she'll sure know about it!"

"Well, Krawlick, that blonde sure is a hottie," Wendeck said with spittle dropping to the ground. Demons understood all about temptation.

Andola went straight through the security gates. She stopped to ensure that the female security guard would do the body check of the long-legged blonde who'd set the metal detector off.

Andola watched Zhou approach the Immigration booths. "Almost there," she said.

* * *

"Father, we intercede for both Zhou and Marie Verheyen."

It was Jack. He and Thierry had just returned from the police station. "You love them both dearly and we seek your divine protection over them, physically, emotionally, and spiritually. Keep them safe, loving Father."

* * *

Zhou stood in line, one person in front of him. He'd chosen an Asian attendant, thinking she might go easy on him.

His heart was beating fast; he could feel the sweat under his arms, on his back and even on his stomach. It was hot in his suit, with the temperature in the high eighties.

He took his jacket off, feeling the immediate relief from a soft breeze that blew onto his sweat-soaked back. His shiny head glistened in the heat.

He approached the booth, the attendant sitting high up in her chair.

He handed her his passport, ticket, and departure card.

She studied it, looking from one document to another and then at her computer screen. She didn't say a word. She pulled the passport up to the screen, comparing two pictures side by side. The one on the screen showed a bespectacled longhaired Zhou Chau taken four years ago.

It seemed to be taking for ever. His heart was racing.

Finally she spoke.

"And what is your business in England, Mr. Zhou?" she asked, staring intently into his eyes, looking for any slight something that might cause him to slip up.

"Telecoms, miss," Zhou said confidently.

"That's a big field, Mr. Zhou. What, specifically?"

"Cell phone services. I'm a partner in a business that develops applications for use over cell phones."

"It's a lucrative area?" The attendant's attention was already moving on to the next in line.

"Certainly is," he said, feeling immediate relief from the conversational tone in her voice.

"Thank you," she said, handing his documents back, minus the departure card.

He moved through the booth.

He sighed once again and the pounding of his heart subsided.

You little beauty!

Zhou picked up his step.

He wasn't the only relieved one. Andola had watched him from a distance while she waited in line for the long-legged blonde to go through her inspection.

* * *

"You won't believe this, sir! Minister Verheyen plans to meet Jack Haines and Zhou Chau outside the Ritz Hotel in London at 5 p.m." Grosch listened intently to the news.

"Excellent. Get Farkad's team mobilized. Instructions to follow."

"Yes, sir."

Grosch hung up. He watched as the crowds cheered on the men and women on horseback. He never did like polo, football being his first love.

He soon spotted Marie, engrossed in conversation with the prime minister and his wife.

A very brief pang passed through him. He turned back to the tedious game.

Chapter 30

It was almost time for Loren to leave for the airport.

She and Jack were seated on a picnic rug in a small, apparently little used, park around the corner from Thierry and Ruth's home. The grass was overgrown and the swings were badly in need of repair. Graffiti covered a concrete wall that bordered one boundary of the netball-court-sized park.

She was dressed simply but in her usual elegant style. This was one of the many attributes that Jack found particularly attractive about her.

"Loren, I'm sorry that my announcement this morning was so difficult for you," he said. They had said very little since the meeting at the breakfast table.

"It's OK," she said as her eyes filled. She tilted her head back, deliberately, in an attempt to control her tears.

They sat for a few moments in silence, neither sure what to say.

"Jack, I—" she started, then stopped, choosing her words carefully. His fears heightened as he anticipated the next few words. He sat with head bowed, not wanting to look at her, not wanting to reveal his hurt and disappointment.

"This has been an incredible experience for me, not just these past two weeks but the last five months, ever since the bomb attack. I've never felt such extreme emotions. I've cried more than I've ever done, I've experienced real grief and sadness like I didn't know existed, plus I've had moments of terrifying fear, like almost being kidnapped on my way to Insead."

She paused. He now looked at her.

"And then I met you… and experienced a renewed hope…" Her eyes filled again and her chin quivered. "It's been a long time since I've fallen so strongly for a man, and… I don't want to leave you!" she said, tears breaking through and rolling down her cheeks.

He reached over and hugged her. She sighed loudly and drew a deep breath to restore her strength. But it didn't last long, as she broke down on his chest. She cried quietly as he stroked her hair. The lump in his throat soon led to his eyes welling up with tears. He felt this strange mixture of euphoria, sadness and a burning desire to heal her heart from all the pain she had suffered.

He started to pray, aloud, as he continued to hug her.

"Jesus, I praise you and thank you for Loren. I praise you for the wonderful woman you've made her, the wonderful employee, boss, friend, and mother. She has been through so much in these past few months, and I praise you that throughout all the terror, adversity and really difficult times you have always been there for her. Please heal her of the pain she feels, the pain of losing friends and work colleagues, the pain in losing her ex-husband, the father of her children… Oh, loving Jesus, I know you can heal all things and desire to do so. Fill Loren's heart with peace; renew her soul with freshness and hunger to enjoy all that life has to offer. Thank you for loving her, like no one else can. Amen."

She said nothing. She felt soothing warmth descend through her body. Her tears dried up as fresh hope brought a smile to her face.

She drew herself back from Jack and whispered, "Thank you."

Using his thumbs, he ever so tenderly wiped the residue of tears away from underneath her eyes, not saying a word.

"I'm sorry that I sort of went AWOL this morning. Everything from the past few months just boiled over and I didn't know how to react or respond. You know, the fact you were dealing – sorry, that's not the right word, but a better one doesn't immediately come to mind – with something that involved both Tom and Ray just, I don't know, baffled me. It wasn't that I thought you were deliberately holding something back from me, but more that you knew something I didn't, especially about two men who have been such a big part of my life."

She paused and grimaced.

"Does that babble make any sense?" She gripped both of his hands tighter.

"Yes, very much," he replied, pushing a stray lock of hair off her face. "And you don't have to apologize. Over the past week or so, I've been especially torn up about what to tell you and what not to, and in the end I decided not to say anything. But after my discussion last night with Zhou, and knowing the magnitude of what this thing seemed to be about, I just had to tell you. It was only fair and appropriate!"

"I'm glad you did," she said, taking one of his hands and rubbing it gently against her cheek.

He looked at his watch. "We'd better get you off to the airport, or else you'll be scratching to get your flight," he said as he got to his knees on his way to standing up.

She yanked him back down.

"I'm not going!" she said. "Well, not yet, anyway!"

Jack looked at her. "I don't understand."

"You can't expect me to board a plane and not know the outcome of your meeting with this Belgian politician. It's too big a deal." She smiled playfully. "And anyway, I don't want to leave you just yet."

"Loren, I'm going to be on a plane heading for Sydney at midnight and you'll have to wait until tomorrow for another flight."

"I don't care. I'm sure Ruth and Thierry won't mind me staying another night."

"But what about the kids? And Marcie?"

"Oh, they'll survive without me for another day. And anyway, I wasn't getting home till tomorrow morning, and if I can get on the right connections I can probably get back home late tomorrow, time difference and all."

"You know this could be dangerous?"

"I know that, but… for some reason I reckon there's someone looking out for you and it's all going to be all right in the end."

He smiled.

"You sure I can't get you to change your mind?" he asked.

"No way. It's made up and I'm staying!"

He got to his feet and pulled her up. She fell into his arms and they looked into each other's eyes for a moment. A hint of her perfume teased his nose. He put his right hand gently under her chin as he drew her mouth to his and kissed her softly. He drew away slightly, and then repeated it, kissing her a little longer this time, only to pull away again, fleetingly, before putting his hand through her hair and kissing her passionately.

It was electric. That tingle she felt only moments ago returned, but this time it came with a flood of passion that made her go weak at the knees. She felt like she was drifting on a cloud. Nothing else mattered except this moment.

She didn't want it to end.

The kiss ended in its own time. He softly ran his forefinger down her cheek, kissing the tip of her nose tenderly.

Jack drew away and took her hand. She responded like she was on autopilot, a huge smile radiating joy as her eyes sparkled. She didn't want to go back into the real world, didn't want to leave this cocoon of wonder, this new intensity of awe and passion.

He didn't either but he knew he had to. He struggled to bring his mind back to the dire situation at hand. Zhou would be arriving shortly.

He didn't have a plan yet, other than to be honest. If things with Ms. Verheyen didn't work out, he was back to Scotland Yard and calling in the NYPD. He was determined to finish his role in this, and let the people whose job it is to protect the leaders of the world do their job, so he could go home.

Home.

It seemed so far away but he yearned to see his girls. But now he was torn. He wanted to enjoy this wonderful closeness with Loren for as long as he could.

She interrupted his thoughts.

"Ah… it never ceases to amaze me how − for Marcie and you and even talking to Ruth this morning − how faith is just such an intrinsic part of your being, your makeup. You wouldn't be the same people that you are without it."

"I guess so," Jack said contemplatively.

"I hope I can develop something as strong," she said as they approached the house and made their way up to the front door.

"Giving your life to Jesus like you did the other night is the first *big* step to take. The rest is a piece of cake." Jack laughed a little. "We should take this up again once I'm finished with a certain Belgian politician." He opened the door.

"I'd like that."

"Hellooo, anyone home?" Jack called out.

"In the kitchen," he heard Ruth reply.

"You'd best sort out your flight plans before it's too late," Jack said. He kissed Loren softly on the lips before they entered the kitchen.

* * *

"Hello, Professor Haines," Zhou said, approaching Jack, who was waiting at the taxi stand, Thierry next to him.

"Ah… Zhou… is that you?"

"Yes, Professor, it's me."

"I almost didn't recognize you," Jack grinned, staring at Zhou's bare scalp. "Can I introduce a friend of mine? Thierry Le Bon."

"Hello."

"Good to meet you, Zhou." Thierry took Zhou's hand in his.

"I just received a message from Minister Verheyen," said Jack. "She'll be at the Ritz in the next half hour. We'd better get moving."

* * *

"Oh, hello, Stevie, lovely to hear your voice!" Louise Haines sat up and wiped the sleep from her eyes.

"I got the time difference wrong again, didn't I, Mum?" Stephen replied.

"No bother, my dear. I sleep very lightly these days, with you and Jack on the other side of the world. I half expect to be woken up."

"Sorry, Mum."

"Please, no sorries. Life is too short to worry about being woken up by a loved one. How are you, dear? I've left you a few messages in the past week or so and wondered if you'd gone away for a few days."

"I've resigned, Mum, and I'm coming home."

"What wonderful news! What's caused this change?"

"I've had enough over here. I'm struggling with what I'm doing: it doesn't have a point. I want to start living with... you know... purpose, again."

"This sounds like a big talk is in order. Do you mind if I grab a cup of tea, dear?"

"Mum, yes, there is a lot to talk about but I don't have time just now. But when I get home I'll share all."

"Oh, ah, OK."

"But, Mum, I sure could do with your prayers."

"You're always in my prayers, Stevie. Is there something specific you'd like me to pray about?"

"I'm in a bit of a sticky situation with my bosses, and the police are also involved."

"Oh dear, that doesn't sound good."

"It's going to be OK, I think. It may take a little time to sort through. Jack's kinda also involved."

"Really? In what way?"

"It's a long story, but Jack also needs some prayer, as he's stuck in a right old mess."

"Oh, no! I knew there were strange things going on over in France, but I didn't realize they were dangerous. What can I do?"

"Pray, Mum. Pray. And maybe ask some of your church friends to pray too."

"Yes, certainly, Stevie. We've met every night since the attack, without fail."

"Are you OK, Mum?"

"Nothing that our Lord can't fix."

"I gotta go, Mum. I'll call in a few days to let you know what's happened and when I'm leaving New York. Bye."

"Righto, Stevie-dear." She heard him hang up.

She got out of her bed and went to her knees.

"Heavenly Father..."

Chapter 31

Royalty of a different kind presently occupied the rooftop of Buckingham Palace, official residence of the Queen of England.

Lord Bacchazar nodded to the messenger who had landed respectfully in front of him.

"Time for some action," the demonic leader said to the small group of able and willing demon sentinels standing at attention. In unison, the demons' wings clapped open as they took to the air, unseen by the tourists merrily taking photos below.

They didn't have far to go.

***

"Here they come," Tagan said, looking up as he came out from behind an air-conditioning unit on the roof of a building down the road from the Ritz. "Perfect timing. Ms. Verheyen is about to arrive."

"Good, now the fun really begins!" Athaniel said eagerly.

Tagan grimaced. He grabbed the hilt of his long sword as he watched the dark mass descend onto the building directly across from the hotel's entrance.

***

Ruth and Loren saw the black Peugeot pull up opposite the hotel. A lady dressed casually, but smartly, got out of the passenger door, then shut it. The car pulled away from the curb and sped off.

"That might just be her, right on time," Ruth said, looking at her watch, recalling the description Jack had provided.

Marie Verheyen was wearing black slacks with a matching purple knitted top-and-cardigan combination. She carried an overcoat in her left hand, being used to London's habitual drizzle, together with a briefcase. She crossed the busy street confidently; obviously she was looking for someone.

"Why would her car have left?" Loren asked.

"Maybe because that spot is actually a no parking zone!" Ruth replied.

"I'm surprised she has come without any protection," Loren said.

"Hmmm… perhaps she doesn't think she's in any danger."

"Ahh… there it is," Loren said, pointing out the black Peugeot. It had parked down the end of the street.

Ruth felt the phone in her hand vibrate.

"Jack, that you?" she asked.

"Yep, I think she's here." Jack's voice came through the phone loud enough that Loren could also hear his voice. "Purple top, black slacks."

"OK," Ruth said.

"Turn the voice recorder on. We've just made eye contact."

"Good luck, Jack," she said, switching the application on.

Loren was noticeably on edge, struggling to keep it together.

"It's going to be OK," Ruth said, putting her arm around Loren.

"I hope so, Ruth," Loren said, a grim expression on her face.

"Dear God, please protect them all," Ruth prayed aloud.

They waited, eager to hear the first words of contact.

* * *

"Hello, Minister Verheyen," Jack said, extending his hand.

She took it, Jack sensing some tension.

"Hello, Professor Haines," she responded coldly. "Where's your friend?"

"He'll join us when the time is right." Jack led the way into the hotel foyer.

"I trust he's the only surprise you have in store for me?" Marie Verheyen stood stock still to one side of the busy door, ignoring the elegant decor.

"Absolutely. I just thought it best if we feel safe together before I bring him into the picture."

"You don't trust me?"

"I'm just being careful."

"So what have you got to show me?" She wanted this to be as brief as possible.

"It's all here." Jack reached into his coat and produced the documents his brother had sent him a few days ago.

"The first few pages are a series of emails from Ray Malone to Tom Mayer that outline a large sum of money being transferred from one to the other," Jack began.

Her bag at her feet, Marie started to read. "And who are these gentlemen? What do they have to do with Leopold Grosch?"

"Tom Mayer is an investment banker based out of New York who was raising money for a particular venture," Jack explained carefully. "We now know he was using his friend and sometime business associate, Ray Malone, CEO of an LA-based advertising agency, Swain & Peters, to procure some of the funds for this venture. Mayer had tricked Malone to believe the funds would be used to assist in a significant acquisition. Mayer tempted Malone with the carrot of being made CEO of the new and much larger merged entity."

Marie looked up from the papers. "What makes you believe it was all a ruse?"

"It was a sham. There wasn't any such merger proposed and Mayer was raising funds for some other purpose. Which then leads us to the second set of documents." Jack pulled a second sheaf of papers from his pocket.

"Oh, before I go on. You may find it of interest to know that Tom Mayer was killed in a hit-and-run car accident two days ago. The NYPD aren't yet convinced it was an accident. Also, Ray Malone has gone missing, after hearing the news of Mayer's death."

"Missing? How do you mean?"

"Missing. He's disappeared. No one can find him."

"Foul play, again?"

"No one knows. In fact, I'm in the unenviable position of being the last person to have seen him."

"Gee, for a professor who specializes in Organizational Behavior, you sure have an unusual hobby." This comment broke some of the tension between them.

"Yes, I've been racking my mind trying to work out why I've been drawn into this maze of corporate corruption. But it's probably one of those things I won't get an answer to." Jack paused. "So you understand the gist of these first documents, then?"

"Sure, Tom Mayer used his friend, Ray someone or other, to extort a large sum of money for some venture. Mayer's now dead, Ray's gone walkabout or been done in, and I don't see how this has anything to do with Leopold Grosch!"

"Good, you got it so far. Now I'll show you the linkage to your Belgian billionaire."

From the look in her eyes she didn't like Jack's inference, but she didn't say a word.

"Go on." She knew she had to be careful not to reveal the true nature of her relationship with Grosch.

"The next two documents, grouped under the heading of 'Bryggia', involve correspondence between Mayer and an individual known only as 'King'."

Her heart sank hearing the name "King". She recalled the memo she had stumbled upon a week ago. It had to be more than coincidence.

"Are you alright, Ms. Verheyen?" Jack asked, seeing her mind slip away, distracted.

"Yep, keep going."

"The emails make specific reference to the moneys raised from Malone. They were to be used for some other major 'investment' and Mayer expected a sizeable commission check from 'King' for raising the funds."

He paused.

"So that's it?"

"No, as I mentioned on the phone, you may find this particularly interesting. Read this sentence." He took the documents back from her, turned a page and pointed to the sentence he wanted her to read.

For some reason she read it aloud. She recalled their earlier conversation: "We now only require the final contribution from MV to complete the pot of gold that will give us sufficient ammunition to shake up the world!"

That stung her into a stunned silence. She dared not look at Jack for fear that culpability for aiding this man would be written all over her face. She turned away, leaving the documents in Jack's hand.

She didn't know what to say. It was all true. She knew it. And her name was associated with it. She would be ruined.

"Ms. Verheyen," Jack said quietly, "are you OK?"

She didn't respond. Thoughts were racing through her mind. She became aware of the rage that she had been keeping a lid on these past few weeks now bubbling up below the surface.

Suddenly she muttered a curse, her eyes fixed on nothing.

"Are you OK?"

"Yeah." She took a deep breath, and turned to face Jack. "Professor, on the face of it you have a case. If so, Grosch is in trouble."

"Great. That's just what I wanted to hear. How 'bout I bring Zhou over so that he can add fuel to the fire?"

"Yes, please. Is he far away?"

"No, they're just outside." Jack ducked out of the hotel's door, eyes searching for two men standing under a tree fifty feet down the street. He waved Zhou and Thierry to join them and slipped back into the foyer.

"I thought there was only one other involved?" she asked, surprised.

"Thierry is a good friend helping me out, that's all," he offered sheepishly, wondering whether involving him was a good idea. Too late.

Before she could respond, the duo had joined them. Thierry stood slightly back from the others, not wanting to overcrowd Ms. Verheyen.

"Marie Verheyen, I'd like to introduce you to Zhou Chau."

She hesitated, watching both men intently. "And this is Thierry Le Bon."

Thierry shook hands, nodding acknowledgment. He then stepped back.

Minister Verheyen turned to the exotic-looking Chinese. "Professor Haines tells me you have quite a story, Mr. Chau?"

* * *

As the foursome left the hotel, a large white vehicle, a strange cross between an ambulance and a classic old Bedford van, drew up to the curb directly in front. It blocked Ruth and Loren's view.

The angelguards saw it too. They knew what it meant.

As did Bacchazar. An evil scowl gripped his face.

"Drakkin, get ready to go to work!"

The monstrous demon in Viking finery stepped off the roof and sailed down, landing on top of the vehicle.

* * *

"*Drakkin!* He's mine, Tagan!" yelled Hannen, readying himself to launch.

"Stand fast, Hannen! You too, Darius," Tagan snapped. "Not yet. We watch and follow for now."

Hannen said nothing. He sat back on his perch, all the muscles on his angelic frame trembling with urgency.

Darius leant over the building's edge to gain an even better view. Holding back was not his idea of combating these sentinels.

"Hannen, be patient for now. I know it's hard. Your time will come, and very soon!"

Hannen reluctantly nodded, his eyes firmly set on his rival.

* * *

Five men, all wearing black, were on top of them before they could move. Each held a gun close to his body.

"You are surrounded. Come with us quietly and no one will

get hurt." The accent had the guttural resonance of an Afrikaans speaker. "Resist and you will be shot."

Jack, Zhou, Thierry, and Marie looked at each other, stunned and scared.

Suddenly Marie started to scream: *"Help, someb——"* She was crisply pistol-whipped from behind. Her senseless body collapsed into the arms of the leader. Another picked her up easily and toted her deadweight body towards the white vehicle.

"Hey——" Jack's protest was silenced by the leader's suddenly visible gun.

Passers-by thought the situation looked suspicious, but did nothing.

The three were swiftly frisked, losing their concealed phones, wallets and carry bags.

The captives complied with the leader's orders and followed the man carrying Marie's body. The van was only twenty steps away. They hopped into a surprisingly plush interior, including leather seats and a small mounted TV.

Jack was pushed into one seat directly opposite the sliding door on the side of the van, followed by one of the five assailants. Zhou sat two seats behind; Thierry sat further back. Jack looked around to see Marie dumped on the back seat up against the side of the van.

The door slammed shut.

Jack silently prayed.

Not a word was spoken. A brute with a military crew cut sitting next to Jack abruptly pushed a cloth into his face, forcing him to inhale deeply. There was an intense alcohol odor. He struggled but his arms were held. He tried desperately to breathe. His heart started palpitating, fast; his mind slowed.

He slumped forward.

* * *

Loren was beside herself as she heard the voice of the lead abductor.

"Oh God, protect them, please! Keep them safe!" Ruth said through gritted teeth, still disbelieving what was going down.

They saw their three men and Minister Verheyen roughly handled into the van before it raced off. It then turned left onto Piccadilly.

Loren felt way out of her depth. This wasn't her city. "Ruth, what do we do?"

"We do exactly as we discussed with Tee and Jack," Ruth replied calmly. "We go to the police. New Scotland Yard is ten minutes away, and then we can get them to speak to…" She hesitated, pulling a notepad from her handbag. "Here it is, an Inspector Williams is the one we ask for. The NYPD cop is a guy called Detective Sabatini, if we need to contact him."

"OK, let's get going then, Ruth." Loren grabbed Ruth's hand and headed off down the street.

* * *

"Hannen, Andola, Grindor, Landen, and Darius," said Tagan. "You will come with me. We will follow at a distance and observe for the present. Athaniel, Elijah and Arlia – stay behind and watch over Loren and Ruth."

Nods all round.

"Let's go!"

The group of six stealthily rose into the air. They quickly ascertained the direction in which the abductors were heading.

"Where's Bacchazar?" Andola asked, noticing the roof he was previously occupying was now deserted except for some small birds.

"He left immediately Drakkin had taken hold of the white van," Tagan said.

They picked up speed and soon had the white vehicle firmly in their sights. Drakkin had now been joined by five other demons, all similar in shape and size to him. These were no sentinel imps. They had brought out the heavy artillery in anticipation of combat with the enemy.

Hannen leapt to the front of the angelic troop. He was itching to have it out with his old foe once again.

Chapter 32

Ruth and Loren ran down the street to Marie Verheyen's parked Peugeot. It hadn't moved.

They came up alongside the vehicle on the curbside, seeing two men occupying the driver and passenger seats.

"Hey, aren't you going to help Ms. Verheyen?" Ruth said, sticking her head close to the open window of the passenger door.

"Ohhh, no!" She recoiled back from the door, holding her hand to her mouth.

"What's wrong?"

Ruth, unable to speak, just pointed to the car.

Loren approached. Her heart sank as she saw the small hole in the passenger's temple, and a dribble of blood rolling down the side of his head. His eyes were still open as he lay back in the seat.

She walked around to the driver's door and found the driver in the same state.

They'd gotten to them first.

Loren slumped to her knees on the pavement, and wept as Ruth looked helplessly at her. These were merciless killers. And they had Jack. He was going to die, she was sure of it.

Some force within her drove her back to her feet. She grabbed Ruth and clasped her tight, the tears ceasing.

Loren had a new resolve, a new determination.

She saw a police car coming down the street. She let go of Ruth, ran into the middle of the road and hailed it down.

The two officers, shocked to see Loren jumping out into their path, braked just in time.

Little did they realize that Arlia stood between the police car and Loren. There was no way that car was going to hit Loren.

"Help, help, please!" Loren cried out desperately as she ran around to the driver's door.

"Hang on, love," said a lady constable, hopping out of the passenger side.

Loren told the two officers a gabbled story of kidnap, terrorist attack on the G8, Belgian government ministers and the NYPD whilst they attended to the two dead men. The black Peugeot was a rental, picked up from Stansted airport only ninety minutes previously.

Loren used her persuasive powers to convince them to call Inspector Williams at South Croydon. Unfortunately, he'd finished his shift for the day and wasn't currently contactable.

"Isn't there someone else at that station who knew about Jack's visit there this morning and the contact with the NYPD?" Loren asked, frustrated.

"No, sorry, ma'am, there isn't," the lady constable replied. "We think it's best we take you both to our station where you can tell us all about it."

"I'm sorry, constable, we don't have time to waste. My friend Jack Haines has been kidnapped along with two other people, one a Belgian MP, and—"

"We know all that, you've told us!" the lady constable interrupted Loren. "But we've got two dead men here and you two have some knowledge of why. So we're going to take you down to the station and get a statement from you both, and then attend to your concerns!"

"Oh, come off it!" Loren said forcefully. "We don't have time for this! They might be dead!"

"Hey, Ms. Summers, that's enough! You can do this the easy way or we'll cuff you as suspects to a murder investigation. So what's it going to be?" The lady constable stepped into Loren's personal space, her face only inches away.

"Loren, let's do what the officers say," Ruth said, trying to inject some calm into the situation.

Loren's eyes were raging with fury and frustration.

"All right, well, let's get to it. Let's go! *Now!*" Loren said, walking over to the small silver four-door police car and hopping into its back seat.

The area surrounding the dead men's car was now filling up: additional police, ambulance personnel, news crews who had heard of the situation over the police radio, and everyday citizens.

* * *

"What's the latest from Farkad?" Grosch asked over his cell phone. He was seated in his luxuriously decorated study.

"They have just arrived at the town of Romsey, about ninety minutes south-west of London," Vincent responded. "Pienaar and his men will board shortly and head to the Mull of Galloway in the south of Scotland."

"Mull of...?"

"Ah, Galloway, sir. I understand Pienaar has connections there. There's a lighthouse with some cabins overlooking the North Channel which separates Scotland from Northern Ireland."

"OK."

"Pienaar will do whatever is required to obtain the names of the other people who have been told about our plans. He'll pass that information on to me and I'll have people deal with them. We'll keep our guests captive until after tomorrow night, then dump them in the sea."

"Good. What of her pilot and two guards who went with her to London?"

"The pilot is dead and disposed of. Her two guards were both shot dead in their car. Metropolitan Police are all over it. The assassin is most likely safely back home watching the results of his handiwork on the six o'clock news."

Grosch nodded to himself. "You're satisfied with their work?"

"Yes, certainly. These mercenaries are good value."

"All sounds like it's going to plan," Grosch grunted, already moving on to his next agenda.

"Indeed it is, sir." Vincent paused fractionally, familiar with his employer's impatience, but needing to tie down a detail. "Sir, what did that chief of police, Witsel, have to say about his conversation with Ms. Verheyen?"

"Not a great deal. Just that she may need to speak to him quite urgently this evening about a serious matter of national importance. Always sensible to make sure you have the chief of police on your side," Grosch said with a certain satisfaction.

"Thank you, sir." Vincent made a note. "Best go, sir. Matters to attend to."

"Yes, absolutely, Vincent. It's all coming together perfectly!" said Grosch, with uncharacteristic warmth.

Bacchazar was enjoying the moment. He towered over Grosch. His venomous eyes bore down on his human captive. His black lips quirked in a sinister grin, baring brown fangs.

The General would have to eat his words.

Romsey, southern England, early evening

Jack's eyes opened to blackness. Fog filled his mind. Fear gripped him as he recalled being thrust into the van.

The man with the Afrikaans accent appeared at Jack's door, a semi-automatic on his hip.

"Time to take a little joyride!" he said.

"Can't wait," Jack replied.

"Turn around, I got to put these on." He held up a shiny set of handcuffs.

Jack started to protest, but the big man waved his gun.

"Hey, be thankful, the boss said no blindfold, so you'll get to see all the pretty scenery," the thug sniggered as he cuffed Jack.

"Great."

"This way." He led Jack through the door. Haines winced from the sharpness of the cuffs digging into his wrists, breaking the skin.

"Hey, Jack," he heard from behind. Zhou.

Thank you, God.

"There's to be no communication between the captives!" another voice said. It was the leader of the group.

Jack looked behind quickly, catching a glimpse of Thierry. His head was bowed as he was dragged out by one of the kidnappers. Jack grimaced to see his friend in such a state, still obviously suffering from the effects of the drug.

They were soon outside, in a clearing surrounded by dark forest. Several of their captors held flashlights, and Jack could see the outlines of men ahead. A vacant-looking Marie Verheyen came up alongside him but ignored him. Jack noticed the bruise from a growing welt under her left eye and dry blood at the corner of her mouth. Sadness filled his heart when he thought of what these men might have done to her.

Please forgive these men, Jesus. Please heal Ms. Verheyen of the wounds inflicted on her; bind Satan and his workers as they attack her spirit, please, Lord God!

"Move the prisoners forward." The demand came from behind Jack.

The group was herded towards a narrow man-made gap in the forest.

***

"We've told you over and over again. How many times do we have to tell you before you believe us?" Loren said in frustration. She sat in a sparsely furnished interrogation room, a plain-clothed policeman sitting directly in front of her. A uniformed officer stood behind. Ruth was nowhere to be seen, having been taken to a separate room soon after their arrival.

"Ms. Summers," the seated policeman spoke, "I understand your frustration but we are dealing with a double murder here, and you two come in here with a story that, frankly, some might describe as wild and fanciful. But I'm prepared to take your word on it for the present—"

Another plain-clothed officer entered the room.

"Inspector, may I have a word with you, please?" the intruding officer requested.

"Excuse me, Ms. Summers, I'll only be a moment!" The inspector got up and followed the other officer outside.

Loren dropped her head in her hands.

"Hold on, Jack, hold on," she whispered to herself, followed by, "God, protect him, please. I couldn't stand to lose him!"

Arlia smiled. She placed her hands over Loren's head and prayed.

Warmth and calm soothed Loren's racing heart and mind.

The inspector soon returned to the room.

"Ms. Summers, looks like you're both telling the same story, which is a good thing!" He sat back down.

"Detective Inspector… Cole, is it? Have you called Detective Sabatini of the NYPD yet?" she asked.

"Yes, we have, and he's able to corroborate some of your story… the death of this Mayer person in New York, the disappearance of the other man and the documents that you talked about."

"Have you played him the audio on the phone?"

"No, not yet, we're checking it out for validity, you know, making sure it's the real thing, not some fake!"

Loren rolled her eyes. "And how long is that going to take? Have you checked the GPS app on Ruth's phone yet?"

"Hang on, one at a time. The audio should be validated shortly and yes, Mrs. Le Bon showed us the application and a few moments ago it appeared to indicate they are now at Romsey, south-west of London. We've contacted the local station and requested immediate assistance in checking their position."

"Good grief, can't you speed this up somehow?" Loren said, getting to her feet. "These are killers and they've got our men."

"We're moving as fast as we can, Ms. Summers. Please be patient. Can I get you another drink, a coffee perhaps?"

Loren shook her head in dismay. *This can't be happening!*

* * *

The heavenly team, sitting in a cluster of tall birch trees, watched eagerly as they saw Drakkin and his monstrous mates traverse the airfield, looking for them. The thick canopy sufficiently concealed those watching whilst allowing them to follow the enemy's movements.

"When will we attack, Athaniel?" Hannen asked, a little too loudly. His heart was pumping at the thought of Thierry being left to his own devices against the highly trained African guns for hire.

"Not here, Hannen!" was the reply.

"What? And let Thierry and Jack continue to suffer?" Hannen said agitatedly.

"For now, if that is to happen, yes. But I very much doubt they will eliminate them yet. They wouldn't have gone to all this trouble to pop them now. No, I think they will try to understand who else knows about Grosch's plans to ensure tomorrow night goes swimmingly."

"Athaniel, I don't understand. This is madness. We can take Drakkin and his buddies, take control of the plane, and all will be safe," Hannen said, fuming.

"I understand your frustration and anger, Hannen. But please trust me on this."

"But can you guarantee no further harm will come to Thierry or Jack or the others?" Hannen asked.

"No, I can't guarantee that. But we *must* not jeopardize the chance of bringing a stop to Grosch's plan at the G8. Unfortunately, and I know how hard this is to appreciate, that has to be our first priority, at this time."

Hannen gripped both sides of his head, shaking it in anguish. He always found this part of being an angelguard the hardest: standing by and watching the potential harming and possible death of your human charge. He knew that Thierry, if he died, would soon be in heaven, but he couldn't stand to see him suffer needlessly.

He had no other option but to obey.

* * *

The trees came to an end, revealing a peculiar-looking aircraft sitting in a large field.

"What's that?" Jack said. His voice sounded unnaturally loud in his ears.

"Our transport," replied his keeper. "An Osprey is what it's called. Looking forward to this. Haven't been on one before. Told it's a beaut ride."

They approached the aircraft: half helicopter, half airplane. Jack had a confused expression on his face as the party made its way towards the open rear-loading ramp, common to air force planes. Further forward, twin rotors sat on each wing, and a glass cockpit fronted the craft.

Soon inside, it was typically sparse – basic folding seats facing each other.

"To the front seats," commanded the leader who stood just behind the cockpit.

Six minutes later, the twin rotors had lifted the aircraft vertically into the night air, before hovering for a moment whilst the pilot shifted into plane mode. Climbing to 10,000 feet, he guided the aircraft north in the direction of the bright half moon partly sheltered by slowly drifting rain clouds.

Jack sat in the middle, two guards on either side, still handcuffed. Zhou was directly opposite whilst Thierry was on his side of the plane, closer to the back, Minister Verheyen directly opposite him. Both of them were still very groggy, struggling to keep their heads upright. Zhou was pensive, but seemingly intrigued by all the gadgetry visible on the walls and ceiling.

Even though a very modern aircraft, it was not equipped for civilian comfort, and the noise of the engines made it hard to hear anyone speak. Jack closed his eyes, and prayed quietly. Frightened and uncertain about whether he'd live to share this story with anyone, he sought God's peace and protection for the four of them.

"Fear not, for I am with you, says the Lord," he repeated to himself. It was one of his favorite Bible verses.

The angels, not far away in hot pursuit, heard his prayers, and they too felt greater assurance and comfort from heaven.

They watched from a discreet distance as the six monsters clung tightly to the smooth exterior lines of the unusual beast of the air.

Chapter 33

"Pienaar here!" Jacques Pienaar said through his radio mic. He was seated in the cockpit, behind the pilot and co-pilot.

"Pienaar, Farkad!" came the reply. "You must be about to land?"

"Yes, we started our descent a few minutes ago."

"You know this place well?"

"Very well. My uncle and his family immigrated here when I was a kid, and I spent a number of vacations with them. He still does maintenance work, that's how I found that it was closed for a few days. Perfect timing, hey?"

"Perfect."

"When do we dispose of the hostages?"

"Not until you receive my order. First you need to find out who else knows what they know."

"Well, I'm sure my uncle won't be carrying any truth serum."

"I suppose not. You'll just have to use more primitive measures!"

Pienaar grunted. "We'll enjoy that!"

"Just tell your men not to get trigger happy too soon."

"My men know their business," the South African growled. Then a thought struck him. "Are we likely to have a reception committee waiting for us?"

"No. The police got to Romsey soon after you were airborne, but I've been tracking you and there's been no other aircraft in any close vicinity."

"How'd they track us so quickly to Romsey? We didn't have a tail at any time during the drive there."

"Come on, Pienaar, the police here in the UK aren't

amateurs. They have their methods. A politician being kidnapped is big news anywhere in the world. The word's spreading fast but it appears they still believe the hostages to be somewhere in England."

"Yeah, just keep 'em away as long as you can."

"Absolutely. I don't think you'll have any interruptions for the next twelve hours or so whilst they interrogate all flight data. That'll take some time. Just make sure you get the information out of the hostages soonest. The sea support will be arriving in the morning, if you need to make an earlier than expected departure."

"'Kay."

"Signing off." Pienaar heard the call disconnect in his earpiece.

* * *

"Get ready for landing." The command came from the cockpit.

The Osprey had slowed and now hovered as the twin rotors went horizontal to begin the landing procedure. The craft was being buffeted by strong wind squalls and pelting rain from the Irish Sea.

Jack's body tensed. He had no armrests, so clasped his hands tightly together. Memories of that horror flight from Chicago years ago came flooding back into his mind.

All ten of the mercenaries were on high alert. Zhou appeared unconcerned. Both Marie Verheyen and Thierry were back in the land of the living, fear etched on the Minister's face. Thierry gave Jack a wink. Jack replied with a nod of the head. *Glad you're here with us, mate,* he said to himself.

WHUMP, WHUMP, WHUMP!

The rotors were working overtime as the descent commenced.

"Not enjoying this, huh?" said the huge man sitting next to Jack, nodding to his tightly wrung hands.

"Ah, no. Flying's not one of my preferred pastimes."

"What was that?!" one of the other thugs shouted as they hit an air pocket, forcing the aircraft to drop.

Jack's stomach was in his throat.

"Don't worry, the guv's one of the best," said the giant next to Jack.

And with that the craft made contact with solid ground – remarkably lightly, considering the conditions. It bounced slightly, then stopped.

"Thank you, Lord," Jack said under his breath.

"Told ya. Perfect record, the guv has." The giant unbuckled his belt and then Jack's.

The door to the rear-loading ramp began to open, the howling wind and rain blasting a strong burst of frigid air into each person's face.

"Ah, the Irish Sea, you blow so cold," said Jack's vast guard, becoming instantly more imposing as he inhaled the frosty breeze.

"Hey nigger, get to your feet!" Pienaar's disdainful voice cut through the din of rain and wind as he stood over Thierry. His face was now protected by a black balaclava and a hooded jacket. Only his eyes and mouth were visible.

Thierry ignored him.

"When I speak to you, *nigger*, I expect an immediate response. You hear me?"

Thierry nodded as he rose to his feet, meeting the mercenary leader eye to eye.

Pienaar eyed the lashing rain. His mouth smiled. "You can lead us out."

"Be my pleasure," Thierry replied as icily as the air now gushing inside. The loading ramp was now fully extended.

Pienaar whipped around, and shoved his semi-automatic violently into Thierry's ribs, winding him. Thierry buckled over.

"Now you don't take a tone with me, ya hear, nigger!"

Thierry didn't react as he straightened himself, struggling for breath, his years of RAF hostile-situation training flooding back.

Jack took a step forward to remonstrate but was pushed back by his guard. Jack was surprised to see compassion in his eyes: they were telling him to sit tight, that playing the hero wouldn't help him or Thierry. Jack nodded comprehension.

"Release the prisoners from their shackles," Pienaar yelled. "And bring them to me!"

Jack, Minister Verheyen and Zhou plus an assassin each stood facing Pienaar.

"Now, don't try anything heroic or my men will have no hesitation in shooting you. Do you understand?"

"Yes," Jack spoke for all of them.

Thierry didn't say a word. He stood his ground, staring Pienaar in the eye.

Thierry saw it coming but couldn't stop it. The butt of Pienaar's semi-automatic smashed into his jaw, snapping a molar out of his mouth. Blood welled over his tongue and down his throat, making him nauseous.

"Hey—" Jack objected.

"You want some action too, do ya?" Pienaar said venomously as he leant into Jack.

"Leave him… please," said Thierry.

He braced himself for the next hit. It didn't come.

"That would have flattened most men," remarked Pienaar. "Armed forces background, hey? I can see it in ya."

Thierry didn't respond. He held his throbbing jaw with one hand. The pain was excruciating.

"We're not going to kill you, not just yet." Pienaar's expression was almost cheerful. "Before we do, we gotta find out some information from you all."

"Nooo…" Fear stuck daggers in Minister Verheyen's heart.

Jack put a reassuring arm on her shoulder.

We need you, Father, he silently prayed.

"We're leaving now. Swartbooi and du Preez here will lead." Two stepped forward, Swartbooi being Jack's attendant. "Do what they say and follow them."

The group stepped forward, but Pienaar grabbed Thierry's arm, halting his progress. He winced from the agonizing pain in his torso and jaw.

"What should I call you?"

"Le Bon!" Thierry shouted over the noise of the elements.

Pienaar pushed him forward with the butt of his firearm. Thierry was hit by a treacherous gust of wind and rain so strong that he had to grab hold of the inside of the door to keep from falling over.

His eyes adjusted to the darkness caused by the heavy rainclouds and he started out after the others. The driving wind and rain were invading his clothes, soaking him to the core. Pienaar jabbed the semi-automatic into Thierry's back as he kept in step behind him.

* * *

"Hey, it looks like they've landed somewhere in Scotland," said one of the detectives as he entered the coffee room of the station.

"Really, whereabouts?" Loren replied excitedly, Ruth raising her head expectantly.

"Ah, Cairngaan looks like the nearest town of any note. Um… but the GPS is saying their current position is in the North Channel… no, it's the southernmost tip of Scotland, the Mull of Galloway."

"Got it," said a second detective as he displayed a map of southern Scotland on the wall using a projector connected to his laptop. He panned closer and there it was, a satellite image of a lighthouse, overlooking the Irish Sea.

"Good work," said the other, holding Ruth's phone. "It was very clever of your husband to set this up, ma'am."

Ruth simply nodded.

"So can we get after them?" Loren asked, jumping to her feet.

* * *

It wasn't long before they reached the others standing in front of a lighthouse. Jack, Zhou, and Minister Verheyen stood looking like drenched rats next to the two killers, who were well protected from the elements in their camouflage gear.

"Swartbooi, here's the key to the first cabin over there," Pienaar said to the man mountain. "Take the prisoners and lock them in there. We'll take the second one further along."

Swartbooi obeyed, leading the foursome to their confinement.

Thierry hesitated.

"You wouldn't believe how much pleasure it would give me to kick you off this cliff and see your body flailing in the wind as you plummet to your death," Pienaar said, raising his semi-automatic again.

Drakkin stood directly behind Pienaar. The demon didn't care for the wait. "Time for all four to die," he spoke into Pienaar's heart, causing his captive to release the safety on the firearm now aimed directly at Thierry.

Thierry set off, not looking back, Pienaar keeping his weapon locked on him.

Dear God, help us all, please! prayed Thierry. *Bind Satan and his evil workers. Free us from their grasp!*

Pienaar lowered his weapon and returned to the aircraft.

* * *

Thierry was shoved through the door, sprawling on the ground, coming to a stop against Marie Verheyen's legs.

The tiny room, barely big enough to house the four of them, was lit by a single lightbulb hanging from the ceiling.

"You OK, mate?" Jack asked as Thierry sat up, crossing his legs, relieved to be protected from the raging elements.

"Yeah, I'll live, Jack," he replied, holding his aching ribs as he gingerly got to his feet. "He hit the same spot on my ribs that just healed from the January attack. Lost a molar, I think, and feels like a couple of others might be cracked."

Jack hissed sympathetically. "I'd stay seated, if I were you."

"It's nothing compared to what I reckon we're all going to experience over the next few hours if help doesn't arrive soon. The GPS on my watch appears to be working, so hopefully, the girls have managed to get the right people's attention so a rescue mission can commence." Thierry slid his sleeve back over his watch, which his captors had overlooked in their haste.

"Great that you're a gadget freak, Tee," Jack said.

"You OK, Ms. Verheyen?" Thierry asked, seeing her shivering on the cold wooden bench.

"Yes, thank you. Just very, very cold," she said, her teeth chattering. She had pulled her legs up into her chest, trying to conserve her body heat.

"It must be below zero," Zhou said.

"What do you think they will do with us?" Ms. Verheyen asked to no one in particular. "Do you think they will kill us?"

"No, well, not straight away. If they had just wanted to kill us, they would have done that back in London," Jack replied. "You heard him back in the plane, they're after information."

Thierry took over. "They want to know who else knows what we know, so they can remove any threat to their plans. If I was in Grosch's shoes I'd make sure I got to everyone to minimize any risk of exposure."

"The girls!" Jack's expression was grim.

Thierry nodded, a concerned look on his face.

"What girls?" Zhou asked.

"Thierry's wife Ruth and my friend Loren. They know everything. Hopefully they are safely under police protection as we speak."

"What about you, Ms. Verheyen?" Thierry asked. "Did you speak to anyone about it?"

"No!" she said truthfully but so bluntly that the men didn't appear to believe her, judging by the responses on their faces. "No, honestly, I didn't tell anyone. I spoke briefly to my chief of police but simply told him that I would need to speak to him later about a matter of national importance. That's all, I swear!"

"OK, Ms. Verheyen, we believe you," Jack said. "Sounds like there's not much for them to get out of us. So what do we tell them?"

"Nothing," Thierry proposed. "Absolutely nothing."

Brussels, after midnight

Grosch was wide awake, sitting in front of the TV, his mind elsewhere.

One of his three cell phones started vibrating on the smooth glass coffee table.

"Hello," he said abruptly, recognizing the caller's number on the screen. It was his secure phone and couldn't be tapped.

"You near your TV?" asked Vincent.

"Yes, why?"

"Channel 28."

Grosch reached for the remote control.

The channel changed. A scene showing the Ritz Hotel crowded with people; then police cars surrounding a black Peugeot. A female reporter came onto the screen:

"Tonight in London, Belgian Deputy Prime Minister Marie Verheyen has, we believe, been kidnapped, along with three men she was meeting. In addition, two of her security guards have been found dead with gunshot wounds to the head. They were seated in their car just a hundred yards away from where the Minister was taken."

She continued: "At this stage, police have received no demands for ransom nor do they have any leads on the kidnappers. However, some information has recently come to hand that suggests the kidnappers may have taken the four away by private plane. There is some conjecture that the kidnapping may be associated with the G8 Summit that commences tomorrow in Berlin. However, this has not been confirmed…"

"No surprise! The London constabulary aren't dummies," Grosch said, muting the TV, trying to ignore his burgeoning rage.

"What the news broadcast failed to add," said Vincent, "was that the FBI, the CIA, the US Secretary of Defense, the UN Security Council and all the other major security agencies round the world have been advised of the situation."

"What did you expect?"

"Sir, there is some bad news, however." Vincent ignored Grosch's rhetorical question.

"Yes?"

"It would appear the British police have identified our men's location. We've been watching the amount of air traffic in the vicinity and it's clear that in the last thirty minutes two reconnaissance planes have targeted the specific area around the south of Scotland."

"It was only a matter of time, Vincent," Grosch replied, sounding unperturbed. "We were never going to keep them at bay for more than twelve hours." His voice hardened. "And Vincent, they've still got to get through our men and recover the hostages. We are in a powerful position."

"They'll have an SAS team there before we know it." Vincent's voice betrayed his strain. Grosch was not tolerant of failure.

"Yes, no doubt, but we've got time to extract the information. Then they can do whatever they want. If they kill Pienaar it will save us the trouble. Any word on Berlin?" he asked, coolly.

Vincent recovered quickly from the abrupt change of subject. "Still working on that. What we know so far is that security has been advised of the possible situation. Extra security is coming in and they have commenced a full search of the hotel and its surrounds."

"A predictable response. The Head of Security will earn his money."

"Yes, sir. They won't find anything, he'll make sure of it. What about the decoy?"

"At this stage, stick with the plan. See what develops over the next few hours."

"Sir, do you think—" But Grosch had cut the call.

Chapter 34

Mull of Galloway, very early Sunday morning

They all heard it simultaneously, even through the howling storm outside and the crashing of the huge waves on the rocks immediately below them.

They looked at each other, all knowing what they had just heard.

The engine of a low-flying plane. But not any plane.

A Tornado reconnaissance jet.

* * *

Thierry, next door, heard it too.

"Help is at hand, folks," he said cautiously.

"Really, where?" Ms. Verheyen asked, looking quizzically at Thierry.

"That sounded like a recon jet and I don't think it would be standard practice to carry out a reconnaissance drill over the Irish Sea at this time on a Saturday night, do you?"

The other three all got to their feet excitedly.

"Hang in there, people," Thierry warned. "Our friends next door aren't going to give us up easily, you can be sure of that."

* * *

"Whatya see?" Pienaar asked as the enormous soaking shape of Swartbooi re-entered the room.

"Two of 'em completed two pass-overs," Swartbooi said, removing his balaclava.

"So they now know we're here," Pienaar said.

"Whatya reckon, boss?" one of the others asked.

"Hmmm…" Pienaar grinned. "Looks like we might just have a fight on our hands after all!"

There was a chorus of cheers and wolf whistles.

"Cool it. We're here to do a job. Du Preez, bring the lady in here. Swartbooi, take the others and start unloading the weapons from the plane."

* * *

The heavy steel door opened suddenly, caught by the wind. Du Preez, dressed all in black, filled the doorway, inadvertently shielding the four from the lashing wind and rain.

"Madame, your presence is required next door," he said almost politely, unaware of his uncivilized appearance.

Thierry stood up, extending his full six-foot-four frame between the hoodlum and Marie Verheyen.

"Hey, nigger, it won't serve you or the lady any good, getting in my way!" du Preez said, meeting him eye to eye. He shoved Thierry aside like a marionette, sending him crashing into the corner of the bench seat. His shoulder hit a protruding snag, piercing the skin and causing Thierry to wince in pain. *This sure isn't my day!*

Seeing that Marie was not moving in response to his request, du Preez grabbed her and thrust her against his hefty torso.

"Hey, go easy, buddy!" Jack said, moving toward him.

"Back soon," said the mercenary, turning to leave. "It'll be your turn next!" Marie took the full impact of the rain and wind as he held her easily in the doorframe. Jack could sense the grin under his hood.

"She doesn't know anything. I'm the one you want," Jack pleaded.

That stopped du Preez's progress momentarily, but then he lurched out, slamming the door shut with a clang behind him.

"Damn it!" Jack said, kicking the ground.

* * *

Louise Haines and two of her girlfriends were sitting around a computer in her study. They were typing the daily prayer bulletin.

"That should do it," one of the others said.

"Make sure you ask them to send it on to all their other friends," Louise stressed, "and encourage them to text or use Facebook or whatever to spread the word."

"We are modern, aren't we, dear?" said the third.

"It's the only way I manage to communicate with Jane these days. Via Facebook, that is," Louise explained.

"There, it's gone. Into the ether."

"Super, girls. Thank you so much. The prayer army is going global for my Jack. Praise the Lord!" Louise hugged her friends warmly.

* * *

Within minutes, the message flew around the globe, far and wide.

Prayers were being said.

Heaven was listening.

And so the message was relayed to a certain angelic squad stationed on the foghorn down the cliff from the Mull of Galloway lighthouse.

"People are praying!" Athaniel announced to his team. "Thousands and thousands of them. Singing their praises and beseeching the Lord's goodness and mercy!"

The team of six could sense it, feel it. The Spirit was at work.

"And here comes the cavalry!" Athaniel said, pointing to a cloud of light speeding towards them.

* * *

He wasn't the only one in the supernatural who heard the prayers.

"We gotta stop this!" Drakkin yelled. "This praying is driving me mad!"

"I think they're singing now," one of his evil sentinels suggested.

"This has gotta stop! *Nowww!*" Drakkin screamed in fury as he stepped through the concrete wall of the room that housed the team of assassins.

* * *

"What's that noise next door?" Pienaar asked, a puzzled expression on his face.

"Dunno," du Preez replied, not particularly bothered or interested.

"Find out!" Pienaar snapped. "And make them stop!"

Drakkin's huge muscular body dwarfed the hefty six-foot-five frame of the leader, one oversized clawed paw resting on his head.

Ms. Verheyen sat terrified in the corner on a single steel chair. Her face was already bearing the results of their first questions. Welts on both cheeks and under both eyes were beginning to become visible, blood flowing freely from a cut lip.

* * *

The heavy steel door smashed against the wall.

"Shut that racket up, will ya!" du Preez yelled, seeing the three men sitting cross-legged in a circle on the cold rock floor.

They stopped.

He slammed the door shut behind him.

* * *

Du Preez resumed his station in the other hut, standing over Ms. Verheyen with Pienaar, ready to inflict another blow to her battered face. Du Preez enjoyed his work, but the finer points of interrogation were beyond him.

All three of them heard it this time.

"Didn't you tell them to shut up?" Pienaar yelled furiously. "Stay here, I'll do it this time!"

* * *

He went to open the door to the second room, the rain drenching him.

A piercing ray of light stung his eyes, momentarily blinding him. He leant up against the door, unable to move.

The rain and wind dropped. The storm hadn't ceased elsewhere, but the beam of light was cocooned from it. The buffets of air and water were still lashing the cabin's walls.

Twenty angels, swords drawn, glowed in the powerful radiance. It was unmistakable, but only visible to those in the supernatural.

They hadn't come for the humans.

"Leave them! They are His!" said one from within the group.

It was a command. Drakkin, at Pienaar's shoulder, knew he stood no chance against this company. Snarling, the giant demon turned and leapt up into the wild night.

"Go back inside!" said the angelic leader. Pienaar heard this in his heart.

The dark of the night descended upon Pienaar once again. The rain and wind resumed using his body as a punch-bag.

He turned and went back into the cabin, wondering what he had been doing outside.

* * *

"Wow, did you see that?" Andola said, both exasperated and overwhelmed.

Hannen and the others stood awestruck, tears streaming down their cheeks.

"Praise to you, Lord Jesus, the Lion of Judah!" Athaniel said.

* * *

"She hasn't told anyone anything," du Preez said as Pienaar walked back into the room, drenched to the bone.

"Hey?" Pienaar said, obviously distracted.

"Boss, you OK?"

"Ah, yeah! Peachy."

"They're still singing next door."

"Let them. It's not hurting anyone, I guess," Pienaar said, ignoring the look of surprise on du Preez's face. He'd never seen his boss change his mind so completely about something so quickly.

Marie Verheyen was crying softly. The welts on her face were now clearly evident, her right eye was beginning to close and her top lip was bleeding heavily.

Her soaked purple cardigan had been ripped off. Her left shoulder was a bright shade of pink, as was most of her left arm.

She had told them the truth.

"So you haven't told anyone then, have you, Minister Verheyen?" du Preez said, pushing his face into hers.

"No more, please, please, no more!" she squeaked as tears cascaded down her cheeks. She was beyond breaking point.

He lifted her up by the throat like a rag doll and whispered: "I think I can guess what you're afraid of. Tell me what I want to hear."

He paused, holding her at arm's length by her neck. She was struggling to breathe. She tried to talk but nothing came out.

He dropped her back in the chair. She reached for her aching throat.

"As... I... told... you... before," she whispered, struggling with each word, his grip having bruised her vocal cords, "I... spoke... to... my—"

"Yeah, yeah, we know that," du Preez said, preparing his right hand to slap her again. She cowered.

"No... no... no... please... no more... The... men next door... they mentioned... two women who... knew... everything."

"Now that's more like it," Pienaar said from behind his subordinate.

"Names, *Minister*, what are their names?" Pienaar demanded aggressively.

"The black man's wife... Ruth, I think he said her name was," her voice was starting to improve, "and the other one was someone called Loren."

"Thank you, Ms. Verheyen," Pienaar said sincerely. "Get the Aussie and bring him to me!" he ordered. "And take her back!"

She tried to get to her feet and collapsed, du Preez catching her before she hit the ground. She let herself be lifted. Pienaar opened the door for his colleague. He looked away, suddenly uncomfortable.

***

The worship had ceased. Jack and Thierry were pacing the floor and Zhou was stretching when du Preez entered, carrying a battered Marie Verheyen.

"You scum!" Zhou said, going for him. "What have you done to her?"

Thierry stepped in and took her in his arms, the other two helping him.

"Haines, your turn now!" du Preez said ominously.

Jack's stomach turned. *Jesus, help me, please. Please soothe Marie's wounds both physically and spiritually. Help me to be strong!*

Jack went straight for the door, resigned to his impending ordeal but feeling renewed and refreshed in his heart. He knew he wouldn't be alone.

"Stay strong for Jesus, Jack!" said Thierry.

As he took the ten steps to the next building he heard the voice clearly in his mind: *Trust me, I will not leave you.*

***

Jack was sitting in the steel chair awaiting his fate.

Du Preez had come, gone back out and returned while Pienaar stood near the door talking on his satellite phone, the aerial to which was as long as the oversized phone. Du Preez and Jack were listening to the conversation.

"Yeah, yeah, we know they know. Two of 'em just completed two pass-overs twenty minutes ago… yeah… the men are just getting the gear now, should be here any minute… not a great deal from the woman, but enough. She mentioned that two other women know everything…"

Pienaar looked over at Jack as he said it. Jack's heart sank.

"… She didn't know anything else… What, you already know about the women?… And you're absolutely certain about that?… Yeah, well, we've got him in here now and are about to interrogate him… will let you know as soon as we find out anything more… Yeah, right!"

He pulled the phone from his ear, pressed a button to end the call and flipped the antenna down.

"Now, Mr. Haines," he said menacingly as he stood directly in front of Jack. "Oh, sorry, *Professor* Haines."

"What do you want to know?" Jack asked pensively.

"Who knows what you know? It's that simple. You tell us everything quick and you'll get to live the last few hours of your life in relative comfort!"

"Unlike Ms. Verheyen?"

SLAP!

Jack winced at the backhander. He hadn't seen it coming. *Can the sarcasm, Jack.* His right cheek throbbed.

"Minister Verheyen did extremely well, considering the love pats du Preez gave her. Few women would have lasted as long."

"You already know about the other two women."

"Yes, we do, but why don't you tell us who they are, just to make sure?"

BANG!

The three men were jolted by the sudden impact of the heavy door crashing open. Swartbooi was carrying a large rocket launcher over his right shoulder. Two other balaclava-clad men followed him, carrying similar weapons. Two others soon entered carrying large bags.

The fifteen-by-fifteen-foot room suddenly became very crowded.

"Is that it?" Pienaar asked, looking over the small arsenal.

"We picked up everything we could carry, boss!" Swartbooi said. "There's another RPG-7 and two more semi-automatics."

"Go get 'em. Never know what we're going to need!"

The five dropped their loads and resignedly went back out into the storm.

Jack was unsure of what to do. How much did they know about Ruth and Loren? The last thing he wanted was to place them in danger.

Lord God, please protect Ruth and Loren. Send some angels to keep them safe from the enemy, oh great and loving God, protector of all, Lord over all dominions.

"So who are these women?" Pienaar asked, holding up the end of his semi-automatic.

Jack stared straight into Pienaar's eyes. Didn't say a thing. But prepared himself for a second hit.

BANG!

The door clattered against the rock wall once again.

"Colonel," the balaclava-clad soldier said, short of breath, "choppers, twelve o'clock from the north!"

"How many?"

"Two, sir!"

"Where's Swartbooi and the others?"

"Still at the plane."

Pienaar went to the door, stepped out and dialed a number on the sat-phone.

"What's your position?… Stay there… We'll bring what we can and meet you there… Have the first grenade ready to fire – only launch on my command. Got it?" He hung up, giving the thumbs up to Swartbooi fifty feet away at the bottom of the plane's rear-loading ramp.

"Du Preez, take Haines back to the other cabin. Then I want the two of you to grab a launcher each. I'll bring the ammo!" Pienaar barked.

Thank you, Lord. Jack got to his feet and started making for the door.

"You know this is only a postponement of the inevitable, don't ya, Haines?" du Preez snarled.

Jack didn't respond and made his way through the door. The rain and wind had finally started to ease.

* * *

"You're on your own!" Farkad's voice said over the sat-phone.

"We don't stand a chance against a hundred armed troops, Farkad, and you know it!" Pienaar screamed down the phone. "They'll pick us off one by one."

"You knew this was a distinct possibility when you took the job!"

"Sure, but—"

"But nothing. You and your men are one of the most feared mercenary groups in the world, that's why we employed you. You've beaten bigger odds than this one. Well, your résumé says you have!"

"All right. Now I know we can't expect any back-up, we'll have to do it ourselves!"

"How much ammo ya got?" Farkad asked.

"Enough grenades to last a couple of days, I reckon, and sufficient ammo for the semis for a week!"

"See, no problem. You've gotta hold out until the sub arrives. After that we don't care what you do with your touring party!"

"Yeah, and what about the fact I'm holding hostage a minister of the Belgian government?"

"If you play your cards right you'll be long gone before anyone can get a hold of you. You just get your friends on that sub working overtime to get to you."

"Another ten hours, maybe less, before they get here. Depends on the currents."

"There ya go. Ten hours to hold out. I'm sure you and your extremely capable crew can manage that now, can't you!"

"Over and *out*!" Pienaar said loudly, having had enough of Farkad's supercilious tone.

* * *

"What is it, Vincent?" Grosch asked through a yawn. He was still in his study, not having slept. The TV was on with the sound muted.

"The wires confirm the various security agencies are pursuing some information provided by the NYPD in its investigation into Mayer's death. There is a theory that is being considered overnight in America that *you* are implicated in both Mayer's death and this attack on Minister Verheyen."

Silence.

Grosch was shocked. He had thought his plan was foolproof.

"How?" he finally asked quietly.

"We're not sure at this stage. We think it must be something that the two ladies relayed to the police, which was then passed on to the FBI and so on."

"What do you recommend?"

Vincent was worried: he had never heard his boss rattled. "We put the decoy in play as soon as possible this morning rather than the original plan for the afternoon. That should then remove fears about G8. It may not remove entirely the conjecture about your involvement, but they need proof and a motive before they can start laying charges against you. It will take months of the best investigative minds to connect our three comrades to you."

"Hmmm…" Grosch rallied quickly. "We cannot have any more slip-ups. All communication must be via this secure line, understood?"

"Certainly, sir!"

"All right, do as you propose. I will be leaving for Berlin at 8 a.m., in two hours' time. I'll obviously be heavily watched and all my correspondence will be closely monitored. I'll have this phone with me at all times, except in the meetings."

Vincent heard the line go dead. It was curiously comforting to know his graceless boss was back in control.

Chapter 35

The morning brought some soothing warm sunshine to the south of Scotland. The battering storms of the night had blown back into the North Atlantic, headed towards the Icelandic coast.

The thin line of brightness that edged under the steel door was all the four captives could see of the vastly improved weather. The temperature had only reached 6 degrees Celsius, but that was a significant improvement on the freezing conditions of a few hours past.

Jack and Thierry paced the tiny hut, trying to build some adrenalin to warm their bodies. They prayed quietly as they moved in step with each other.

"Ah, excuse me, gentlemen. I wonder if you would help me sit up on the bench, please?" Marie asked, having been silent in her own thoughts since waking a while ago.

Jack and Thierry went to her assistance, helping her up onto the bench.

"Morning," Jack said. "How's the arm?"

"Extremely sore," she winced as she moved it.

"And morning to you too!" Jack said, noticing Zhou stretching as he got to his feet.

"Did I miss anything?" Zhou asked.

"Absolutely nothing," Thierry replied. "Our friends have been outside since you fell asleep and we haven't heard a peep out of them."

"What no shots, nothing?" Thierry and Jack responded with a shake of their heads.

Zhou took a seat next to Marie.

Jack and Thierry returned to their pacing. No one said a word.

"You know I've been having an affair with him for four years?" Marie said out of the blue, stopping the two pacers in their tracks. She suddenly had the men's full attention.

"Grosch, you mean?" Jack asked.

She nodded.

"My husband and I have a sort of open marriage. We tolerate each other's fantasies, is perhaps a better way of expressing it."

She paused, waiting for some reaction. None was forthcoming.

"I'd known Leopold for many years. We first met when I was a junior minister and his business interests were taking on greater significance within government circles. We saw each other occasionally at various functions over a few years, but nothing happened until one particular function about four years ago. It was in Antwerp, a party fundraiser, and we were seated on the same table. That was the night our affair started. It wasn't long before we began meeting regularly twice a week at a city hotel, one he owned of course, and more often than not we just talked."

Suddenly Marie needed to make them understand. "It wasn't always about sex, that wasn't the most important aspect of the relationship. He's a very, very smart man who is incredibly well connected. I don't think either of us loves the other, certainly there have been moments when I was convinced I did, but it was more about mutual admiration... well, at least I admired him," she finished painfully.

"Did your husband know about him?" Zhou asked, for all of them.

"I don't know. I'm sure he is aware I've been seeing someone, but we never discussed it. Never discussed any of them. His or mine. Soon after we had our first child we agreed that seeing someone else was OK as long as it didn't mess up the children. At the time I wasn't that thrilled about the idea," she went on candidly, "but I also loved my husband deeply. He had admitted to me that he had taken up with an old girlfriend of his during my first pregnancy. It hurt, but I... well, I loved him. In my mind I decided it was OK to share him so long as we stayed together."

Once again she paused. The three men were intrigued.

The compassion in Jack's face, in particular, was evident. She wasn't sure why she was telling these three strangers her story but somehow it made her feel better.

"He has been very good to me. Leopold, that is. It's only been in the last few months that his demeanor has changed. He didn't seem as interested in me, especially once the practicalities of the finance package had been sorted out."

"Finance package?" Thierry asked.

"Oh, the natural gas pipeline project that the Grosch Group are building, with significant government financial assistance. I approved it." She paused to compose herself.

"I still think the project is right for the country." She could hear her tone growing more defensive. "As it's essential infrastructure, the government should provide finance, but..." She shook her head. "I know now he's used me. I keep going over and over in my mind all the budget meetings, trying to see whether they could have acted as a buffer to finance some other activity. The detail Grosch's team provided was extraordinary. Could some of the money be used for other purposes? Yes, I guess it could, and we'd never know." She shook her head, profoundly disappointed in herself.

"This must be very hard for you," said Thierry.

"I had hoped to be prime minister one day." Her voice was tinged with sadness. "I will advise the prime minister of my intention to resign immediately we get back!"

It happened almost instantly. The men could see it on her face. Marie went from struggling to defend herself to suddenly switching sides.

"We have to stop him! We can't let him get away with this!" She spoke angrily, trying to get to her feet, but the pain in her arm kept her in her seat. She was abruptly seething with rage inside: at Grosch, certainly, but more truly at herself. She had let her own lust for power distract her from doing what she was paid to do: protect and serve the country she loved.

"We're sure in agreement with you on that point!' Jack said as he sat down alongside her.

***

They had planned well. They left the mercenaries waiting for over four hours, so mental fatigue was setting in as the mid-morning sun dried their black uniforms.

The SAS hit them from the air and the ground. The two Chinook helicopters armed with two M-134 six-barreled mini-guns and an M-60 machine gun came ranging up from the sea cliffs behind the guerillas, unloading a number of rounds before Pienaar and his men could respond. It was a lethal attack, taking out six of the mercenaries, three each from Pienaar's team on the cliff's edge, and Swartbooi's team guarding the parking area directly in front of the lighthouse. They were now down to only four.

Both of Pienaar's teams discharged a number of rocket grenades. The helicopter pilots were smart enough to withdraw to a distance where the grenades would disintegrate before striking them.

"Du Preez, get the Minister!" barked Pienaar. He now had sufficient shelter behind the facilities building at the back of the lighthouse to minimize any barrage from the sea by the Chinooks. But he could no longer see the ground troops, who were taking orders from those in the choppers, who had complete vision of the battle arena.

The SAS troops approached the parking lot in three groups of ten, one on each flank, and the third down the central driveway. The group on the cliff's edge quickly made considerable ground, realizing Pienaar was unable to deal with the double-barreled sea-and-ground assault.

"Boss," Swartbooi's voice came over the sat-phone, "troops a hundred feet from your position. You better get outta there or you're a sitting duck!"

"Launch some grenades to hold them back so that we can get the Minister here. They won't risk shooting her!"

"Aye-aye, sir!"

Pienaar knew he had to move. He followed du Preez's tracks back around between the facilities building and the lighthouse, meaning he had protection on both sides. The path led back to the hostages' cabin.

BANG!

He'd only moved a little way when he was thrown to the ground by the impact as the facilities building was destroyed. This left him exposed except, fortunately for Pienaar, the explosion created a mini dust-storm.

Come on, Johannesburg, now would be a good time to arrive!

He was thirty feet away from the first cabin when he saw du Preez carrying the feebly struggling figure of Minister Verheyen over his shoulder.

"Get back to the cabins!" Pienaar yelled, sprinting towards them, ducking instinctively from another hail of bullets from the choppers. They struck the concrete wall that served as a barrier at the cliff's edge.

The cabins were just twenty feet ahead but they would have to expose themselves in order to get back to them.

Grenades continued to explode outside and in the parking lot. Pienaar couldn't tell whose they were but the fact that they hadn't stopped for the last few minutes was a positive sign that Swartbooi was still alive.

"Give me the woman!" Pienaar shouted.

He grabbed her around the waist and stepped out through a hole in the concrete barrier towards the cliff's edge in full view of the hovering Chinooks, his semi pointed at her head.

* * *

"I can't keep them back for much longer!" Swartbooi's voice boomed over the phone.

"How far away?"

"About thirty feet from your location, and I've got twenty bearing down on me. The Chinooks fly over every few minutes, picking the exact time we shoot off a grenade."

"Focus on us, Swarty. We can do this as long as they don't send troops up the cliff."

"Aye-aye, over!"

Du Preez had another rocket locked and loaded, ready to fire.

Come close again, my friends, and you'll feel my heat this time!

* * *

"Why don't we help them out and make a run for Marie?" Zhou suggested.

"Too dangerous!" Thierry replied, hanging his head out the door. He could see Pienaar holding Marie out on the cliff's edge. "He's got a gun on her."

A deafening explosion from the sea jolted them. A blinding flash of light invaded the air directly in front of them, the blast shaking the ground.

Thierry peered out of the door.

"What was that?" Jack asked, coming alongside, Zhou right behind him.

They all looked in stunned amazement as they watched the mangled remains of a Chinook falling to the sea below, a trail of thick orange and black smoke following its descent.

"Oh, dear Lord!" Jack cried out.

* * *

"You little ripper!" du Preez yelled, a huge smile on his face.

"Did you do that?" Pienaar asked, having gotten to his feet.

"Nope!" du Preez responded, shaking his head in disbelief.

"Colonel Pienaar." The voice came from the sat-phone. "This is Captain Bischoff of the *Johannesburg*, come in!"

Pienaar grabbed the phone off du Preez.

"About time," Pienaar said eagerly.

"Did you like our welcome?" Bischoff's voice came through loud and clear.

"Sensational!"

"Should be surfaced in five, then have a pickup on the shore within another five."

"Can you make that five all up?" Pienaar exclaimed, looking over his shoulder, feeling the explosions from the surface getting stronger and stronger.

"Do our best, over and out!"

"Call Swartbooi and tell him the situation. We won't wait for him!" Pienaar said, handing the phone to du Preez.

We're going to do this! Pienaar dragged Ms. Verheyen with him as he raced back towards the mercenaries' cabin.

* * *

For a minute, then two, there was a lull in the fighting. Pienaar and Marie had disappeared.

Thierry, curiosity overcoming good sense, took a tentative step out of the open cabin door.

Pienaar stepped out of the adjoining cabin. "Not another inch, nigger!" he said, jamming the muzzle of his gun into Thierry's face.

Thierry immediately put his hands up, stepping back from the gun. *I've got to buy some time!*

"Leaving, are we?" Thierry asked.

"Yeah! Well, we are," Pienaar said, glancing at a distraught-looking Marie. "Unfortunately, you and your buddies are staying here!"

Thierry noticed that Pienaar and Marie were now wearing abseiling harnesses.

"That's right, nigger, we're going off the edge!" said Pienaar, answering Thierry's silent question. "Straight down there!" He indicated with the gun.

Thierry saw the dark-grey submarine on the water's surface. A crew of four had disembarked on a green inflatable boat headed towards the shoreline.

Du Preez stepped up alongside. He ignored Thierry.

"They're going to try to come around the cliff's edge!" he said to Pienaar.

"Get ya harness on," Pienaar barked. "We're going down!"

Before he could reply, du Preez collapsed to the ground, startling Pienaar.

"Get up!" he screamed.

No response. He kicked him, but du Preez did not move. As Pienaar stared, a trickle of blood ran from du Preez's slack mouth.

Pienaar lifted his head to see four M4 carbine rifles pointed directly at him twenty feet away. He fastened his grip on

Marie, moving closer to the cliff's edge so that he could still see Thierry.

"Let her go!" The demand came from the lead SAS soldier.

More SAS troops appeared around the back of the cabin.

"I'm going to take Minister Verheyen here for a little ride down the cliff and you're all going to stay here and watch us. Otherwise, I'll put a bullet through her brain right now! *Ya hear me!*"

"Loud and clear," came the SAS response. "Don't be a fool; you've got nowhere to go! Our other chopper will be around here soon and will pick off the men in your rescue boat and then your getaway is sunk!"

"No way, buddy! Who took the other chopper down, huh? We'll take the second one down too if it comes too close!" Pienaar hissed, a little crazed despite his training.

Thierry could see the venom in his eyes, now red with rage. There was no sign of fear in him at all.

Marie kicked out at Pienaar, causing him to lose balance. Thierry, seeing what was going to happen, reached out for Marie, grabbed hold of one arm and pulled her closer.

Pienaar dropped his semi-automatic, trying to right his balance, but it was too late. He was going over the edge. He was still holding onto Marie's other arm. More significantly, she was locked into his harness.

"Help!" Marie screamed.

Thierry's grip on her arm was tight but he knew Pienaar's weight was going to be too much for him. He was going to have to let go, or he would go down with them.

Jack saw it all from the room. He rushed out, leaping for Marie.

"The harness, Jack!" Thierry yelled.

Jack fumbled around her waist, frantically trying to work out how to unlock her from the harness. Thierry was struggling to keep her on her feet against the dragging weight of the falling Pienaar.

Marie screamed.

"Quickly, Jack, quickly… I can't hold on for much longer!"

Thierry cried out, a painful grimace fixed o̶...

After what seemed an eternity Jack mana̶...
from the harness. It had little effect. Her arm w̶...
Pienaar's vise-like grip.

Jack reared up on his knees, crashing all his weight dow̶...
on Pienaar's corded arm. It felt like he'd just hit concrete. He
winced as a sharp stabbing pain shot up his arms. He fell face
first to the ground, inches from the edge.

But it had the desired effect.

Pienaar cried out, releasing Marie's arm.

She fell back into Thierry, who lost his balance, collapsing
backwards onto the ground. Marie fell back onto him, her right
elbow smashing into his jaw. Instantly, she tried to sit up.

Pienaar had somehow managed to hold onto the rock ledge
with his left arm. He brought his semi round as he struggled for
his own life.

As the gun fired, one of the SAS soldiers standing ten feet
away put two bullets through his head. Pienaar died instantly, his
body going limp. He let go of the ledge and fell the 200 feet to
the rocky shoreline below.

Marie had fallen off Thierry, a look of despair in her eyes.
Jack, on hands and knees, scrambled over to her.

"I've been shot!" she whispered.

"No!" Jack cried out.

He saw a small hole in her purple cardigan. Pienaar's single
shot had pierced her chest just under her ribcage.

"Quick, she's been hit!' Jack screamed to the approaching
SAS soldiers.

Jack cushioned her head with his arm.

His heart cried out for her. *Please, God, no!*

He saw no fear in her eyes, only inevitability.

Blood was now seeping out of her mouth as her lungs filled
up.

"Tell them all…" she coughed and spluttered blood, "I'm
sorry…"

After a moment, Jack got to his feet, covering his head with
his arms, in emotional agony, while Thierry closed her eyes and
whispered a quiet prayer.

God, I don't know where Marie stands with you, but
, she find peace now."

* * *

The mood in the large tree at the end of the makeshift airfield
was grim.

They watched as her spirit was escorted away. Two of
Drakkin's henchmen gladly received her soul and flew off into
the distance.

The heavenly crew grieved as Pienaar's men and Marie
Verheyen were lost for all eternity. It saddened them greatly.
They had seen it many times before, but it never got easier.

Not a word was spoken, all five lost in their own thoughts
and prayers.

London

"Everything ready?" Vincent asked, answering his secure cell
phone.

"Yes. Everything is in position." Farkad was in his car, having
just left the hotel where the three loyal subjects of Leopold
Grosch were staying. Little did they suspect that their loyalty was
not to be reciprocated.

"Good work, Farkad."

Farkad's voice grew harder. "I've just had word from Bischoff
aboard the *Johannesburg*. Pienaar's crew has been compromised,
all likely dead. Bischoff's had to submerge after being chased by
an SAS Chinook."

Vincent swore, but his mind quickly started thinking of
options. Pienaar had simply been a means to an end. "Any word
on our four captives?"

"No. Bischoff believed they are likely to be all alive but
couldn't be sure."

"OK." Vincent was confident the situation could be turned
around. "You continue with your mission this morning. I'll go
to the wires to find out what's happening. The SAS or RAF will
update the situation." Different thoughts were racing through
his head. "You go, do what you must and let me know when it's
done."

"Au revoir!" Farkad signed off.

Vincent didn't respond.

Where will you go now, my Chinese friend? Your Aussie pal appears to be a good luck charm. Luck always runs out, my friend, especially when you're dealing with Grosch.

Chapter 36

Somewhere above the North Sea

Berlin.

Thierry had set the German capital into the navigation system of the Osprey. He was co-pilot to Major Bill Lancaster of the SAS, who had volunteered to "escort" this party to the German capital. His superior would not be privy to the assignment nor approve the use of any SAS aircraft; hence the decision to "borrow" the Afrikaans mercenaries' aircraft.

All was ready. The party comprised Thierry, Jack, and Zhou, together with five of Lancaster's team who had also volunteered for the mission. They had left Marie Verheyen's body at the Royal Air Force base at Fife, where they refueled, Lancaster shaking his head as he signed the paperwork. This could get him busted to private.

He wore the widely recognized sandy beret adorned with the Excalibur wreathed in flames – the "Who Dares Wins" insignia. His heavily lined face and silver military buzz-cut confirmed he was well into his fifties.

Jack's impassioned pleas, plus Zhou's extraordinary story, had finally convinced Lancaster to support their mission. He'd heard these G8 terrorist theories. Frankly, he was a little unsure how believable they were, but there was something about this Australian. Jack was either a crazy man or he thoroughly believed there was going to be an attack on the G8 today. Lancaster was a man accustomed to hard quick decisions. The military even had an acronym for it: TCUP, Thinking Correctly Under Pressure. For some reason, he still wasn't sure what, he decided to give Jack the benefit of the doubt and back his judgment.

"Where'd you learn to fly, Thierry?"

"I was a Flight Lieutenant, 43rd Squadron. Got out after the Gulf War."

Lancaster nodded his head in understanding.

"Bet this Osprey is a new experience for you, though?"

"Not really. I flew choppers for a few years when I first left the RAF, so it's not too much of a stretch."

"Flight time to Berlin, Major?" Jack called from the open cabin.

"Around four hours!" he yelled back.

Jack grunted, then sank back in his folding removable seat, trying to get comfortable, and reflected on the last few hours. His right cheek, now a purplish black, was still throbbing from Pienaar's backhander. At least it would take his mind off the flight.

Jack closed his eyes.

Jesus, thank you for protecting us. You're amazing. We could have been killed so many times but you kept death away. As King David praised you in the Psalms: "Though I walk in the midst of trouble, you preserve my life; you stretch out your hand against the anger of my foes, with your right hand you save me." Thank you. Thank you. Thank you.

Please continue to protect us. Guide Major Lancaster and Thierry as they fly this plane. Guide our every action as we land in Berlin and work out how to stop this tragedy from occurring. In your name I pray you will bind Satan's workers, keep them away, so this tragedy can be avoided. Oh, loving Father, arm us with the right words so we can get to the authorities, give them hearts and minds to hear us and to act.

He didn't notice the bump caused by turbulence.

Lord, I pray for Marie. She may have known you, I don't know. Grant her peace, Lord. She was a very brave lady. Thank you that she had the chance to share what she shared with us this morning. Be with her husband and family as they grieve her passing. Care for them, love them, cherish them, and comfort them, dear Lord God.

Father, please keep Loren and Ruth safe, wherever they are. Wrap your loving arms around them. Keep them free from all evil and keep them strong. Thank you, Lord.

Jesus, I intercede for Zhou. He joined us in worshipping you this morning, but may he know you as Lord and Savior. Give me the words to share with him on this trip so he can be assured of his salvation, no matter what happens in Berlin. Thank you, Jesus.

* * *

Louise Haines and her two girlfriends hadn't ceased praying and worshipping. They all had a strong conviction that God wanted them to keep praying.

So they did.

And so did the many from all corners of the globe who had responded down the prayer chain they had started a few hours ago.

The Holy Spirit was striking hard at the barricade of evil that hung over the world. Little by little, inch by inch, He was taking hold of people who had been bound by Satan's influence.

Churches all around the world were noticing an increase in attendance. Talk of revival was becoming a common topic of sermons. Worship times were growing louder and more enthusiastic. Parishioners talked over morning tea of how they sensed the Spirit at work, old enthusiasms rising to their lips.

Satan and his brood were infuriated. They had no intention of sitting back and letting good penetrate the world they had worked so hard to infect.

* * *

Vincent had finished updating Grosch on the events at the Mull of Galloway. Grosch was seated on the balcony of his Berlin hotel suite. It opened onto the internal courtyard where the welcome function would be held in less than one hour.

"They're headed for Berlin, sir!" Vincent announced.

Grosch was surprisingly unconcerned by the news.

"Hmmm… did Chau survive?"

"Yes, sir, all three of the men survived, only Minister Verheyen perished."

Grosch didn't respond. He disliked waste. Marie had been useful, and − he admitted it to himself − very nearly his intellectual equal.

"What of the men, sir? What shall we do with them?"

Volkyre snarled: *Get their women!*

"How about we have a bit of fun with them," Grosch said, rubbing his chin, "Where are their women?"

"I believe they are holed up in a swanky city hotel not far from the police station they went to last night. Farkad tells me it's heavily patrolled."

"That's OK, we're just testing their resolve. Let our heroes *in my plane* believe we will kill their women. Give them one hour to change their destination to London, and if they don't comply, their ladies will be executed. That will give them something to think about!"

"Yes, sir!"

"Good, that is all."

"But, sir, what happens if they don't comply?"

"Vincent, they'll comply. They're not going to take that chance, are they?"

"I'm sure you're right, sir. Oh, one last thing, sir. Is the device completely ready?"

"I'm expecting the two of them any minute to discuss it."

"Two? I thought it was only one, Ballack." Concern, verging on irritation, was very apparent in Vincent's tone. Grosch usually left operational details to him.

"I brought along some insurance," responded Grosch flatly. Sometimes Vincent got above himself. "He's part of the security team here working for Ballack."

"And his name?" Vincent's peremptory tone annoyed Grosch, but he held on to his temper.

"You remember Tank, don't you?"

"Yes, I do." Grosch could hear Vincent relaxing. "He helped us a few years ago with those meddling Russians?"

"That's the one. I was able to convince him that we needed his services. A million for the heads of the twenty most prominent leaders of the world is a pretty fair price, wouldn't you say – cheap, even?"

"Definitely, a steal at that price." Vincent particularly admired Grosch's ability to execute his plans.

"My sentiments exactly."

"Sir, I must be off, I must take care of Farkad."

"Certainly. Has he completed his assignment?"

"Any minute now, sir. You'll be formally advised of the situation as soon as the news breaks."

"I look forward to hearing it."

"Enjoy your afternoon with the kings and queens of the world. May they enjoy their final hours."

Grosch chuckled, and cut the connection.

Vincent sat for a moment. Had the old man actually laughed? He shivered.

* * *

Thierry desperately wanted to make contact with Ruth, but every time he tried her cell number it just diverted to her voicemail. *Where are you, Ruthie?*

The plane's intercom clicked. "Mr. Le Bon, pick up please?" the unfamiliar voice said.

"This is Le Bon, who am I speaking to?" Thierry said, surprised by the unusual accent. Air traffic controllers typically referred to the plane they were calling and identified themselves immediately.

"You don't need to know!" The voice was curt.

This doesn't sound like an air traffic controller.

"Then why are you calling me?" Thierry felt a flicker of unease.

"To let you know of a development concerning your women," the voice replied.

"How do you mean?"

"While you and your Australian friend were playing commandos in the south of Scotland, we decided to take responsibility for their welfare."

"So you're with Scotland Yard?" Thierry's tone was suspicious.

The speaker's response held a tinge of amusement. "Not exactly. I rang to let you know that your actions have put your two ladies' lives at risk. If you don't change your course to London within the next thirty minutes, we will kill one of them. If you still haven't changed your course within one hour, the second one will be killed. Have I made myself clear?"

Gulp!

"Who are you?" Thierry said, not really sure what to say. "How can I know you're telling the truth?"

But Vincent had hung up.

Berlin

The ornately decorated outdoor terrace was bathed in midday sun. The leaders of the world's most powerful countries and organizations were seated while their host for the two-day summit, the German Chancellor, warmly welcomed them all.

Platoons of security people stood alert, visible and concealed, around the outskirts of the terrace.

The group of leaders had been expanded to include members of the developing world so that the issues of famine, disease and inequality could be more effectively confronted. Despite the nod to multilateralism, the ongoing financial crisis was highlighting the significant power that two or three nations had over the welfare of all. Resentment was rife, and Germany now struggled with a dark mood of pessimism and uncertainty driven by its pivotal role in keeping Europe afloat.

As the Chancellor urged all in attendance to come together in a spirit of unity, Leopold Grosch sat easily in full view of all. He stood to be a significant beneficiary of the increased defense and security spending in response to the rising tide of fear and apprehension.

Finally it was over. The audience warmly recognized the Chancellor's address with a unified seated ovation. She handed over to the Head of Security, who had an update on the terrorist threat that hung over the Summit.

A large monitor came to life. The face of a male BBC reporter filled the screen. He was delivering an urgent news report:

"News has just come to hand that Scotland Yard has foiled a major terrorist plot. The target was the G8 Summit that has commenced today in Berlin. Details are still sketchy at this time but Scotland Yard has been able to reveal that five men of multiple nationalities have been taken into custody.

"They were arrested at their London hotel after police had been given a tip-off from an anonymous source. Police found the men harboring documents detailing plans to fly an executive jet, with a bomb concealed in its engine, directly into the Berlin hotel where the Summit is being held.

"Scotland Yard's covert operation located the plane at Stansted Airport and traced ownership papers to one of the arrested men.

"We will bring you any further news immediately it comes to hand.

"This is Martin Sidwell for the BBC."

The response from the delegates was a mixture of surprise and relief. Judging by their reactions, most had considered the overnight reports to be bogus.

The German Chancellor rose to her feet.

"Ladies and gentlemen, it is with good fortune that we hear this news," she said, in her careful but accented English. "The threat of an attack has now been averted thanks to the excellent work of the British police." She nodded to the British Prime Minister. "We can now commence proceedings in the full knowledge that we are safe and are unlikely to be interrupted.

"I look forward to joining with you all to present a united front to the world. Let us move forward with great encouragement in the knowledge that our security forces have once again defeated the recurrent scourge of terrorism."

Grosch was soon in deep conversation with the Director General of the World Trade Organization, an acquaintance of many years' standing.

All was going according to plan.

* * *

Flashes of white light dropped like falling stars into hiding across the city. They awaited the call from their leader, Tagan.

"The Lord has answered your request, Tagan." Athaniel stood with Tagan in the rafters of one of Berlin's famous museums situated directly across from the hotel.

"Yes, though we are still well short. Bacchazar's company is closer to 20,000 strong. But I know the Father will provide." Tagan, a veteran, spoke with confidence, but even experienced angels were not privy to the Almighty's timing. He reproached himself privately for a case of the jitters.

"So Grosch's diversion may have worked!" Athaniel said, acknowledging the human's cunning.

"It certainly seems to have duped the leaders of the nations, judging by their reactions." Tagan was worried by the sudden lessening of caution.

"The people of God are praying, Tagan."

* * *

Jack was standing at the cockpit door, raking his fingers through his hair in frustration.

"So what do we do?" he asked, stooping to look into the cockpit. "Do we keep heading for Berlin and risk the girls being killed, or do we give in to their demands?"

"Jack, I'm not going to risk Ruth's life!" Thierry replied firmly.

"Thierry, I'm not sure that's right. God has gotten us this far…" Jack hesitated.

"But Jack, this is my Ruthie we're talking about, and Loren!"

"Mate, I know, but I keep getting this sense we're supposed to trust God, and let Him look after the girls. It's the world's leaders in our hands, Tee…"

Thierry glared at Jack. He didn't want to hear that!

"Tee, you know the story of Abraham and Isaac − it's a bit like that." Jack met his friend's gaze steadily.

Thierry was battling with himself and his faith. He finally made a decision. "Jack, I've trusted your judgment all along. As hard as it is to say this, I'm gonna keep trusting you and God."

Jack grabbed Thierry's shoulder. "Don't trust me, mate, trust Jesus!"

Thierry placed his hand on Jack's, wordlessly.

"Wow, you sure about this?" Lancaster asked, having observed the discussion. He thought, *These guys are seriously weird!*

"As sure as I can be," Jack said, turning to walk back to his seat next to the SAS team, most of whom were taking the chance to doze. He felt peace in his heart, a calmness that he hadn't experienced for a long time.

Over to you, Father!

Darius, riding on top of the Osprey, smiled enormously and high-fived Hannen.

* * *

The German Chancellor occupied the Presidential Suite during the two-day Summit. Little did she realize she shared her spacious room with some invisible entities.

The General and Agramon were deep in collective contemplation as Lord Bacchazar finally arrived at their luxurious hiding place.

"Well, Bacchazar, all appears to be going smoothly!" the General said with a smirk of derision on his face.

"You doubted it would, dear General?" Bacchazar replied disrespectfully.

"You may think it is going well, Bacchazar, but we have a worldful of people praying, which is the last thing we need at this time!" the General snarled.

"Only a few more hours, General, and it will be done. A few humans' prayers aren't going to stop us now."

"I wish I had your confidence, or should I call it foolhardiness?" the General snapped back.

"What are you sniggering at, Agramon?" Bacchazar bawled suddenly, leaping to stand intimidatingly in front of his adversary.

"*No!* This is not the time for you two to start squaring off at each other!" The General was weary of pulling his two belligerent lieutenants apart. "You will have plenty of time for that in due course. Now focus on our plans for the Heavenly Host!"

* * *

An enormous explosion shook the Paddington Green police station, smashing all its windows as well as those of adjoining buildings. Glass rained down.

The first thought that entered people's minds was *terrorism*. All the horrible memories of the Boxing Day football stadium attack flooded back.

Dozens of police officers came rushing out of the station. There was no obvious perpetrator, but their gaze soon fixed on a police vehicle, popularly called a paddy wagon, now utterly destroyed.

The wagon had only moments earlier pulled up outside the station.

Two uniformed police officers, a desk sergeant and five suspects brought into the station for questioning were now dead.

Chapter 37

"Two o'clock, gents!" Jack announced. "Only four hours to go."

"You don't believe this story about the foiled terrorist attack, then?" Lancaster asked, having just briefed the others on the news.

"Not for a second!" Zhou said. "That's a decoy, purely to put everyone off the scent."

"But Jack, look at the evidence they've got: five men, a plane, a bomb, a set of documents confirming the destination – it's all there!" Lancaster added.

"Sure, it's a very good decoy," Jack said dismissively. "Grosch probably even fooled his own men into believing it. Those five suckers who were captured probably really believed they were going to be responsible for the biggest ever attack on the leaders of the world!"

"Oh Jack, I just can't see it. Gone to all that trouble, bought a bomb, probably had to pay a lot of money, millions to pay off the people who worked on what you're saying is just a decoy?!" Lancaster was increasingly worried he'd bet his career on a bunch of nutters.

"And what about Zhou here, Major?" Jack asked. "Why did Grosch try to kidnap him? 'Cause he knows too much about the *real* bomb!"

"True, I can't dispute that," Lancaster said, shrugging his shoulders. Zhou had been convincing. "Jack, I can't believe he'd go to such lengths to set up a fancy decoy."

"How do you know the decoy was Grosch's anyway?" Thierry interjected. "There may have in fact been two separate plots, completely unconnected to each other."

"Thierry's right," Jack replied, "We are all presuming Grosch had something to do with the foiled plot. Either way, Major, there's still a bomb going off in two hours."

The intercom crackled. "Mr. Le Bon," Vincent's distinctive voice interrupted the discussion. "You disobeyed my orders. Your women will die, but not well." The voice was cold. "You will be next." The connection died.

Thierry slumped in his seat. "Jack, you better be right on this."

Jack's arms were wrapped tightly around his body, stress oozing out of his clenched jaw. *God, only you can save Ruth and Loren! Please…*

***

"Hello?" replied a male voice.

Blast!

Fear suddenly gripped Thierry's heart.

"Ah, this is Thierry Le Bon. Why you are answering my wife's phone?"

"Oh, hello, Mr. Le Bon, good to hear your voice. Where are you?"

"Please, who are you?"

"I'm Detective Cole, from Scotland Yard. I've been handling your wife's case."

"Do you know where Ruth and Ms. Summers are located at the present time?"

"Certainly. If you wait a moment you can probably speak to them."

Thierry heard a knocking on a door. Lancaster, in the adjacent seat, listened intently.

Please, God, please…

"Hello, Detective," said a female voice, "come in. The ladies have been resting but some food is on the way up, so they're both awake. I'll go get them."

Thierry held his breath.

A door opened. Some more knocking.

337

"Detective Cole… are you there?" Thierry finally said, not able to wait any longer.

"Thierry, it's me!"

"Ruthie?" Thierry was trembling violently.

Jack and Zhou, now seated immediately behind the pilots, leant forward to listen in to the conversation.

"It's me, Tee, where are you? Loren and I have been worried sick!" she said, the relief in her voice clearly audible over the poor connection.

"I've been trying your phone for hours, what happened?" Thierry asked, his eyes filling with tears.

"Oh, the police had our phones for their investigation. Detective Cole has just now handed mine back to me."

"Where are you?" Thierry asked.

"In a lovely London hotel, about to enjoy room service, and praying feverishly for you. But more to the point, where are you? The police said you got away from the kidnappers and are on your way back."

"Oh, Ruthie, it's a long story, and yes, we're heading back, but first we've got to pop into Berlin to try to stop a maniac." Thierry was trying to keep his tone light.

"No, Tee, you've done your job!" she cried out in exasperation.

"Hi, Ruth, it's Jack here." Jack moved in closer to the phone. "I know it's hard to understand but I sense this is something God wants us to do. Are the police protecting the hotel?"

"Jack, I so hope you're right." Ruth liked and trusted Jack, but it didn't relieve her anxiety. "And yes, there are police all over the hotel, two outside the door and lots downstairs."

Jack sighed loudly as he lifted his head. *Thank you, Father!*

"Oh, baby, it's going to be OK," Thierry said through gritted teeth.

"Is Loren there?" Jack asked quietly.

"Yeah, Jack, she's right here. I'll put her on."

"Jack?" Loren said, taking the phone from Ruth.

"Hey, Loren," Jack replied, trying for casual.

"Oh, Jack, it's—" She stopped as she burst into tears. Jack too wept openly as he listened to Loren's sobbing.

These are two of the gutsiest men I've ever encountered, Lancaster told himself, turning his attention back to the flight path. The career soldier knew there were many battlefields.

* * *

"They're still headed to Berlin, sir."

"Hmmm, perhaps we've underestimated them, Vincent," Grosch said calmly. "So we still have a loose cannon in Mr. Chau. Does anyone believe their story?"

"Everything I've heard on the wires at the moment tells me that the threat has been extinguished with the capture, and now very unfortunate demise of our five colleagues."

"Who specifically?"

"Scotland Yard, Special Ops, FBI?"

"That's good."

"I hope so, sir, I really do! But, it's like they have the Midas touch or something. They've managed to escape everything we've thrown at them."

"Relax, Vincent." Grosch was not in the habit of explaining himself, but he needed Vincent to get a grip. "If by some miracle of Midas they get to land, they've still got to get to the hotel, then get through security here. They've got no chance; security is so tight. The protesters haven't made any headway, so what are three men with a crazy story going to do? And if they get through security, Tank will look after them."

"Yes, sir." Grosch could hear Vincent mastering himself.

"But we do need to dispose of Chau and his companions urgently. No detonation can take place with them alive to sell their stories. So follow their progress and see how far they get. If they don't land in Berlin, we will need to track them down. Put your London assassin on alert in case they return there. Also, sound out the network in Germany. Prepare them, with a chopper if need be, to go into action at any moment. If Chau and his friends have no luck landing in Berlin they'll land somewhere very nearby. Got it?"

"Yes, sir! All in hand."

* * *

Grosch was tied up in the Enlarged Dialogue working session, a group of twenty, mostly heads of state, chaired by the Secretary General of the United Nations. It would finish at 5:30, giving him sufficient time to prepare for his dinner that evening.

The entire group of Heads of Delegation of the G8 and the Enlarged Dialogue group of twenty would all convene at 6:30 for cocktails and then dinner in the hotel ballroom. Being a senior adviser to the European Commission, he wasn't expected at the evening function.

Grosch was having dinner with the German minister of finance instead, giving him the perfect alibi.

* * *

Ruth and Loren were in the lounge, drinking tea.

The familiar opening tune to the BBC News sounded faintly from the TV opposite. Ruth turned up the sound as the well-known face of a leading anchorman appeared on screen:

"Further to our earlier story about the foiled terrorist attempt on the G8 Summit, news has just come to hand confirming that the five men taken into custody for questioning were the victims of a bomb attack outside Paddington Green Police Station, together with three police officers. No group has yet admitted responsibility for the attack.

"In other breaking news, our Paris bureau has this morning announced that Paris police have recently found the body of a man that fits the description of Ray Malone, an American advertising executive. He had been missing for the past forty-eight hours. Police have confirmed the man's body was found deep in the forest of Fontainebleau, with a single gunshot wound to the head. At this time, police do not consider there are any suspicious circumstances surrounding the death of Mr. Malone, all evidence suggesting he took his own life."

Ruth reached out with both hands to hold Loren's. *May the peace that transcends all understanding fill Loren's heart, Lord.*

Loren smiled sadly, but her mind was elsewhere.

"Oh, Ray, you didn't need to do this," she said under her breath.

In the air approaching Berlin, ninety minutes till detonation

"Jack, it's that easy. I wanted someone else to know how to disarm the device if something happens to me," Zhou said to Jack as they huddled together in the open cabin.

"You're right, Zhou, it does sound easy. But I reckon I won't need to use it, as we're all going to get out of this safely." Jack grinned at his young former student.

Zhou shook his head. "I've always admired your faith, Jack." He looked back seriously at his mentor. "It was amazing to see you and Thierry this morning singing and praying whilst the mercenaries threatened us."

"Yeah, I've been meaning to ask you what you thought. You joined in, which was fantastic."

Zhou grinned in turn. "It seemed the right thing to do."

Jack faced Zhou, his back to the watching SAS men, privacy granted by the roaring engines. "Would you like to know Him, Zhou?"

"Who?"

"Jesus."

The Chinese lad suddenly looked very vulnerable. "I would love to. How do I meet Him?"

"You ask Him into your heart. That's all."

"Really? Could you show me?"

"Sure, I'd be honored."

Jack put his hand on the young man's shoulder, and bowed his head.

"Pray these words after me."

Jack watched as Zhou closed his eyes.

"Jesus, thank you for loving me," he began, waiting to hear Zhou repeat it. "I want to meet you and have you fill my heart, soul, mind, and body. I believe you are the Son of God. Forgive me for ignoring you and leading a rebellious life. I want you. I need you. Teach me how to how love and worship you. Thank you. Amen."

Zhou was crying very quietly. Jack held him while the SAS men looked on, uncomprehending.

* * *

"They're not going to let us land!" Thierry said to Lancaster, exasperated.

Lancaster shook his head.

"Hey, Jack, you there?" Thierry yelled.

"Yup, what's up?" Jack said, poking his head into the confined space.

"Just had word from Tegel air traffic control. They're not going to let us land."

"What? They can't be serious! What did they say to you?"

"Said we are an unauthorized aircraft and they had no intention of giving us landing clearance!"

"Grosch. It's gotta be! He's got his tentacles everywhere."

Lancaster ignored Jack's comment, picking up one of the plane's phones.

"Thierry, take over while I speak to the people I know on the ground."

Jack and Thierry listened to the one-sided conversation. It ended abruptly.

"So where do we stand, Bill?" Jack was still on his feet.

"He's not sure what's going on and is off to speak to the airport security. Said he'd get back to me as soon he knew anything further."

"What would happen if we just land it?" Jack asked.

Thierry rolled his eyes. "Jack, you just can't do that."

"Surely it happens all the time," Jack insisted.

"Yeah, by madmen who shouldn't be in the air in the first place," Thierry threw back.

"Look, we can't buy ourselves any further time. We need to get on the ground pretty quick, or else the emergency crews are going to be picking bodies out of the rubble in downtown Berlin."

"What's the very latest time Zhou reckons we've got?" Lancaster asked.

"It's set to go off at 6:30. If we don't get there in time, the leaders of the world all get murdered."

"Yes, Jack's got it right," Zhou interjected, poking his head into the cockpit. "Grosch or someone else will set the timer off thirty minutes in advance, with detonation to occur once the thirty minutes have elapsed."

Jack was pacing in the confined cabin.

Lord God, help us, please! Anything, please!

The cabin phone started ringing. Lancaster picked it up.

"*Ja*... no good?" His eyes said everything. "Stay close to your phone, we've gotta devise another plan, 'cause we'll need a vehicle to get downtown... over..."

Jack's blood pressure was rising. They were stuck 20,000 feet in the air above the target site, and running out of time.

Chapter 38

Berlin

Lancaster had brought the plane down below the clouds so they could find a suitable field in which to land. If Berlin wasn't going to let them land in official landing space, then they were just going to land in unofficial landing space.

It didn't take them long to find what they needed. Between Jack, Lancaster, and Thierry they found the ideal spot: an unoccupied multi-field football park. It appeared to be an oasis in the middle of Berlin suburbia, houses and unit blocks surrounding the slightly browning grass of the football complex.

"Better buckle up, Jack, as we're going in!" Thierry said, pushing him out of the cockpit with his stern tone. "Tell the others too."

"Damn it," Lancaster said, slamming the phone down, and stopping Jack's exit. "Smitty reckons it's going to take him twenty minutes to get to our landing field!"

"We might just have to compromise a little when we're on the ground," Jack replied.

"Whatya mean, Jack?"

"I noticed a number of cars parked nearby." Jack was never happier than when breaking rules. "We might have to borrow one or two. I'm sure the owners won't mind, especially as it involves the safety of their nation!"

"It may in fact make it easier for us to get closer to the hotel too," Thierry chimed in. "Grosch will have instructed security to keep at bay any unidentified Special Forces vehicle. We should be able to get to within running distance of the hotel in a civilian car."

"Good point, Tee. Bill, tell your friend Smitty to turn around and give us backup at the hotel."

"Aye-aye, sir, Jack!" Lancaster ruefully admitted to himself that he had lost command of the task-force, if he had ever had it.

"Now, I like the sound of that, Bill!"

"Whoa, hang on a minute, guys." The plane lurched forward abruptly, forcing Jack to brace himself against the wall. Zhou, who hadn't buckled himself in, was sent flying. He landed with a thud on the floor of the cabin, leaving his body with a few more bumps and bruises. Lancaster's men, all strapped in, watched his antics with amusement.

"Sorry 'bout that, chaps!" Thierry yelled through the open cockpit door. "Everyone OK?"

"Yeah, only Zhou went for a tumble, but no broken bones, by the look of it!" Jack replied, watching Zhou get gingerly to his feet, holding his right hip.

The plane dropped again in altitude just as Zhou fell back into his seat. He hurriedly reached for his seatbelt.

Thierry now had the plane on course to land.

"Here we go!" he screamed fearlessly, aware of a hot rising tide of exhilaration.

Jack especially wasn't appreciating the bumping around. He had his arms under the fold-back seat, head bowed.

Jesus, protect us, please. Please get us to ground safely. Help us get to the hotel. Father, protect us all, give us the courage to go, the wisdom to say and do the right things, and the speed and clarity of mind to act quickly and decisively. May your glory reign supreme and may your angels protect the men and women of the G8 and the hotel workers.

The landing gear kissed the ground gently.

A perfect landing.

The men all applauded in appreciation. So too did the angelic crew accompanying them.

It was 5:30.

* * *

It hadn't taken long for a number of interested onlookers to start making the short trip to the football complex. Others were watching from their homes, curious as to why an unusual armed forces aircraft had parked itself on their neighborhood football field.

They would learn soon enough.

"Got just the one for a short journey!" Jack announced, pointing in the direction of a series of cars parked in the side street.

"Which one, Jack?" Thierry asked.

"Whatya think? The silver Range Rover, of course! The best of British luxury, doncher know?" He ended his sentence with a poor attempt at a snobbish English accent.

"Don't ever think of taking up acting, Haines," Lancaster retorted.

"The four of us take it and there's that big charcoal Beemer, five cars further down, which Collins and the rest of your men can use." Jack was running, the others quickly followed.

They covered the distance surprisingly quickly.

"Any good at jump starting cars, Bill?" Jack asked as he grabbed the SAS commander's semi-automatic, smashing the driver door's window, setting off a screeching alarm.

Without replying, Lancaster swung himself into the driver's seat, cut the flex to the alarm and disengaged the key ignition with his all-purpose knife within seconds. He had the pristine cruiser's engine roaring when the alarm to a second car down the street erupted.

The Range Rover was off before its owner could get to the curb. Jack, embarrassed, slid down the passenger seat, avoiding the outraged stare of a man who was yelling something in German, as he watched his newly purchased car being hijacked by an oddball foursome: one Caucasian male dressed in military fatigues, a second disheveled Caucasian in civvies, a sloppily dressed black man and a bald-headed Asian.

Jack prayed quietly.

Thank you, Jesus, for getting us safely on the ground. Please bless us now with the speed of angels so we can get to the hotel on time.

Lancaster was operating the GPS as he drove, plugging in various details. Jack watched with admiration: how was this man so able to multitask while carrying the weight of the lives of the world's leaders on his broad shoulders?

Little did Jack know that Darius, Andola, and Hannen were hugging the luxury 4WD, soothing, instructing, focusing. Only Darius was watching as Athaniel swooped in to join them, having emerged from his Berlin hideout.

"Arlia and her crew will line the streets as we head for the hotel," Athaniel informed his team. "They'll then pick up the rear so that by the time we reach the hotel we will be a thousand strong!"

"Yes, but will that be enough?" Darius replied.

"We'll be OK, Darius. The Father has it all under control. Guard this car and get them to the city!" Athaniel shot off in the direction of the city.

* * *

They'd only been traveling for a little over five minutes when the sound of distant sirens invaded the tense air within the cruiser.

"Think that's for us?" Thierry asked, pushing his head between the two front seats.

"Hand me the phone, Jack!" Lancaster ordered as he looked suspiciously into his side mirror, seeing nothing untoward.

He pressed the recall button on the sat-phone as he held the steering wheel with one hand. "Smitty, would the cops know about us?... Well, can you talk to one of your contacts and make sure they don't get in our way? We don't have any time to waste on dodging coppers!"

Something about that conversation was strange. Lancaster couldn't pick it, but there was something odd about it. He could feel it in his gut. His gut was rarely wrong.

He felt the eyes of the others upon him.

"He doesn't know! Could be the owners of the cars, but he'll get them off our back!"

The siren sounds were coming closer and actually appeared to be coming from two different directions, one behind, fast approaching, and another one to their left.

Lancaster swore. "They're right on Collins' tail now," he announced, seeing the small police car through the side mirror.

All three passengers turned to see the clearly distinguishable blue and red lights flashing atop the car.

"Whoa!" Lancaster shouted. The vehicle jolted sideways as he swerved viciously to avoid a second, larger police car that was shooting out from a side street.

"Haines, grab the wheel, quickly!" He thumbed another key. "Just keep going!" Lancaster yelled through his phone. "We don't have time to stop! Just follow me… I'm following the route the GPS has provided, mostly major roads… over!"

Panic swept over Jack.

Not now, Lord, pleeease! We're so close, please keep us safe. Guide Lancaster and Collins as they drive.

Lancaster had taken the luxury cruiser up to 100 miles per hour, Collins in hot pursuit. Even though his Beemer was a good ten years old, it was doing a great job keeping up. The two police cars, however, had no trouble staying right on Collins' tail.

* * *

"See those two police cars approaching from the north?" Darius pointed out to the others. "We need to cut them off. They're the only real chance of stopping us; the two trailing will struggle to get in front of our two cars!"

"No problems, Darius. On our way!" Andola said as she, Grindor, and Hannen dropped towards the ground.

* * *

"More sirens approaching from in front of us!' Jack announced as sweat streaked his forehead.

"Not what we wanted!" Lancaster replied. "Come on! Come on!" he cajoled the powerful brute of a vehicle to greater feats of speed, hunching closer to the steering wheel.

All four of them could glimpse the now familiar blue and red flashing lights of two more police cars fifty yards in front of them in the street parallel to their own. A T-intersection could only be moments ahead.

"They're gonna try and cut us off!" Thierry burst out.

"Not if I can help it!" Lancaster said as he floored the accelerator, all four pushed back in their seats as the fine V8 engine reached maximum revs.

They all watched as the two police cars turned onto the cross street. They weren't going to make it; the police would block them off.

Oh, Lord, please keep us safe, protect us!

From the intent on Lancaster's face, Jack knew he wasn't going to slow down. They were either going to beat them or they were going crashing through. Hitting something at this speed was going to be messy.

Closer, closer, but it was clearly apparent the cops would beat them. Lancaster kept his foot flat to the floor.

They weren't going to make it. The police cars would cover the width of the road, and there was no passing space on either side.

Lancaster was just going to plow through them, by the look of it.

This is it!

They all braced themselves for the inevitable impact.

Please, dear God, save us!

Jack opened his eyes just as he expected to be hitting the police cars, but they were still going. The police cars had overshot the street and gone straight through the intersection.

Jack shook his head as tears welled up in his eyes.

"Praise you, Jesus!" he screamed, kicking the dash and punching the air with relief and joy.

"Hallelujah!" Thierry chimed in.

The two cars kept charging ahead. Two other police cars were now holding fast right behind them, mystified as to why their colleagues had overshot the street.

"Thank you, Jesus, thank you, thank you," Jack whispered.

* * *

"Excellent work, team, excellent!" The three white knights had returned to their positions alongside Darius. He swatted away two overly bold small demons who thought they could be heroes.

Not today.

"And now for the real enemy!" He turned his gaze to the enormous black cloud of evil that hung over the three blocks surrounding their ultimate destination.

"Come, Jesus, bring your mighty army and eradicate this vermin!"

***

Tagan and Athaniel watched it too from their vantage point within the museum. The massive black cloud had built up over the past hour as the sentinel squadron left their various hiding places.

The cloud squirmed and hissed as the demon masses prepared themselves for battle.

"There must be over 30,000 now, Tagan!"

"At least!"

The two senior angelguards could feel the tension. The air got thicker with evil as the marauding assassins badgered each other. Numerous airborne scuffles broke out as they fought for the best positions.

It was almost time. Time for death. But not just for anyone. No, it was the time for the white knights, the angelguards of heaven, to meet their worst enemy. To confront their lifelong foe: the hordes of Hades.

Tagan and Athaniel were on edge, awaiting the battle cry that would launch the strike. The two mighty keepers of the faith embraced each other in the knowledge there was only one who knew the outcome of what lay ahead.

But they knew that whatever happened to the other, God's glory would reign. Not just now but forever more.

***

"All is in readiness, General!" Bacchazar said from his elevated position in the Presidential Suite. It was presently unoccupied by any human, and the three leaders, the General, Agramon, and Lord Bacchazar, freely roamed its plush surrounds.

"Good, good. Bacchazar. It is looking very positive," the General replied, somewhat surprised they were in such a favorable position.

"White knights approach from the main highway, estimate about 1,000 strong, closing in fast, due to arrive in five minutes!" Agramon reported.

"Let's send them a welcoming party, shall we?" Bacchazar said haughtily.

"Yes, do that now!" the General replied.

Bacchazar rose to the exterior of the roof, sniffing appreciatively: the air was smotheringly thick and vile. He signaled the one whom he sought for this assignment: Drakkin, the Viking assassin.

On receiving his orders, Drakkin exploded into the air, emitting a high-pitched whistle, whereupon 5,000 snarling sentinels broke away from the main swarm. They formed themselves into a tight unit as they took to the early evening sky and quickly made some distance from the hotel.

"It is done!" said Bacchazar, returning to the Presidential Suite.

"Now, white knights of heaven, show us whether you can stand the wrath of Satan!" the General roared, laughing hideously.

* * *

The meeting had broken up. Grosch had excused himself from the crowd that gathered in the conference room.

His demeanor was calm but the tremor of excitement had gradually increased during the course of the past hour. He hurried to the lift. As soon as the doors opened, he stepped inside and pressed the button for the sixth floor. He turned his phone on and read a message, then deleted it before dialing a number.

"Receive them into the hotel and make sure Chau is killed. You can let the others die with the leaders of the world." He cut the connection, stretched his back and enjoyed the release of pressure that had built up over the course of the day.

Volkyre released his grip on the base of Grosch's neck. He grinned, sensing victory.

Grosch felt invigorated. In less than an hour all that he had spent the last five years planning would finally come to fruition. His business revenues had grown tenfold in that time. The next wave of defense orders would soon arrive. Then, and only then, the Chinese would pay him exactly what he wanted for a stake in Grosch Industries.

*　*　*

Jack's uneasiness was growing as fast as they covered the ever-diminishing distance to the hotel. He saw dark clouds hovering unusually low to the ground and moving very quickly towards them.

Something big was going down. Doubt invaded his mind. Fear slithered into his heart.

Dear Jesus, please give me the courage to act decisively. Satan, in Jesus' name, I rebuke this fear and your plans to kill innocent people. Jesus, may your will be done, and may I be obedient to your will.

The cloud of doubt receded, but a seed had been planted in a hidden part of his mind.

It really is happening, Lord, isn't it? It must be, I can just feel it in my heart. Protect us, shield us, cover us from the enemy, please, Jesus.

"Jack, can you feel it?" Thierry asked quietly.

"Feel what?" Lancaster didn't allow Jack to respond.

"Yeah! Something big is about to happen," Jack's words were very deliberate. "We're right, it's going to happen, I'm now absolutely convinced of it!"

"Yeah, likewise!" Thierry replied.

"What? What's going to happen?" Lancaster asked, irritated he was missing out on whatever Jack and Thierry "knew". "What are you two going on about? Is this some spiritual mumbo-jumbo or what?"

"Angels and demons, Bill − ever thought about 'em?" Jack replied.

"What, like in horror movies?"

"Not exactly, but kinda. We don't have time to discuss it now, but let's just say that a battle in the spiritual world is brewing!"

"Oh, that's just—"

"Watch out!" Zhou yelled from the back seat just before a late-model Renault ran through a "Stop" sign, missing their front fender by inches.

"Phew, that was close, too close!" Lancaster sighed, his stomach returning to its usual position in his abdomen, having momentarily exploded into his throat.

"How much further?" Thierry asked, sounding keen to get out of this car chase.

"Coupla minutes, judging by the GPS here," Lancaster replied. "We'll stop as close as we can to the hotel, make a run for it, while Collins and his men fend off the chasing coppers."

"Sounds like a good plan, I guess," Thierry said quizzically, "and how are we going to get into the hotel through all that security?"

"Smitty should help us, and if that fails, we push our way in!" Lancaster stated with surprising confidence.

"Who's this Smitty character you keep referring to?" Jack asked.

"Colonel Charles Smithson, an old buddy of mine from the Green Jacket days. He now works for himself, security you know, gun for hire. He's part of the security team for the Summit."

"Just who we need, by the sound of it!" Jack's mind eased on hearing Lancaster's description.

"Absolutely! Smitty's a good man. I'd trust him with my life." He recalled the strange reaction he got from Smitty the last time they spoke. He let it go.

* * *

They collided with surprising force. Arlia, Landen, and their army of white knights were outnumbered five to one.

The superior swordsmanship of the white knights punished the marauding demon squadron. It wasn't long before their ranks began to lessen as one white knight after another struck truly.

But the demon squadron just kept coming and coming. Soon chinks in the white knight army appeared as they tired from the intensity of the battle. The demons, led by an enraged Drakkin, were pushing them further away from the hotel. The street brawler was maniacal, thrashing his oversized battle-axe in tandem with his heavy rounded shield. He screamed commands to his underlings, enjoying the thrill, the thirst of battle.

But he wanted one white knight in particular. The one who had haunted him all those years, the one whom he felt it was his destiny to extinguish once and for all. Hannen: the tall Scandinavian, the graceful fighter, the demon-killing machine.

The Viking had sensed his adversary's presence nearby. He knew Hannen was watching, and waiting. But Drakkin knew there would be only one victor tonight. And he was sure going to enjoy it.

* * *

Landen, the huge white knight, was smashing his way through one demon sentinel after another. His extra two, sometimes three, feet in height gave him a tremendous advantage. He surprised them with his incredible speed and mobility for one so large. They soon regretted chancing their arm.

Arlia, another veteran of such battles, kept knocking the sentinels down and out as they came at her with relentless abandon. Her fearsome attack was too powerful for the sentinels, with their inferior fighting ability.

But just as the hordes of demons appeared to diminish, their ranks were replenished. There was only so much the white knights could withstand. Their numbers began to reflect that. More and more of the white knights succumbed to the sheer volume of demons set upon them.

"We can't hold out for much longer, Arlia!" Landen yelled as he struck three impish demons that foolishly challenged him.

"Yes, I know, Landen, but we *must* prevail!" Arlia replied more bravely than she felt. She saw that their numbers were now less than half what they started with.

* * *

The sovereign threesome of Bacchazar, the General, and Agramon stood on the roof of the luxury hotel enjoying all they saw. Bacchazar kept sending wave after wave after wave of demonic swordsmen to join the battle.

"We will have the victory, General!" Bacchazar exclaimed in his deep voice.

"Don't let up, don't let up, kill them, kill them all!" the General replied, enraptured by the prospect of victory. His blood-red eyes bulged with excitement watching the white knights take a beating as they were overrun by his hordes of killers.

Chapter 39

Forty minutes to detonation

The silver Range Rover pulled up a few blocks away from the hotel. Barricades had been set up, limiting the traffic to the hotel to essential services and VIPs.

The four jumped out running as Lancaster left the car's engine on.

Jack's heart was pounding, but his mind was clearly focused on the one objective: finding Leopold Grosch.

They reached the temporary security perimeter ring that kept unwanted people away from the hotel. Lancaster spoke to one of the security guards manning a temporary entry gate.

Jack scanned the front of the hotel, adrenalin pumping, the familiar seeds of panic hitting the base of his spine. He looked up and noticed a dark, almost slimy haze casting an ominous shadow over the entire hotel. *But it's too early for nightfall!*

He suddenly felt nauseous from the thick air and struggled to breathe.

He couldn't throw this sense of fear. Something dreadful was about to happen. He could feel it in his bones, in his water. *If we don't find the bomb we're going up with it!*

"Where do you think he might be?" Thierry asked him, catching his breath.

"Not the foggiest idea. I'm hoping Bill's buddy might lead us to him."

"He's got us in! Quickly!" Lancaster said, the gate opening to allow the odd-looking foursome entry to the hotel.

They were still fifty feet from the car drop-off area immediately in front of the hotel's front doors. A single black stretch limousine pulled up outside the front of the hotel. Three men stepped out of the hotel lobby, two dressed in immaculate black suits wearing poorly concealed earpieces. They deferred to the third, a pudgy man dressed in a classic charcoal business suit.

One of the security men opened the door for the businessman. He stopped and leant up against the opened door.

"Oh no!" Zhou stopped in his tracks, grabbing Jack and Thierry, who were either side of him, forcing them to stop. Lancaster stopped too on losing his flank men.

"What, Zhou? What's wrong?" Jack asked, hurriedly looking at Zhou, whose skin was now a parchment white as the blood rushed from his face.

"It's him!"

"Who?"

The businessman turned in their direction. He just stared. And then smiled. A cocky, conceited smile.

He hopped in the back seat, the door shut, the tinted windows concealing him from prying eyes. The car slowly moved off. Volkyre, Bacchazar's personal aide, rode proudly on its roof.

Zhou gulped, "Grosch!"

"What? Where?"

"He just got in that limo that's driving out now!"

Jack, Thierry, and Lancaster followed Zhou's gaze as the limo made its way through the perimeter fencing.

"You serious, Zhou?"

"Absolutely, Jack. He's just left the hotel!"

"Ummm… hmmm…" Jack was thrown completely. He didn't know what to do now.

Fortunately, somebody approached them and distracted him.

"Bill! Good to see you, man!" A security man dressed all in black approached the foursome. He was relatively short for a security type, but stocky. His head was shaven to reveal an unattractive scalp covered in scratches and scars. A prominent tattoo of a red scorpion on his neck added to his intimidating demeanor.

"Smitty, how's business?" Lancaster replied, shaking his hand firmly.

"Excellent, my friend."

"Let me introduce you to my colleagues: Jack Haines, Thierry Le Bon, and Zhou Chau." Lancaster indicated each with his hand.

"G'day, Jack Haines," Jack said, grimacing a little from the very tight handshake. A shiver shot up Jack's spine as he took in this new man's eyes. They were pitch black, uncaring, even inhuman.

"Gud day to you too, Jack. Other than Bill here, most people call me Tank." His hot breath smelt stale.

He shook Thierry's hand but basically ignored him. He took a real interest in Zhou.

"Sorry, I missed your name?" He gripped Zhou's right hand.

"Zhou Chau. Tight grip you've got there, Tank."

Tank grinned, releasing Zhou's hand after a longer-than-usual handshake.

"Come inside, gentlemen, then we can discuss your particular concerns. But first, Bill, you'd best give me your semi. Don't want to be frightening the tourists, do we now?" Lancaster complied grudgingly.

On entering the lobby Zhou gasped at the astonishing craftsmanship. The intricacy and extravagance reminded him of St. Peter's in Rome.

Tank led the foursome directly towards a magnificent marble staircase.

"Let's take the stairs to the first level, where we can talk in private."

Jack scanned the lobby. It seemed surprisingly quiet for such a significant event. Various security personnel had taken up conspicuous positions scattered around the floor, some talking into their handsets. Eyes followed their progress.

His anxiety was increasing. The muscles in his lower back tightened, bracing for some impending strike. The opulently decorated lobby seemed rather dim, he vaguely thought. A massive chandelier only produced a sepia glow, each of its small bulbs cocooned in a shadowy fog. The carpet and the many large vases of flowers would normally be radiant with color, but not tonight. Any color was dulled by the sepia haze.

And it smelt: of stale air and intense mold.

Jack's senses were on high alert, but the dullness and staleness created confusion.

Was I wrong all along? Was the decoy not really a decoy but the real thing? What a fool I am!

But what about Zhou's story? And why were they kidnapped? Perhaps someone else wanted them dead and not Grosch? Perhaps Zhou is involved in other things that I've been innocently thrown into? But why kidnap Marie? Oh, Lord Jesus, have I just believed what I wanted to believe?

"Tank, was that Leopold Grosch that just left the hotel?" Thierry asked, interrupting Jack's thoughts.

"Indeed, Thierry. He has a dinner engagement this evening."

Obviously he's not going to blow himself up! But who's going to lead us to the bomb? Who's going to activate it?

Jack stopped at the foot of the staircase. He sensed a presence behind him, and turned to look. A flash of light shone brightly through the glass atrium, but it wasn't from the descending sun. He followed the light to where it ended on the plush carpet a few feet away. To his amazement, there stood three winged beings, apparition-like. They were significantly taller than any human, and very beautiful. All were dressed in platinum tunics. They each held a long sword against their chest. He had never seen anything so splendid.

Is this a dream?

Oh, Jesus, give me clarity, please. Give me the courage to follow what you've put in my heart.

Then they were gone. The light beam vanished.

"Jack?" Thierry asked, three steps up the staircase. "You alright?"

Everything was moving in slow motion. He looked up at Thierry, then at Lancaster and Tank who had advanced further up the stairs. All were looking at Jack, awaiting a response to Thierry's question.

Zhou. Where's Zhou?

He looked left. Zhou was still by his side.

And then he saw it clearly. It all fell into place. He knew their plan.

They're going to kill us!

They wanted us to come here so we could die like everyone else in the hotel. Then Grosch would get away with it.

Of course!

His eyes blinked and everything was back to normal speed.

"Yeah," he started to say, "I'm fine, Thierry, just fine!" and put his feet on the first step.

"Thought we'd lost ya there, guv," Thierry replied. The three in front turned to continue their advance.

Thank you, Lord, for sending those three angels. I now know you are here with us and I have a job to do. Save us, please.

The others had reached the top. They turned, waiting on Zhou and Jack to join them.

* * *

The sound of a text arriving was masked by the hum of the air-conditioning units in the specially designed room that managed the temperature within the hotel.

A timer on one of the controllers clicked alive: 0:29:59, 0:29:58…

* * *

"Come, Jesus, come," repeated Louise Haines and her three girlfriends, stretched out face-down on the carpet, quiet worship music in the background.

* * *

Arlia, Landen, and the shrinking army of white knights were bravely soldiering on against a relentless foe. The hopelessly outnumbered white knights somehow managed to keep taking down demon after demon.

But Bacchazar's multitude of assassins kept pushing them further and further away. A long line of demons manned a ten-mile track from the hotel to where the remnant of the white knights clung on. Their numbers just kept on growing; it was like there was a never-ending supply of sentinels that came up out of the hotel's basement.

Bacchazar was screaming, exhorting his hordes to kill and destroy. He had watched Grosch leave the hotel and the melee of death that pervaded the air around it. That evil would soon spread its tentacles through the hotel's rooms, strangling the hope and will out of its occupants. Grosch would be safe. The wickedness in his heart was unconstrained by any semblance of good.

The final act was near its end; the curtain was ready to come down; the ruler of the world would reign once again!

* * *

Bacchazar, distracted by the battle, had failed to notice the three angelguards that walked straight in the front door, unannounced and unimpeded.

Darius, Hannen and Elijah too felt the thickness in the air, the muck of demonic possession.

"The roof?" Elijah indicated.

"Our orders are to stick with Jack and his team," Hannen advised.

"But if we infiltrate their leaders now, we can save Arlia and the others!" he said pleadingly.

"No, Elijah, we follow Tagan's orders!"

Elijah nodded reluctantly. They followed their charges up the staircase.

Fifteen minutes to detonation

Conference rooms filled the first floor. The relative peace and calm on the ground floor was replaced by bustle as waiters, caterers, decorators all rushed around making the final preparations for the meeting in the ballroom.

The sepia haze also flowed onto this floor.

"The venue for this evening's cocktail function and then the working dinner for the Summit," Tank pointed out as they passed the open door to the elegantly garlanded ballroom.

"What time does it start?" Jack asked.

"The Heads of Delegation should be arriving in fifteen minutes or so," Tank replied easily. "The German Chancellor and the US President arrive last, five minutes later. They are presently in the auditorium, giving the first press conference of the Summit."

How do they plan to do it? Blow the entire building up? No, that would have required an incredible amount of dynamite spread all around the hotel, and surely that would have been uncovered by the security checks. They must have some other plan.

Fear and panic racked Jack's mind once again, his muscles still taut. His head hurt.

Tank showed them into a small meeting room that was devoid of furniture except for a few classroom-style chairs sitting idly. Jack entered last and stood back from the other three, while Tank stood at the door.

Another man was waiting for them: the other security guard they had seen at the front of the hotel.

An imposing man, he must have been six foot six, his smooth shaved head much more attractive than Tank's. His nose was flat at the bridge, evidently broken on more than one occasion. A diamond solitaire earring in his left earlobe shone brilliantly in contrast to his black suit and skin.

"Gentlemen, may I introduce you to Mr. Ballack, Head of Security for the G8 Summit?" Tank said as he closed the door. Distracted by Ballack's presence, no one noticed as Tank turned the key.

Jack's senses were swimming. The air was so dense, it suffocated him, and nausea rose rapidly up into the back of his mouth. He coughed that first dry cough that was a precursor to vomiting. But he swallowed hard, managing to push the sensation back.

His head was throbbing. He needed to sit down. He stumbled for a chair, grabbing it just in time. He closed his eyes, took a few deep breaths.

Oh, Jesus, come and save us, please! Oh, Lamb of God, Lion of Judah, roar! Come and rescue your people!

The fluorescent lights blinked, causing the others to look

to the ceiling in surprise. Every strip continued to stutter, to Ballack's obvious irritation.

He turned his back and started speaking into his handset.

"What's up with the lights, Smitty?" Lancaster asked pleasantly enough.

"Shut up, Bill, just *shut up!*" he snapped back.

"Hey, what's eating you, buddy?" Lancaster replied, disconcerted by his old friend's reaction.

Tank didn't get a chance to reply.

"Good to make your acquaintance, gentlemen," Ballack said, turning back. "The lights will right themselves in a few minutes."

Jack continued to sit, breathing deeply, as he prayed silently.

"Please take a seat, gentlemen, and make yourselves comfortable," Ballack offered courteously.

They complied.

"Well, Mr. Ballack," Lancaster started to say, "Jack here has a story that he thinks is important you hear."

"Sorry, I didn't get your name?"

"Lancaster. Major Bill Lancaster, British SAS," he replied, getting to his feet, extending his hand.

"Well, Mr. Lancaster," Ballack said slowly. From inside his jacket he smoothly drew a nine-millimeter with silencer and shot Lancaster right between the eyes. Lancaster's head snapped back. His lifeless body collapsed, hitting a chair on the way down.

Zhou swore, jumping to his feet.

"Sit back down, Mr. Chau!" Ballack said venomously.

"How… how do you know my name?" Zhou asked, foolishly.

"Because they were expecting us, Zhou!" Jack muttered. He felt sick.

"Very good, Mr. Haines!" Ballack acknowledged him with a small clap. Tank smiled as he stood near the door.

"And I presume the story you wanted to tell me had something to do with Mr. Grosch setting off some sort of bomb, sending the leaders of the world to a premature death, is that right, *Jack*?" He was standing over Jack, his nine-millimeter still in his hand.

"Something like that, yes," Jack replied.

Come, Jesus, come!

"Well, Jack, I don't need to listen to your story, because it's not a story… I must commend you for coming all this way, especially when our little decoy in London this morning satisfied the rest of the world. You just kept on coming, thinking you could save the world, just the three of you!"

He stopped, and gestured to Tank. Tank pulled out two pairs of handcuffs, then walked up behind Thierry and roughly cuffed his wrists behind the chair. Thierry kicked out but almost toppled over, correcting himself at the last moment.

"No use struggling, or else I'll just put a bullet through you right now!" Ballack said. He raised one eyebrow at Jack.

Jack let Tank put the cuffs on him.

No cuffs for Zhou.

Jack had a quizzical expression on his face. *What are they doing with Zhou?*

"Mr. Grosch," Ballack said as he walked ominously up behind Zhou, "especially wanted to say goodbye to you, Mr. Chau—"

He raised his pistol and shot Zhou in the back of the head. Zhou fell face forward to the ground.

"Nooo!" Jack screamed, thrashing around in his chair.

Ballack turned, aiming the gun at Jack. A trail of smoke drifted from the muzzle.

"That'll do, Ballack. Let's go," Tank intervened, pulling Ballack's gun down. "We gotta get out of here."

"Enjoy your last *breaths*, gentlemen," Ballack said. Jack caught the emphasis. His mind clicked into gear.

The two of them walked out the door, locking it behind them.

"Oh, Zhou, I'm so sorry!" Jack was trembling, devastated. "God, oh God, why?"

Thierry started praying, tears welling up in his eyes. He'd seen death first-hand in his military past but it still didn't make it any easier.

"Dear God, please take your son Zhou into your bosom and welcome him into the room you've prepared. He is now with you, Father, and for that we are thankful."

Andola was devastated at Zhou's violent death, but at the same time joyful that he was about to meet his Maker. She took Zhou's spirit and leapt skyward. "It's time to go home, my friend."

"Jack, Jack," Thierry pleaded, "we need to kick into gear, or else we're going as well, and I'm not ready yet!"

"Come, Jesus, come. Pleeeassse," Jack prayed softly.

"Come, Jesus, come," now stronger.

"Come, Jesus, come!" with steely determination in his voice and face.

Suddenly, the door unlocked. A porter stuck his head in the room. "Ah, you gents shouldn't be in here," he said in a strong German accent.

"Help us!" Thierry cried out.

The porter rushed in, Darius and Hannen in tow.

"What's happened here?" he said, noticing Zhou's and Lancaster's lifeless bodies.

"What's the time?" Jack asked. "There's a bomb going off at 6:30! Quick, get some help!"

"Ah, really?" the porter said dubiously. "It's 6:24."

"We don't have time to talk… these two are friends of ours and were shot dead… can you get us out of these cuffs?"

Thierry had an idea.

"Bill will have cuffs too. He'll have a key. They're universal, one sits fits all. This man over here – quick – search him for handcuffs!"

Darius gave the porter a nudge. He knelt down next to Lancaster and searched his pockets. He pulled out a set of handcuffs with a key, and started working on Thierry's wrists.

"One down," the porter said, pleased, moving over to Jack.

Thierry was on his feet.

"Where's the main air-conditioning control room?" Jack interrupted.

"The roof," replied the porter.

Jack got to his feet, "Four minutes. Come on, Tee, we can still do this!"

"Buddy, you get as many people in these conference rooms as you can out of the hotel," Jack said as he dashed out the door, Thierry and two angels in pursuit.

"Ah, OK," said the porter. He didn't move, staring numbly at the bodies on the floor.

The lights continued to splutter.

Chapter 40

A cool breeze whipped up, blowing the leaves and assorted rubbish into the air, then died away.

A sudden calm fell on the city of Berlin, the capital of Germany.

A single trumpet blast pierced the air, only heard by those in the supernatural.

Tagan stared out of the window directly opposite the hotel.

"Athaniel, it's time for us to go," he said, drawing his sword from its metallic silver sheath.

"Aye-aye, sir," his partner acknowledged, knowing what was about to happen.

"COME, JESUS, COME!" Tagan roared. "THE LION OF JUDAH HAS ARISEN!"

"HE HAS ARISEN INDEED!" Athaniel yelled.

The two white knights lifted up out of their temporary headquarters, straight for the roof of the hotel.

* * *

All the lights in Berlin suddenly dulled. The air shook. A howling cyclonic wind erupted through the streets, smashing windows, felling trees, sending pedestrians rushing for cover.

Darkness descended on the German capital.

* * *

"It has started!" the General screamed from the main bedroom of the Presidential Suite.

* * *

They came from out of the clouds. An army the size of which had not been seen this side of heaven. Tens of thousands of angelguards mounted on silver horses, majestic in their brilliant splendor, set upon Bacchazar's hordes of demonic swordsmen. The tide was now reversed, the angelguards outnumbering the demon sentinels by at least ten to one. The demons didn't stand a chance and were fleeing for their lives. The angelguards would not let them go, chasing and harassing them to eternal oblivion.

The angelguard army consumed the demons in a matter of minutes.

Arlia, Landen and their weary remnant now fought with renewed vigor, their hearts leaping to see their heavenly helpers who had arrived at just the right time.

The ten-mile black trail of satanic sentinels was smashed to pieces all the way to the demonic wasteland.

The angelguard legions departed as quickly as they had arrived, vanishing back to their king!

* * *

"Ughhh…" Bacchazar shrieked, from the hotel's roof, seeing his ghastly hordes decimated before his eyes.

"You filthy righteous scum!" he yelled, waving his sword in the air as the few surviving sentinels sought the safety of the Presidential Suite immediately below the roof.

Then he became aware of the presence of another. He turned instinctively, to see the radiant brightness of the silver blade fifty feet away, raised high in the air.

Held by the one he least wanted to see.

* * *

"So you needed your heavenly help again, did you, Tagan?" Bacchazar barked, edging closer, fury leaking from every pore.

"You should know well enough, Bacchazar, the heavenly host will always come to the rescue of its people!" Tagan replied.

Bacchazar joined the six demons standing armed and ready for battle. They stood in front of a door clearly marked in German: KLIMAANLAGE. Behind the door were the hotel's air conditioning control systems.

"Do not leave this door unattended!" he said calmly, even though his blood was fizzing with rage. "Tagan, you're not going to save them this time. It's too late and you know it!" he snarled. Bacchazar shot into the air, his sinister black sword drawn and eager for angel blood.

With a sweep of his wings Tagan was airborne, ever watchful. "Bacchazar, it's never too late!"

"C'mon, then, Tagan. Let's do this, once and for all. I'm going to do what I should have done a long time ago!"

CRASH!

An exit door smashed open. Jack and Thierry raced out into the open. Jack immediately pointed to the door to the air-conditioning room. "Two minutes!"

"See, Bacchazar, there's still time to stop this madness!"

"No, my old opponent, it's too late for your humans, they won't do it in time. My demons will make sure of that."

"Don't bet on it," said Tagan as Darius, Andola, Hannen and Elijah roared out of the hotel's roof. Blazing white light pierced the blackness as they smashed through Bacchazar's demonic guard in seconds.

The demon lord shook his head. He rushed Tagan with his huge black sword. Tagan parried it with his silver blade. The clanging sound of two lethal weapons that had seen thousands of years of service erupted into the night air.

Jack and Thierry were completely oblivious to the brawl immediately above them as they yanked open the now unguarded and unlocked door to the air-conditioning room.

Darius and Andola followed them inside whilst Hannen and Elijah stayed outside, high-fiving their success. They watched the battle in the air above them.

The supernatural leaders struck viciously against each other. They both knew this was likely to take a while, as all their previous battles had. But they threw themselves into the fray with no thought of their own safety, each clearly focused on bringing the other down.

* * *

A light in the middle of the ceiling automatically flashed on, having sensed the two humans at the door. It illuminated a larger than expected room where three enormous air-conditioning units sat side by side.

"Which one, Jack?"

Jack moved to the second one as Thierry inspected the first. They were both shaking.

"God, help us, please!" prayed Jack.

He reached the unit and stared at it. Nothing seemed out of place.

"Ninety seconds, Jack!"

Jack scanned the set of instructions in English and German hanging over the unit.

"It's this one, Tee! The sign here says it's for the conference rooms."

Thierry joined him. "What are we looking for?"

Jack swung around the back of the supply duct that took the air into the hotel. Feverishly he scanned behind the six-foot water tank. Water tank? He looked left and right. Neither of the other systems had water tanks. He dropped to his knees.

He traced his hand along a small metal pipe that joined the tank to the supply duct. Underneath the pipe on the tank was a control unit housed in a box.

He yanked it open.

"Tee, over here."

"Sixty seconds…" Thierry knelt down beside Jack.

"This sure doesn't look like a bomb," Jack said dubiously, desperately missing Zhou's expertise.

Inside the control unit were two devices. One they both knew very well: a cell phone.

And next to it was a colored screen that now read: "00:00:58, 00:00:57…"

"This must be it, Tee. But what's in the tank?"

"Gas, Jack." Thierry saw the small logo on the inside of the unit. "It's sarin gas. They're going to gas everyone through the air conditioning!"

"Ah—"

Jack knew what he had to do.

* * *

The ferocity with which the two spiritual leaders fought was frightening and remarkable. Their fighting skills and repertoire were simply awe-inspiring, as was their capacity to persevere. At times the fight resembled a heavyweight boxing slugfest, at other times an engrossing fencing match. But the longer it went, the looser and scrappier it became, as both grew more desperate.

* * *

A dark shadow landed without a sound on the roof, took in the brawl over the other side and stepped menacingly towards the light. He had managed to evade heaven's knights.

He had come for one angel in particular.

"You lookin' for me, by any chance?" Hannen said as he turned away from Elijah to face the dark shadow.

Drakkin charged out of the shadows straight for Hannen's midriff. Hannen, though, was too quick and somersaulted over the fast-advancing Viking warlord.

The two enemies stood fifteen feet from each other. Drakkin's hideous helmet couldn't conceal his vicious intentions.

"Your time is up, white knight!"

"We'll see about that!" Hannen darted for the Viking with his long sword, only for the demon to repel it, pushing Hannen back in the process.

The street brawler of a demon tackled the angelguard with battle-axe in one hand, long dagger in the other, snarling and spitting. "You will not prevail this time! I will make a necklace out of your teeth!"

Hannen didn't respond. He just swung hard and fast repeatedly, trying to find a way through Drakkin's tough defense.

Incredibly, Drakkin was still full of energy, even after having spent the past sixty minutes in direct combat.

This fight too would not be over quickly.

* * *

The countdown flicked remorselessly: "00:00:05, 00:00:04…"

SMASH!

"00:00:03, 00:00:03, 00:00:03…"

"Jack, you've done it! It's stopped!" Thierry cried out. "THANK YOU, JESUS!"

Jack fell backwards, sprawled on the ground, cradling his bleeding right hand, hair stuck to his sweat-soaked face. His heart raced.

"Thank you, thank you, thank you!" whispered Jack.

Thierry pulled him up and hugged him.

"Gas, who would have thought?" Jack said, drawing himself away. "I was sure there was going to be an explosion."

"Sarin gas, a deadly nerve agent!" Thierry replied. "Do you remember a story in the mid nineties about an attack on a Tokyo subway by some cult that killed a handful of people but incapacitated thousands of others?"

Jack nodded his head.

"I learnt about it in Gulf War training. Apparently a pinhead of the stuff can kill a human. Asphyxiation."

"So there would have been a hotel full of asphyxiated bodies lying around? Incredible."

"Well, not now. Thanks to you."

"And you, Tee — it was a team effort." Jack clumsily high-fived his friend with his left hand as they got to their feet. So too did Darius and Andola.

"We better get downstairs."

* * *

Tagan was struggling. Bacchazar was hammering him with one blow after another of his gigantic blade. Tagan was fending him off but only just. He had already taken a savage cut to his right arm, but the white knight leader had never before backed down, and tonight wasn't the night to start.

Suddenly Bacchazar's attention was diverted by something out of the corner of his eye. That split second was just enough for Tagan to force his adversary back and away, giving him a moment to catch a breath before the next onslaught.

Bacchazar looked grim as whatever it was below stole his attention.

Tagan turned to follow Bacchazar's gaze and smiled.

Jack led Thierry out of the air-conditioning vault, headed for the exit door leading back into the hotel. The huge smiles on their faces said everything.

"Praise be to God!" Tagan said quietly to himself. "It's over, Bacchazar! Give it up!" he yelled.

The demon leader didn't immediately respond. Tagan watched as the anger rose up in his opponent and the grip on his black sword tightened. Tagan knew there would be one huge last struggle as the fury in his foe raged.

Bacchazar flew at Tagan in uncontrollable frenzy, screaming obscenities, his menacing blade swinging furiously.

Tagan had anticipated this move and spun away at the last moment, nicking Bacchazar's torso on the way through with his razor-sharp blade. Bacchazar swung around in shock and astonishment, ready to come again. Once again Tagan foresaw his opponent's move, spinning away and striking harder through the demon's leathery torso.

That strike hurt Bacchazar. Black ichor flowed from the gaping hole in his side. But he would not yield. He knew Tagan's hide was his only hope now of keeping some semblance of respect with the General.

Out of the corner of his eye Bacchazar watched as the victorious human duo stepped into the hotel.

Ignoring his badly beaten body, Bacchazar attacked with one final lunge of his mighty sword. The raging fury inside him was unquenched and unrelenting.

It was only when Tagan smashed his sword out of his hands that the demonic leader realized how weak he actually had become. He stood completely defenseless for the first time, with four critical wounds to his torso.

Shame suddenly gripped his mind.

"Goodbye, my old foe!" Tagan spoke confidently, with a hint of respect for Bacchazar. He felt no remorse for what he was about to do. But nor would he rejoice. That wasn't in God's design.

Bacchazar just nodded.

He could try to run, but he knew Tagan would quickly catch him. Why not die with some honor?

Tagan's powerful right arm swung hard, his keen blade decapitating his old rival. Bacchazar's huge body simply disintegrated.

* * *

On reaching the ground floor Jack and Thierry ran towards the reception area, which was abuzz with people.

They slowed on entering the main lobby, trying to appear calm and in control. Their hearts were pounding as the adrenaline surged through their bodies, giving them surprising clarity.

They headed straight for the elaborate and ornate staircase.

"Excuse me, gentlemen," said a voice behind them, "that's a restricted area." At the same time, four German Secret Service agents stood in their way. A porter was standing with them.

"That's them," he said.

Jack and Thierry were surrounded.

* * *

Tagan raced down the side of the hotel. Ḥannen was flush up against the hotel wall, with Drakkin snarling and hissing as he kept repeatedly hammering the angel with his double-pronged attack.

"Give it up, Drakkin! Your leader has been extinguished. You don't stand a chance!" Tagan said, entering the fray, his first strike crashing into Drakkin's huge battle-axe.

"Is Bacchazar dead? I don't believe it!" the Viking warlord hissed back, swinging wildly and missing with his thick and extremely heavy sword that had replaced the long dagger in his other fighting hand.

"Believe it! Why would I be here if he wasn't?" Tagan replied. He and Hannen combined, coming at Drakkin from both sides. He evaded their two blades with a nimble jump which turned into a backwards somersault. An elusive move for someone so bulky.

But that move, deft as it was, put him on the defensive.

The two angels came flying at him blades blazing. Drakkin fended Hannen off with his axe, Tagan with his sword. Tagan's lusty blows were coming faster and harder, whilst Hannen, clearly weakening, kept up the onslaught. It could only be a matter of time before Drakkin faltered.

* * *

On glancing inside a window of the hotel, an idea suddenly struck Drakkin.

He shot into the room, Tagan and Hannen right on his tail.

It was only when inside that he realized he'd made the wrong call.

Athaniel and Arlia had seen him coming and just waited.

He was completely surrounded. He hissed and snarled like a cornered snake, lunging with both lethal weapons simultaneously but to no avail.

But he wasn't going to surrender. Not Drakkin. He had grander aspirations still to be fulfilled, even more so if what the white knight leader said was in fact true and Bacchazar was now no longer.

Drakkin cannoned up into the air as fast as his exhausted body would take him, turned and dived for cover amongst the buildings of Berlin.

* * *

"We understand you have some story to tell us," said the leading Secret Service agent.

"Ah… it's a long story," Jack replied.

"We've got all night, gentlemen, so start talking!"

"Be our pleasure," Jack responded. He didn't care how long it took. It was over.

Four angelguards – Tagan, Athaniel, Darius, and Arlia – stood at the back of the room and cheered. But another lay on the ground, exhausted and wounded: Hannen.

Epilogue

Washington DC. A few weeks later

Jack and Loren had flown into Washington Dulles International Airport that morning from LA, accompanied by Loren's parents. A black stretch limousine with presidential markings met them and drove them the fifty-minute journey to the White House.

They were ushered into the Diplomatic Reception Room, soon joined by Thierry, Ruth, and Mikey, their son, who had come in from London the previous evening. Jack's brother Stephen, his mother Louise, and his two daughters were also on hand.

The occasion was the recognition by both the United States and the United Nations of this motley group of people who had stopped a madman from further cementing evil's reign over the world. Two of those rescued from harm, the President of the United States and the leader of the United Nations, would be personally presenting them with their medals.

The first was the United States Presidential Medal of Freedom, bestowed upon people who have made outstanding contributions to the security or national interest of the United States or to world peace, or who have made a significant public or private accomplishment. Previous recipients included former presidents and leaders of business, politics and the entertainment world. This would be the first time the medal would be bestowed upon non-US residents. The president himself had personally recommended this particular group for the medal.

The second medal was the UN Medal, recognizing their role in maintaining peace in the world.

The group were led out to the Rose Garden, located just outside the Oval Office, specially designed for outdoor ceremonies such as the one that was about to begin. A series of chairs with pristine white covers had been set up on the perfectly manicured central lawn. Hedges of different colored roses as well as magnolias and crab-apple trees bordered the lawn. Before taking their seats, the guests were greeted by numerous government authorities whose names would all be soon forgotten.

Even though he was very hot in his charcoal suit on this midsummer's day, Jack was glad to take a seat while they waited for the arrival of the leader of the free world.

The last few weeks had been a blur for him. He'd spent the best part of the first week in Berlin with Thierry, successfully convincing various security groups of their innocence. Jack then flew home. Thierry had flown back to London to be reunited with Ruth and Mickey.

Grosch's dinner with the German finance minister was rudely interrupted by the Secret Service, who took him into custody. Ballack and Tank were rounded up at Tegel Airport as they were boarding separate flights.

Unfortunately, after being held in custody for a week, both were found dead in their respective cells. Poisoned, the autopsies revealed. How or by whom nobody was able to tell.

The case against Grosch had become a media frenzy not just in Europe but also in the US. All sorts of different theories were canvassed, the most popular being that he was a distant relative of Hitler. Unfortunately most of the evidence was circumstantial. Losing Ballack and Tank was going to make it even harder for the prosecutors to get a guilty verdict.

Jack knew he would have to spend some time back in Berlin when the case against Grosch finally came to trial. Judging by the smokescreen presented by his very large defense team, it wasn't likely to be soon. The case would take a long time to get started, let alone reach a point where a jury would convict the man.

Jack found unwanted celebrity status back in Sydney. He had little time for all the fuss and couldn't have cared less about it all. Prior to flying to the US, he had had afternoon tea with the prime minister and his wife at their Sydney residence.

Loren sat down next to him, gripping his hand. Jack had no idea what the future held for the two of them. They had been inseparable over the weekend just gone, with their parents as loving chaperones. But he did not know whether they should pursue a relationship. He was convinced God had brought them together, but perhaps for a specific purpose that had now taken place. He knew time would tell. God would continue to instruct, direct and guide him. He was content at this time to leave it at that.

Loren had flown home to be with her children. She had attended Tom's funeral, which had been postponed until she got home. It was important for Taylor and Luke to say goodbye to their dad.

A few days later, fearing a breakdown and after some stern words from Marcie, Loren checked herself into a women's hospice. There, some very godly women cared for her, giving her some time to sort through all that had happened in the past few months. She expected to stay two days, but left after five, her heart and mind still grieving somewhat but far better able to cope once again. That Sunday, for the first time, she took the kids to her girlfriends' church. She found solace there: it felt like a home away from home. She felt hungry to know all there was to know about Jesus. This was an adventure she was really going to enjoy.

The audience was now stirring. The ceremony was about to start.

Jack was tired of all the pomp and fuss. He just wanted to get on with his life, being a father to his twins, a brother to Stephen and Jane, a son to his ever-helpful mother. As well as grappling with the complexities of a long-distance relationship with Loren, he looked forward to just spending time with his buddies, watching the football at home and inspiring his students to dream their dreams.

A man he didn't know sat down next to him. His navy suit was well worn; he had a slightly disheveled appearance, and was wearing too much cheap cologne.

"You Jack Haines, by any chance?" the man asked, removing his dark Blues Brothers sunglasses.

Jack nodded, cautiously.

"Good to meet ya finally!" the man said, extending his right arm. "Tony Sabatini's my name!"

"Detective Sabatini, good to meet you too," Jack replied, responding with a very warm handshake. "I was hoping I'd see you here."

"Wouldn't have missed it."

"We'd probably still be locked up in Berlin if it hadn't been for your evidence in linking Malone and Mayer. Hey, you caught Mayer's killer yet?"

"You betcha, nailed the guy a few days ago. Florida Quays. He was about to set sail for Cuba."

"Wow! Congratulations. No doubt they'll want to use his testimony against Grosch as well."

"That's what I thought. But he had nothing to do with Grosch, doesn't know who he is. Received anonymous instructions from someone out of London."

"Any idea from whom?"

"Not at this stage."

The doors to the Oval Office opened, with Secret Service agents taking up positions on either side. The President stepped out of the building and made the short walk to the grey lectern with the US Coat of Arms proudly adorning it. Following him was a small group consisting of the Secretary General of the United Nations, two well-known high-ranking senior officials in the US government and more Secret Service agents.

Jack thought of the golf game he was playing with Stephen the next day. It had been too long since their last round together.

***

Tagan and Athaniel led the small troop of white knights that looked on from the back of the lawn as the President opened proceedings. Darius, Arlia, and Hannen had taken up positions closer to the seated block of government officials.

They knew one battle had been won, but the war against the enemy of God and man would rage on. Too many people had been lost, too many souls captured by the evil one and his workers. There were still billions that needed the presence of heaven's angelguards.

The Chronicles of the Angelguard continue in

Wrestling with Shadows